THE
JUDAS
KISS

NORMAN KATKOV

THE JUDAS KISS

A DUTTON BOOK

DUTTON
Published by the Penguin Group
Penguin Books USA Inc., 375 Hudson Street,
New York, New York 10014, U.S.A.
Penguin Books Ltd, 27 Wrights Lane,
London W8 5TZ, England
Penguin Books Australia Ltd, Ringwood,
Victoria, Australia
Penguin Books Canada Ltd, 10 Alcorn Avenue,
Toronto, Ontario, Canada M4V 3B2
Penguin Books (N.Z.) Ltd, 182-190 Wairau Road,
Auckland 10, New Zealand

Penguin Books Ltd, Registered Offices:
Harmondsworth, Middlesex, England

First published by Dutton, an imprint of New American Library,
a division of Penguin Books USA Inc.
Distributed in Canada by McClelland & Stewart Inc.

First Printing, October, 1991
10 9 8 7 6 5 4 3 2 1

 REGISTERED TRADEMARK—MARCA REGISTRADA

LIBRARY OF CONGRESS CATALOGING IN PUBLICATION DATA:

Katkov, Norman.
  The Judas kiss / Norman Katkov.
    p.   cm.
  ISBN 0-525-93366-2
  I. Title.
PS3521.A654J84   1991
813'.54—dc20   91-2577
                                                     CIP

Printed in the United States of America
Set in Goudy Oldstyle

Designed by Steven N. Stathakis

PUBLISHER'S NOTE
This is a work of fiction. Names, characters, places, and incidents either are the products of
the author's imagination or are used fictitiously, and any resemblance to actual persons, living
or dead, events, or locales is entirely coincidental.

In memory of
Harold Matson
and for Jonathan Matson

THE
JUDAS
KISS

— 1 —

AROUND NOON ONE DAY in the autumn of 1937, Carly left her bedroom clutching a small purse of petit point, hurrying through the apartment in Vienna's District I. She scooped up her coat and scarf from the chair beside the telephone in the foyer.

"Carly!"

Her mother came after her. "Where are you going?" Carly opened the door. She hated to lie, so she didn't answer. "Wait!" said Helga Siefermann, and then, almost in a whisper, "Your father's birthday."

Carlotta Siefermann, whom her mother had named after the Empress of Mexico, Maximilian's queen, had forgotten a present for her father in the past. "What should I get him?" She shoved the purse into her coat pocket.

"Oh, anything," Helga said. "A book."

The sunny day was brisk and windy, raising the tail of Carly's scarf, which lay across her back as she ran down Kruger Strasse to a taxi. "The Dorotheum, please."

In the taxi, riding to the huge government pawnshop, Carly took the purse from her coat pocket and opened it. Inside, wrapped in white tissue paper, lay a gold ring, a gift of her Grandmother Melzer. The ring was an heirloom, made for a Valkyrie, but Carly had never worn it.

"Which entrance?" she asked the driver.

Carly had never been in the Dorotheum, had rarely ever passed the enormous building. "The busiest," she said.

"Dorotheergasse," said the driver.

Carly had given herself thirty minutes for the Dorotheum, but she was back on the street in less than fifteen, standing in the sun in the lunch crowd as though she had lost her way. She and Lisl were meeting at one o'clock. Carly decided she would walk to District III.

She saw Lisl first, standing at an angle near the flower stand on the corner as though trying to hide. Lisl Schott was a knockout, tall, although not as tall as Carly, with white baby skin and russet hair and hazel eyes. "Lisl."

The young beauty shuddered, startled, but seeing Carly, ran to her. "I thought you wouldn't come," she said. "I was praying when I heard my name."

"Now you owe God a favor," Carly said as they came to the apartment building.

"How can you joke now?"

"I have to joke now," Carly said, making herself smile for Lisl. They had been friends forever, since their nannies had sat together in the park watching them play.

As they went past the elevators, Lisl whirled. "Will everything be all right?"

"Dr. Stepnitz said everything will be fine. You heard him."

They had come the week before, after Lisl had seen her family doctor, who had delivered her. "You'll be in good hands," he said. "Stepnitz is very good, a gifted physician."

"And he does . . . that?"

"Someone must do . . . that," said her doctor. "Lucky for you, child."

Lisl went from her doctor to Kruger Strasse, and in Carly's bedroom she said, sobbing, "I've missed two periods." She tried to smother herself in the pillows. "I didn't want to. I told him to stop." Carly lay down on the bed beside the woman so recently a virgin, holding her until she cried herself into exhaustion. "Promise you'll go with me," Lisl said.

Now, before a door with "STEPNITZ" etched into a brass rectangle, Lisl held on to Carly. "I'll never do it again," she said. "Never. With anyone. Not until I'm married." Her face began to fall. "If anyone will want me."

A buzzer sounded in the consulting room when anyone entered, so Otto Stepnitz knew they had arrived. He always made such appointments for one o'clock, when his nurse went to lunch and he was alone. Dr. Stepnitz sat at his desk reading a journal for another fifteen minutes before appearing in the reception room. "Ladies."

He was a fastidious man, plump and shorter than average, almost bald, with a pencil mustache. He looked like a banker or a haberdasher. Stepnitz gestured at the two chairs in front of his desk. "Please."

He sat down facing them. The tall one, the one he preferred, remained standing. Stepnitz liked both, but the one in trouble, all peaches and cream, was a silly young creature. "We brought the money," Carly said.

From her purse she took the money she had been given for her ring, and turned to take Lisl's money. "One hundred schillings," Carly said, setting the bills on the desk.

"Two hundred," Stepnitz said.

"You told us . . . !" Lisl began, and broke off, staring up at Carly.

"There are problems," Stepnitz said. "I have expenses, you know. Medical and nonmedical, especially nonmedical. People need to be paid. And since you were here, my payments have been raised."

"This is all we have," Lisl said.

"Two hundred." Stepnitz never offered his alternative until they were more frantic, ready to surrender to panic. The tall one was a long distance from panic. She was furious and, to Stepnitz, even more desirable.

"You gave your word," Carly said.

"My word?" He sat back in his chair. "What word? I have no word. Look around you. Everything here is a lie. My life is a lie." He pointed at Lisl. "She is part of the lie. You two, with your few schillings, are part of the lie."

Carly advanced to the desk, interposing herself between Lisl and the doctor. "You must help us."

"Do not say 'must,' " Stepnitz said. "Not to me."

Carly wanted to slap him. He reminded her of boys at school, the cowards that yelled dirty words from a distance. "You'll do it," she said.

"Because you say so."

"You will do it or I will tell everyone what happens here," Carly said. "I'll go out into the street right in front of this building and tell everyone. I'll point at your windows. And they'll believe me. People want to believe such things. And why should I lie? I'm not a liar. You're the liar."

He loathed the young, arrogant bitch. Stepnitz came out of his chair. "Tuesday," he said. "One o'clock Tuesday."

"Carly!" Lisl reached for her, terrified.

"She must remain afterward," Stepnitz said. "Several hours. And today I have patients coming at two o'clock." He reached for the money, but Carly snatched it up, stuffing the bills into her coat pocket.

"Tuesday," she said.

In the street, Lisl said, "What would I have done without you? I would have killed myself."

Carly felt woozy. The ordeal of pawning her grandmother's ring, the doctor's callous behavior, Lisl's whimpering dependence, made her head spin. She stopped at the flower stand. "Call me tonight."

Lisl threw her arms around Carly, kissing her again and again. "You're my best friend, my only friend."

On the other side of the Ring, in District VIII, Nick Gallanz followed Dolly Stacker out of a café. "I'd like to see the matinee of *Mourning Becomes Electra*," Nick said.

"I'd like to play Electra," said Dolly Stacker.

"If we had a theater, you would play her."

"We cannot afford a theater." Dolly Stacker was a bright, sensible woman, a bookkeeper for a furniture dealer, but she shared Nick's addiction to the theater. She had brought him into a group of amateurs like herself, actors, actresses, playwrights, directors, song writers, lyricists, set designers, most of whom earned a living at lackluster jobs and dreamed of the footlights. The pair stopped on a corner. "Meanwhile, you owe me a lunch," Dolly said.

"Put it on the bill," Nick said.

"If you'll kiss me good-bye," Dolly said. She was a little woman, soft and round, who used bright lipstick on full lips.

Nick put his arms around her, holding her as though they were behind locked doors while he kissed her. People stared at the pair. Dolly clung to him. "You never say you love me."

Nick kissed her again. "I love you," he said, and left her, dodging cars. He was always late, always impatient. Dolly watched her bareheaded Tatar moving like a cat in the traffic. He was lean as an acrobat, with high cheekbones. His skin lay tight across his face, and his hair, the color of sable, was cut short. He seemed atavistic, out of place in Vienna's midday bustle. Dolly stayed until he disappeared before walking in the opposite direction, warm and oozy inside.

Two blocks away, Nick turned into Josefstadter Strasse, taking a shortcut. He passed a cobbler's shop, a barber, and a storefront with a door set into the base of a V made by two angled show windows. A man was locking the door, and as Nick passed, he spotted the "FOR RENT" sign over his head and the empty store inside. Nick spun around. "*Mein herr!*"

Oscar Benedick saw a young man leap forward, trapping him. "Are you the landlord?" Nick asked, nodding to make it true.

"I own the building."

"And you can't rent this shop," Nick said.

"I'll rent it, I'll rent it," Benedick said. He had dealt with clients since his first job in Budapest.

"Maybe," Nick said. "Open up."

Benedick had never turned away a single human being. He unlocked the door. "What did you have in mind?"

"Space," Nick said, walking into the shop. "Pray you have the right space."

Benedick followed him. "For what?" Nick didn't stop, but paced off the length. "What kind of business?" Benedick asked. "What do you sell?"

Nick reached a door at the rear. The space would work. "Dreams," he said, moving to the side wall so he could pace off the width.

"I have no time for these monkeyshines," Benedick said. "I am a businessman."

"Does the back door lead to an alley?" Nick asked.

"Where else? Good-bye," Benedick said. "Out, out."

"I'll take it," Nick said.

Benedick stopped. The stranger wore decent clothes. He jumped around and spoke in riddles, but he was young. And the last two tenants, a milliner and a radio repairman, had failed. "I am a law-abiding citizen," Benedick said. "Tell me your trade."

"The theater," Nick said. He spread his arms, an impresario welcoming his audience. "I am in the theater."

"You want to make a theater *here?*" Benedick shook his head. "Impossible."

"I'm an architect," Nick said. His poor high school grades had not qualified him for the university, but the influence of one of his father's customers had gained him admittance into the Technische Hochschule, where he had graduated last in his class. "I'll make this place a showplace," Nick said. "Lights, color, crowds. Your building will be a magnet. You won't recognize your own property." Nick shook his finger at the landlord. "Promise you won't raise the rent."

"A theater," Benedick said. "A back door." He started for the entrance. He had worked in two countries and thought he knew every synonym for a brothel. "You take me for some kind of fool," he said. "You hear my accent and decide I'm a provincial. Back door. For the customers, *your* kind of customers, correct? Wrong! Get out!"

"I'm giving you a second chance," Nick said. "The rear door is for deliveries, for the sets. I'll design a portable ticket booth. We'll bring it in every night." Nick took out his checkbook. "Yes or no? Quickly!"

"Who ever heard of a theater in a store?"

"Tell me your name and how much."

"Upstairs," Benedick said.

Nick followed him up to an office, where Benedick demanded Nick's signature on a lease. The landlord asked for references. Nick gave him Dolly Stacker and Peter Dietrich, an insurance salesman who hoped to direct plays. When Nick came out of the storefront, he pulled the FOR RENT sign from the transom.

As he crossed the Ring and hurried across the Burggarten, Nick saw a mass of men in civilian clothes trying to maintain military ranks while they marched toward the Hofburg. They carried no flags, no banners, they were badly clothed, and they were silent. Their silence was eerie. Yet they were a commonplace.

Austria had become a nation half insane. And Vienna, still gleaming with the architectural monuments of an imperial city, had turned into a battlefield.

Depending on the political party you favored, or the coffee house oracle you overheard, or the street corner orator who shouted after you, Austria either had at last embarked on a stable course, or Austria writhed under the tyranny of Chancellor Kurt Schuschnigg, or Austria in her latest convulsion had succumbed to anarchy, or Austria had fallen under the rule of an oligarchy whose private army, the Landswehr, would soon establish a slave state here beneath the Alps.

The year of 1937 had begun with the customary charade: masked balls, commemorative concerts, holiday performances by the Philharmonic, the Staatsoper, by the Burgtheatre. At the midnight mass on January 1 in St. Stephen's Cathedral, Cardinal Innitzer promised new beginnings and fresh hope, and while few of his parishioners wanted for anything, people were hungry and cold in Vienna, in Graz, in Salzburg, and all along the Danube.

Twenty years of folly, of ignorance, of an archaic and bloated government apparatus, of official ineptitude and military defeats on the battlefield and in the corridors and cloakrooms of diplomacy; an endless plague of consecutive disasters, in war and in the forums of its leaders and representatives, had taken Austria from a world power with a polyglot empire of forty-seven million subjects to a dismembered country of less than seven.

On the map Austria had shrunk to what seemed the size of a postage stamp, and even this tiny nation reeled in disarray. The country had been mauled too often and too deeply. Its wounds seemed fatal. Austria seemed to be exsanguinating.

While the single event which signaled the start of Austria's finish came with its entry into World War I in 1914, the empire had been on the brink for half a century, since 1848. There had been uprisings. The people had revolted. They had walked into guns and cannon. Emperor Ferdinand and his court fled, leaving Vienna and holing up in Innsbruck.

The Hapsburgs appeared doomed. The army could not stop the monarchy from toppling. A woman saved the empire, one woman, alone.

Archduchess Sophie of Bavaria had a husband, a Hapsburg, whom she ignored, and two sons whom she adored. She combined the obsessions of Joan of Arc with the skill and determination of Metternich and Richelieu. When her sons were born, Archduchess Sophie decided they would be kings. Her chance came in 1848. The emperor, hiding in Innsbruck, had been born retarded. Archduchess Sophie made him abdicate. She made the army accept her son, Franz Josef, as the new emperor. She watched Franz Josef crowned, in 1848, before his eighteenth birthday.

He was eighty-four years old when he signed the articles of war in 1914. Franz Josef had ruled for sixty-six years. His wife had long before been murdered on a quay in Geneva. His son, Crown Prince Rudolf, had committed suicide. And his heir, Franz Ferdinand, had just been assassinated in Sarajevo. Franz Josef was very old and very frail, and he died in 1916.

His successor, Archduke Karl, ruled for two years. The Austrian army lost everywhere in those two years. Generals sent boys into the line. Parents watched pubescent sons herded into trains and never saw them again.

When the Central Powers surrendered in November 1918, Kaiser Wilhelm of Germany abdicated. He left Germany, fast. In Russia the czar and his family left, but not fast enough. The Communists killed them. In Turkey the Ottoman Empire collapsed, and in Austria the people took to the streets. The new emperor lost his throne. After nine hundred years the Habsburg monarchy expired.

The Allies were not charitable victors. In Versailles, where Wilson, Clemenceau, Orlando, and Lloyd George met to write the peace, they changed the maps of Europe and Asia Minor. When they finished at Versailles, they had dissolved an empire and turned Austria into a republic.

The new republic produced a constitution which the people accepted. Political parties were formed. Candidates campaigned for election to the Nationalrat and the Bundesrat, the two chambers which constituted the new Parliament. The nation would be led by a chancellor chosen from the political party with a majority of the seats in the Parliament. If no majority emerged from an election, the chancellor would be selected from a coalition.

Alas, the Parliament could not govern, and the chancellor could not lead. The ancient country had become, in a flash, a new country. There were political parties all over the place. Nobody agreed. Demonstrators began to appear in the streets. There were counter-demonstrations. So there were riots. The riots became endemic in the land of the waltz and the torte.

Austria had been impoverished. Its people were a defeated and bewildered people. They were exhausted. The country could not feed itself. All through the Twenties governments were elected and fell with regularity. Chancellors came and went.

In the midst of this turmoil an Austrian who had adopted Germany after the war attracted a small band of followers. His name was Adolf Hitler, and he had a messianic belief in himself. His initial cadre soon attracted a following among the Bavarian rabble in and around Munich.

He soon attracted a following among the Austrian rabble as well, and there were Brown Shirts in Vienna almost as soon as they appeared in Germany.

Suddenly—it seemed suddenly, especially to Jews—Adolf Hitler became Chancellor of Germany. The Nazis controlled the country. The Bavarian gangsters ruled the Reich. And from the day of his ascendancy

Hitler's plans for Lebensraum began with Austria, above all, Austria. Adolf Hitler lusted for the land of his birth.

To keep his country free from Hitler, Engelbert Dollfuss, the Austrian Chancellor, dissolved Parliament, suspended civil liberties, abolished the free press, and announced he would fight Anschluss, the Nazi word for coupling, to the death. Dollfuss established a dictatorship to confront the predatory dictatorship on Austria's border.

In July 1936, Dollfuss was murdered in his office. Everyone knew German Nazis were in the gang which stormed the Hofburg, shooting guards on their way to kill the chancellor.

For a few days his death created chaos. Hitler was prepared. He had troops and tanks on the border waiting for word from his agents, telling him Austria could be forced to surrender.

One Austrian, Kurt Schuschnigg, who had been Attorney General in Dollfuss's cabinet, refused to turn over his country. He went to the generals of the army, who put their troops on alert and called up the reserves. Kurt Schuschnigg moved into the dead chancellor's office and became the new chancellor. He said all emergency measures instituted by his predecessor would be continued because of the current emergency. So Austria remained a dictatorship. And Austrians continued to demonstrate. And Nick could never ignore a show.

"What's happening?"

Nick saw the girl who had come out of nowhere, a bareheaded girl with long, straight, sand-colored hair. "They're headed for the Hofburg," he replied.

"Are they Communists?" Carly stayed abreast of him. "Who are they?"

"Austrians," he said. "Citizens." He glanced at her once more and this time did not look away. She wore a long tweed coat like an infantryman's coat, with a bright orange scarf tied around the collar. The girl looked straight at him as though he had the answers to all the world's mysteries. "There could be trouble," he said. "They're breaking the law already, blocking traffic. You'd better leave."

"Are you leaving?" There were less than two hundred marchers following their leaders, four middle-aged men walking ahead of the rest. "You're not leaving," Carly said.

"Go home." Nick watched the two rows of policemen facing the marchers. The policemen blocked the street from curb to curb. They were shoulder to shoulder, all with clubs held across their chests, all set to swing.

"Will the police hurt them?" Carly asked.

"Go home," Nick said, stepping into the street. Cupping his mouth with his hands, he yelled at the four leaders: "Stop! Stop!"

Nobody listened, nobody looked at him. Carly stayed in the street with Nick. "Do you know them?" she asked.

He ran, passing the marchers. The cops would break heads, break bones. Someone had to stop the slaughter. He forgot the girl.

Captain Konrad Schoonover, the police captain, wanted the marchers to disperse, but they kept coming. "They're harmless," Nick said. "Just send them home."

The captain almost wrapped his club around the man's head. The girl saved him. She acted goofy, charging a line of cops, but she was a stunner. Captain Schoonover pushed the butt of his club into the man's chest. "Beat it. Take her with you."

"Talk to them," Nick said. "It's your job. Keep the peace."

"Ten seconds," said Captain Schoonover, "or you're in jail." He shoved the club into Nick's ribs, and Carly grabbed it.

"You coward!" she said, holding on to the club with both hands. Nick got her around the waist, trying to pull her away from the captain, who pushed her aside as one of the cops yelled, "Now!"

The marchers had broken ranks and were running directly at the rows of cops. Captain Schoonover shouted, "Tighten up! Tighten up!" waving at his men to stand fast, but the cops were already attacking.

They plunged ahead in a pack, clubs raised. They came at the demonstrators swinging, and as the first marchers fell, moaning and screaming in pain, as the first blood spurted from the first wounds, Carly and Nick were caught in a massacre. The street became impassable. Cops fought cops to be the first at the enemy, and marchers trampled and ran over each other trying to escape.

Starting to run, Nick grabbed Carly. She heard the clubs landing on flesh, on bone, heard the cries of marchers being maimed. She saw blood everywhere, bright, shining red blood. She stumbled and almost fell, but Nick held on to her, kept her erect. The police scared him, and his fear made him furious. He raged at Carly, "You want to die?"

He kept running, kept her running, staying clear of the marchers until the cops and their prey were behind them. Nick slowed to a walk, puffing. "We're all right," he said as the first troops of an army twelve abreast in green dress uniforms wheeled around the corner, all with sidearms or clubs, bearing down on the few helpless marchers who had escaped from the cops.

Carly said, "Who . . . ?" and Nick, really scared now, said, "Landswehr."

The pair were encircled. The Landswehr were vigilantes, trained and disciplined, sworn to protect Austria from its enemies, within and without its sacred borders. As the green uniforms filled the street, their commander, Lieutenant Ludwig Kemp, raised a whistle and sounded one sharp blast. "Extended order! Extended order!" His men fanned out, and Lieutenant Kemp pointed his club like a saber to lead the charge.

The marchers were trapped. Carly and Nick were trapped, caught between cops in blue running at them and Landswehr in green closing the pincers.

Spotting the pair, three of the Landswehr sprinted toward them: fifty feet, forty, thirty. "In here!" Nick yelled, yanking Carly and plunging down some worn stone stairs leading to the basement of Mikkleman and Sons, Milliners.

Below, a porter came out of the Mikkleman basement, wheeling a mountain of cartons. Nick took Carly into the freight elevator and they rode to the first floor, walked into the stockroom, past employees, through the delivery door to the loading dock in the alley.

Nick jumped into the alley. He turned and raised his hands for Carly, but she already stood beside him, falling back against the loading dock, panting and very frightened. "You saved my life."

He looked away, embarrassed. They walked through the alley. He looked at his wristwatch, but it had stopped. "What time is it?"

Carly shook her head. She had never carried a watch. "I'm awfully late," he said, waving and running. Ernst Auerfeld, his employer, had warned him again and again.

Carly didn't want to lose him. She had a stack of questions. She couldn't forget the marchers. She saw them and *heard* them. She wrinkled her nose, blinking hard so she wouldn't cry. She watched the stranger disappear around the corner. Carly didn't even know his name.

She began to walk, an attractive young woman at whom men stared frankly as they passed. In all her twenty-one years Carly had never seen a deliberate act of violence, a conscious, eager, anticipatory outburst of cruelty. A man came toward her reading a book, and Carly remembered her father's birthday present. She walked faster, and at the intersection she stopped to get her bearings so she could proceed to a bookstore.

Later that day, when Nick left Ernst Auerfeld's drafting room, he telephoned Dolly Stacker. "Let's meet tonight, the whole group," Nick said. "You call and I'll call. We can meet at your apartment."

"Why tonight, Nick? *Nick?*"

"You'll know everything when we meet," Nick said. He had to collect enough money to cover the check for the storefront rental.

Waiting for the trolley, he smiled broadly and clapped his hands. "Zwischentheatre," he said aloud. "Zwischentheatre." He walked toward a streetlamp like a host welcoming his guest. "Zwischentheatre," Nick said, enjoying the word. Night after night the group had talked of the plays they would offer, the classics no less than the experimental. The Between Theatre, between the old and the new.

That same evening, in the Ottakring, a neighborhood of workingmen and drifters, Lieutenant Ludwig Kemp came out of a saloon where he had been celebrating the day's victory. He staggered slightly, stopping frequently until his head cleared.

Behind him, returning to his rooming house, Emil Huebner saw the soldier and recognized him. The soldier lived in the block. Emil Huebner envied the man, any man, his uniform.

Emil was a loyal, passionate Austrian. His parents were Austrian, his grandparents, his great-grandparents were Austrian. There had been Huebners and Schmidts and Lesters in and around the village near Steyr for generations. They were Aryans. Emil Huebner, though, looked like an Oriental. Some physical anomaly, some ancestor from the East, had invaded the genetic structure and endowed him with the inheritance which became the determining element in his life. He had been born a Chinese: straight black hair, olive skin, round face, almond eyes.

He was always called Chinese, Der Chineser in German, pronounced Der Kin-aiz-er, with the accent on the second syllable. Only his family and teachers called him Emil. He had been a foreigner from birth.

He was always the butt: in the village streets, on the playing fields, along the school corridors. His peers, with the distinctive cruelty of the young, extended and elaborated on the Oriental theme, breaking into singsong, shuffling along with arms raised before them, palms pressed together, heads bobbing. Even the town drunks jeered, "Der Chineser."

Der Chineser mourned the fall of the Hapsburgs, the dissolution of the empire as though he had suffered a death in the family. Austria became his family. The new, tiny country of less than seven million was even more precious to Der Chineser.

He left his village as quickly as he could. In Vienna he could live unnoticed. But people still stared, and some laughed at the sight of him. Friendless, he despised the riffraff, the dregs who filled the streets in constant protest. He loathed the new rulers of Austria, pallid little men in suits. The Emperor Franz Josef had lived in a uniform like the man approaching Der Chineser now. He saw the man raise his arm to salute.

Emil shivered with the excitement of being acknowledged. "I suppose you're returning from field exercises."

"From combat!" Kemp said. "From victory. The republic is in crisis." Kemp wrapped his arm around Der Chineser, who had never been embraced. "Join me in a beer, my friend."

In the saloon, Kemp paid for two steins. They chose a table beside the window, away from the sleeping drunks and neighborhood bullies. Kemp raised his stein. "To Austria!" As they drank, Kemp repeated his account of the day's rout. Der Chineser could hear the ringing slogans of the Landswehr, the pleas of the Communist traitors. As Kemp drained his stein, Der Chineser leaped to his feet. "Allow me, please."

They drank once more to Austria, and Kemp, his sodden brain riveted on victory, told Der Chineser once more how the Landswehr had destroyed Austria's malevolent foe. Der Chineser would have listened all night. He could see it all, see the loyal Landswehr troops gallantly charging the foreigners who had ruined Austria. "If only I could have been there," he said, and then, recklessly, "been with you."

Lieutenant Kemp swayed in his chair. He liked his new comrade, a true patriot. "You could be with us," Kemp said. Der Chineser felt faint as Kemp raised his stein. "To the Landswehr."

Der Chineser's voice shook. "To the Landswehr."

2

ONCE A YEAR ERNST
Auerfeld, the society architect, invited everyone in the drafting room
to a party, including the wives of the married architects. They were
never the only guests, however. Magda Auerfeld's parties were famous,
even in Vienna. Her admirers, and detractors, were legion.

Ernst started the custom intending it to be an office party. Magda
banged her fist on the breakfast table. "It is an insult!"

He watched the coffee which had sloshed from his cup spreading
over the white damask tablecloth. He gestured at the apartment. "This
is an insult?"

Magda faced him as though they were duelists. She was a heavy
woman whose height made her imposing instead of fat. She had blond
hair which had never been cut and lay coiled in layers and gathered at
the nape of her neck. "You cannot treat architects like servants, Ernst.
You yourself taught me an architect is a creative man, an artist."

When he insisted on limiting the guests to employees, Magda

15

dropped her napkin on the table. "Find yourself a hostess," she said, leaving him.

She was on the telephone with her father, making a date for dinner with her parents on the night of the party, when Auerfeld capitulated.

The episode was a trifle. Magda and Ernst had been at each other's throats even before their marriage. For that time and for Vienna, Magda had married late, being well into her twenties when Ernst Auerfeld came into her life. Before him, Magda had dismissed the men she encountered as dwarfs, midgets, puppets, and mannequins, despite the fact her parents were worried she would remain a spinster. Sophie and Simon Kalbeck had come to Vienna from Poland with Magda because they had not wanted their only child to grow up in a backwater and marry some hick who would bore her.

Their fear for Magda's future became an obsession, and to escape, Magda said she had found her beloved. "Promise you will tell no one." When they swore, she said, "Rudi Ludwig."

The young man's father, one of Vienna's leading furriers, had apprenticed his son to the owner of an African animal farm to prepare him for the Ludwig salon. "He'll be gone three years," Magda said. "I promised to wait."

Rudi Ludwig returned to Vienna in less than two months, a victim of allergies which had immobilized him in the tropics. Back in Austria Rudi recovered quickly, thrusting Magda into a panic.

To celebrate their reunion, Rudi took her to a ball given by the students of architecture at the University of Vienna. The gala was modeled after the Beaux Arts in Paris.

Magda was about to complain of a headache when Rudi introduced her to a strapping young man, half naked, wrapped in a leopard skin which did not reach his knees. He was tall and had a cavalryman's mustache. She looked up at him while they danced, her arm across his naked back, and she didn't release him when the music stopped. "Do you waltz as well?"

"Better."

"Prove it," Magda said, and after the first waltz, still holding him, she said, "You didn't prove it."

Magda met Ernst on a Saturday night. Monday afternoon she happened to be on the university campus, happened to be in Ernst Auerfeld's path. In a coffee house nearby, Magda asked him to a party and then went home to invite everyone else.

She was soon inviting him to her parents' hunting lodge for the weekend, and one weekend when her parents remained in Vienna, she drove Ernst to the lodge for the day. They spent most of the day in front of the fireplace, and that night Magda told her parents she was marrying Ernst.

For one of their wedding presents Magda's father gave her and Ernst two matching apartments and furnished both: one as their home, the other as an architectural drafting room. And when they returned from their honeymoon in Venice, almost before they unpacked, Magda's father had furnished Ernst with a full roster of clients.

Because Ernst Auerfeld could not resist the largesse, he never forgave Simon Kalbeck—or Magda. "I can get my own clients."

"Then you'll have an even larger practice," she said.

In 1937, Nick's first year with Ernst Auerfeld, the party fell on a harsh October night. Nick came out of the trolley, running across Este Platz to keep warm.

He rode up in a crowded elevator, with women in furs and men in tailored coats, one with an astrakhan collar. On the sixth floor everyone emerged. They were all guests of the Auerfelds that Saturday night.

Nick had never seen his employer's wife. She seemed to fill the doorway, wearing a purple velvet gown cut low in front and back and dropping to the floor. Her blond hair was gathered in a bun. She wore pearls and diamonds and gold everywhere: hair, ears, throat, hands, wrists. "I am Magda Auerfeld."

"Nicholas Gallanz," he said. "From the atelier."

"Atelier," she said, smiling at the young stranger, a cossack who belonged on a horse in boots and tunic. "Gal-l-l-l-anz," she said, making the name a mile long. "Ernst talks about Gal-l-l-lanz, his burden, always tardy." Magda raised her arm, covered with gold bracelets, gesturing at the doors of the drafting room across the corridor. "Grow up, *Gaspadin* Gallanz," she said, using the Russian word for friend. "This is not a kindergarten. Berte!"

Magda waved to an elderly uniformed maid who moved like an arthritic. "Make this one eat, Berte," Magda said, pushing Nick at the maid. "He needs some meat on his bones."

Magda left to welcome other arrivals, and Nick gave Berte his coat and entered an enormous parlor. To the left, at the far end, a brocade curtain hid a winter garden. Nick faced a series of oriels, like chapels in a cathedral.

He crossed the living room, ready to leave. In Josefstadter Strasse the Zwischentheatre were assembled for the first run-through of their first play, *Camouflage*. Nick had fought for the play, written by Sepp Wiegend, a chief clerk in the government tobacco monopoly. Nick had influenced the casting. He felt like a deserter. "Thirty minutes," he said to himself.

Berte followed him with a tray of hors d'oeuvres. "Take one," she said. Nick obeyed, and Berte pushed the tray into his chest. "More." She had come to Magda's parents when a girl in her teens, and she had raised their only child. When Magda had married, her parents sent Berte to care for the bride. Berte nudged Nick. "Another." The old woman had become like her employer.

Someone somewhere said, "Nick." He turned in a circle until he saw Alfred Slavin, who had been Ernst Auerfeld's classmate at the university and his first employee. "Over here," said Slavin, waving.

The architects were all in a bunch, Slavin and his wife, Anton Wiesner and his wife, all behind an open grand piano which shielded them from the other guests. They were neither eating nor drinking. To Nick they were tourists waiting to leave so they could dissect the great party. He abandoned them.

As he stopped another maid with another tray, Magda Auerfeld said, "Slow. Don't fill your belly." She sailed past him to the brocade curtain. "Ladies and gentlemen," she said, and, louder, "Attention!" She repeated, "Attention!" until she silenced the guests. "Dinner!" Magda pulled a cord, and the drape moved to one side like a stage curtain. Her guests faced a large U-shaped table with heaping platters of beef, ham, veal, venison, game in aspic, almost hiding the waiters behind the food. Magda spread her arms. "I cannot eat alone."

Nick hugged the walls, avoiding the stampede. For a while the party stopped as everyone ate. Nick pushed back his sleeve to check the time, and remembered his broken wristwatch left on the chest of drawers. He looked around for a clock and almost bumped into someone. He said, "Sorry," and the girl said something, and then he really saw her, a tall girl with a red ribbon holding back her long hair.

She said, "We meet again."

Nick said, "Again?" He studied the strange girl until, all of a sudden, she wasn't strange. She began to smile, so he began to smile. "You," Nick said, recognizing her. "That day near the Hofburg."

"You saved me," Carly said. "I'm Carly Siefermann."

"Nick Gallanz," he said.

Then they were silent, both trying desperately to say something, until, feeling stupid, Carly offered, "You know Magda."

"I work for her—for Ernst Auerfeld," Nick said. "I'm an architect."

Magda passed them, crossing the room full of guests as though it were empty. "Fritz!" She waved. "Fritz!"

In the entrance, a man Nick's age gave Berte his coat. He was taller than Nick, taller than any man in the room except Ernst Auerfeld. He made Berte smile just looking at him. He had perfect features, nose, mouth, chin. His eyes were Nordic, a luminous blue, setting off his hair, jet black and curly. He was spectacular.

He gestured at Magda. He didn't like parties, didn't like Austrians or anyone else en masse. Except for the obligatory events at which Fritz represented the House of Von Gottisberg, he did not respond to invitations. But he had known Magda forever. And she had nerve and style. And he had made money with Magda's father. So Fritz had come by for a drink.

As he came out of the entrance, waiting for Magda, some of the guests caught sight of him. Several bent their heads, whispering and gesturing. Others, puzzled by the whispering around them, turned, and they, too, were affected by the appearance of Magda's tardy guest.

Behind the piano, Alfred Slavin said to his wife, "I-I'll be back," leaving her and the other architects. He crossed the room, his heart pounding.

Fritz took Magda's hands, kissing each hand. "I'm late," he said.

"Not in my house." Magda put her arm through his. She liked Fritz. She had always favored a handsome man. Her father was handsome, and she had married another.

"Excuse me," said Alfred Slavin. He had never confronted a stranger in his life. "Excuse me, Baron, for this intrusion. I wanted to say . . . I saw you on that jumper last month. At the horse show. You were . . . well, no one came near, Baron."

"Too kind," Fritz said.

At that moment Magda saw Anton Wiesner. The little snob, who wouldn't talk to anyone in the drafting room, was making a beeline for them. "Come, Fritz."

Wiesner trapped them, gushing all over Fritz about the Von Gottisberg collection. Once a year Fritz opened the palace so the public could see the paintings.

By that time Fritz commanded the attention of most of the guests. Women wanted to touch him, men wanted to be with him, and not because of his title. Vienna teemed with titles, barons and counts and princes. Fritz had something else, an indefinable allure, a magnetism which could neither be defined nor denied. His attraction was universal. A vain person would have exploited and thus diluted the effect he created. Fritz had always been bored with the reaction of the hoi polloi, and was often annoyed by these small storms of attention.

Magda finally dumped Anton Wiesner and took Fritz to her parents. "Greetings, Simon," Fritz said. He bent over Sophie Kalbeck's hand. "Marry me."

"Tonight," she said.

Magda knew her parents enjoyed Fritz, so she listened patiently for a time. "Mama, you cannot keep him to yourself," she said. Magda intended to introduce the Baron Von Gottisberg to a favored few of her guests. She took his arm. "You can indulge an old lady."

She couldn't avoid Helga Siefermann. The envious pest dragged her husband halfway across the room, making certain she would not be omitted. Magda said, "Baron, let me present Helga and Klaus Siefermann."

Helga had seen the new, young baron, but only at a distance, in a crowded lobby between the acts, on a crowded staircase. She didn't care if Magda Auerfeld never spoke to her again. "Carly!"

Standing beside Nick, Carly saw her mother in a crowd with Magda. "Come and meet my parents."

Fritz saw the girl. She was a good-looking piece. Her mother introduced her, and Carly gave him her hand. Nick watched the baron bow, holding Carly's hand and smiling at her like they were alone. "Nick Gallanz," he said, ending the tête-à-tête.

"I need a glass of champagne," Fritz said, abandoning Magda and her court. He took Carly with him, and Carly took Nick. The baron was the most attractive man she had ever seen, and Nick looked like someone from the Arctic, someone from a primitive race. Carly couldn't keep from smiling.

A waiter filled three flutes, and Nick took one. He didn't like champagne. "Do you think Austria is in terrible trouble?" Carly asked.

"Austria is always in terrible trouble," Fritz said.

"You're teasing," she said.

"Never about Austria," Fritz said.

"We saw a terrible battle," she said, including Nick. "We saw harmless men beaten, Austrian citizens beaten to the ground and bleeding. First the police and then those terrible Landswehr. Using clubs on innocent men who couldn't fight back. Cowards!"

Fritz saw the color rise in her face, making her even more attractive. "The streets are no longer safe," he said, and to Nick, "Agreed?"

"I still go out every day," Nick said. "And every night." When Carly set down her glass, Nick put his beside it, finished with royalty and forsaking the run-through of *Camouflage*. "We're leaving," he told Carly, taking her arm.

She said, startled, "Leaving . . . ?" and Fritz said, "Not without me. We can settle Austria's future in peace. This way."

Fritz had parked his coupe near the building. They squeezed into the little car. "Where are we going?" Carly asked.

"Trust me," Fritz said.

He drove to the Hotel Imperial, and in the café they sat at a small table, almost touching, like three conspirators, until Fritz grew bored with the pair's sophomoric prattle. "I think we can stop worrying about Austria for the rest of the night," he said. "I'll drive you home. Nick, where do you live?"

Nick had no choice. "Sternwalter Strasse in the Eighteenth," he said, raising his arm for a waiter. "I'll get the check," he said, forfeiting lunch for the week.

"There is no check," Fritz said. The Imperial mailed him a statement every month.

They squeezed into the coupe with Carly between them once more. Nick could feel her against him. Fritz drove fast, making sharp turns, and Carly's hair fell across Nick's face. As they reached District XVIII, he said, "Straight ahead," and then, "Turn here. You can leave me on the corner."

"I'm glad we saw each other again," Carly said.

"Then we'll see each other again," Nick said, not wanting to leave her with the baron.

"*Wiedersehen*," Fritz said.

Nick boosted himself out of the coupe and crossed the street. He let himself into the ornate lobby of an old apartment building and rode the elevator to the fifth floor.

In the apartment, he dropped his coat on a chair. He stood over the chair, ready to kick something or hit something. He went to the cabinet and took out a bottle of slivovitz, but set it down on a tray of glasses. He didn't like slivovitz. He took off his jacket, throwing it at his coat and walking into the master suite with its massive bed, like a barge between the windows. He left the bedroom, roaming through the apartment. He couldn't even remember how she looked, but as he paused under the arched entrance to the dark dining room, Nick said aloud, "Carly."

Back in the coupe, Fritz watched Nick walk into the building.

Fritz's left arm lay across the steering wheel, and he faced Carly in the green glow of the instrument panel. "Shall we go somewhere to see the sunrise?"

She shook her head, smiling slightly. "Some other night."

He leaned forward and kissed her. Her lips were soft, pliant. She was pliant. He could feel her breasts, firm and full, as he kissed her. Fritz moved his left arm, taking her shoulder, bringing her closer, letting his hand drift slowly, slowly along her spine, into the small of her back. He raised his head but did not release her, looking at the lovely child, the fresh, warm, fertile, lovely child.

Carly clung to him. Without preface, he had captured her completely. His body against hers, his hand touching, barely, her buttocks, his lips against hers, had triumphed. Carly had been kissing for years, in other cars, front and back seats, in corridors, hasty kisses at parties and lingering kisses in lobbies and stairwells, standing kisses, and, a few times, kisses on a sofa, and once on a riverbank with a blind date whom she had to fight before she could escape. Now, in Fritz's arms, she could not resist. Fritz kissed her again, gently.

He took her breath away, made her tremble, and he frightened her because he made her frightened of herself. He had almost instantly brought her to the forbidden edge beyond which she refused to venture, especially since Lisl Schott's narrow escape. Carly had to stop him while she could. She turned her face. "Please. I'd like to go home now."

Fritz took her chin until he could see her clearly and she could see him. "Are you certain?"

She could still feel his mouth on hers. "Yes, I am," she said, and knew she lied, and knew he knew she lied.

Fritz made a sort of nod and released her, setting her free. She felt as though she had been defeated, as though she had been given a prize which had been immediately snatched away from her. As the car moved, Carly sat beside him adrift, bewildered, unable to sort out her feelings. She felt certain that as he drove, he laughed inwardly.

He shifted through the gears, picking up speed. He had a baby beside him, a child. She should be rolling a hoop in the park, playing hopscotch in the park. "Tell me once more where you live."

In Kruger Strasse, in front of Carly's apartment, Fritz left the coupe before she had opened the door. He helped her out and followed her into the building. "Auf Wiedersehen," he said, lying. Fritz blamed himself. He should have discarded Magda Auerfeld's invitation.

Alone, Carly crossed the lobby like an ice skater, taking long, and his brother, Sam, in the chair in the corner with all the newspapers.

Lottie Gallanz was taller than most women of her generation, and slim like Nick. She had black eyes and a sculpted nose. She dressed in black. Every day but Saturday she returned from buying her family's food, scurrying into the kitchen as though she had escaped from a battlefield. Lottie came from generations of people crouching behind bolted doors.

She stood on tiptoe to kiss Nick. Lottie had her family, her world was complete, here in her tiny fortress. "Now we'll eat," she said. "Give me your coat, Nicki."

She asked for it every week, and every week Nick said, "I can handle my coat. Hello, Papa. Hello, Sam."

Nick went to his father, a watchmaker, who hugged him. "I kissed my father all my life," Boris Gallanz once told his sons. He held on to Nick, studying him as had Lottie. "You're all right, Nicki? You need something?"

Neither the ritual nor the language varied. "Nothing, Papa, nothing," he said, and then, "My wristwatch!" Nick patted his pockets. He had left it behind. "It stopped."

"Bring it to me," Boris said. He worked for Schunemann, one of the best jewelers in the city.

"I need a watch," Nick said. "We're having run-throughs at the Zwischentheatre all week, and the timing must be right."

"Here," Sam said, raising his left arm to remove his watch.

Boris followed Nick across the small room. "Sam, this is your watch," Boris said. "I gave *you* this watch."

"He'll give it back," Sam said. He looked at Nick, grinning. "Won't you, kid?"

"Cross my heart," Nick said, and then, "Big Ben!" Sam's watch was oversized, in a heavily scored silver case. The thick leather band was scored as well, and as Nick fumbled with it, Boris took his wrist.

"Here, let me," he said, buckling the wristband as Lottie summoned them to dinner.

Their places at the table were immutable. Boris faced Lottie, and Sam, the eldest, sat at his right. Sam, like his father short and plump, was a lawyer who avoided the courtroom, content to remain hidden in the large firm which employed him.

As she served them, Lottie always told her family not to wait for her, and when she took her place, always began an interminable series of questions concerning the food, asking for candid answers, and Nick

rhythmic strides in a lazy series of arcs: right, left, right, left, her hands in her coat pockets. She could hardly wait to tell Lisl. Everything had been so much fun. Carly giggled, remembering how she had fought with her mother about the Auerfeld party, how reluctantly she had dressed for it. Finding Nick Gallanz at the party seemed like a chapter in a story. Carly had never encountered anyone so . . . wild. "We're leaving," she said aloud, giggling again. Nick Gallanz *belonged* in a story.

The elevator stopped. Carly stepped into the corridor. She had never, anywhere, met anyone like the baron. Rich people, some with titles, had come to the Siefermann home all her life. Fritz was . . . "different," she said. She took her keys from her pocket, and later, in bed, she unexpectedly felt his lips once more and turned, pushing her face into the pillow, her cheeks flushed, her heart beating fast, her naked body warm and tingling.

Fritz sped through Vienna like someone in a race. In less than five minutes he turned into a narrow lane built for horse carts. Only a flickering flame on his right broke the darkness.

The light came from a gas lamp hanging beside a thick door with the number 11 in brass, at eye level. Fritz pressed an enamel button beside the door.

He waited because Katharina did not accept a client, even the Baron Fritz Von Gottisberg, until she herself had identified the guest. A rectangle lay in the door through which Katharina could see out but no one could see in.

An elderly porter in livery with white gloves admitted Fritz. Neither he nor Fritz spoke in the overheated house, which smelled, now in October, of roses, a heavy, sticky smell. The house was deathly still, almost spooky, like an undertaker's parlor.

The porter left, walking beneath a flight of stairs, and Fritz turned familiarly to his right, entering a room lit by candles in candelabra. He took off his coat, and as he dropped it, Katharina stopped in the entrance. "I've missed you, Baron."

Katharina dressed for the turn of the century, telling clients to call her Katharina, after Katharina Schratt, the Burgtheatre actress who had been the great friend and solace of the Emperor Franz Josef. Katharina named all her girls after queens, empresses, mistresses of monarchs. She wore lipstick and mascara and rouge, and made her hair a lunatic shade of orange. She looked crazy, but she owned, including the building, the most restricted, selective, profitable whorehouse in Eastern Europe. "Did you have any fun at Magda Auerfeld's party?"

Fritz grinned. He didn't know or care how Katharina had learned of the party. "I hated her dessert."

"She doesn't understand the flavors you prefer." Katharina raised her hand, wiggling her fingers, summoning him as she walked to the staircase. "Giselle has been asking for you, Baron."

"Alexandra?"

Katharina put her hand on the bannister. "Alexandra has left me," she said. Katharina had herself put the gypsy under surveillance and caught her stealing from clients: petty thefts, gypsy thefts, anything that hadn't been nailed down. Katharina waited until she personally arranged for the girl to be deported before kicking her into the street, where the police waited. Katharina looked over her shoulder. "Have I ever disappointed you?"

At the head of the stairs she turned to the left and knocked on the third door. A young woman with black hair bobbed and parted in the center opened the door. She wore a silk robe which fell apart at her breasts. Katharina said, "This is Victoria."

Victoria took Fritz's hand, just his fingertips, raising them to her mouth and stepping back, bringing him with her so Katharina could close the door. Victoria tugged at a sash around her hips, and the robe opened wide.

On the bed, a four-poster with a white canopy, lay a buxom young woman propped high on white pillows, one leg drawn up and a scarf across her thighs. "Welcome, my darling," Giselle said as Fritz pulled off his clothes.

"Go ahead," he said, undressing. "Go ahead, go ahead."

Giselle sat up on the bed, reaching for Victoria and falling back into the mountain of pillows. Giselle's thighs parted to admit the other woman. Fritz saw her link her ankles across Victoria's hips, taking her prisoner, saw the pair merge into a tangle of arms, legs, torsos, quivering, twisting, moaning, groaning, as he became naked and flung himself onto the bed, and they parted to fall upon him like beasts of prey.

Sunday morning, the telephone rang like a fire alarm. In his clothes on the sofa, Nick rolled, half awake, slipping off the couch, hitting the floor with his knee. The phone rang again, and Nick ran to it, believing Carly was calling him.

He said happily, "Greetings." By then he was fully awake, and realized Carly didn't have his telephone number.

A woman asked for Elsie. Someone banged on the apartment door. Nick finished with the woman and then heard a muffled, "N-Nick?"

When he opened the door, a glowing Max Ingster said, "Y-you shoul have b-b-been at the r-run-through." He swung Nick around like dance partner. Max, a compact, wiry man, was a gym teacher in a hig school near the Grinzing. "N-Nick, we were g-great. Everybody. J-Juditl Emmerich, Rex Mulhall. They had everyone crying. Sepp s-said the made his little p-play a big play. He's right, Nick. They're t-t-terrific."

"You? Were you terrific?" Nick had chosen the gym teacher to play the military attaché, the villain, and had fought with Sepp and Peter Dietrich, the director, knowing that Max never stuttered under pressure, or in real or possible danger, or in any emergency anywhere.

"N-nobody complained so I guess I passed," Max said, whacking Nick across the shoulders. "The run-through was a hit. And if we g-get an audience, we'll be a hit."

"We'll have an audience," Nick said. "People will come and they'll tell other people."

"Right," Max said. "Hey, let's celebrate. I'll buy breakfast."

"Sunday," Nick said. "I'm with the family for dinner."

Max followed him through the apartment. "Dinner," he said. "This is breakfast."

Nick entered the bathroom to shave. "Sunday I fast till two o'clock," he said. "His name is Klaus!" Nick shoved Max into the wall, racing through the corridor.

Nick had tried to find Carly's phone number the night before, but she was not listed. She had introduced him to her parents, and Nick had fallen asleep trying to remember their names. He opened the telephone book. "Klaus Siefermann," he said, and put his forefinger under the number. He called but there was no answer.

Max Ingster left, looking for company. Nick shaved and bathed and dressed in clean clothes. He called Carly again, then tried a third time without luck before leaving the apartment.

In the trolley Nick rode across Vienna like someone entering another country. He had left Leopoldstadt, the ghetto, before his eighteenth birthday, and now, at twenty-five, he returned like a penitent.

The apartment building he entered had a narrow, clammy entrance with stairs near the rear and people on the stairs all the way to the top: kids playing and neighbors gossiping. Nick's family lived on the third floor.

He used his key to please his mother. By the time he opened the door, Lottie Gallanz had flung herself out of the kitchen to greet him. "Nicki," she said. She clasped Nick's face in her hands. "Let me look at you." He had been gone six days. Nick saw his father in the kitchen,

tried to join Sam and his father in their praise. Every dinner was Lottie's triumph, her distinction. And every Sunday Nick wanted to protest, wanted to shake his mother and lift her out of the chair, out of the kitchen, out of the shabby apartment into the *world*. He wanted to end the succession of empty days which made up his mother's life. "It's marvelous," Nick said. "Everything is wonderful."

They were on the fruit compote when Lottie said, "I called you this week, Nicki. Wednesday, I think. Yes, Wednesday."

Nick looked at Sam, who had insisted he give his parents the telephone number: "There could be an emergency. They might need you."

"A woman answered," Lottie said.

Nick wanted to tell both his mother and his father, wanted to stop the adolescent *hiding*, but Sam stared at him and he could *hear* Sam: "They can't understand your life. You'll hurt them."

"Who is she, Nicki?"

"A friend from the Zwischentheatre," Nick said. Sam bent over the bowl of fruit compote.

The ritual crept through the afternoon. On Sunday Lottie delayed cleaning the dishes, instead joining her family in the living room. Within moments Boris plodded to the bedroom for a nap, and Sam sat in his chair, head drooping. Lottie's eyes closed. They made Nick angry and sad. If he skipped a Sunday, he felt guilty, but whenever he came to Leopoldstadt, he wanted to run.

And he loved them, loved them without restraint. He loved his shy, reclusive, brainy older brother. He loved Boris Gallanz, the frightened, bowing and scraping alien, the perpetual stranger living on sufferance, always trying to please, to slip through the traps and hazards ready to engulf and destroy him and his family. And Nick loved the terrified woman who crept through the streets like a wraith, asking only to be left alone, to be spared another day. He wanted to shield her, wrap her in furs, hold her close and promise to keep her safe.

On Sunday he never left until his mother returned to the kitchen. If Sam was asleep, Nick didn't wake him, and he never woke his father.

At the trolley stop, Nick went into a tobacco shop and called Carly, but there was no answer. She and her parents did not return from their country house on the Danube until nearly midnight, and the maid never worked on Sunday.

At noon Monday, Nick slipped off his stool and reached for his jacket and coat. As he hurried through the drafting room, Ernst Auerfeld said, "Come back on time or don't come back."

In the Caravan, the nearest coffee house, Nick dropped coins into a pay telephone. "Answer!" he said just before he heard a woman's voice. Finally! "Let me speak with Carly."

"She is out," said Helga Siefermann. "Who is calling?"

"I am Nick Gallanz. When will she be home?"

"Around dinner," Helga said. "Gallanz? How do you spell Gallanz?"

"Like gallant," Nick said, "but with a z instead of a t."

Later that afternoon, while writing to her mother, Helga heard Carly in the foyer. Carly joined her, plopping down in a chair and pushing off her shoes. "Where were you today?"

"With Lisl Schott," Carly said, raising her legs, curling up on the chair and facing the coal fire in the grate. The raucous sounds of traffic in the street were only a murmur here, eight floors above Kruger Strasse. The fire made odd shapes on the walls and ceilings.

Helga wrote, "Carly has returned, the usual tornado. You should see her, Mama, with the color in her cheeks and her hair tumbled from the wind. She is wearing a skirt and a sweater, both without color. She buys coal miner's shoes and her coat, that same old tweed, belongs on a donkey. She doesn't care how she looks, and still she is the most beautiful young thing in Vienna."

As her mother continued, Carly rose, bending for her shoes. Helga didn't look up from the paper. "Your hair is a mop, child. Fix your hair for dinner." Carly walked toward her room. "Who is Nick Gallanz?"

Carly whirled around, her skirt billowing. "Nick Gallanz? He's . . . why?"

Helga said something which Carly could not hear.

"I can't hear you."

Helga said loudly, "He telephoned today. Who is he?"

"An architect," Carly said, sorry she hadn't left Lisl immediately after lunch. "You met him at Magda Auerfeld's party."

"I *met* him," Helga said, and then, flatly, "Oh, yes," remembering the man who had attached himself to Carly and the baron. "Why did he call?"

"Mama, he's a boy and I'm a girl," Carly said, carrying the shoes to the telephone in the foyer.

Less than five minutes later, Magda Auerfeld entered her husband's drafting room. She wore her karakul coat and a matching karakul turban which sat at a rakish angle over her left eye. Her blond hair seemed golden against the gleaming black fur. Work stopped at every drafting table. Ernst Auerfeld intercepted her. "Magda? What happened?"

"A personal matter," she said, passing him. "Gal-l-l-l-anz!"

Nick slid off his stool. "Carly Siefermann called you," Magda said. Her telephone had been ringing when she returned to the apartment.

"I need to use your phone," Nick said.

Magda shook her head. He had more gall than an alley cat. She pointed at Ernst's desk. "There is the telephone."

"That one is strictly business," he said. "No exceptions."

"I am not a social secretary, sonny," Magda said.

"Thank you for your message," he said, getting back on his stool. Magda watched the sassy bugger, and as he picked up a pencil, she took his wrist.

"Find a barber before you go to Carly Siefermann," Magda said, pulling him off the stool. She marched him through the drafting room to the open door of her apartment.

Carly beat the maid to the telephone. "Hello!"

"At last," Nick said. "I called all day yesterday. Where were you?" Carly stared into the telephone as though she could see him. She had never been cross-examined. Nick said, "Hello. Come back."

She said, "I'm here," and he told her everything: his discovery of the Zwischentheatre, the group of stage-struck men and women who had banded together to produce plays, the selection of their first play, Camouflage. "You must come to opening night," he said.

When he was gone, Carly dropped into the chair beside the tab-oret, her legs extended and her arms hanging at her sides. She felt as though she had finished a race. Her mother saw her sprawled in the chair and came close. "Are you well?"

"Wonderful," she said. She pushed herself erect. "Wonderful," she repeated, on her way to a bath, forgetting her shoes.

In a rathskeller after work, Nick ate standing and hurried to the Zwischentheatre. Peter Dietrich, the director, and Abe Feiner, a book-seller in the group, were discussing motivations of the characters in Camouflage. Max Ingster followed Nick into the storefront, and Sepp Wiegend, the author of the play, followed Max. Others in the cast and in the group arrived. "Let's clear the stage," Peter said, and more loudly, "Judith, we're waiting."

"Let me," Nick said, crossing the stage to a line of doors along the rear wall. Nick had designed a row of large closets for dressing rooms. He knocked on a door and opened it. Judith Emmerich and another woman owned a fashionable beauty salon. Judith had dressed for her role since the first reading of *Camouflage*. "Peter Dietrich has no sensitivity," she said to the mirror.

Nick extended his hand. "Forgive him."

Sitting between Peter and Sepp Wiegend, Nick held Sam's wristwatch and timed the run-through. Afterward, the group left the storefront for a nearby café they had adopted to dissect the performances. "Not tonight," Nick said, running for a trolley.

He rode to District XVIII. The trolley stopped across from the apartment building where Fritz had parked Saturday night.

Lights burned in the apartment, and Nick crossed the living room wearing his coat. "Nick? Nicki?"

Dolly Stacker lay in the center of the big bed. She had been in Brno for the weekend visiting her brother. That morning she had gone from the train to her office in the furniture showroom, staying late to catch up with her work. Dolly thought of Nick on the train from Brno, and all through the day she caught herself thinking of him. She liked him more than she had ever liked any man. He was never dull, and he could see through people, could see the truth. Now and then he made Dolly uncomfortable with the truth.

Because Dolly's brother married into one of the richest families in Czechoslovakia, her parents left her the sprawling apartment. She lived alone and enjoyed her privacy until that spring. Six months earlier, in her bed, she opened Nick's hand and closed his fingers around a key to the apartment.

When Nick stopped in the doorway of the bedroom, Dolly raised her arms. "Come to Mama."

"Not tonight," Nick said, and then, impatient with himself, he walked into the bedroom. "I'm leaving."

He didn't make sense to her. "Is the building on fire?"

"Funny," he said. "I met someone, someone else."

"You're sleeping everywhere," she said.

"Not true."

"But you finally decided to tell me now."

"I met her now," he said. "Saturday night at the Auerfelds'."

"Love at first sight," she said.

"I met a girl I want to see again. And again."

"Don't be so goddamn noble," she said, and softly, "I'm not greedy, Nicki." She beckoned him. "There is enough for two."

"I'm not a sultan who keeps a harem."

"Yak, yak, yak, yak," she said. "I'm tired. Come to bed. We'll talk in the morning."

"I won't be here in the morning," he said. He went to the closet Dolly had emptied for his clothes, and brought out his suitcase, setting the luggage on a chair and raising the cover.

Dolly sat up in bed. "Come here, Nick." He took an armful of his clothes from the closet and dumped everything into the suitcase. "You're afraid," she said.

Nick came to the bed. "We had fun," he said. "We'll still have fun. We'll be together at the Zwischentheatre."

"Kiss me," she said. "I dare you."

He bent over the bed and she locked her hands around him. He kissed her, and she gave him everything she had. He reached up to free himself. "I'll finish," he said, returning to the closet.

"You bastard."

He grinned. "You don't mean that."

"I do mean it," she said. "Bastard, bastard, bastard." As he stuffed his shoes into his coat pockets, though, she relented. "Nick? Keep the key."

"It's on the cabinet with the slivovitz," he said, closing the suitcase. "Can I borrow a few schillings till payday?"

She pointed at her purse on the chest of drawers. "Help yourself." Nick brought her the purse, and Dolly gave him some money. "Enough?"

"Plenty," he said. "Thanks." He took the suitcase from the chair. "Thanks."

"Nick—"

"I'll see you," he said. "We'll see each other."

Saturday night Nick took Carly through an alley into Josefstadter Strasse, opposite the butcher shop. "Stop," he said.

Nick had transformed the storefront. The big windows were blacked out. A powerful light bulb within a metal reflector hung over the sidewalk. Above the light, fastened to the building wall, on a white sign with a red border Carly read, "ZwISCHENTHEATRE." "My work," Nick said, writing in the air. He steered her toward Dora Ertle, a midwife, in the ticket booth. "Do we have an audience, Dora?"

"Not enough." Dora wore a coat over a sweater, and wool gloves. Above her on the wall hung a photograph of the group.

"I brought a customer," he said.

Dora saw money in his hand. "Are you crazy?"

"I'm buying a ticket," he said. "Sell me a ticket."

"Sell?" She tore a ticket from a large roll. "Here's a ticket."

"Take the money," he said. Dora hid her hands. "It's not for me," he said. "Carly Siefermann. Dora Ertle."

Carly said, "Hello," and Dora smiled and put the ticket in her hand.

"Welcome, my dear," Dora said. She leaned out of the booth. "Judith Emmerich is having a nervous breakdown!"

"Thank you very much," Nick said.

Inside, Carly paused between two rows of benches which could seat two hundred people. The walls were a neutral color, but the curtain was a brilliant blue. "Did you do all this?"

"You are not in Epidaurus," Nick said, very pleased. There were eight people, three women and five men, on the benches. "I hope you can find a place," he said, gesturing. "I must go backstage."

"Can I come?" Carly asked, but then shook her head. "No, I shouldn't interfere."

He took her hand, walking down the aisle between the benches. "Around here everyone interferes." He pushed the curtain aside and let her in.

They passed Rex Mulhall, playing a squire, his lips moving as he rehearsed silently. "His real name is Egon Burghofer," Nick said. "He is a pharmacist with his own shop, but in the Zwischentheatre he becomes Rex Mulhall. Rex, king, and Mulhall by using half of each grandmother's name. He is afraid if his customers learn he is an actor, they will stop trusting him with their prescriptions."

Sepp Wiegend faced them. "The audience is the same size as the cast," he said.

"Wrong," Nick said. "Carly makes nine to your eight." He introduced her to Sepp.

"M-make it s-seven," said Max Ingster. "The famous J-Judith Emmerich is s-sulking in her tent."

Nick pointed at the row of dressing rooms. "Here are the tents," he told Carly, and to Max, "Let me try."

Judith Emmerich's door stood ajar, so she could hear her enemies and her friends. Nick knocked and entered the tiny dressing room, closing the door. "I'm late," he said, a faithful courtier begging his liege lord's indulgence.

"Peter sent you," Judith said, aware of the plot against her. "The coward," she said. "He hates me, Nick. He orders me to play in the wings. In every scene I am out of sight while Rex Mulhall, the pill pusher, is up front."

Nick put his hands on her shoulders and turned her around to face the mirror. "Sarah Bernhardt played tragedies with her back to the audience," he said.

Judith felt behind her, groping for him. "Stay with me."

Out front, Carly took a place in the first row of benches. Nick had brought her to a new land, strange and enchanting. The perky woman in the ticket booth, the men behind the curtain, the distraught actress whom only Nick could save, seemed to be caught up in disasters, large and small, and all seemed, somehow, elated.

A man and a woman arrived, choosing the front bench across the aisle from Carly. Then she heard footsteps and looked back as two men walked toward the stage, removing their coats. She counted the audience again and again until she saw Dora come into the storefront and disappear behind the curtain. Soon the lights dimmed. She heard someone moving. "Carly?" Nick whispered. Bumping into her, he sat down.

She leaned toward him. "Twenty-eight!" she whispered, excited and happy.

The play enchanted Carly. She chose no favorites in the cast, liking all equally, liking them especially because they acted out of love for the theater, out of dedication. She hoped the play would never end. When the blue curtain moved across the stage, creaking along the overhead track, she applauded louder and longer than anyone except Nick. The cast responded extravagantly, bowing and beaming, and when Judith Emmerich reached for Rex Mulhall's hand, raising their hands high, and Nick rose, crying, "Bravo! Bravo!" Carly jumped up. "Bravo! Bravo!"

The men and women in the audience moved to the aisle, leaving the storefront. Carly tugged Nick's arm. "Can I meet them? I think they're wonderful!"

"They will agree," Nick said.

The ensemble assembled in front of the Zwischentheatre, and the critique of the night's performance began immediately, like a war. They left the storefront without a break in the battle, and to Carly, their voices sounded like firecrackers exploding. "You will like this place," Nick said, taking her into a café.

Inside, the men pushed tables together, and everyone dragged chairs across the floor, all while everyone continued talking. When the wine came, Judith stood up with her glass. Her lips quivered. "To Peter, my director, who believed in me, and to Sepp, who gave me the role of a lifetime."

Sepp followed Judith and Peter followed him. One at a time the cast spoke. Love poured over everyone like lava. They remained in the café until Erik Ekstrom, the owner, showed them out so he could close. Max Ingster took Carly and Nick in his car. There were seven all told, and Carly sat on Nick's lap. In Kruger Strasse in front of Carly's apartment, Nick followed her out of the car. "Good night, Max."

As Carly pressed the night bell for the porter, Nick looked at the city in the shadows. "I love Vienna now, late and quiet," he said. "Sometimes I believe if I listen, hold my breath without moving, I can hear the footsteps of all the armies which have marched across Vienna." Behind them the porter turned the key and opened the door. "Fraulein."

"How will you get home?" she asked. Nick had moved in with Max Ingster, promising to share the rent.

"I'll walk until there is a trolley. Now is the best time to walk. And I can sleep tomorrow."

"It *is* tomorrow," Carly said.

"Fraulein," said the porter.

"I have to go," she said. She extended her hand. "Thank you."

Nick took her hand and discovered that he didn't want to let go. "Fraulein."

"Good night," she said. She opened the door, and Nick closed it, keeping her with him.

"Next Saturday," he said. "Seven o'clock next Saturday, all right?"

She nodded, and the porter opened the door. "Fraulein, please." She slipped by him into the lobby, and Nick grabbed the door away from the porter. "Wait!"

He caught up with her. "How about Wednesday?" he asked, then changed his mind. Wednesday lay beyond the horizon. "Tuesday! I'll come Tuesday. I'll come from work."

Carly couldn't sleep. Nick and his gang had left her wide awake. In her room with the door closed, she went to the windows, parting the drapes to look out at the silent, darkened city. She listened hard, trying to hear the soldiers whom Nick had resurrected.

The men and women of the Zwischentheatre had flipped her world topsy-turvy. Bits and pieces of the long night returned vividly. She left the windows and sat down on her bed, hugging herself. They were all wild at the Zwischentheatre.

She discovered she was hungry, and realized she had not eaten since lunch. It seemed to Carly she had lived for years since noon. She crossed the bedroom on her way to the kitchen but stopped before she came to the door. Gnawing on a chicken leg or a cold chop or a cold sausage seemed dull. Carly unbuttoned her blouse. She decided to ask Nick for a tour of Vienna, his Vienna.

From the instant he woke that same Saturday, Emil Huebner, Der Chineser, was counting the minutes. Before the day ended, he would be a soldier, a rifleman in the Landswehr. He would meet Lieutenant Ludwig Kemp, his new friend, at seven o'clock, in the saloon where they had shared a beer. Der Chineser faced an eternity.

He tried not to look at his watch. Der Chineser shaved, bathed, completed his week's laundry in the freezing basement of the rooming house. In a café he lingered over his breakfast. In another he extended his lunch. By five o'clock that afternoon he could no longer stay away from the saloon, where he began to circle the block.

By seven-thirty, alone on the corner, Der Chineser knew he had been cast aside once more. As he crossed the street, on his way to his rooming house, he saw a large flatbed truck with stakes along the sides and across the rear. Men stood in the rear. The flatbed swerved, heading for him. Der Chineser dashed back to the sidewalk as someone yelled, "Huebner!"

Someone yelled "Emil!" and Der Chineser recognized Lieutenant Kemp, in uniform, leaning out of the truck cab. "Hop in!" Kemp yelled. "Give this guy a hand!" In the rear, men raised stakes from slots and others bent over the side, and for the first time in his life, Der Chineser faced helping hands. Strangers yanked him off his feet and onto the flatbed.

Someone banged on the roof of the cab. "Go! Go! Go!" The truck moved out. Der Chineser heard greetings from all sides. One person slapped him on the back. Someone else offered him a cigarette. He heard the word *kamerad*, comrade. He leaned against the truck cab, dazed.

In Vienna the Landswehr used an old laundry building with boarded-up windows for an armory. They assembled on Wednesday and Saturday nights for close-order drill, care and cleaning of equipment, and other basic-training routines. With the others Der Chineser went through an enormous door once used by the wagons which collected and delivered the laundry. Inside, the building had been stripped. Der Chineser could barely see. Lieutenant Kemp hurried ahead to a switchboard beside a wooden platform. Searchlights made the laundry bright as day.

Everyone except Der Chineser wore a Landswehr uniform. Every-

one had a rifle as well, and as other troops arrived, they went to crates
of weapons beside the stairs leading to the wooden platform.

Kemp left Der Chineser and crossed the building, saluting Major
Manfred Oster, the ranking Landswehr officer for the night's training.
The major stared at Kemp's companion. "Are we recruiting Orientals
now?"

"He's a good man," Kemp said. "Loyal."

"Where did he get that face?"

"With respect, sir, this man is a good man," Kemp said. "I've
checked on him," he added, lying. "Sir, we're not running a beauty
contest."

"You've proven that, Lieutenant," said the major. "He's your recruit, so you can swear him in later."

Der Chineser watched Kemp execute an about-face. The lieutenant looked grim. Der Chineser didn't know how he would get back to
the rooming house. "Welcome, Huebner."

Der Chineser turned his head, fast, and sucked in his breath. "I'm
swearing you in," Kemp said. "We always do it after training."

Kemp brought him to the supply sergeant, who issued a uniform
to the recruit. "Wear the blouse tonight," Kemp said. Der Chineser
thought, happily, of sleeping in it.

When the troops massed for close-order drill, Kemp placed him in
the rear of the column. "Follow the man in front of you," Kemp said.
"Don't worry about mistakes. We all had to learn."

Der Chineser made error after error, turning left when the others
turned right, continuing to march when everyone halted, constantly
walking into the soldier in front of him. The man never complained.

After a ten-minute break, Major Oster called the men to attention.
"Fix bayonets!" Watching the others, Der Chineser fastened his bayonet beneath the rifle muzzle. The troops faced bales of hay. Each man
had his turn. Der Chineser had memorized stories of battle, of bayonet
charges. He ran in a crouch, ran with all his strength, imagining the
enemy before him as he crossed the laundry to bury his bayonet in the
hay. When he returned to his place, he heard Major Oster:

"If I ever led this pathetic gang into combat, I'd be charged with
first-degree murder," said the major. "Only one man used his bayonet
like a soldier." Der Chineser hoped he meant Lieutenant Kemp. But
the major came straight for him. "Show these veterans how it's done,
soldier."

Der Chineser raised his rifle. He crouched and took off, hearing
the sound of gunfire around him, ignoring the danger to his life, charg-

ing into the bale of hay at full speed. "Well done," said the major, and to his troops, "Let's try it once more. Try to remember you're carrying a rifle, not a lollipop."

Kemp stopped beside Der Chineser. "You were great, Huebner. I'm proud of . . . Jesus," Kemp said, his voice dropping to a hush, "it's the baron!"

Der Chineser saw beside the major at the platform a bareheaded man with thick, glossy black hair. He stood like a diver at the edge of a diving board. He wore a silk turtleneck sweater and over it, buttoned to the throat, a loden cloth après-ski jacket. "Baron Fritz Von Gottisberg, the commander-in-chief," Kemp said. Der Chineser was entranced. The baron made everyone else in the laundry look deformed. "He started the Landswehr," Kemp said. "He did it all by himself, bought the building, the rifles, bought the blouse you're wearing. He's a . . . genius."

Major Oster would not have called for bayonet drill if he had expected an audience. On Thursday Fritz had telephoned from the *schloss*, the Von Gottisberg castle near Innsbruck. Their conversation had been on ordinary matters. Fritz had suggested dinner some night after he returned. Now Major Oster winced. Fritz had returned, all right, watching those clods hopping around like old men in a sack race.

Fritz had come to the laundry so he could select a spy. The assassination of Chancellor Dollfuss the previous year had convinced Fritz that Hitler intended to invade Austria. Fritz believed if the Austrian army would fight, they could win. And if the General Staff knew when the invasion was coming, the army would have a better chance. All that week in the castle, Fritz had tried to decide whom he would choose to join the Nazis and report to him.

Manfred Oster seemed halfway intelligent. Fritz left the castle early Saturday morning, planning to reach Vienna in time for an early dinner with Manfred, but the Daimler's clutch began to slip on the journey, delaying him.

Fritz watched his troops finish the bayonet drill. "Enough!" said the major. "Platoon leaders, dismiss your men." He pulled off his gloves. "No excuses, Fritz. It's my responsibility. They behave like a pack of amateurs. I'll stay on their tails."

All around them rose the hoots and hollers of men released from captivity, from the suffocating and demeaning discipline imposed by a displeased military superior. Fritz, who never failed to reward the Landswehr, asked, "Is there enough beer, Manfred?"

"Take a look." Men were rolling three barrels across the laundry floor, coming straight at Fritz and the major. Others carried crates of steins. "If there wasn't enough, you'd really see a bayonet charge," Oster said. "They would crucify me. There is enough beer to float this ark."

"You expect too much, Manfred," Fritz said as he and the major moved aside. "They *are* amateurs. Butchers, bakers, candlestick makers. Those with a trade are the cream of the crop. Most come from the saloons and the street. And they come on Saturday night, their night to howl. They give up their fun to let us insult them."

After Der Chineser turned in his rifle, he couldn't find Lieutenant Kemp. Everyone lined up for beer, three lines for the three barrels. Der Chineser walked back and forth, back and forth. The lieutenant could have forgotten him and left. Der Chineser half ran to the door, pulling with both hands. In front of the laundry stood a glistening Daimler limousine and to the right, the truck which had brought him. He whirled around, rushing back to the barrels.

Kemp saw Huebner, the recruit, in the Landswehr blouse and civvy pants. "Grab yourself a beer, Emil."

"Later, maybe," said Der Chineser. "The oath, Lieutenant."

"The oath!" Kemp said. "Done and done." Kemp drained his stein. "Okay, raise your right hand . . . *No!* Come on!" He yanked Der Chineser's arm. "Come on with me!"

Der Chineser said, "How about the oath? You said you would administer the oath."

"Relax." Kemp didn't want any interruptions. The baron and Major Oster were with an officer whose name Kemp couldn't remember. "Excuse me, sir." At first they didn't hear him. "Sir? Baron?"

Fritz saw that idiot, Kemp. He had another idiot with him, wearing half a uniform. A Chinese! The League of Nations had moved into the laundry. "Yes, Kemp."

"Excuse me, sir," Kemp said. "I'm sorry to interrupt, sir. I thought . . . sir, this is Emil Huebner, a new recruit to be sworn in. Major Oster said I should swear him in, but I thought . . . it would be such an honor since you're here tonight. If you didn't . . . don't object, sir."

"My honor, Lieutenant," Fritz said. He put his stein into Manfred's hand. "Private Huebner?" Der Chineser merely nodded, unable to speak. "Follow me," Fritz said.

They climbed onto the platform. "Comrades!" Fritz raised his voice. "Comrades!" He waited until the laundry fell silent. "Men of the Landswehr. A loyal Austrian has volunteered to join our ranks. Emil Huebner, like all of us, is determined to keep Austria safe from its enemies within and without its borders." Fritz looked down at the slobs holding their mugs. "Within and without its borders."

He turned to Der Chineser. Where had Kemp found this specimen? "Raise your right hand and repeat after me," Fritz said. Der Chineser obeyed. "Before God, I, Emil Huebner . . ." Fritz said.

"Before God, I, Emil Huebner . . ."

". . . swear to protect Austria from all enemies, foreign and domestic . . ." Fritz said. Der Chineser repeated every word. Fritz continued, reciting the oath which he had composed, using every bloodthirsty, chauvinistic phrase he could employ. Der Chineser did not falter, and as he finished, Fritz extended his hand. "Welcome."

Der Chineser took the baron's hand, a firm, strong hand, a leader's hand. Nobody in the village near Steyr, from whose taunts and jibes and daily cruelties Der Chineser had fled, would believe Emil Huebner stood shoulder to shoulder with the Baron Fritz Von Gottisberg.

Fritz bent for a stein. "You deserve a beer, my friend." He handed Der Chineser the stein and made his escape, beckoning Manfred Oster.

They walked toward the entrance. "I'll call you next week, Manfred. We'll arrange an evening," Fritz said. He would make their dinner a casual event, two young bucks enjoying themselves. Long after the food and wine and brandy, Fritz would speak of the Landswehr's critical need for intelligence, of his search for a man he could trust to infiltrate the enemy's ranks and report only to him. The major followed Fritz to the Daimler.

"Late date, Fritz?"

"Only with my bed," Fritz said. "I crawled down from the schloss. Bad clutch."

"I thought we could stop somewhere in town," the major said.

"I don't feel like drinking," Fritz said.

"Neither do I," said Oster, grinning. "I had another idea. We could meet at Number Eleven, at Katharina's. She'll revive you, Fritz. I'll stop on the way and call."

He caught Fritz off guard, making himself a crony. Fritz did not encourage intimacy. He had never needed help with women, and he never took witnesses to a whorehouse. "Some other night, Manfred."

Fritz drove away from the laundry. He had nearly committed a serious error. He could not send Manfred Oster to spy for him. Fritz needed a lackey, not a buddy, not someone who declared himself an equal.

The exchange with Manfred left Fritz on edge and in no rush to return to the palace and hear his solitary footsteps in the empty corridors. Fritz would have enjoyed a romp in the silks and satins of a darkened bordello. But he had tired of Katharina's pod of trained seals. He sought someone fresh and unspoiled, someone he, not Katharina, could initiate. But the solitary life he fostered, the privacy he guarded, kept him isolated. He didn't know anyone young. As Fritz stopped for a red light, he remembered the girl at Magda's party, the Siefermann girl.

She was *too* young. She probably believed in the tooth fairy. The girl had behaved so innocently she deserved to be slapped.

Early Monday morning, Fritz nursed the crippled Daimler through empty streets to the specialist whom he allowed to care for the limousine. Fritz drove down the ramp into the spotless garage, and as he stepped off the running board, he saw Der Chineser pushing a four-wheeled cart.

Herman Spangenberg, the owner, all in white like a doctor, joined Fritz and saw him watching Der Chineser. "Would you believe he's Austrian? He is," Spangenberg said. "Our new apprentice. Best I've ever had."

Der Chineser stopped beside the Daimler, as though Fritz was invisible. He took a linen sheet from the cart and spread it across the front seat. He slipped a felt sleeve over the steering wheel and covered the floor mat with paper. "In my stall, Emil," Spangenberg said.

"Yes, sir," said Der Chineser. He wiped his hands and stepped into the limousine.

"Let's take a look at that clutch," Spangenberg said as he and Fritz followed the car.

"While you're looking, yank it," Fritz said. "Put in a new one."

"Count on three days, Baron," Spangenberg said. "The clutch comes from Munich."

"Munich," Fritz said. Hitler and his cutthroats had founded their master race in the lovely old city. Der Chineser came out of the Daimler, and as he raised the hood, Fritz smiled. He had planned to walk back to the palace. "Can you spare your apprentice? I need a ride."

"Emil, use my car and take the baron wherever he wishes to go," Spangenberg said.

When Der Chineser rolled up in Spangenberg's sedan, Fritz deliberately chose the backseat. Up front Der Chineser sat at attention. Fritz wanted to call him Private . . . , but couldn't remember the man's name. "This seems preordained," Fritz said, low. "Can you hear me?"

"Yes, sir."

"Good. I've been thinking of you since Saturday night," Fritz said.

"You're a new man in the Landswehr, a stranger. You fit the requirements." Fritz paused. "I have a secret mission," he said, and stopped again. "A dangerous mission," he said. "I'm asking for a volunteer."

"I volunteer! *Sir!*"

Fritz leaned forward, speaking softly once more. "Do you know the old brewery in the Simmering, the Tenth District? The old brewery? There are two. The old brewery is nearest the cemetery."

Der Chineser could not lie to his commanding officer. "I'll find it, sir," he said, begging. "You can trust me, sir. I'll find it."

"I know you will," Fritz said. "I have full confidence in you." Fritz moved back, settling himself beside the rear window. "Tomorrow night," he said. "Midnight."

At the palace, Fritz waited for Der Chineser to open the rear door. "This is between you and me," Fritz said. "Not between you and me and Kemp."

"I swear to you, sir," said Der Chineser. "Baron, sir, I swear on my honor."

"Until midnight tomorrow."

Der Chineser couldn't salute because of the secret nature of the mission. He couldn't thank the baron. He couldn't run after him to kiss his hand. Der Chineser returned to the boss's car. He had two endless days to endure. He drove into the Himmelpfortgasse. How could he survive until tomorrow night?

Crossing the courtyard, Fritz chuckled. Der Chineser would be a loyal Nazi, a real superman among the supermen from the sewers. Fritz could have given the man his assignment in Spangenberg's car during the ride to the palace, but he had deliberately manufactured drama by setting the rendezvous for midnight in a cemetery. Fritz opened the door of the servants' entrance. He had found his spy.

3

ONE SUNDAY EARLY IN November Magda Auerfeld said, "Give me your glasses, Ernst," refusing to have her own and be marked old.

She held several pages of a letter which Dieter Rantzau, the portraitist, had brought her. "His name is Benno Karon," Dieter said. "Karonsky. I knew him in Berlin. We were young, starting out. I would be another Rembrandt, and he would be the new Garrick. Now I paint rich ladies if they'll hire me, but Benno could have made a mark. I myself never saw his equal."

"*Ja, ja,* let me read," Magda said. With her husband's glasses far down on her nose, she looked like a schoolteacher on the alert for mischief. Dieter had telephoned the day before, a few hours after receiving the letter and after he and his wife, Fanny, had read it over and over. Magda told them to come for Sunday breakfast.

Although Dieter and Fanny knew the letter by heart, Magda read aloud. "Dear Friend Dieter," she began.

43

Here is a voice from the past. Maybe I have not the right to intrude on you. Maybe I would not intrude if I had a choice. Dear friend, I have no choice. I have come to the end here, I, my wife, my son. Maybe you remember our son, Leo. He is a little slow. I say slow when in fact he is mongoloid. Twelve years old and he cannot dress himself, and Inge gives away her life to him.

Dear friend, I am desperate. I cannot work, cannot find a role. Nothing. I cannot pick up a bit, a few lines, a walk-on. Do you remember the old days? One year I took a taxi from one theater to the other, playing in two shows.

I cannot work anywhere, at anything. I asked for jobs in stores, in factories. The post office hires extra men during Christmas. They would not hire me. I went to the railroad yards, where they take on laborers day to day. You stand in a crowd, and the foreman points. He points all around me, but me he does not see.

How do we live? Inge's parents help, but they are almost out of money themselves. We have been selling possessions, sacred possessions. We live from day to day and many days now we fast, or we eat little so we have enough for Leo.

They have abolished us in Germany. We do not exist. This is the fact. We are in Berlin, but we are like papier-mâché, we are without dimension. And every day is worse. We cannot work, attend schools, check into a hotel. Do you remember Hermann Kiel? The lanky drink of water always quoting Goethe? We were best friends for twenty years, from long before either of us married. We worked together, ate together, drank together. We went out with women together. I remember two sisters we took for a weekend, all of us in the same bed. Hermann Kiel will no longer talk to me.

I am like a pariah dog, the one everyone hates. I feel like a dog which has never known a home, which is always in the street, dirty, matted, mangy, full of fleas, tail between legs, dodging cars, horses, carts, bicycles, trucks, slinking around people, half starving, waiting until darkness to dig in the garbage for a crust of bread, always running, afraid of everyone and everything, whose appearance angers everyone, even children, even other dogs.

Every day, all day I torment myself. Hitler did not win overnight. We had our chance. We had years to leave. Why didn't we leave?

We stayed because here is our home. Berlin is our home.

Germany is our home. We are Germans. No, dear friend, we were Germans.

I tell you it is more than the human mind can comprehend. One day you are living a life, working, sleeping, dealing with good times, bad times, planning for Christmas, for a vacation. Should we see Italy this summer? Should we take a place on the beach on the Baltic? Should we book a cruise? Should we paint the apartment or move? Should we move to a larger apartment, to a house, to the suburbs? Should we buy a car? One day we have a date with the barber, we keep a dentist's appointment, take shirts to the laundry, suits to the tailor.

And all this business of living disappears in a flash. Overnight. We are illegal in Germany.

Dear friend, you knew from the beginning money is why I write. I have no money, and I beg you to help me. I have no shame or embarrassment because I am begging. Without money we will die. I know this now for a certainty. I was stupid earlier. I am no longer stupid. There are three of us, Inge, Leo, and I. I am not counting Inge's parents, Catholics, or my father. I must turn my back on them so we can escape.

Dear friend, without you we cannot escape. Please help.

Forever yours,
Benno Karon.

Magda lowered the letter, sniffling. She lowered the glasses. Her husband took the glasses out of her hand. "It's a bad business over there," Ernst said.

Magda came out of her chair as though she were alone, crossing the room to a table with a cluster of cut-glass decanters. Each had a silver necklace with a disc: SCOTCH, SLIVOVITZ, BRANDY, GIN, SHERRY. Magda removed the glass stopper from the scotch bottle and took a tumbler from a stack. "Magda!" Ernst glared at her. "It's not even noon!"

She poured three fingers of whisky into the tumbler and drank, emptying the glass. Magda made a face and walked toward the others, waving the letter. "For him it's already midnight! After midnight!"

"I'll tell you straight, Magda, even in front of our friends: I don't like this drinking in the morning," Ernst said.

"Don't drink," Magda said, solving his problem. She folded the letter, flattening it against her bosom and offering it to Dieter. "I never liked the Germans," Magda said. "My father never liked them. Ernst, bring me your checkbook."

"You have a checkbook," Ernst said.

She said quietly, "Please, I am not for jousting now." Ernst went into the bedroom. Magda rubbed her eyes. "I suppose you're going to other people," she said.

"We'll all give what we can," Dieter said.

"I have a message for your friend," Magda said. "He must take his father. My check will be enough for his father."

"You're a good person, Magda," said Fanny Rantzau.

"Ja, ja," Magda said, bored with the housewife homilies. She left them, walking into the winter garden, standing among the ferns and Diefenbachia, looking through the graceful oriel at the Vienna rooftops, turned inside out by the letter from the man with the Mongoloid son.

"Here is your checkbook," Ernst said.

She sat down, scribbling quickly. "Now maybe we can have some breakfast in this house."

When they had eaten and been served fresh coffee, Dieter tapped a glass with his spoon. "Magda, Ernst. I have other news. We are leaving. We are selling everything and leaving."

Magda hated him. "Running away?"

Fanny said, "You're not fair," but Dieter shook his head at his wife.

"Correct, Magda," he said. "We *are* running. While we can run."

"Coward!" Magda said. "Afraid of your own shadow. How many times must I tell you? You are not in Germany, mister. Austria is not Germany."

"Not yet," Dieter said. "He'll come, Magda. He is an Austrian. He won't rest until he has Austria. The Austrians will welcome him. Look!" Dieter opened his wallet, taking out Magda's check. "The National Bank and Trust. Your banker, Helmut Weber, is a Nazi. The great patriot, artillery major, the war hero who helped write the constitution for the republic."

Ernst set down his knife and fork. "Helmut Weber?"

"Bigger men than Weber are Nazis," Dieter said. "They see Hitler coming. They will jump from the sinking ship. Hitler is coming, Magda."

"Never!" Storming out, Magda left them at the table. Dieter went to her. "This is not good-bye," he said. He kissed her on both cheeks. "We'll come to say good-bye." Magda didn't move, didn't blink.

* * *

That week Helmut Weber telephoned Fritz. "Am I intruding?"

"Never," Fritz said. "How are you, old friend?"

"A banker is always tip-top," Weber said. "I won't keep you, Fritz. This is a business call. The mortgage you hold on the Altmayer property is due. Altmayer asks if he can refinance. He is in good shape, Fritz. The terms are good."

"You lead, I'll follow," Fritz said.

"I'll need your signature," Weber said. "Can you come by in a day or two?"

Normally a junior officer would have sent the papers over with a messenger. Fritz knew Weber intended to corner him. Fritz could hear the Nazi traitor saying: "Either you are with us or against us."

Fritz remained at the desk in the study long after the telephone call. He didn't see Zinn enter. "Are you ready for lunch, Baron?" asked the butler.

"Take your lunch and—" Fritz said, and stopped. He despised men who brutalized their servants. "I'm sorry, Zinn. No lunch."

Fritz left the study, crossing the palace to the Great Hall. The vast chamber, with its heirlooms and portraits on the walls, comforted him. If Helmut Weber had offered Fritz's grandfather membership in the Nazis, the old goat would have buckled on his sword to kill the banker. Fritz remembered his grandfather. The Baron Ferdinand Von Gottisberg had been one of the century's ranking fools, roaming through the forests below the schloss, shooting anything which moved or flew. Fritz stopped, facing the entrance as though guests had arrived. Every Friday morning Helmut Weber went to his lodge to hunt through the weekend.

Just before noon Friday, Fritz drove to the National Bank and Trust. Weber's secretary brought him the Altmayer documents, and he signed the papers. "Tell Helmut I'm sorry I missed him," Fritz said.

Near the doors Fritz stopped to slip on his beret. "Hello, Baron." Turning around, Fritz saw a man in a black chesterfield, a beautifully dressed man holding a derby. "It's Klaus Siefermann, Baron."

"Yes, yes," Fritz said. "How are you? Good to see you," Fritz said, remembering the girl. "How is your daughter?"

"Thank you, very well. I'll tell Carly you asked." Fritz opened the door for the Beau Brummell.

Fritz walked slowly to his car. He had sidestepped Helmut Weber, the treasonous swine, and he deserved a celebration. He could take the Siefermann girl somewhere. He remembered a pretty girl.

He drove back to the palace and called. "Carly Siefermann, please."

Carly and Lisl Schott were in the bedroom when the maid stopped in the hall. "For you."

"Who?"

"A man. He didn't give his name." Nick began with his name, Carly followed the maid who returned to the kitchen.

"This is Fritz Von Gottisberg." Carly leaned against the wall. She was back in his little car with his lips on her lips and his confident body against hers. "Are you there?"

"Yes, I'm here," she said, feeling moronic.

"Have dinner with me tonight?"

"Tonight?" Her voice squeaked. Carly hated herself. She tossed her head, throwing back her hair, digging her fingers into her scalp. Why did he call now, for tonight? Lisl was sleeping over.

"Tomorrow night," Fritz said.

"Tomorrow night?"

In the palace Fritz looked at the ceiling. He had made contact with a juvenile. "Yes, Miss Siefermann. Tomorrow night."

Nick! Carly pushed away from the wall. "I can't tomorrow night."

Fritz laughed. He couldn't even manage to bag a birdbrain like the Siefermann tot. "Pick a night," he said. "Sunday, Monday, Tuesday, New Year's Eve."

"Well . . . Sunday night."

"Sunday," Fritz said. "Very good, Miss Siefermann," he said, sorry he had called, sorry her father had hailed him in the bank.

Carly felt parched and her cheeks were hot. But when Lisl heard Carly coming and looked across the bedroom, she saw her best friend smiling.

Sunday night at the Zwischentheatre, Nick walked into a war backstage. "We'll refund," said Peter Dietrich.

"Never, ever use that word," Nick said.

"We have no cast," said Sepp Wiegend. "They went skiing and the car broke down on the way back."

"We finally picked up an audience," Nick said. "We finally see some people out front."

"Madman!" Egon Burghofer, the pharmacist who had taken Rex Mulhall for a stage name, raised his forefinger. "We have one actor tonight who knows the play." He hit his chest. "One!"

"We'll do something else," Nick said. "We are in a theater. Anything which entertains an audience is theater: a play, a recitation, dogs jumping through hoops, a magician."

"I don't see any magicians," said Peter.

"Someone should go out front," Nick said. "Sepp, you have a desk full of plays. Recite one of them."

"We must refund," said Peter.

Nick stood in his way. "You're a director, always telling someone else how to act. Go out and act."

Dolly Stacker, who had been in the ticket booth, joined them, carrying a large cloth bag with the night's receipts. "You're still arguing?"

"I'll finish this," Sepp said, but Nick pushed him aside, slipping through the curtain. "Ladies and gentlemen . . ."

The men and women on the benches facing him stopped Nick. The modest audience became a horde. He couldn't leave, or hide. He refused to return their money, so he had only the truth left. "We cannot offer you our play. You're entitled to a refund. But we need the money."

"If you're stealing, at least point a gun," a man said. Others spoke, including women. Men rose, shouting. Nick moved across the stage. The protests formed a chant. Nick returned to the center of the stage and saw Carly in the audience, smiling at him. Carly saved him. Nick spread his legs, planting himself on the stage, and put two fingers in his mouth.

The high-pitched whistle tore through the storefront like a siren, silencing the audience. "Sit down," Nick said. "Give me a chance." He squatted, facing a man in the first row. "You, give me a chance."

The man's wife poked him, pulling him down. Another man sat down. Then another and his wife sat down. Nick became erect, and soon only he stood in the storefront.

"I told you there is no play tonight," he said, talking to Carly. "The cast is somewhere on the Schneeberg. One man committed this crime. Call him Max." Max Ingster had driven the cast to the Schneeberg, a mountain about fifty miles from Vienna. "This morning he learned the first snow had fallen. He couldn't wait. He had to be in the bindings." Nick saw Carly turn to someone beside her. Nick saw a man turn so their heads were together. Then they separated and Nick saw the Baron Von Gottisberg.

"Everyone is happy on the slopes," Nick said. "They ski all morning," he said, and began to ski across the stage, his hands with the ski poles extended. Nick turned, skiing back across the stage. "They have a quick lunch." He raised his hands to gobble his food. "They pile into Max's car." He turned the ignition key and said, "Bbbbrrrnnnggg," as the engine sputtered and caught. "After ten minutes the car stops. They can see the church steeples in Payerbach.

"Everyone leaves the car," he said. "They must be here, on this stage, at eight o'clock. They take their skis, their poles, their boots. Payerbach is a village, not an imperial city. One train in the afternoon, one at night. They must board the afternoon train. They walk," Nick said, walking. "They hurry," he said, running across the stage. "They hitchhike." Nick stopped, extending his arm and wiggling his thumb at cars and trucks passing.

He paused, winded by his exertions, and in the audience someone said, "You'll miss the train."

Men and women laughed, and when they subsided, Nick said, "Exactly what the cast told Max. They said, 'Max, we'll miss the train.' And Max said, 'We're not taking the train. I know this car. It is a good car. Probably needs a spark plug or something.'

"The cast argued with Max," Nick said. "They refused to be treated like sheep, but to Max they *were* sheep. He knew the first law of command. To rule you must silence the opposition."

In the audience a woman tittered, then a man laughed and said, "Careful," and others laughed. In the autocracy which Kurt Schuschnigg led in Austria, there was no political opposition. Democracy in Austria had died in 1934.

"So Max stopped the debate," Nick said, continuing. "He told the cast he would telephone a garage in Payerbach, bring out a mechanic, and one, two, three, they'll be in Vienna." Nick saw the baron whispering to Carly. "Now the cast decided to vote, the train or the car.

"Max also knew the second law of command," Nick said. "Nobody votes." As he shook his head, laughter came from all through the Zwischentheatre—from both sides of the curtain. Now it became clear to everyone that Nick was offering a parody of Austria's repressive government, which had long since suspended the franchise.

In the audience someone said loudly, "The walls have ears," and someone else said, "Ssshh." Laughter rose once more, and Nick, grinning, waited for the tiny theater to subside.

Then he ran his forefinger across his throat. "On the spot Max abolished free elections," Nick said. "Max waved them to the train. He would be thinking of them in his warm bath in Vienna." Nick raised three fingers. "Max had learned the third rule. You are smart and everyone else is dumb."

"Including you," said a man in the audience. Another man said, "Let him talk," and to Nick, "Give it to 'em, friend." Others urged Nick to continue, and Nick whistled once more.

"If you stop, I'll go," he said. "Back to Payerbach. Naturally, Max won. The opposition collapsed. Max found a telephone and soon, slipping and sliding in the fresh snow, came a truck with a mechanic. To save time Max raised the hood. 'Start loading your stuff,' he told the opposition. 'We're on our way.' "

Nick wiped his forehead. "The mechanic changed Max's mind. 'You need a new transmission,' he said. He chained the car to the truck and dragged it, backward, with the cast in the rear in the open and Max in the truck cab with the mechanic and a heater. Even so, they might have made the train, but a mile from Payerbach the truck had a flat tire. While the mechanic jacked up the wheel, they could see the train leaving the station."

Nick didn't stop. He had to keep talking so the audience would keep laughing, had to watch Carly with the baron. Everything Nick said had its roots in the abrogation of civil liberties in Austria. The audience understood every reference he made, and his daring, his originality, captivated the men and women he faced.

The storefront was poorly heated and drafty, but long before he finished Nick began to perspire. His throat hurt, and he wanted to stop for a drink of water. He couldn't stop, couldn't give the audience a chance to consider a refund. Moving constantly across the stage, he continued until he could no longer think. He crossed the stage again, stopping at the wings. "Anyway," he said, waving, "see you all tomorrow night."

They mobbed him backstage, and while they passed him around like a medicine ball, the storefront erupted. No one in the Zwischentheatre had ever heard such applause. They were clapping, whistling, stamping their feet. Some yelled, "More! More!" and some yelled, "Come back! Come back!" Dora Ertle had him in a bear hug, one hand squeezing his face so she could kiss him on the lips. Sepp pulled Nick away from her. "Get out there, man!" Sepp said, pulling back the curtain to push Nick onto the stage.

Nick said, "Thanks," and "Thank you," looking for Carly. He turned to slip through the curtain, but the audience shouted, "No! No! No!" He faced them and the applause subsided. "Thanks. Thanks a lot. You're all wonderful," he said, escaping.

Backstage the group claimed him once more. "Stop, I need a glass of water," he said.

"Not for you," Peter said. "You're drinking wine, the best we can buy."

They streamed into the café, removing caps, hats, gloves, mittens, coats, scarves, en route to their usual corner. They brought more chairs and pushed tables together. "Let's have some wine, Erik," Sepp said. "Not your usual bilge. Bring us something we can swallow."

Nick picked up a chair and, carrying it across the café, saw Carly and Fritz on the other side. Candles burned on a shelf behind them, and the soft amber made a nimbus around Carly. "I'll be right back," Nick said to nobody in particular, leaving the chair and crossing the café. "Hello."

Carly said, "You were wonderful. We've been talking about your performance."

"Join us," Fritz said.

"I'm with them," Nick said. "Join us."

"Do you want to, Fritz?" Carly asked. "I do."

"Then I do," Fritz said.

In the corner Nick said, "Attention! I've brought two friends, Carly Siefermann and the Baron Von Gottisberg."

The exuberant band fell silent. Those who greeted the newcomers spoke softly. The group behaved like students in a dormitory after the "Lights out!" command. Even Sepp was subdued. Seeing them subside around him, Fritz said, "Nick forgot my name. My name is Fritz. Thank you for including us."

Nick poured wine and Fritz raised his glass. "To the Zwischentheatre," he said. "Long life and continued success."

Everyone liked the baron. He seemed like a regular fellow. The corner revived, picking up steam. People were talking but not in the usual style, not all at once, and the conversation seemed directed exclusively at Fritz. Although he sat in the middle of a table, he seemed to be at the head.

Fritz sipped his second glass of wine but did not finish it. "I can't keep up with you youngsters," he said. He did not intend to drive Nick home again. "I hate to spoil your evening, Carly."

Erik Ekstrom escorted the honored guest to the door. Dora Ertle said, "He made me weak just looking at him." Someone else said, "Now I can tell my grandchildren I once drank wine with a baron," and someone else said, "I like his taste in women."

"So does Nick," said Peter. "Hey, Nick! The baron stole your girl!"

Nick's throat hurt and he felt hollow inside. Sepp nudged him. "Say something."

Egon Burghofer, a pharmacist again, pushed back his chair. "I'll say something. I must open up tomorrow morning."

Nick watched Carly disappear. "Let's settle up with Erik," he said. "Erik!"

They dug for money as Erik lumbered through the café. "The check," said Egon.

"No check," Erik said. They stared at him. Erik would take money from his children. "The baron paid the check."

"He's my favorite baron," Peter said.

Nick had always needed an alarm clock, and that night he woke in the dark. He tried to sleep and could not, tried not to disturb Max and failed. "Go away!" Max said. The train from Payerbach had been late, arriving in Vienna after midnight.

On his way to work, Nick stopped in the Caravan to call Carly. "She is asleep," the maid said.

He called at noon. "She has gone out," said the maid.

All afternoon Nick tried to avoid the clock and failed. Years passed in the drafting room. When the day ended, Nick ran out, carrying his coat. He called from the Caravan. Carly hadn't returned. He came out of the café in a rush, pushing his arms through the coat sleeves.

As he reached the far side of Kruger Strasse, Nick saw a taxi stop in front of Carly's building. In November, night came early, and although the lamp lights burned, he could not see clearly. He ran into the street, but a truck blocked his path, and when it passed, the taxi pulled away. He followed the doorman. "Was that Miss Siefermann in the cab?" he asked. Then he saw her approaching. His heart turned over.

"Carly!" He held on to her, passing the lobby. "Let's go somewhere."

"Nick, I can't," Carly said. "My parents have opera tickets, so it's an early dinner."

"You'll be home for dinner."

Carly looked at him, excited by his mysterious appearance. "Where are you taking me?"

"Here," he said, turning the corner and stopping beside the building, facing her. Nick raised his hand, touching her face. "Carly, I love

you. I never meant these words before. Never. Now I do. I love you."
He came close and kissed her.

When she felt his lips, his arms enfolding her, Carly pressed him
to her. Time stopped but only until Nick said, "I love you, Carly. I
love you."

Nick knew her. He could see straight into her. "Don't be afraid,"
he said, and kissed her again.

"Nick . . ." She shook her head. "I'm not . . ." she said, stepping
back, away from the edge. "I'm late," she said. They walked back to
the lobby doors. "I'll see you tomorrow," Nick said.

She had a date with Fritz. "I can't."

"Wednesday," he said.

"We're having dinner at my uncle and aunt's."

"Friday." He had promised his parents he would be in Leopoldstadt Thursday night to meet a relative who had escaped from Russia.
"Friday."

"Yes, all right," she said, leaving. "Bye."

The elevator didn't come for a year, and when the doors opened,
Carly faced a mob. She had to greet the Vogels and the Kierhavens,
and their little boy who tried to look under her dress whenever he saw
her. Mrs. Vogel remained, wrapping her boa around her neck until
Carly stepped into the elevator and pressed the floor button.

She tried to forget Nick. She couldn't forget him. She tried to
forget everything he had said. She couldn't forget anything. "I love
you, Carly. I love you." She could hear him. "I love you, I love you,
I love you, I love you," as though Nick had climbed into the elevator
shaft.

Carly's parents returned from the opera around midnight. Helga
walked through the darkened corridors to Carly's room. "Are you
awake?"

"How did you know?"

"I'm a mother," Helga said.

"Mama?" Carly turned up the bed lamp. Helga entered and sat
down on the bed. "I didn't tell you why I was late for dinner," Carly
said, looking at the cross on the wall. "I wasn't late, really. When I
came home, I found Nick outside. We went for a walk." Carly turned
to her mother. "He said he loves me."

Helga almost cried out, blaming Carly for the Leopoldstadter who
had wormed his way into their home. Helga bit her lip, thinking, thinking. "And you? What did you say?"

Carly's head moved from side to side across the pillow. "I didn't say anything."

Helga leaned forward to kiss her daughter. She left the bedroom, walking slowly, a besieged queen on the battlements. In the master bedroom she removed her earrings. "Klaus?"

"Let me sleep, Helga."

She undressed and got into bed beside her husband. "Nick Gallanz told Carly he loves her."

Helga could not evade the tragedy which loomed over them. He was like all his kind, a Rasputin, wily and hypnotic. He had cast a spell over Carly; otherwise he would have been forgotten long ago. Helga had to keep him away.

Nick loved everyone that Tuesday, even Ernst Auerfeld. He loved the working drawings for the bathroom he had to complete by the end of the day or be fired.

After work, Nick ate standing. The Zwischentheatre had always been dark Monday, and every Tuesday turned into a reunion. In Josefstadter Strasse Nick walked into a crowd. He caught up with two men. "Where is the party?"

One fellow with a cavalryman's mustache said, "My boss's sister saw a show Sunday night here in the neighborhood. She and her husband came for a play, but the cast went skiing and their car broke down. So this one bird came out on stage. My boss's sister said she laughed until she almost wet her pants." Nick grinned. "You heard about it, too?" Nick nodded, stepping into the street. He saw people lined up in front of the box office.

Backstage, he entered another war zone. "Goddamn it, this is a theater, n-not a music hall," Max said. He had brought his girl, Ruth Posner, a math teacher in his school, and she held his arm, stroking his hair to comfort him.

"If we ring up on my play tonight, they'll lynch us," said Sepp Wiegend. "This audience didn't pay to see *Camouflage*. They heard about Sunday night. The people who were here Sunday night gave us this audience."

"You have a short memory, Sepp," said Judith Emmerich. "You stood right here the first time Nick showed us this place and swore we would present plays. *Plays!*"

Peter Dietrich pushed himself into the center of the fight. "I'm the director. No one is more anxious to see this play than I. But we can't."

Nick tried to be heard, and when he failed, put two fingers in his mouth. His whistle stopped the battle long enough for him to say, "You're killing the Zwischentheatre. You're committing hara-kiri. You're not even doing that right. The Japanese stab themselves when they lose. You've picked a night when you won. We won! After all our work, all our dreams, all our bad luck, we finally had good luck. Max's car saved the Zwischentheatre. We couldn't give the audience a play Sunday night, but we gave them a show. And they liked the show. They .. liked . . . the . . . show. They came to see that same kind of show. Somebody better get out front fast."

Peter grinned. "Good luck, Nick."

"I had my turn," Nick said. "I used up everything Sunday." He looked at the others as though facing a jury. "I have nothing left."

"You'll think of something," Sepp said. Dora Ertle moved the curtain aside, hiding behind it. "Save us," Sepp said. "Nick, I am serious."

Out front, the size of the audience stopped Nick cold. The benches were filled and people lined the walls. People sat in the aisle, on the floor. Nick pulled at the knot of his tie and unbuttoned his shirt collar. "I suppose you heard about the mix-up Sunday night," he said. "We couldn't give a performance because the cast were up on the Schnee-berg, in the snow. They were in a car, the car broke down, they missed a train, they had to take the late train.

"Some train, this late train," he said, making up a story. "The cast told me they are sorry they didn't walk to Vienna. They said boarding that train is like entering a foreign country. The conductor of that train is the head of the country. He decides where you sit, where you smoke, when you smoke, when you eat, go you-know-where—women first, men second." Someone tittered, and another person laughed.

"This conductor's train is the cleanest, quietest, the most orderly train in Austria," he said. "With this conductor you will have the safest ride of your life. You might wonder whether you are in Austria or across the border." Nick simulated coming to attention. "You must obey on this train. No questions asked and no arguments allowed. Nothing allowed."

People were laughing. He took off his jacket and dropped it on the stage, repeating what he had said Sunday, using the train conductor instead of Max as a stand-in for Kurt Schuschnigg and Adolf Hitler.

He was a hero once more, on both sides of the curtain. When his gang released him, Nick could not stay still. "We need material," he said, walking from wall to wall. "We need sketches, skits. From everyone. If you can't write something, find someone who can." He went to the curtain, bunching it in his fist. "Twenty-four hours from now they will expect a new show."

While the Zwischentheatre confronted a bizarre crisis, Helga Siefermann sat alone beside her writing table. She could not keep Carly chained, could not banish Rasputin.

Nick proved it quickly. He called the next morning. "I can't wait till Friday. Come to lunch."

Carly returned to the apartment glowing, bringing the day's mail from the lobby. She told Helga of Nick's triumph. "The audience loves him. They love him."

Alone, Helga picked up the mail. She saw a letter from her mother and set it aside. She could recite the complaints from the old woman in Salzburg.

Later, Helga helped Carly dress for the evening. "Where are you going with the baron?"

Carly smiled. "I can't take him back to the Zwischentheatre."

Carly never kept anyone waiting, so Helga had only an instant with the baron. She watched Carly leave with him. Only Rasputin blighted her happiness.

Helga intended to wait up for Carly so she could listen to an account of the evening. When she was alone, she opened her mother's letter. She glanced through the sheaf of pages and dropped the letter on her writing desk to make herself tea. She was walking into the kitchen when she abruptly turned back. She said, "I am desperate!" fiercely, hurrying to the telephone. Her mother had always been a night owl. Helga called Salzburg. "I must get her away from him, Mama."

"He'll be there when she comes back," said the old woman.

"Carly will forget him," Helga said. "He loves her. She does not love him. She feels sorry for him. Carly feels sorry for people. She has a big heart, too big. You must do this for me, Mama."

Helga's mother telephoned just after ten o'clock the next morning. "Carly, it's your grandmother Melzer!" Helga said.

In Salzburg the old woman said, "Carly, I'm having terrible trouble." She said her most trusted servant had left without giving notice. "Stay with me until I find someone on whom I can depend. Put me back with your mother."

They didn't give Carly a chance. "She'll do it, Mama," Helga said, and ended the conversation. Helga put her arm around Carly.

"I'll help you pack." She sent her husband to buy the railroad ticket. "One way, Klaus."

He adjusted his homburg. "Are we giving her up for adoption?"

"She can buy a return when she is ready to return." Helga went to Carly's room. "Take something for the evening."

"I'm not going to Salzburg for my debut," Carly said.

Helga had won and indulged herself. "You and your father: how could I live without your answers?"

Carly left a message for Nick with Ernst Auerfeld in the drafting room. When Nick called, she said, "I can't see you Friday. My grandmother in Salzburg needs me."

"You're leaving? When will you come home?" Nick asked. Vienna had just become a desert.

Carly laughed. He made every incident a melodrama. Nick kept talking until Helga said, "You haven't packed."

Three days later Fritz telephoned. "Carly is in Salzburg, Baron," Helga said. "She is with her grandmother. She will be sorry she missed you, Baron."

In his study Fritz lay back in his chair. Such a pretty girl. And she behaved, she didn't crawl all over him, praying for wedding bells. Fritz swung around, opening his date book. Anna and Willie Blucher's dinner. Ugh! The preview of the French prints show at the Albertina, of which he was a patron. Ugh! Fritz closed the date book. He left the study. "Zinn! Help me pack!"

Fritz left Vienna in the Daimler the next day. The road ran beside the foothills of the Alps. High above, the mountains were white, and below a thin sprinkling of snow covered the ground. "Like a bride's veil," he said.

His description was apt. Snow lay across the countryside like gossamer. The trees were bare and the branches were laced with snow. He drove over a river where light refracted from the surface like bolts of lightning. Around one o'clock he turned off at Taurnsee, stopping at a lakeshore inn. He had lunch on the terrace above the water, sitting in the sun in his coat, sipping hot chocolate and watching the ducks move solemnly across the lake in long columns. He stayed until his chocolate became cold, leaving the ducks reluctantly.

After Taurnsee, he drove steadily but without extending the Daimler, and in a little over two hours, he caught his first glimpse of the Hohensalzburg, the ancient fortress guarding the city below. A few miles beyond, he left the highway and started the climb to Salzburg.

There are always tourists in Salzburg, and the medieval streets, which seem no wider than a wheelbarrow, are always impassable. Fritz drove in first gear. He could have run faster, crawling block after block until he reached Marketplatz and stopped in front of the hotel.

Inside, crossing the lobby, Fritz heard someone playing Mendelssohn's Second Piano Concerto. At the desk he said, "I called yesterday. Von Gottisberg."

The clerk said, "Yes, of course, Baron. Welcome. A pleasure to have you with us, Baron Von Gottisberg. An honor." Behind the mail rack, the day manager heard everything and rushed out, so Fritz had to endure an encore. Then he had to wait while the day manager got the key from the desk clerk to personally escort the baron.

The pianist finished the Mendelssohn concerto. "Lovely," Fritz said.

"He is rehearsing for a wedding Sunday," said the day manager. "We have the wedding and a reception."

When he had evicted everyone from his suite, Fritz spoke to the hotel switchboard. "There is a Melzer out near the Mirabel. Find the number and ring it for me."

A maid answered. "Carly Siefermann, please," Fritz said.

"Not in," said the maid. "She went . . . wait! Here she comes. Fraulein Carly."

Then Carly said, "Hello," said Fritz stretched out on the bed. She always sounded as though she had been given a present.

"Can you leave your grandmother long enough to dine with me?"

"Who is this?" she asked, and instantly, "Fritz? Fritz! Where are you? Are you in Salzburg?"

"I am here," he said. "You can show me the sights. Have we settled dinner?"

"Yes, yes, yes, yes," Carly said, walking toward the heavy staircase of the old, gloomy house, happy for the first time since leaving Vienna. She had known, almost from her arrival that her mother and grandmother had tricked her. There were enough servants in the house to maintain a hotel. "You lied to me," Carly told her grandmother. "Mama lied and you lied. Why did you lie?"

The old woman could not betray her daughter. "You are so cruel. Look at me, alone day after day."

"You have a mob here," Carly said.

"Strangers," said her grandmother, like someone left on an ice floe. "Strange faces. Alien faces." She pressed Carly's hand between hers. "Do you know how it feels to dine alone night after night after night?"

So Carly remained in the fortress, inventing tasks and excursions, and sitting across the table from the aged, scheming woman.

When Fritz arrived, Carly went to greet him. He stood under the light in front of the double doors with the colored glass panels, and he could see only the outline of a figure approaching. Then a door opened and Carly said, "Hello," bringing him inside. Fritz had a sudden impulse to abduct her. His reaction astonished him. "You haven't changed," he said. "I'd recognize you anywhere." He kissed her cheek.

"You have to meet Grandmother Melzer," Carly said. "She made me promise."

"I'm just a prisoner of love," he said.

In the parlor Fritz saw an aged woman in a Queen Anne chair, an old Carly who had once been as tall and as striking, with the same hair and eyes, and with the same bones in her face. "An honor," Fritz said, bowing.

In a restaurant in Monchsberg, high in the hills, the captain escorted the baron and his lady to a table overlooking Salzburg. Fritz leaned forward, his arms crossed on the table. "You're a mystery woman," he said. "Zip, you disappear. Why did you run away?"

"I didn't run away."

"You were shanghaied," he said.

"You're joking, but it's true," she said. She could not belittle her mother. "My grandmother is lonely."

"Tough luck," Fritz said. "My tough luck. I drive all the way to Salzburg because I thought we could have some fun, but you must nurse your grandmother."

"I'm not chained," Carly said. "I come and go, in and out. I *am* out. I'm here."

"Bravo!" Fritz said. He filled her glass. "Tomorrow?"

"Yes, tomorrow!" Carly said decisively. He swallowed a smile. He enjoyed being with her, talking to her.

He came in a taxi the following day. "The Old City," Fritz told the driver. As they approached, Fritz asked the cabbie to leave them near the Getreidegasse, one of Salzburg's oldest. They walked into a market day with sellers and buyers jamming the streets. "We are approaching the beginning of Salzburg," Fritz said. He gave Carly a detailed history.

"You and Nick," said Carly. "He knows everything, too."

They ate in the streets, stopping at one stand after another. Then

Fritz took her to a coffee house. "Tired?" She shook her head. "Good," he said. "We'll dine early. There is a concert at the Residenz."

The next day, Fritz took her on a tour of the Hohensalzburg, a guide once more. He fascinated Carly with his stories. "How do you know so much?"

"I suppose it's mixed up with my family," he said. "We've been here a long time, so we believe we're part of Austria's history."

That same day they rode the funicular up the Untersberg, six thousand feet above the city. Fritz watched her hair blowing every which way. "Hungry?" he asked, waiting for the quick nod which had become familiar. They had lunch at the summit before riding down to Salzburg. That night he kissed her, kissed her once. "Sweet dreams."

Fritz produced an adventure with an itinerary for each day. Once he drove into the country to a rural hotel, where they dined at a communal table, served from huge platters and drinking wine from a single pitcher. One of the waiters broke into a song, and soon the entire room rang with voices. They stayed late, and in driving back to Salzburg, Carly dropped her head to Fritz's shoulder, and they sang again.

In the dining room of the hotel the following morning, Fritz sent for the wedding pianist. The young man appeared. "Good morning, Baron."

Fritz pointed his knife at a chair. "Have some breakfast."

Fritz came for Carly late that afternoon. He drove back to the hotel, leaving the Daimler with the doorman. "Surprise," he said, bringing Carly into the hotel. He caught the concierge's eye. Fritz took Carly into the spacious lobby to a sofa and chairs arranged around a coffee table near a piano.

A headwaiter approached. "Good afternoon, Baron." He bowed. "Mademoiselle. A pleasure to serve you, Baron. An honor."

"We're having tea," Fritz said.

"Certainly," said the headwaiter. He gestured. "At your service, Baron. In the Trianon. Over here."

"No," Fritz said. "Here." he patted the headwaiter's shoulder. "Good man." Soon a waiter appeared, carrying a large tray which he set down on the table.

Carly poured tea for them. The tray was heaped with sweets. "Where do we begin?"

Fritz took a cookie. "Open wide," he said, and put the cookie in Carly's mouth. "Now you're on your own."

They sampled almost everything, and were on their second cups of tea when the pianist took his place, adjusting the piano bench. Fritz had told him to come at four o'clock. "Chopin," Fritz said, paying him. "Only Chopin."

As Carly raised her cup, she heard the first chords of a Chopin nocturne. The delicate, haunting refrain silenced the lobby. Carly set down her cup, looking at Fritz as though they shared a prize.

Two women entered the lobby, walking to the elevators, but they stopped, and on tiptoe went to chairs near the piano. Another woman, leading a boy by the hand, sat down. Other guests, alone or in pairs, entered silently and joined the others. The lobby seemed to become intimate. The pianist played on and on, and when he finished and rose, his audience applauded. Fritz helped Carly from the sofa. "These shoes will cripple me if I don't discard them," he said.

Fritz had kept his room key when he left the hotel. He opened the door of the suite, following Carly. "Give me a moment."

In the dressing room he removed his black shoes, among his favorites. He slipped on another pair, and as he tied his laces, he heard Carly humming one of the nocturnes. When he emerged from the dressing room, she stood at the windows, hugging herself and humming, her voice low and sensuous. His breath came quickly. Her voice was like a web enfolding him. He could not stay away. Fritz crossed the bedroom and put his arms around her.

She did not resist. When he stepped back and moved her away from the window to kiss her, she welcomed him, closing her eyes, content to drift for a little while, to drift, drift . . .

"If our chancellor had the brains of a gnat, he would put you on a postage stamp," Fritz said. "Princess Carly. May I have this waltz, Princess?" As they circled the room, Fritz sang the waltz from *The Merry Widow*. "Da dee da, dee da da da, dee da . . . da . . . da." He brought Carly closer and closer to the bed, and when he felt it against his legs, he dropped with her and atop her.

Carly felt his arms tightening, claiming her. His hands were strong and demanding, and she felt, low and deep within her, a warm, increasing tingling, a vibration in her body, spreading from her belly. She felt his kisses, his lips on her throat, his leg seeking to part hers. "No."

She refused to admit him. She did not know why she resisted. She felt ashamed, but she was not ready, not yet, not with Fritz, not with anyone. "Stop," she said. "Stop."

He could not stop. He kept her captive, his hands everywhere. "No, Fritz," she said, fighting him. He began to undo her dress, but she managed to get one hand free and then the other. "Stop, I said. Stop!"

She put her hands against his chest, trying to push him aside, but he had her trapped, and as she fought, he forced his leg between hers. "You can't!" she said. "I won't!"

He didn't believe her. He had waited all week. He had left Vienna to reach this goal. He had traipsed through Salzburg, through the countryside, sat through lunch with Carly's grandmother. He had enlisted the pianist, invented the amateur ploy with his shoes, to get Carly here with him. And she had joined in from the first. She had followed him willingly, happily. She must have known how the game would end. Fritz fumbled with her dress. He had lain awake imagining her breasts. Rolling from side to side, Carly finally pulled one arm free and swung hard into Fritz's middle, knocking the wind out of him as she rolled clear, using hands and feet, crawling like an infant and escaping.

As he lost her, Fritz left the bed. They faced each other, panting, like combatants. Carly straightened her dress. "I didn't mean to hurt you."

"Only a flesh wound," he said. From somewhere in the distance they heard the resonant boom of a drum. "I'll survive." He had never lost anywhere, at anything, and now he had to endure the presence of a witness to his failure. He wanted to get out of sight until he could compose himself, but he didn't move, facing her as though he had been brought up on charges. Again they heard the drum far off.

"I guess I'm not what you expected," she said. "I suppose I behaved like I would do . . . it." Carly knew she appeared silly, unsophisticated.

"Your grandmother will be worrying about you," Fritz said. He called the concierge and ordered his car. They heard the measured cadence of the drum approaching: boom, boom, boom.

"I can get home," she said.

"Perish the thought," he said. He opened the door, hoping to find a crowd, but the corridor was deserted and they remained alone.

They were alone in the elevator, and when they reached the lobby, he said, "I would consider it a supreme act of Christian kindness if you dined with me." He had never come as close to apologizing.

"We've just had tea," she said, and then looked at Fritz, discarding the lie. "I'd rather go home, go back to my grandmother."

"Agreed," he said, weary of being punished. "To grandmother's house we go."

They emerged from the hotel into a crowd. There were people everywhere. They heard the drum, much closer, boom . . . boom . . . boom. "It could be a circus," he said.

A fat man with a fat wife swung around, full of hate. "You think you're funny, mister? You're not funny. You won't be joking very long, you and the rest of your gang."

"Rather unfriendly," he said, as they were pushed in all directions by the crowd.

"Do you see your car?" Carly asked.

"Alas, no."

The encounter in Fritz's room had drained Carly. She hated Salzburg, hated being shut up with her grandmother, hated herself for behaving like a schoolgirl. "I'll take a taxi," she said.

"Not while chivalry is still in flower," he said. She infuriated him. She had already turned him away twice, in his room and in the lobby, refusing the chance to dine and bury the fiasco. Now she wanted to make it worse, dismissing him like some kid in dancing class. He took her arm, holding her firmly. "This way."

The hotel stood in an X formed by two streets which crossed at an angle in front of the entrance. The garage was in the basement at the far end of the building on their left. As Carly and Fritz walked toward the garage, they saw an army. The street was bright as day, lit by scores of torches. Approaching them, jamming the street from curb to curb, were row after row of Austrian Nazis in uniform. The flames of their torches were reflected in the shop windows, and the buildings looked spooky. The spaced boom of the drum silenced the crowd. Fritz inched his way forward. "Pardon," he said. "Excuse me. Sorry. Let us through. Coming through." He didn't stop. "Coming through."

Fritz moved on the diagonal until he and Carly came to the street. Ahead, a group of Nazis stood in an arc. He heard voices, but they were too far away. Beside Carly, several girls bored with waiting crossed the street to look for a better show, and in the hole they made in the wall of the crowd, Fritz saw the Daimler.

The limousine stood several feet from the garage entrance, in the middle of a turn, blocking the street and the Nazis on parade. The driver's door hung open, and beside it Fritz saw the hotel doorman with a gang of Nazis. He glanced at Carly. "Go home."

She could not desert him now. She began to run, keeping up with him. She heard Nazis cursing the doorman, threatening to turn him and the car upside down. "I'm your man!" Fritz yelled. "You want me!"

As the Nazis spun around, Fritz stopped Carly. "Stay back," he said, and came straight at the Nazis, smiling. "*Meine herren,*" he said, and reached the Daimler, putting his hand on the radiator. "How can I serve you?"

"Butt out," said one Nazi, a solid, heavy man who wore more armbands, swastikas, insignias on his epaulettes than the others. "Nobody sent for you."

"Baron!" The doorman circled the Nazis bunched around the limousine, staying clear of them to come up beside and behind Fritz. "The car stalled. I couldn't help it, Baron!" The Nazis had terrorized him. "I came out of the garage and this guy rode right up on his bike. I had to slam on the brakes. I would have killed him otherwise. So the car stalled." The doorman pointed at the heavy Nazi. "They told me to get moving. I must have flooded the engine."

"We've wasted enough time," said the Nazi. He waved at the others. "Get this douche bag out of here!"

"No, wait!" The doorman pointed at the Daimler. "This is the baron's car!" He pointed at Fritz. "This is the Baron Von Gottisberg!"

The Nazi came close, facing Fritz. "Fuck the baron," said the Nazi. He put his hands on his hips. "Baron Fuck Von Gottisberg." He looked at his troops. "This is the Baron Fuck Von Gottisberg." He turned back to Fritz. "Now you know what we think of barons around here." He waved his arm. "Get rid of this clunk! Get it out of my sight or I'll put a match to the goddamn thing!"

Fritz leaped forward. "One word, please," he said. "One word, Commandant."

"Fuck you is the word," said the Nazi, leaving Fritz to charge into his men, pushing and shoving. "You heard me, clear this street! Clear ... this ... street!" Fritz followed him.

"Please, Commandant," Fritz said. "I don't ask for myself. It's my wife," Fritz said, gesturing at Carly. "My wife is pregnant."

Carly wanted to scream, "Liar!" Fritz had disgraced them, dragging her down with him, fawning over the Nazis, begging them for mercy. She saw the Nazi leader looking at her, and she wanted to open her coat, spread it wide to show him her flat belly.

"She's having a hard time, Commandant," Fritz said. He spoke quietly, man to man with the Nazi. "Morning sickness, that kind of business. She looks strong but the doctor says it's touch and go whether she makes it. Lots of rest. The doctor said the main thing is rest and no excitement. Carly!" Fritz said sharply.

He had trapped her. She could not expose him and leave him to the horde of Nazis massed in the streets with their torches. She walked toward the Daimler as Fritz said, "I can start this car, Commandant.

Give me one minute to start the car. Sixty seconds." Fritz waved. "*Carly!*" he shouted, and to the Nazi, "Sixty seconds. I'll be very grateful. Not for myself, for my sake, Commandant, for my wife." Fritz took a big step. "*Liebchen,*" he said, grabbing the sleeve of Carly's coat. "Remember, Commandant, she is bringing Austria the future. We'll be out of your way in a jiffy. Thank you, Commandant. Thank you."

"Don't call me Commandant!" said the Nazi. He put his hands on his hips as Fritz helped Carly into the Daimler and closed the door. "Sixty seconds," said the Nazi.

Fritz ran around the front of the car and jumped inside beside Carly. He pushed the accelerator to the floor and kept it there as he turned the key and stepped on the starter with his left foot. "We're on our way." The engine didn't catch. "Almost," Fritz said, and began to pump the accelerator.

"Sixty seconds!" the Nazi shouted.

"It's coming," Fritz said, pumping. He saw the Nazi gesturing to his pals, and as they moved in on the Daimler, the engine caught and roared. Keeping the accelerator against the floorboard, Fritz shifted gears, released the clutch, and the limousine bucked, bucked, bucked, and then hurtled down the street at full throttle.

Fritz waited until the Nazis were far behind before easing off on the gas pedal. The crowds on both sides of the street stared at the limousine with the young couple inside, uncertain whether or not to cheer. "You might acknowledge your subjects," Fritz said.

Carly looked straight ahead, seething. She loathed Fritz's performance with the Nazis. He had kowtowed to the ugly barbarians, bowing and scraping. She sat in the Daimler as though a brick wall separated her from him.

When he turned away from the parade route, Fritz realized most of Salzburg had been in the streets to cheer the Nazis. He turned again, doubling back toward the Mirabel, glancing at the self-righteous virgin beside him. "You are disappointed in me," he said. "Sick inside because of my craven performance, dragging you into it, my pregnant wife. A word to the wise. He who runs away lives to live another day."

When he stopped in front of the stately home, Carly had the door open. "Thank you. Good night." She left the car fast, but Fritz caught up with her at the entrance. "You're a big girl now, living in the real world—cruel, treacherous, sadistic from one end to the other. Come out of the nursery."

"I don't need a civics lessons from you," she said, raging. She reached for the door, but he took her wrist, and when she faced him defiantly, she was very nearly irresistible. More than he had ever wanted anything, he longed to kiss her. "Let me go!"

"Listen, then," he said, and released her. "Don't run away believing a white knight will always appear to rescue you. There are no white knights. Those vermin who trapped us are thirsty for blood. Month after month, year after year, they have been promised a war. They are ready to shoot you, stomp on you, string you up, skewer you, hang you from a pole. They would have been happy to kill us right there in front of the hotel. If they had been ordered to burn us alive, we would be ashes now. Remember all this when you slip between your safe sheets tonight, and maybe you will offer up a prayer for your savior, Fritz." She stepped aside. "Now you can go," he said, and he went, leaving Carly at the doors of the dark house.

Inside, she blamed herself for the debacle in Fritz's room, the struggle on his bed, the distressing end of their day, of all the days with him in Salzburg. The encounter with the Nazis sickened her. She heard Fritz over and over: "My wife is pregnant." She walked toward the stairs as the telephone rang. She knew he was calling, and she refused to talk to him. The telephone rang again, and she stopped on the stairs, ashamed and angry. He would only lecture her, make her feel silly and stupid. She could see him daring her to face him, and when she heard the third ring, she raced down the stairs, ran to the telephone ready for battle.

"Carly, is it you?"

"Nick!" She felt as though they had been apart forever. "Where are you?"

"At the Zwischentheatre," he said. "Carly, we are the biggest hit in town! They are coming from all over town, from *out* of town!" Nick said the evenings of satire, born in an emergency, were the rage of Vienna. "Nobody sleeps," he said. "Everyone is writing sketches, bits and pieces, jokes. Strangers come, offering material. Free! When are you coming home?"

She listened happily to the familiar wild man. "Soon."

"Come now!" he said. "We have trouble backstage," he said, as though Carly could cure everything. "Some in the group are afraid of offending the high and mighty. Some quit."

"Quit the Zwischentheatre?" More cowards. "Who?"

"Egon Burghofer. Abe Feiner, the bookseller. Dora Ertle will quit. She shakes all over, every night. I'm out of money. Good-bye."

"I'll call you," she said. "Tell me your number and I'll call you! Nick!" But she heard the click as he hung up.

Carly climbed the stairs of her grandmother's house, completely alone. Salzburg had become threatening and Vienna was safe. Nick and his gang were in Vienna except for the few cowards. She passed her grandmother's room. They had lied to her, Grandmother Melzer and her mother. She undressed rapidly, throwing her clothes aside, angry with both, and when Fritz telephoned around noon, he learned she had taken the morning train to Vienna.

Carly's father met her at the station, and in the taxi she asked a thousand questions. "Daughter, you were gone one week," said Klaus Siefermann.

She held on to him. "I missed you, Daddy. I missed everything."

In the apartment Helga kissed her. "You gave us no notice."

Carly looked directly at her mother. "You gave me no notice."

Later, on the bed in her bedroom, she heard her mother. "Carly-y-y-y!"

In the long corridor Helga stood beside a forest, an enormous basket choked with flowers. "For you," she said, praying she was correct. No one but the baron could have sent the basket, could afford such a garden.

"Here," Klaus said, finding the small white envelope pinned to the satin around the birds of paradise. He removed the envelope, extending it to Carly. "I thought it was for me."

Helga could see *"Carly Siefermann"* written across the envelope. "Open it!"

Carly removed a card and read, *"Wiedersehen?"* Below, Fritz had written, "F."

Carly slipped the card into the pocket of her robe. Safe in Vienna once more, in her own home, the unhappy memory of Fritz's room in the hotel in Salzburg grew dim and faint, and when he called the following day, Carly wore one of his roses in her hair. "Thank you for the flowers," she said. "We're living in a jungle."

"Small token of my esteem," Fritz said. "Where would you like to dine?"

"Tonight?"

"Starting tonight," he said.

Carly made a face. "Fritz, I can't."

So the actor had won again. "Better luck next time," Fritz said.

The palace seemed deserted, barren. The sound of his footsteps was a lonely echo. Fritz got into a fleece-lined short coat and slipped a beret over his head, coming out into Himmelpfortgasse to walk away the afternoon.

Thoughts of Nick Gallanz went with him. Fritz could not rid himself of Carly's jumping jack, forever circling her like a court jester. He and his impoverished band of amateurs had corrupted Carly, seducing her with their cheap wine and high-minded ambitions. Fritz returned to the palace in less than an hour, ambushed by Nick Gallanz.

Fritz sat in the study all through the afternoon, leaving his chair to pace, returning to sit, turning his letter opener over and over and over. At twilight Zinn appeared with ice, setting the bucket on the bar beside the desk, although Fritz never drank alone. Hours later, Fritz opened a desk drawer and took a personal card which bore the Von Gottisberg crest. He wrote, "Come to dinner Saturday week, 12 November, eight o'clock," and below, "F." Fritz addressed an envelope to Carly. Then he copied her invitation and sent it to Nick Gallanz in care of Ernst Auerfeld.

Now, deep into fall, Vienna feasted on game, choosing from venison, wild boar, rabbit, and birds from the fields and ponds of Austria. On Thursday of the following week, Fritz sat in the kitchen with Matilda choosing a hunt menu for Saturday night.

Two nights later, Carly arrived a few minutes before eight. "I'm early," she said. "You can blame the nuns. Ever since grade school, I've been afraid of arriving late."

"I'm lucky," Fritz said, taking her hands in his. "Greetings, Carly."

"Greetings," she said, discarding Salzburg forever. "Greetings, Fritz."

Around six o'clock Nick rode to the Zwischentheatre with Max Ingster. Max and Judith Emmerich were playing husband and wife in a lengthy skit. "She's b-been skittish the last few nights," Max said. "I w-wish you could hang around."

"I'll talk with her," Nick said.

Judith didn't reach the Zwischentheatre until after seven-thirty. "Those animals!" she said of her clients in the beauty parlor. "You cannot satisfy them. Look at me, Nick. I'm shaking like a leaf. How can I go on tonight?" She put her face in her hands.

Nick pushed back his sleeve to check the time. "Dolly Stacker knows your lines," he said. "I'll tell Dolly," he said, opening the dressing-room door.

Judith lunged forward, grabbing his coat with both hands. "I'll try."

He was late already. "We need a performance, Judith, not an audition."

She rose, big as Nick, shoving him into the wall of the tiny dressing room. "You will see a performance, Mr. Gallanz."

"Bravo!" he said, escaping through the rear door of the storefront
and running for a taxi.

Nick had not deceived himself. He had gone to the Zwischentheatre deliberately to delay the evening. For more than a week, from
the day he had received Fritz's invitation, Nick had kept the envelope
out of sight, kept his mind closed to everything Fritz had not written
on the crested card. He had kept Fritz out of his thoughts until, riding
in the taxi, he could no longer avoid his host. Baron Von Gottisberg
was not searching for new friends, not from Leopoldstadt. Nick and
Fritz moved on different continents. Nick knew the moment he removed the card from the envelope why he had been invited to dinner.
Carly. "You're here," said the taxi driver.

In the palace Zinn took Nick's coat as though it smelled. He said,
"This way," and Nick followed him through the palace until the butler
stopped at the head of the marble steps down to the Great Hall.

Nick saw Fritz come away from the fireplace, arms out. He saw the
splendid, soaring chamber with its massive trusses crossing the ceiling,
with its massive furnishings scattered willy-nilly around the Great Hall,
saw the portraits on the wall, Baron Von Gottisberg following Baron
Von Gottisberg, back to antiquity. Fritz said, "Nick," and behind him,
at the fireplace, Nick saw Carly. Fritz had not opened the palace to
bring strange young lovers together. "Gang's all here!" Fritz announced.

Carly waved and then clapped her hands, delighted with Fritz's
surprise.

"Welcome to the palace," Fritz said, putting his arm over Nick's
shoulders. "Place needs a paint job, but I'm too lazy."

Nick grinned. "You could hire someone."

"I like the old place as is," Fritz said.

"I, too," Nick said. "Here is the place to stage *Macbeth.*"

"It's a thought," Fritz said.

They joined Carly. "Did you know?" she asked. Nick shook his
head.

Fritz said, "I sort of owed Nick an evening after that night in the
café." Nick didn't believe a word.

Zinn entered with champagne. "Let me," Fritz said, wrapping a
towel around the bottle to spring the cork. Fritz filled the flutes on the
tray Zinn held. "Who has a toast? Nick?"

"Sure," Nick said, raising his glass. "To Austria."

"To Austria," Carly said, and louder, "To Austria!"

"Our Austria," Fritz said. "Ours, not Germany's. Not Herr Schickelgruber's. Ours!" he said, sharing his secret for the first time.

"Yes, Fritz, yes!" Carly said. Why had he not been this way with the Nazis in Salzburg? "Forever!"

"Drink up," Fritz said, annoyed because he had exposed himself, showing off in front of Carly. "To old friends and new friends."

Fritz brought them to the Petit Salon for dinner. The small room, exquisitely furnished, hidden from the rest of the palace, seemed hidden from the world as well. "I love it, Fritz," Carly said.

Nick watched Carly, then Fritz. He watched their eyes, their hands, like someone seeing a magic act. Fritz was the magician, offering Carly the best of everything in his little corner, showing her what she could have instead of a seedy storefront and the café in District VIII.

Carly drank more wine than usual. "I've never been drunk!" she said, feeling woozy.

"You're safe with us, eh, Nick?" Fritz set down his knife and fork. "Hey! All this game we've been eating gives me an idea," he said. "Why don't we go up to the schloss for a few days? The weather is still good for hunting."

So Nick knew why Fritz had sent him an invitation, why Carly had been invited to dinner. The Baron Von Gottisberg was smooth as silk. He wanted Nick to play on his playground but only in front of the only witness he wanted. "I am a city boy," Nick said.

"City boys hunt," Fritz said.

"I'm not a hunter," Nick said.

"I'll teach you both," Fritz said. "Carly?"

"I've just come home," she said.

"The schloss is not a military installation," Fritz said. "You can leave when you wish."

Nick tried to elude him. "I've had my vacation."

"Carly, if Nick goes, will you?" Fritz asked.

"I cannot," Nick said, and Carly said, "He can't."

Fritz pushed back his chair. "Carry on," he said, leaving them. He went into the study, closing the door. Fritz found Magda Auerfeld's telephone number. "Am I disturbing you?"

"Not enough," Magda said. "Are you hiding? Nobody sees you or I would be jealous. I am anyway jealous. You live like a hermit, like an old man. You are a young man. Join the world, Fritz. One day you will be sorry."

"I've committed every word to memory," Fritz said. "Meanwhile,

I am running up to the schloss for a few days, thinking of making some structural changes in the castle, odds and ends. I should have an architect. Let me take Nick Gallanz for a week."

"Nick Gallanz!"

"He's here now," Fritz said. "All right? Shall I wait while you ask Ernst?"

"If I ask Ernst, he will say the same as I. You want Nick Gallanz, take Nick Gallanz." Magda returned to the living room. "Ernst!"

Magda's husband watched her approaching, her face bright with emotion. "The gall of that little bugger."

"What little bugger? Who is the latest villain, Magda?"

"Your boulevardier," Magda said. *"Cher maître* of the Zwischen-theatre. The Leopoldstadter, Nick Gallanz. He aims high, I give him credit."

"Would you once in your life tell me what in the hell you are talking about?"

Magda gave her husband a verbatim account of her conversation with Fritz. "Gallanz will come back asking for a raise," she said.

Fritz returned to the Petit Salon. "We can't leave until Tuesday. I'll need to service the car." He raised his glass to Nick. "You have a week."

4

LATE TUESDAY AFTER-
noon Fritz said, "Innsbruck." They were high in the Alps, Carly between Fritz and Nick in the front seat of the Daimler.

"How far to the castle?" she asked.

"Almost there," Fritz said. They came to a pass, and the road
narrowed. The mountains rose on either side like prison walls.

"My father called this our moat," Fritz said. "If we blocked this
pass, we could make the schloss impregnable." The road curved sharply,
and they were in daylight once more. "Don't look down, Nick," Fritz
said.

Nick lowered the window, leaning out over the running board.
Far, far below he saw cattle no bigger than terriers. "Where are the
parachutes?"

Fritz made another turn, and the Daimler plunged down a steep
grade. "Last lap," he said. At the bottom of the hill the road widened.
"Home," Fritz said.

In the distance, high above them, Nick saw towers rising like peaks, and at one side the larger tower, the keep. Closer, he could see the walls and windows of the upper levels. All at once the entire castle was visible.

"Fritz, Fritz," Carly murmured.

"You like it," Fritz said.

"I love it!"

As they reached the schloss, Nick saw a man emerge who dressed and looked like an ambassador. Fritz left the Daimler. "Come on, kids. Fiegel, help Mr. Gallanz."

Fiegel, who commanded the castle staff, took the suitcase which Sam Gallanz had bought used more than ten years earlier for a holiday in Greece. Nick followed the ambassador into the castle and up curving slate steps. Fiegel opened a door, waiting for Nick to precede him into a bedroom which seemed larger than his parents' apartment. "It'll do," Nick said.

Fiegel set the suitcase on a rack and opened it. In Vienna Nick had borrowed clothes from Max, from Peter, from his father. Lottie Gallanz forced Nick to pack the handkerchiefs she embroidered. As Fiegel took clothes from the suitcase, Nick said, "Careful of the handkerchiefs," crossing the bedroom.

"Sir!" Nick looked over his shoulder. "You will probably want to rest after your journey," Fiegel said.

"You probably know," Nick said, turning back.

Fiegel put everything Nick had packed into a single drawer. "Dinner at eight," Fiegel said, closing the door, sealing him inside.

So Nick had hours to endure alone, away form Carly, wondering if Fritz had sealed her in a room, or if she and Fritz were together. He stretched out on the bed and immediately leaped up. "I'm not tired!" He opened a window, feeling the Alpine wind, freezing and cutting like a knife. He closed the window, shivering, and flopped into a chair, pushing off his shoes.

Long before eight he opened the bathroom door, leaning against the doorjamb, watching the corridor. When he saw Carly emerge from her room, he waved and ran to join her.

Fritz led them on a tour before dinner, telling them the history of the castle and of the Von Gottisbergs. When Fiegel summoned them, Fritz said, "Back to the twentieth century. We should have good hunting tomorrow. Fiegel says the men in the village have never seen so many birds."

All three were quiet during dinner. Fritz abandoned his ringmaster role, and when Carly yawned, covering her mouth, he said, "Early to bed. Agreed?"

In his room Nick found a complete hunting wardrobe, jacket with shooting patches in the shoulders, whipcord trousers, wool socks, field shoes with thick, scored rubber soles, heavy shirts, sweaters, and a suede vest.

In the morning they could hear the barking and yelping of dogs. "They're ready," Fritz said.

In front of the castle was an old truck. Beside it, standing with two other men, Nick saw Fiegel, who looked like an advertisement, wearing a Tyrolean hat with a feather. An open shotgun, barrel pointing at the ground, hung over his arm.

The two other men, handlers, carried game bags hanging from their shoulders. Each held two dogs on leashes, a pair of German smooth-haired pointers, an English springer spaniel, and a cocker spaniel, both black and white. At the sight of Fritz all four animals sprang forward, straining at their leashes, barking wildly, trying to get at him. "There are my beauties," he said, joining the dogs and squatting.

The dogs were all over him, licking, slobbering, keening, pushing their rumps into him, nibbling at his fingers, trying to sit in his lap, their blunt, docked tails quivering. Fritz opened his arms, talking to each dog, hugging each dog, rubbing each animal's skull, scratching its withers, slapping its chest, squeezing the four soft, wet muzzles in turn. "You're a good boy," he said. "You too. And you."

Watching Fritz with the dogs, Carly said, "He's different up here, he's . . . younger. The dogs love him."

"Yes, I see," Nick said, and to himself, "I love you."

Fritz rose, the dogs crowding around him and onto him. "You're all good guys, and you're going to send up a lot of birds, aren't you?" He walked to the truck. "Carly. Nick."

On the tailgate of the truck were several shotguns and boxes of shells. Fritz took a shotgun, and with one hand on the barrel and the other on the stock, he opened the weapon, letting the barrel hang. He opened another shotgun and set it over Carly's arm, opened another for Nick. "Fill your pockets," Fritz said, taking handfuls of shotgun shells from the boxes. Carly and Nick obeyed.

Nick had never been around guns. He liked the cold touch of the smooth barrel, liked the feel of the wooden stock. He thought of using the shotgun as a prop onstage. An actor could strut around with a shotgun. Nick tried to think of a subject for a skit using shotguns.

"Nick!" Fritz brought him back from the Zwischentheatre. "The birds are waiting."

The hunting party moved out, the two handlers with their dogs, Fiegel following, and behind him, Carly between Fritz and Nick. "I've been hunting with Fiegel since I could walk," Fritz said. They proceeded into the fields.

At the Innsbruck road Fritz said, "We'll cross soon." They followed the handlers over a narrow wooden bridge, into brush which rose to the ankles. "Let them go," Fiegel said. "Slip the collars."

The handlers gathered up the leashes, bending over their dogs, raising the chain collars over the animals' heads, starting with the German smooth-haired pointers. As each dog came free, it shot forward in a blur. "Look at them," Fritz said. "Look at the springer." He gestured. "Look at the cocker. He won't finish last."

The dogs were beautiful to watch, spreading out, each taking a section of the field, head down, nose deep in the brush. One of the handlers raised a whistle and blew a short blast. All four dogs looked back, waiting for the hand signal. The handler moved them to another field.

Suddenly a pointer stopped in its tracks. The dog froze on the run, right front leg raised, stubby tail horizontal and motionless, liver-and-white flanks expanding and deflating as the animal breathed without a sound, creating a kind of vacuum around itself. Around and behind him, the other three dogs were frozen, honoring the lead dog's point. The four animals were immobilized, as though they had been set down in the field by a sculptor. Somewhere close by, hidden in the brush, were birds. Everyone in the field stopped. "Look!" Carly said, her voice squeaky with excitement.

"Sshhh," Fritz said. Taking her arm and turning her to face the hidden birds, he whispered, "Watch me." He pulled Nick close. "Watch me. Watch Fiegel."

As Fiegel loaded, Fritz took a shotgun shell from his pocket and shoved it into the barrel. Holding the barrel with his left hand, he snapped the stock, locking the shotgun.

The handler looked back, and when Fritz nodded, the handler said, "Flush!" and the pointer charged, leaping into the brush. The other dogs charged as two pheasants came straight up, wings spread and flapping fast, making a whir which seemed like thunder. For an instant the only sound on earth came from the birds' wings as Fritz and Fiegel raised their guns and fired. Both birds seemed to stop in the air and then drop. The pointer sprang forward and the spaniel closest to it followed for the other bird.

Fritz broke open the shotgun, removing the spent shell casing. "Do what I do," he said, taking a shell from his pocket. He waited until Carly and Nick held shells. "Load," Fritz said, watching them load. Fritz pushed his shell into the barrel. "I'm locking," Fritz said, snapping the barrel into place. "Carly." She closed her gun. "Exactly. Nick." Nick locked his shotgun, and then moved it up and down at an angle across his chest, bringing his knees high, marching in step, a drum major leading the parade.

Fritz leaped at him, grabbing the barrel. "No, man, no! This is a gun, a lethal instrument. Never play with a gun."

"Word of honor," Nick said.

Fritz dropped his arm. "You saw me earlier," he said. "You saw Fiegel. Our guns followed the birds." Fritz moved aside and moved his gun in a wide arc, raising the barrel. "Try it, Carly. Up, up, up, up."

Carly swung from right to left, barrel tilting at the sky. "Excellent," Fritz said. "Nick."

Nick took his turn. "Up, Nick, *up*," Fritz said. "The birds will be climbing. You climb with the birds. Carly, *bitte*." He gave Carly his gun and stood directly behind Nick. Fritz put his hand over Nick's hand on the barrel of the shotgun. "Now," he said, and swung Nick's gun around. "Up, up, up." Fritz stepped away. "Again, Nick."

Nick swung again. "You're getting there," Fritz said. He took his gun from Carly. "Remember, the birds deserve a sporting chance."

Ahead, the pointer returned to the handler with the pheasant in its mouth. The handler took the bird, rubbing the dog's head. "Baron?" He raised the bird.

"We'll need a whole lot more for a decent dinner," Fritz said. He gestured at Carly and Nick. "We're counting on you, aren't we, Fiegel?"

"We expect help," Fiegel said.

The spaniel brought back the second pheasant. The dogs crowded in on the handlers, begging to go, their docked tails twitching like minnows. One of the handlers raised his hand, sending them forward.

The dogs spread out. The handlers followed, and behind them came the shooters in a row. "You don't pull the trigger," Fritz said. "You never pull the trigger. You squeeze. You squeeze steadily, all the way back. Carly? Nick?" He looked from one to the other. "Squeeze," he said, and grinning, "And up, Nick, up."

Beside Fritz, Fiegel said, "The cocker." Far to the right, the cocker pointed, almost hidden in the brush. As Fiegel spoke, the two pointers froze, honoring the point, and on their left, the spaniel stood frozen, one leg raised. Everything stopped. Then a crow wheeled and dove and climbed. "Caw, caw, caw, caw."

The silence, the greeting from the faraway crow, the wind which rippled through the brush, the four motionless dogs, perfectly trained, made Carly shiver with pleasure. "So beautiful."

"Quiet," Fritz murmured. He moved forward, and everyone moved with him in a line across the field. "Carly. Nick," Fritz whispered, alerting them. He nodded at the handler.

"Flush!" The silent field erupted. The little cocker spaniel darted forward and a bird rose. As the other dogs tore after the cocker, Fritz said, "Carly," and she fired. She missed, and Fiegel fired and missed.

One of the pointers flushed two birds. As Carly said, "Nick!" Fritz stepped back of the others.

"Up, Nick, up!" Fritz said, and as Nick raised his gun and fired, missing, Fritz crouched, aiming at the pointer and squeezing off. The pointer took the charge full in the muzzle and fell screaming. Carly dropped her gun, running.

The other dogs were terrified. "The leashes! The leashes!" Fritz shouted. "Get the leashes on them!" he shouted as the two handlers ran. The wounded dog, screaming in agony, tried to bury itself in the brush, digging to escape the pain.

Nobody saw Fritz stop beside Nick. "Don't blame yourself," Fritz said.

Carly dropped to her knees beside the pointer. The dog's muzzle was drenched in blood, and blood streamed from the animal's eyes. Carly gagged and couldn't stop, retching, her belly heaving, but she remained on her knees beside the dog, still screaming and trying to dig a hole in the ground and hide the pain. "He's blind!" Carly said, but nobody heard her because the dog screamed. She tried not to look at the blood. She had to look. "He's blind!" She raised her head, shouting. "He's *blind!*"

"Blind!" Fritz said, horrified, throwing his shotgun aside and running. He dropped beside the wounded animal. Watching Fritz and Carly with the dog, Nick wanted to vanish.

Fritz took the pointer in his arms. The dog tried to escape, tried to get away from the pain, but Fritz kept it captive. "Give me a gun!" Fritz yelled, fighting to keep the dog, hands and clothes covered with blood. "Go away, Carly! Goddamn it, I need a gun. Fiegel! Goddamn it!'' Fiegel shook his head, raising his hands helplessly, but one of the handlers pulled a revolver from his jacket. "Baron.''

Fritz took the gun. "Carly, get out of here.'' She didn't look at him, didn't reply. Fritz put the muzzle of the revolver behind the dog's ear and fired. The animal twitched in Fritz's arms and died.

"Baron.'' Fiegel stood over them, extending a handkerchief. Fritz took it, wiping the revolver before giving it to the handler. He wiped Carly's hands and his, rising and bring Carly with him.

"Very sorry, Baron,'' said the handler, and the other said, "I'll . . . we'll take care of things here, Baron.''

Fritz said, "Thanks, thanks.'' He saw Nick alone. "Poor Nick, I feel sorrier for him than I do for the dog. Nick!'' Carly followed Fritz, who put his arm around Nick. "We're leaving. Now.''

They heard the other dogs barking, protesting the aborted day's frolic. "It is not your fault,'' Fritz said. "Tell him, Carly.''

"It was an accident,'' Carly said. "Nick?'' She looked into his eyes until he nodded.

In the castle, Nick said, "I'll be in my room for a while.''

Fritz followed him. "You're not alone,'' he said. "Remember, you're with friends.'' He followed Nick into the bedroom. "Do you want anything?''

Nick tried to smile. "Sure. Close the door.''

Fritz pointed. "If you change your mind, that buzzer works.''

Nick crossed the room to the windows, trying to get away from the dog, the dog's screams. He saw the snow in the Alps, the clouds moving through mountain passes. Far below he saw a field, and without warning, the blinded dog. He could hear the dog. He turned away, knowing he could not escape, sitting on the bed and taking his punishment.

In the morning in the breakfast room, which Fritz had made a bright, cheerful place, he said, "New day, a new start.''

"A new start,'' Carly said, worried about Nick.

"Who's for what?'' Fritz asked. He raised an elaborate cruet and set it in front of Nick. "Rub this magic lantern and make a wish.''

"More coffee,'' Nick said.

Fritz set the cruet in front of Carly. "Fair maiden.''

Carly put her hand over a large salt cellar. "Fun,'' she said. "Let's have fun.''

"Granted,'' Fritz said. In the days which followed, Fritz managed to arrange outings and adventures where nothing would remind them of the awful episode in the field. On Saturday, he said, "This week went too fast. We've just arrived. Let's stay longer."

Nick knew then he had underestimated Fritz, knew Fritz had included this final, secret chapter in the palace in Vienna before proposing the holiday. Nick could not stay, and Fritz knew it. "I have a job," Nick said. "And if I'm not at my drafting table Monday morning, I will not be there Tuesday morning, or ever."

"I'll split the difference with you," Fritz said. "Three more days."

Nick faced a master. "I'm already on probation with Ernst Auerfeld," Nick said. "I must return."

"I give up," Fritz said. "Carly, you can't both desert me."

Nick stopped breathing. Carly said, "We all came together, we should all go home together."

"The trains run Sunday," Fritz said. "Nick can take the train." Nick waited for Carly to override him, but Fritz went on, "Fiegel is counting on us, Carly. There is a ceremony in the village tomorrow night and Monday night. Fiegel vouchsafed our attendance. I can't go alone. I'll undermine his credibility."

Fritz made the evening a celebration. At dinner he stood behind his own chair. "Nick!" Fritz seated him. The wine, the ticking clock tolling the last hours of Nick's presence, made Fritz expansive and the evening memorable.

Later, in front of the fire, Carly said, "I feel protected here, feel safe."

"No one has ever been safe in Austria," Fritz said. "Austria has never been safe, it has only survived. These Alps haven't stopped the conquerors. They have marched on Austria from every direction for a thousand years. The world covets Austria. The world envies us and I agree. We are an enviable people, a learned people, a civilized people. We have given the world an entire pantheon. Metternich, Beethoven, Mozart, Mahler, Schoenberg, Schubert, Strauss and Strauss and Strauss, and Mendel, Mesmer, Freud, Semmelweiss, Wittgenstein, Schnitzler, Egon Shiele, Klimt, Kokoschka, Theodore Herzl, Biedermeier, Von Hofmannsthal, Musel, Karl Kraus, Adolf Loos . . ." Fritz stopped; he rarely boasted, but his love for Austria rivalled Der Chineser's. "Among others," he said.

They rose early Sunday, and soon Fiegel came for Nick in a small sedan. Fritz opened the car door. "Come back."

"Sure," Nick said as Carly leaned forward and brushed his cheek with her lips.

Nick heard Carly and Fritz calling after him: "Bye, bye!" He had to acknowledge them. They stood together, their arms raised. Carly's hair spilled over her shoulders and over Fritz's shoulder.

When the train rolled into the station, Fiegel took Nick to the first-class cars. Fiegel opened a compartment door, stowing Sam's shabby suitcase. "You'll be alone, sir," Fiegel said, giving Nick an envelope with the ticket.

Nick didn't want to be alone, thinking of Carly and Fritz waving at him. When the conductor came for the ticket, Nick said, "Don't close the door." He looked out, trying to find the castle, but saw only Carly's face in the window.

The train arrived in Vienna exactly on schedule. Nick emerged from the station into the early evening bustle. The lights, the noise, the traffic, the vibrant, familiar clamor of the city seemed to enfold Nick, as though an old friend welcomed him. He hurried to the Zwischentheatre.

The night's performance was under way when he arrived, and he used the rear door of the storefront. Backstage, the group passed him around as though he had been rescued from a forsaken island. "Every newspaper in town sent a critic out this week," said Sepp.

"We're f-finally legitimate," Max said. "We're finally a theater."

Peter cornered him. "We need a sketch for next week's show. We're seven minutes short."

"Leave me alone for seven minutes," Nick said.

"Seriously," Peter said. "Any ideas? We're in trouble." Sepp and Max and Dolly joined them, adding their concerns. "We don't even have an *area* to work from," Peter said.

"Hitler," Nick said. "We fill the stage with Adolf Hitler." Nick spread his arms. "A full line, stage right to stage left, like an opera finale. We pack the stage." Nick put his forefinger over his upper lip. "Everyone with a moustache. Everyone. The whole gang!"

Peter behaved as though he had struck gold, delivering a crazy dance. Dolly kissed Nick. Max did a forward somersault and followed it with a back flip. "G-great! Nick, that's great!"

They all threw out ideas for the sketch before Judith Emmerich said glumly, "We're really looking for trouble."

Nick hugged her. "Right! Looking for trouble!" He faced the others. " 'Looking . . . for . . . trouble'!" That's Hitler's song. That's what we sing!" Nick grabbed Sepp. "You could write some lyrics and put them to a familiar song. We sing it for the audience, and then we get the audience to sing along with us."

The sketch came alive among them, and during intermission they expanded the Hitler premise. Finally Nick pulled on his coat. "I am finished."

"Hang around," Sepp said. "I've got a date out front watching the show. We'll go with you."

"Tomorrow," Nick said, picking up his suitcase. "I'm for bed."

He opened the rear door, stepping into the alley. He reached the street and turned toward the trolley stop.

"That's him! I recognize him!" said Der Chineser. He had studied the photograph of the group hanging in the ticket booth in front of the storefront.

Beside Der Chineser in the cramped cab of a three-wheeled van sat Rudi Lofting, an early Nazi, built like a wrestler. They had waited four nights in the van. Nick had used a shortcut from the trolley stop to the rear of the storefront, so Der Chineser missed his arrival. Now he turned the three-wheeler out from the curb, running without lights.

Nick leaned against the lamppost at the trolley stop. He closed his eyes and saw Carly in a long gown, her shoulders bare, dancing with Fritz. He saw her in the Daimler with Fritz. Almost a hundred yards back, on the same side of the street, Rudi Lofting left the cab of the three-wheeler. "Keep the engine running."

Rudi went to the rear of the van. "No noise." He helped a Nazi out of the van. "Quickly," he said, helping another and a third. "Pace yourselves after me."

In the cab Der Chineser could see Austria's enemy under the light. He saw two comrades running across the street. He saw Rudi up ahead, on his way to the trolley stop. The last man, the fourth member of the patrol, stayed well back.

Lofting checked the pair on the far side of the street. They were on a line with him, in position.

One of the pair took out brass knuckles, holding the blunt, destructive loops of metal in his left hand and slipping four fingers of his right hand through the rings, making a war club with four spaced metal heads. "Get dressed," he said, and his companion obeyed.

"Willie!" Rudi strode toward Nick, his big arms out in welcome. "I'll be damned! Willie!" The pair wearing brass knuckles walked into the street, coming fast.

Nick saw the stranger approaching. "You're wrong. My name is not Willie." The man smiled, arms spread. Nick said, "I told you—" as Rudi leaped. Spinning Nick around, he grabbed him from behind and locked his hands across the target's chest. Sam's suitcase fell as Nick twisted, trying to free his arms. He said, "Who . . . ?" and "Let go of—" before Rudi rammed his elbow into Nick's mouth.

Nick could barely breathe, barely see. The two Nazis came at him, and as Rudi released Nick, one man swung.

The brass knuckles landed below Nick's eye, opening his face as though he had been slashed with a knife. Blood gushed from the long, gaping wound in a thick river, across Nick's face, filling his mouth. He staggered helplessly, on fire with pain. Rudi grabbed Nick's hair with both hands, pulling back his head until he stood erect and blind as the second Nazi swung.

The brass knuckles got Nick full in the face, breaking his jaw, squashing his nose, splitting his mouth wide open. Blood erupted, rising in an arc before splattering across Nick and the sidewalk and the street.

He sagged and as he began to fall, senseless, the fourth man swung a blackjack, opening Nick's skull. He dropped, facedown, into a lake of his blood. Rudi kicked him in the head. "Pick him up."

As the Nazis raised Nick—what remained of Nick—from the sidewalk, Sepp and his girl arrived in the intersection. They saw the creature covered with blood, and as Sepp, horrified, noticed the suitcase, she covered her face with her hands and started screaming. The sound filled the entire neighborhood, startling the two Nazis holding Nick. They released him, and he fell heavily, lying in his blood like a sack. Enraged, Rudi turned homicidal. "Stop her!" He shoved his men. "Stop her!" Rudi began to kick Nick in the ribs, then the head.

Sepp saw the man coming at him and grabbed his girl. "Run!" Then he saw men using their boots on Nick. He wanted to run, but he couldn't leave Nick. They were killing him. He looked around wildly for a rock, a stick. Seeing his girl beside him, paralyzed, he yelled, "Run!"

She ran toward the audience spilling into the street from the Zwischentheatre. She and Sepp had been the first to leave, hurrying to beat the others. She began to scream: "They're killing him! They're killing him!"

In the van Der Chineser had watched the entire operation. His comrades had carried out the mission, and now everything depended on him. He shifted into gear, ready to crush anyone in his path.

The Nazi running after Sepp saw the crowd bearing down on the trolley stop. He saw his buddies running to the van, the mission commander running, and he veered, following them.

Halfway down the block the van slammed to a stop, and Rudi opened the rear door. "Come on, come on!" The Nazis dove into the van, and Rudi slammed the door. Der Chineser had the cab door open and was rolling before Rudi could close it.

As the three-wheeler passed, Sepp reached Nick, lying on his belly in a lake of blood. Sepp dropped to his knees and turned Nick over on his back. Nick didn't have a face. "Get someone!" Sepp shouted. "Police! Call an ambulance! He's dying!"

All those who came from the Zwischentheatre for the trolley stopped, and no one crossed the street. A quarter mile to the north, sitting in a parked police car, two cops heard the racket. "Sounds like a massacre," said the driver. He started the engine.

"Sunday night," said his partner. "Why in Christ can't they stay home on Sunday night?"

Max beat the police car. He kneeled and took Nick's wrist, feeling for a pulse. All around them, the audience, emboldened by Max, inched their way toward the creature in the blood. "He's alive!" Max said, forgetting his stutter in the emergency.

"The cops are here," Sepp said. Max looked into headlights. He shielded his eyes and saw legs in uniform.

"Some kind of drunken brawl," said one cop.

"What a mess," said his partner.

"He was beaten!" Sepp said, ready to strangle the police. "They beat him and when he went down, they kept kicking him!"

"Yeah, well," said the cop driving that night. "We'll call for an ambulance."

"He'll die!" Max said, on his knees. He punched Sepp's leg. "Help me," Max said, rising and squatting.

"We'll tell the ambulance," the cop said.

"You're taking him to a hospital," Max said, and to Sepp, "Get his legs."

"You're nuts," said the driver. He would never get the police car clean.

"He belongs in an ambulance," said the other cop.

"Shut up!" Max yelled. He and Sepp raised Nick. "Open the door!"

"Forget it," said the driver, returning to the police car.

"Open the door!" Max yelled. "Open it!" Sepp yelled. His girl began screaming again, screaming, "Open it! Open the door!" Other women began screaming, "Open the door!"

Holding Nick under the shoulders, Max backed into the police car and opened the door. "Give us some room."

"Get a move on," said the driver.

"Thanks for all your help," Max said, ready to kill the cop, kill anyone. "Watch it, you might get your uniform dirty."

"I can handle you without getting dirty," the cop said.

"Max Ingster!" Max yelled. "Without your monkey suit, whenever you're ready!"

Sepp yelled, "Max! He'll die!" Max raised Nick's shoulders, moving backward into the police car. Inside, Max bent double, dropping to the floorboards between the seats. The cops climbed into the police car. "I'm staying," Max said, afraid Nick would die during the ride. He couldn't let Nick die alone.

In the Alps, snow began to fall late that night, and when Fritz woke, the recessed windows were piled high with snow. Fritz went to the windows barefoot, like a boy hurrying to see what the day promised. He looked out on a white world. Perfect.

He dressed quickly and below talked with Fiegel, making plans. "Fix a tray," Fritz said. "Hot chocolate, biscuits, whatever goes with it. And two cups."

When Fiegel brought the tray, Fritz said, "Follow me." Fiegel followed him up the stairs to Carly's room. Knocking once, Fritz opened the door and saw Carly sitting against a wall of pillows looking at the falling snow. Fritz took the tray from Fiegel. "Breakfast."

Carly put her legs together and smoothed the covers for the tray. Fritz set it on her thighs and sat on the bed. He poured the hot chocolate, and Carly took the big, thick cup with both hands. As they drank, a loud, hard thud reverberated through the room. The wind had flung back a window. Fritz jumped up from the bed. The noise startled Carly and the tray on her belly rocked from side to side. Cups toppled and the pitcher fell. Chocolate oozed onto the bed covers. Fritz closed the window. "It's my fault," she said. "I thought I had dropped the latch."

He returned to the bed. "Look what I've done," Carly said. Fritz set the tray on the floor.

"Look what I've done," he said.

She rubbed her sticky hands. "I have to get up."

"Get up."

She said, "Fritz, I—" and stopped, looking away, hating herself for behaving like a baby. "I'm not wearing anything."

He put his hands over his eyes. "I won't look," he promised, facing the windows with his back to Carly. "Cross my heart and hope to die."

Fritz heard the bed creak as she left it. He tipped his hand until it lay like a visor over his eyes. In the mirror beside the windows he saw Carly naked. She raised her hands to gather up her hair and threw it back over her shoulders. Then he saw her enter the open bathroom and stop at the sink, arching her back, her breasts high, her nipples pink as a baby's mouth. He watched her bend over the sink to wash her hands, knees and ankles together. Perfect, she was perfect.

Early in the afternoon, the wind abated. Fritz suggested a walk. "I didn't bring snow gear," Carly said. He took her hand and they climbed the stairs.

Fritz said, "Abracadabra," and opened her door. Winter clothing covered the bed, and on the floor were boots of varying styles and length.

They emerged from the castle into a wonderland. Their boots sank into the snow. Carly loved the silence. They came to the Innsbruck road and walked in the paths made by cars and trucks. Carly climbed a fieldstone wall and Fritz followed. A rabbit appeared from nowhere and she chased the animal, sinking deeper into the snow with every step until she fell. Fritz saw her wriggling like a fish on a hook. As he approached, she pulled one leg free and fell on her back, panting and laughing. He held out his hands, lifting her to her feet. "Where to?"

"I suppose we should start back to the castle," she said.

"You are at the castle," Fritz said. "It's all the castle, wherever you look."

"I love it," she said. "I love it all."

"Claim it," he said. "Establish sovereignty." He put his right hand against his chest like Napoleon. "I, Carlotta of Gottisberg, pronounce these lands and all manner of domicile therein and thereon, large and small, mine forevermore."

For Carly the day was hypnotic. Sitting in front of the fire that night, she felt as though she had entered a new, strange land of enchantment.

"You've left me," Fritz said.

"I'm here," she said. "The snow, the quiet, the . . . safety, nothing seems real."

"There is a kind of magic in the castle," he said. "Not always, but now and then you can fall under a spell." She did not respond, looking past Fritz into the dark corners. He said, "Carly," bringing her back once more. "Everything you wore today—boots, sweater, everything—belonged to someone in the castle. All your clothes are from a baroness—my mother, grandmother, great-grandmother. All your clothes fit.''

Fritz went to her, standing between Carly and the fireplace, facing the beautiful young woman, *his* beauty, the chatelaine he had chosen. ''You like the schloss.'' She looked up at him. The quiet perfection of the castle needed no testimonial from her. ''It's yours,'' he said. ''The castle is yours. This afternoon in the snow we played a game, a charade. The game is over.'' She felt his hand on hers as he brought her to him.

''You belong here,'' he said. ''Belong with me, in Vienna with me. After these days together, you know you belong with me. Baroness Von Gottisberg.''

He terrified her. Fritz had flung Carly into an alien landscape of decisions and pledges, of finality. She wanted to protest, wanted to flee, to be free. First Nick and now Fritz had tricked her, trapping her, bombarding her with vows, with declarations, with demands. They changed everything. She wasn't ready, she wasn't ready!

''We can tell your parents when we return tomorrow,'' Fritz said, and took her in his arms.

She raised her hands. ''Wait,'' but he bent to kiss her. Carly turned her head sharply to free herself. His arms fell and she stepped back, leaving him. ''I'm sorry.''

Fritz looked like he had been shot. His face became pale.

''Fritz, I'm sorry,'' Carly said. ''I didn't expect . . . I didn't know you . . .'' She tried to stop and could not. ''I never thought you . . . I thought we were friends, good friends,'' she said.

Fritz almost raised his hand to hit her in the face, her adolescent, silly, patronizing face. This mindless birdbrain of a juvenile, this alley cat from a pedestrian lump of a lackluster family, had tricked him into offering her his name. She had been playing hide-and-seek with him.

Carly vowed to be alone for the rest of her life, away from Fritz, from *men*. ''I'm very sorry I hurt you.''

''Superficial cuts and bruises,'' he said, fighting the rage within him as he would a stubborn colt he was breaking to the saddle.

''You're awfully nice,'' she said. ''And kind.''

The stupid adolescent mouthing her clichés pulled Fritz away from the precipice. He had been on the verge of succumbing to impulse, but now all that remained was the need to rid the castle of this ingenue. ''We should make an early start tomorrow so we can reach Vienna in daylight.'' He reached for the poker and, bending over the fireplace, dismissed her.

He had planned a leisurely drive from the castle. He lunged at the fireplace, thrusting the poker into a log as though piercing an enemy's heart. *Bride!*

He could not sleep. His mind returned to the scene in front of the fireplace. Over and over he heard himself, heard her snivelling reply.

He had made a mistake, only a mistake. Nothing had been lost; he hadn't lost a schilling. The schloss remained the schloss; the palace in the Himmelpfortgasse would be there when he returned the next day. He had been tormenting himself over a young, senseless, ignorant wench. His vanity had been bruised, nothing more.

In her room, Carly flopped, belly down, onto the bed. She hated the evening's end, hated Fritz's proposal and the turmoil he had unleashed within her. The entire holiday had been ruined. All the excitement, the adventure, the days of exploration and discovery around the castle, had been wiped out. Carly turned on her back. She felt as though she had been caught lying. Fritz hadn't tricked her or cheated. Everything was her fault. Carly turned on her belly as though she had been found out and was trying to hide. She defended herself. She couldn't be blamed if she didn't love anyone. Carly wondered if something was wrong with her. Maybe she was missing something inside. She turned on her back, playing with her fingers.

Why didn't *she* fall in love? She liked Fritz. Why didn't she love him? When Lisl had learned Carly was dating Baron Fritz Von Gottisberg, she almost had a heart attack right in the middle of the Graben. "You're going out with Fritz Von Gottisberg?"

Well, she wasn't Lisl Schott. She liked being with Fritz. They had fun. Carly made a face and turned onto her belly.

In the Daimler leaving the castle the next morning, Fritz said, "I had a Jesuit teacher who would take us out on skis after a snowfall. We would have school on the slopes. Father Sebastian," Fritz said, and gave Carly an interminable account of his years with the priests.

Fritz talked all the way. He behaved as though nothing had happened the night before. He made it easy for Carly.

As they reached Vienna, Carly sat on the edge of the seat, like a sprinter in the blocks, and when she saw the doorman in front of her apartment, she almost rolled down the window to wave. "End of the line," Fritz said. He pushed himself across the front seat, following Carly, and removed his beret. "Good-bye."

She leaned forward and kissed his cheek. "Thank you for everything."

"Anytime," Fritz said, and left her, pushing the beret into his coat pocket. He needed a purgative after his days in the nursery. Fritz drove toward Number 11 and Katharina, and Katharina's varsity, Giselle and the other one whose name he couldn't remember. Victoria. If the pair weren't creative enough, he would tell Katharina to lock the front door and send in the entire team.

Helga Siefermann had stayed home all day so she wouldn't miss Carly. In the kitchen, pouring tea for herself, she heard the maid: "Fraulein is home!"

In moments Helga was trailing after her daughter. "I'll help you unpack."

"I can manage," Carly said sharply. "I'm a big girl now." She went into her bedroom. "I'm sorry," Carly said, hearing herself apologize again, although she was innocent.

"You're tired," Helga said. "We'll talk later. Maybe we'll talk at dinner."

"Mama, wait," Carly said. Her mother was innocent, too. "Fritz asked me to marry him."

Helga said, barely, "Marry . . . ?" She shivered in the overheated apartment. Baron Fritz Von Gottisberg. Baroness Carlotta Von Gottisberg. A miracle had befallen her. As Helga went to embrace her daughter, Carly said, "I said no."

Helga couldn't even cry. "Why did you tell me?"

For almost twenty-four hours Carly had been in a continuous state of remorse, serving penance for her cruelty to Fritz. Now her mother had become another of her victims, and Carly refused to accept the punishment. Her mother could stand there looking like she had a knife in her heart for the rest of the night. Carly bent over her suitcase and when she removed a dress, Helga left her.

Carly threw the dress aside. She didn't have a terrible disease, and she didn't intend to hide forever. She strode into the corridor and telephoned Ernst Auerfeld's drafting room. "Nick Gallanz, please."

Alfred Slavin said, "He's not here. He's sick, I think." Carly asked to speak with Ernst. "He's out. You can call tomorrow."

Carly called Magda. "I'm looking for Nick Gallanz."

"You didn't look in the right place," Magda said. "He's in Prince Eugen Hospital. Some Nazis beat him. Thugs, scum of the earth."

Carly's parents heard her cry out, and when they rushed into the corridor, they saw her taking her coat from the closet. "Nick is in the hospital!"

"You haven't even unpacked," Helga said. "Have you looked outside? There is a flood outside. Wait!" she said as Carly left.

The snowstorm in the Alps had reached the Danube plain and

turned to rain in the warmer, lower altitude. Carly emerged from the building into a deluge. She walked three blocks before a cab driver saw her waving. "Prince Eugen Hospital."

"If we're lucky," said the driver. "You need a boat in something like this." Carly rode for what seemed like hours before he said, "Made it."

She ran into the hospital, ran through the lobby to the information counter. "Where is Nick Gallanz?"

The nurse flipped through a card index. "He's on three but not allowed visitors." She looked at Carly's hair, wet and dripping. "You should have called."

Carly thanked her and walked toward the entrance watching the nurse. When she bent to take something from under the counter, Carly darted into a corridor, turning right and left and right until she saw a sign marked "STAIRS."

At the nurses' station on the third floor, Carly asked for the number of Nick's room. "He's not allowed visitors," said the nurse. "You should have called."

"I won't disturb him," Carly said. Sam Gallanz came out of the elevator as she said, "I'll stay in the doorway. Please let me see him." Sam recognized her immediately from Nick's description.

"There is nothing to see," Sam said. He was an introverted man whose life had changed forever the night before. He blamed everyone in Vienna for Nick's beating, including Nick's girlfriend. "He's more dead than alive," Sam said.

Carly thought the dumpy little man was a doctor, and then she remembered Nick's pride in his brilliant lawyer brother. "You're Sam! I'm Carly Siefermann, a friend of Nick's. I just heard . . . he'll be all right."

"You should share your diagnosis with the doctors." Sam had been awake for almost two days. He had at last managed to send his parents home, and had come up from the lobby after leaving them because he could not desert Nick. He should not have spoken to the girl. He should not have stopped.

"Go home!" he said, ready to hate the tall young woman, but she began to cry. She didn't make a sound, she didn't move. Her eyes filled and the tears fell from her wet lashes. Her lips quivered, and her face began to crumple, and Sam, who could not pass a stray dog without worrying about the animal's next meal, felt as though he was about to face a firing squad. "This way."

When Sam stopped at 307, Carly rubbed her eyes. He opened the door wide and Carly entered the hospital room.

Everything was white, the walls, the bedcovers, the lamp in the corner, the two chairs, even the white tile floor. Carly could see the outline of the figure in the bed, the two small peaks made by the feet beneath the covers, then the two mole tunnels of legs. She saw the bandaged arms on the covers, like tongs, and the white ball of bandage and tape which was Nick's head. He seemed a thousand miles away. Carly had to touch him. Now she could not be stopped, crossing the room to the bed. The doctors had bandaged everything but Nick's eyes and lips, and his eyes were closed. Carly put her hand over his stone-cold hand.

"They broke all his ribs," Sam said, seizing on his audience after lying to his parents since the previous night. "They split his head open, tore his face open. He needed twenty-four stitches in his head alone. They broke his jaw, broke his nose. The doctors closed his jaws with wires, both jaws. He's ripped apart from head to toe."

Sam stood behind the chairs, where he had spent the day tending to his parents. Because he was the eldest, they had always leaned on him. Sam had always been the go-between, the delegate to the outer, hostile world, the family's leader. Nobody knew Sam's true heart. Dealing with city and federal offices, paying taxes, rent, utility bills, buying railroad tickets, writing checks, visiting banks, were chores for a simpleton, done by rote. Sam had never been comfortable in the streets. Nick was the public figure. He thrived in the hurly-burly. The apartment in Leopoldstadt came alive when Nick arrived. They all waited for Nick, the family's true bellwether, and now they had lost him. The bundle on the bed in room 307 was a bag of stuffing, not Nick. The Nazis had eliminated Nick, but his family would not let him go. His family clung to him, waiting like a dog which refuses to leave its master's grave.

Carly had never hated anyone or anything in her life, "Have the police found the men who did this?"

"The police are full of Nazis," Sam said. "They change from one uniform to the other."

At home, Carly's mother heard the key in the lock, and looked out to see Carly removing her coat. "You're soaked, Carly. Take off everything, quick."

In her bedroom Carly stripped naked and rubbed herself with a towel. Helga brought Carly's robe. "Take a hot bath, child."

Carly wrapped the towel around her head. "You haven't asked about Nick."

"How is he?"

"The Nazis tried to kill him," Carly said, watching her mother, who didn't blink. "They tried to kill him! He's unconscious! I can't even see his face." Carly watched her mother. "Are you deaf, Mama?"

"I didn't harm your friend," Helga said.

Her mother's response shot through Carly like a branding iron. "You're not even sorry," Carly said, and, without warning, discovered the real truth. "You're glad!" she said. "You're happy to be rid of Nick, one way or another. I know you sent me off to Salzburg to separate us because Nick is a Jew. Shipped me out to forget a schoolgirl crush on a Jew. But you're ready to see him *die*. You're ready to celebrate."

"Watch your language to me, miss," Helga said.

Her mother's voice infuriated Carly. "Better not talk now," Carly said. "Say nothing now," and louder, "Say nothing now. Maybe you'd better leave now, because you could be in danger. I can't even see straight or think straight. I have never felt this way, felt as I feel now. I don't even know how I feel now. Like throwing something. Like tearing this room apart. Like taking a gun and going out into the streets to find the men, *men*, who did this to Nick, waited in the dark four against one, four against one, to leap on a person they didn't even know, had never met, and tore him apart. They tore him apart! Because he worked in a theater! Because he made jokes! He made *jokes!* They came after Nick to kill him because he made people laugh!"

The towel came loose and dropped, and Carly grabbed it with both hands as though she held a garrote. "And you're celebrating, Mama," Carly said. "You can't hide your feelings from me anymore. Something has happened here tonight, Mama. My mama," Carly said. "I learned who you really are. Everything between us is in the open now. From tonight on, stay away. Don't interfere with me ever again. Ever! Don't coach me from the sidelines and don't try tricks. One more trick and I won't even say good-bye. I won't even take my clothes. I'll leave this apartment with the clothes I'm wearing, and you'll see me once a year at Christmas, and even then I won't stay. I'll leave your present and take mine." Helga believed every word.

As Carly fell silent, she thought of Nick, stiff and still in his bed, and her mother became unimportant. "Go away," Carly said, and when Helga didn't move, she went into the bathroom and closed the door.

Carly could not be alone, unable to help Nick, to breathe life into him. Her mother had gone. Carly called Fritz. "I apologize for disturbing you," she said. "Please forgive me. Nick is in the hospital. Four Nazis attacked him last night near the Zwischentheatre. Fritz, they almost killed him!"

"We're lucky he's alive," Fritz said.

"So far. I don't know how he keeps breathing," Carly said. "He's bandaged like a mummy."

"Can I help?" Fritz asked. "Does he need anything?"

"That's the worst part," Carly said. "There is nothing we can do for him. We can pray for him, but right now I don't believe God . . . don't believe in a God who would allow this."

He let her talk until she exhausted herself. "I guess I shouldn't have called you," Carly said. "You're nice. You're always nice, Fritz."

"I'm here if you need me," he said. When he replaced the receiver, his hand trembled. Carly's call had come minutes after he had entered the palace. He had been at Number 11 for hours, first with Victoria and Giselle, then with two others, a redhead and an imaginative Slav with a silk handkerchief. When she completed her repertoire, he could barely dress himself, barely drive through the Inner City to Himmelpfortgasse. He had fallen across the bed in his clothes, half asleep, when the telephone rang. Fritz pulled off his trousers. He was in deep, deeper than he had ever allowed himself to venture. Just the sound of her voice had flipped him end over end. She had taken possession. The girl owned him.

Early the next morning, Fritz called his florist, ordering flowers for Nick. "Send the same selection each week," Fritz said. "On the card write, 'Only bears hibernate.' "

By that time Carly was in the hospital, going directly to the elevators. On the third floor she tried to avoid the nurses' station. "One moment!" Carly stopped. "Whom do you wish to see?" asked the nurse.

"Nick Gallanz. He's in 307. I'm his sister from Salzburg," Carly said. "I just arrived from Salzburg."

She entered Nick's room to face his family. Sam and his parents sat beside the bed. Carly said, "Hello . . ." Sam and Boris rose together. Lottie looked at Carly as though she faced a housebreaker.

Sam tried to save her. "This is Nick's friend, Carly Siefermann." Boris said, "I am Nick's father," and Lottie nodded at the alien.

Carly saw the same inert bundle on the bed, the lifeless figure, the heap of nothing. "There is no change," Sam said. "You can sit here."

Carly sat beside Lottie Gallanz, who shifted in her chair so nothing of her would touch the czarina. Carly looked up at Sam. "What did the doctors say?"

"The same," Sam said. "They've done everything. Now we must wait."

Carly stayed through the day. At noon Max Ingster and Peter Dietrich came and were stopped in the lobby. Max sent a note with a nurse asking to talk with someone from Nick's family. Sam showed Carly the message. "You know them. Will you go?"

While Carly was with Max and Peter, Dolly Stacker arrived on her lunch hour, and then Sepp Wiegend arrived. Later, Carly told the nurse at the information counter to summon her when someone asked to see Nick. Others from the Zwischentheatre came after work and after dinner, and Carly commuted between 307 and the lobby.

She returned the next day and then each day following. Nick's mother caught a cold, and when a doctor found her beside the bed, he dragged her out of the room. "Do you want to kill him?" The doctor left orders barring Lottie from the hospital until she had recovered and he had examined her.

Boris Gallanz had to return to his bench at Schunemann, the jeweler, and in the following week Sam's superiors summoned him to the law offices. Only Carly remained, arriving every morning and sitting beside Nick's bed through the day and into the evening.

For more than a month, Nick lay without stirring, kept alive by the glucose which dripped steadily from a bottle hanging beside his bed into a needle in his arm. On the Sunday before New Year's of 1938, Carly came to the hospital early, almost an hour before Sam arrived. As he passed the bed, Carly saw Nick's eyes open. "Sam!"

She sprang at the bed and saw Nick's eyes close. She felt Sam beside her. "His eyes opened and then closed! Nick, do you hear me?"

Then neither spoke, afraid to move, standing rigid until their bones ached, and both saw Nick's eyes open and close. "There!" Carly said. "Did you see it, Sam?"

"I saw," Sam said, blinking hard and reaching for his handkerchief. Nick heard the faraway sound, first a sustained buzz. Then he heard voices but not words, as from a distance. He opened his eyes and saw filmy shapes bobbing up and down like toy boats in a fountain. They were all around him, and the voices came from all around him. His eyelids weighed a ton, and he closed his eyes. And opened them. The bobbing figures remained, all in a fog. He tried to see and hear clearly, tried to think. He couldn't think!

The figures moved, and directly in front of him he discovered three Carlys. The three melded into two, melded into one, changed back to two, and split into three. But Carly wasn't in Vienna. She was at the schloss with Fritz.

Nick closed his eyes so he wouldn't see Carly, and when he looked again, he saw three Sams, and heard the voices without words.

That night, Carly called Fritz. "He's conscious!"

"Hallelujah!" Fritz said. "Tell me when I can see him."

He picked up the evening newspaper and read, a third time, a story opposite the editorial page. Chancellor Kurt Schuschnigg had been interviewed by a correspondent for the London Morning Telegram.

"There is no question of ever accepting Nazi representatives in the Austrian cabinet," Schuschnigg told the reporter. "An absolute abyss separates Austria from Nazism. Christendom is anchored in our very soul, and we know but one God; and that is not the State or the Nation, or that elusive thing, Race. Our children are God's children, not to be abased by the State. We abhor terror; Austria has always been a humanitarian State. As a people we are tolerant by disposition. Any change now in the status quo could only be for the worse."

Fritz lowered the newspaper. Maybe Schuschnigg would be as lucky as Nick Gallanz.

For days Nick drifted in and out of consciousness. He saw forms around him, and sometimes one became someone he knew: his mother, father, Sam, Carly. When he became fully conscious, the doctors ended the ban on visitors, but Nick could not talk because of the wires in his jaws. Carly brought him pads and pencils, and for several weeks he wrote to her and to his family, to those from the Zwischentheatre and to the hospital staff.

Late in January, Carly and a nurse began helping Nick out of bed, and he sat in a chair for a little while each day. One Saturday afternoon Fritz came, bringing a stack of books. As he stood beside the bed, he said quietly, "The bastards." He sat down on the bed. "I'm sorry, old friend. I'm very sorry."

Nick wrote, "Me, too," on the pad, holding it up so Fritz could see it.

Fritz nodded. "Good man," he said. "You can't let those swine win." He gestured. "Over there, Carly," he said. She came around the bed and sat down so that Nick was between them. "Good," Fritz said. "Together again."

He stayed most of the afternoon, making the day cheerful. When he rose to leave, he took a pad from Carly and wrote, "Anything special I can get for you?"

Nick read Fritz's message and below it, printed, "G-U-N."

Fritz tore the page from the pad, crumpling it in his hand. "Man talk, Carly," he said.

On Monday, a nurse pushed her way into 307, her face hidden by a large rectangular package wrapped in red paper and tied with a red ribbon. "Fritz!" Carly said. She helped the nurse unwrap the package. "Candy!" Carly said. "There's enough to feed an army, and you can't eat it."

Nick wrote, "You and everyone else can." That night after Carly left, Nick removed the top layer of chocolates. He removed the second layer and saw, taped to the bottom of the candy box, an ordinary brown paper bag. Nick put his hand into the bag and felt the cold touch of metal. He pulled up his legs, making a wall, hiding the box from the door, and took a gun out of the paper bag. He held a Beretta automatic with a short barrel. He ran his hand over the barrel, over the butt. Then he slipped his forefinger through the trigger guard and, his jaws wired, said to himself, "Squeeze."

One morning in February, Carly charged into Nick's room and stopped in front of the door. Nick sat in a chair beside the windows with a mug of coffee. His last bandage had been removed and the doctors had removed the wires in his mouth. His face still carried jagged islands of bruises, but he was clean shaven. He saw Carly smiling at him. "Tell me the joke."

She crossed the room and bent over him, holding the back of the chair with both hands, her open coat making a kind of tent around them. Carly put her rosy, cold face against his and kissed him. "It's you," she said. "You're . . . you again."

Nick said, "You think a gang of Nazis—?" and broke off. They had mangled him so horribly, the weeks in the hospital had been so excruciating, that he could not speak with sophomoric bravado.

Carly dropped her coat on the bed, and when she turned back to Nick the world changed and so did she, inside and out. She felt free and happy, happier than anyone in the world. And although she could feel the tile floor beneath her, she seemed to be floating. "I love you," she said. She could not contain herself. "Nick, I love you."

In her own way she hurt him badly, no less than the Nazis. He felt a different kind of pain, sharp and searing. And she enraged him. She had ruined everything for them, forever. Did she believe he was stupid enough not to see she felt sorry for him? She had patronized him from the day they arrived at the castle. She and Fritz had made allowances for the ignorant city boy. "Stop, Carly."

His voice, harsh and hostile, frightened her. "You decided to help the patient today," Nick said. "You decided to . . . boost my morale. I have survived such a terrible ordeal you feel I deserve this . . . gift. You could have brought flowers or books, like Fritz. Don't you know everyone hates pity?"

She said, incredulous, "Pity!" and dropped to her knees in front of him, wrapping her arms around his legs. She looked up into his eyes. "I love you," Carly said. "I love you," she repeated, and took his hands to kiss them. She cupped his hands and put her face in the cup, kissing. She raised her head. "I love you."

Nick looked down at Carly as though he had her under a microscope. He searched for the lie in her face, in her eyes. She said, ever so softly, "I adore you," and Nick twitched as though he had touched a live wire. Taking her wrists, he came out of the chair, bringing her with him.

He believed her. Carly loved him. He said, "Carly," feeling her yield as she sought his body with hers. When he kissed her, she pressed herself to him. Nick kissed her face and her eyes, and she responded just as urgently.

She threw back her head, thrusting her hips into him, abandoning all restraint. She said huskily, "Nick . . . darling."

He put his hand under her chin, raising her head. "Not here," he said softly. "Not in this . . . laboratory." He kept her close. "I'm leaving. The Nazis keep me in this room."

She wanted to shield his battered body with hers. "The doctors will tell you when it's time."

"I'm going tomorrow," Nick said. He had the Beretta under the pillows. He had thirteen rounds in the clip, thirteen to start. No Nazi would ever touch him again. "You call Max Ingster tonight, Carly. Tell him to bring his car tomorrow morning." He put his hand in her hair, smiling at her. "And you love me?"

She took his hand, kissing it. "And I love you."

Leaving the hospital late that afternoon, Carly decided to cancel her date with Fritz. She decided to postpone the date, ask Fritz if they could see each other later in the week. She didn't want to see him later in the week. She wanted to spend the night with Lisl at her house. Carly hated cowards.

When Carly came home, she called Max. Hearing her on the telephone, Helga ran through the apartment. "You're late."

Carly turned to the wall. "Nick is leaving the hospital," she said. "Can you take him? And me?"

"Yes, b-b-but early," Max said.

"Bring Nick's clothes," Carly said.

When she set down the telephone, Helga followed her. "Look at the time," she said frantically, as though she had the date with Fritz. "You must still bathe and dress. I'll help you."

"No." Carly closed the bedroom door, barring her mother. She began to unbutton her dress, remembering Nick's body against hers, her body against his.

Carly managed to keep thoughts of Nick away while she bathed. She gathered up panties, a bra, stockings, selecting shoes and a dress, dropping everything on the bed. Then, in front of the mirror, she was back with Nick. She could not resist. Helga knocked on the door. "The baron is here."

Carly swung around, caught, as though her mother could see through her. "Hurry," Helga said.

She could hear Fritz with her parents, and as she joined them, she saw her father holding a newspaper and pointing at the front page. A thick black banner headline read, "CHANCELLOR MEETS WITH HITLER," and below, another headline said, "Schuschnigg Seeks Peace in Berchtesgaden."

Seeing Carly, Fritz said, "I seek dinner. Politics makes me ravenous." Carly had never seen him more handsome, in a dark suit and white shirt with a burgundy handkerchief in his breast pocket.

The sight of Carly turned Fritz inside out. She made the room an Eden. He became a truant. They left the building and in the coupe he said, "Let's celebrate something. Anything."

He trapped her. She could not go on. She would be lying, would be a thief. "Fritz? Fritz, wait . . ." She said, "I—" and stopped. She had to face him and say it. "I love Nick."

Fritz's anger actually blinded him. He saw only darkness and red streaks. He held on to the steering wheel to save himself, fighting to survive until he could say, "Nothing like hearing about a good, old-fashioned romance to work up an appetite."

"Don't be clever," Carly said. "I mean, don't . . ." she said, miserable. "I mean . . . I don't know what I mean."

"You love him. Does he love you?" Fritz asked, knowing the answer.

"Yes, he does," Carly said. "He did first. I mean, he told me first." She squeezed one hand with the other. "I hope we'll always be friends, Fritz."

"You have my word."

"Well, I . . ." she said, and stopped, facing Fritz. "I had to tell you or I would be lying. I'd better go," she said, and pushed the door handle. She could not open the door. She looked down at her hand on the handle and felt Fritz's arm across her. He put his hand over hers and opened the door. "Fritz—" she said, and he interrupted:

"Leave now," he said, and harshly, "Leave!" He watched her crouching as she came out of the coupe, watched her disappear as she stood erect, watched her ankles and her shoes as she left him, on her way to her hero, the victor she had chosen for her loins. He almost slid across the seat and followed her, almost asked her to reconsider. The impulse horrified him. Fritz fell across the seat to seize the door handle and slam the door. He pushed himself back behind the wheel, turning the key and depressing the clutch and shifting all in one motion. As the engine caught, the coupe shot forward, aimed directly at a fiacre.

The horse pulling the carriage clomped along, barely moving. The coachman heard the roar of the engine, then saw the small car hurtling at him. He dropped the reins to jump, and heard the squeal of the tires as the coupe turned hard, two wheels off the pavement. Fritz missed the fiacre, then a taxi which had the right-of-way, and turned into a deserted street, stopping so hard the coupe rocked. He sat panting as though he had run a race. He rolled down the window, leaving coupe and leaning over it, his arms on the roof of the car.

He heard a woman laugh and then footsteps. A couple was approaching, arm in arm. He returned to the coupe, driving as though he was being towed. In the Himmelpfortgasse, he put the car into the old stables beside the Daimler, and walked across the courtyard to the dark empty palace, the lonely, sterile hulk rising above Vienna, a faded remnant of past glories.

He did not sleep until late, and then he slept very late. He asked for coffee in the study, and Zinn brought him the tray and the newspapers, his face grim. Fritz saw, ". . . RIAN INDEPENDENCE!" across the top of one folded newspaper, and took it from the tray.

He opened the newspaper and read the complete banner, "SCHUSCHNIGG PLEDGES AUSTRIAN INDEPENDENCE!"

As Zinn poured coffee, Fritz raised the newspaper and read, "Chancellor Kurt Schuschnigg returned last night from a historic rendezvous with Adolf Hitler, vowing that Austria's sovereignty would remain forever intact.

"In a meeting at Berchtesgaden, the German leader's retreat in the Bavarian Alps, the two heads of state conferred for twelve hours without interruption. Chancellor Schuschnigg said he and Der Führer spoke frankly with each other in an atmosphere of mutual trust.

"With peace his overriding goal, Chancellor Schuschnigg agreed to Der Führer's request that all members of Austria's National Socialist Party currently imprisoned be released immediately.

"Chancellor Schuschnigg acknowledged the political importance of Austria's large Nazi membership. As further evidence of his hopes for coexistence with the Greater German Reich, the Chancellor accepted Der Führer's suggestion that Nazis should be represented in the government."

Fritz dropped the newspaper on the desk and saw Zinn watching him. "You're waiting for me to tell you what happened," Fritz said. "Suppose you tell me."

"He gave away the country," Zinn said.

Fritz took his coffee, holding the saucer and raising the cup. "Correct," he said. "He gave away the country, Zinn."

Fritz did not leave the palace. He remained in the study, reading the newspapers and listening to the radio.

Late in the day, Zinn came to ask about dinner. "Bring me a tray," Fritz said. "Some soup and . . . something," he said, facing the radio as though he could see inside it. The evening news only repeated what he had heard many times.

Hours passed and when he left his chair, he felt stiff. He arched his back and stretched, leaving the study and walking through the palace, turning off lights. Zinn and Matilda had long since gone to their room.

Fritz went back into the Great Hall and lit a fire. He returned to the study, opening a safe in the wall. He removed several long boxes like those used for card index files. He carried the boxes, two at a time, to the fireplace. When the fire was hot enough, he set one box on the logs, watching it burn, prodding it constantly with a poker, scattering the contents until nothing remained. When the first box was ashes, he set the second on the fire. These were the records of the Landswehr, the names and numbers and locations of all units, plus the names of all members everywhere in Austria. By midnight the recorded history of the private vigilante army Fritz had founded and supported had vanished forever.

Long before Fritz woke the next morning, Max Ingster drove Carly through Vienna to the hospital. "Hitler is r-running Austria now," Max said. "He's the new chancellor."

The car was crawling through the streets, and she wanted him to go faster. Then she remembered. "Nick's clothes."

"In the trunk," Max said.

In the hospital, Nick sat on the edge of the bed. Every time he heard footsteps, he looked at the door. Once he went to it and looked into the corridor. He returned to the bed and heard footsteps again, listening until the sound receded. He had been waiting for what seemed like an eternity. He got up, taking his robe from the footboard, getting into it as he crossed the room. Max's car could have broken down again. There could be a message at the nurses' station.

It was deserted. Then he saw a nurse far down the corridor, and as he started after her, the elevator doors opened and Carly emerged. Max followed her with a carryall and a parka over his other arm.

Walking to his room, Nick found Carly's hand and laced his fingers through hers. "L-let's get a move on," Max said. "I've got a gym class at nine o'clock."

At his door Nick said, "I'll get dressed." Carly nodded, feeling his hand slip away as though she had lost a life preserver.

In his room Nick opened the carryall and dressed quickly. He pulled on the parka and went to the night table, opening the drawer for the Beretta automatic in a bag. When he opened the door and saw Carly, he felt as though they had been apart for years. "Hello."

Carly rode in the backseat with Nick. They sat touching and she held his hand in both of hers, and although Max never stopped talking, they really didn't hear him. They didn't hear anything or see anything. They rode through Vienna as though they were holding their breath. When Max stopped and said, "We're here," Nick turned to Carly and said, "We're here."

They got out of the car, walking up the stairs of the neglected building to Max's apartment on the second floor. Nick reached for the key atop the doorjamb.

Carly stopped just inside the small apartment, turning to Nick, and as he raised his arms, she raised her arms. Nick kissed her, and Carly's lips parted, and she choked back a sob in a burst of great joy such as she had never known.

He said, "Carly, Carly, Carly," trying to bring her even closer, as though he could not believe he had her.

Kissing, they got out of their coats. Kissing, Nick brought her to his bed against the wall of the single large room he shared with Max. Still kissing, they sank down onto the bed. "My beauty," he said, and put his face in her breasts. He kissed them, kissed her neck, brushed her neck with his lips, her eyes with his lips. He felt her breasts rising and falling, heard her breathing deeply, and as he lowered his hand, raising her dress to move, with infinite tenderness, along her thigh, her hips rose to join his and she said fiercely, "Yes, darling, *yes.*"

She wanted to be free, wanted to discard the wondering, the guessing, the years of endless dialogue with Lisl Schott, with the others. All the whispers in the classrooms and cloakrooms, on the playing fields and in the bedrooms, all the shared fantasies, the fears, the boasting of schoolmates, the warnings of schoolmates were forgotten. "Yes, Nick, yes."

He was endlessly patient, endlessly indulgent, and when at last he slipped between her thighs and joined with her, and heard her long, rapturous sigh of acceptance, of welcome, he thought only of her, setting the tempo to accommodate her, to please her, waiting until he heard her moan, heard her gasp, heard a hoarse demand, waiting until he heard her sustained cry of delight before ending his own voyage.

Afterward, she would not release him. She lay, flushed and damp, in his arms. "My love," she murmured. "My darling lover. Was anyone ever so kind, so gentle?" And when Nick raised himself on his elbow to look down at his great prize, he saw her eyes fill and bent to kiss his beloved.

5

AFTER BERCHTESGADEN, everyone in Austria lived by a clock whose ticking could be heard all the way to Berlin. While the celebrants, the Austrian Nazis and their supporters, were the most conspicuous, there were as many mourners. Triumph and fear walked side by side in Austria after Berchtesgaden.

Austria changed after Berchtesgaden. The change was almost palpable, like a mist or a fog rolling in. Everything and everyone continued as before but almost in slow motion. Nobody laughed. The shouts and cries of those for whom Berchtesgaden had been a victory were bloodthirsty.

Those who were afraid were afraid every waking hour. They had taken on fear like an illness, a persistent cough or a rash. It centered in their heads like a buzzing, leaving some breathless and some with a thickening in their throats as though they were about to choke. Their fear changed all those who were affected. The past seemed to have been stripped from their lives by Berchtesgaden. They forgot the pleasures of family life, of food and wine, of pride in their work. They had been turned into men and women waiting for the worst.

The fear was infectious, sweeping the populace, cities and towns. The fear moved beyond the urban centers into Austria's farmhouses, and into the meeting halls and churches of the countryside.

The Zwischentheatre was one of the first casualties of Berchtesgaden. People stopped daring to laugh, so the audiences in the little storefront evaporated. People stopped coming to the Zwischentheatre, and those who had bought tickets in advance stayed home.

The gang at the Zwischentheatre, founders and acolytes, and bright, aspiring actors and writers, were also casualties of Berchtesgaden. No one could find humor in the meeting at Berchtesgaden, no one could write satirically about the Greater German Reich. Der Führer had stopped being funny.

So the Zwischentheatre closed down. The storefront remained dark. The gang congregated in Erik Ekstrom's boozy café waiting for the worst.

For seven days after his return from Berchtesgaden, Kurt Schuschnigg believed he had saved Austria by agreeing to share his country with the Nazis. Exactly one week later, Adolf Hitler announced in the Reichstag in Berlin: "Ten million Germans living beyond our borders can no longer be victimized by foreign leaders.

"Never will I abandon those of our people who are today at the mercy of autocratic rule," Hitler continued. "Ten million Germans belong with all Germans. We are one people. We will not be separated. We must not be separated. Here and now I pledge to those Germans, I have not forsaken you. We who share a common heritage belong together. We have been patient. No one can accuse Germany of not being patient. We have waited for a thaw in the icy climate which separates two sister nations who share a common heritage.

"We share a common history. We share a common language. We are two halves of a whole. We must come together. We must unite."

In the Hofburg in Vienna, Kurt Schuschnigg listened to Hitler's address on a shortwave radio. With him was his military aide, General Michael Mertz. "How can there be ten million Germans in a country with six million people?" asked the general.

Schuschnigg snuffed out his cigarette and took another from the pack on his desk. "He never stops," he said. He had been denied cigarettes at Berchtesgaden, kept at a table for twelve hours, surrounded by Hitler, von Ribbentrop, Goering, coming at him in turn like hyenas gnawing on a carcass.

"He will never stop," Schuschnigg said. That same week the chancellor announced a plebiscite for March 13, 1938, a Sunday. He believed Austria would choose independence over Der Führer.

In Vienna, starting Monday, March 7, the Hotel Metropole became a favorite of guests traveling on German passports. All the Germans were male, and they registered from cities and towns all over Germany, but they all came from Berlin, and all were important in the Gestapo, in the SS, and in the Counter-Intelligence Corps of the German Army.

Friday morning, two days before the plebiscite, Nick crossed Este Platz, walking down the block to the Caravan. In the coffee house the regulars were established at their regular tables, but plenty of newspapers remained on the racks and Nick took a load. A waiter followed him. "Do you have enough?"

"Coffee," Nick said, dropping into a chair and reading rapidly, changing newspapers after a few paragraphs.

"Hi."

Looking up, Nick forgot Hitler, forgot Austria. Carly wore a floppy coat with a bright green scarf that trailed down her back. Her hair fell over the scarf and her coat collar. She sat down beside Nick, touching his face as though needing to make certain he hadn't changed.

The waiter brought coffee for Carly, but they didn't see him, didn't see him take the newspapers. They sat over the small round table, safe, until Nick said, "Time for work."

"I'll meet you," Carly said. She waited in Este Platz every day.

Outside, the street was covered with leaflets and more fell from the sky. People reached into the air for them, and Carly and Nick grabbed a pair as the airplanes flew by. Austrians were urged to vote in the plebiscite. The chancellor asked for a united Austria. *Ein Volk!* One People!

Carly held on to Nick. "I can't let you go."

"I never leave you," Nick said, kissing her.

In the drafting room, everyone came to work with a leaflet. Everyone talked about the plebiscite, and when Ernst Auerfeld appeared, he joined in the discussion.

The day dragged. Everyone watched the clock. Ernst used the telephone all day, calling friends for news. Late in the afternoon, a low rumble reached the drafting room. When the sound increased, Ernst went to the windows, and Alfred Slavin slid off his stool, following him. Nick and then Anton Wiesner and the other architects joined them. "They're all wearing swastikas!" said Slavin. A trickle of fear ran down Nick's back and into his buttocks.

"They're all Nazis!" Ernst said. "The streets are full of Nazis." He opened a window. Nick pushed through to another window, raising it as well. "Something about the plebiscite," Slavin said.

Leaning out of the window, Nick saw a mob in the streets. Men plastered swastikas on cars and buildings, on lamp poles, across shop windows. "Ernst!"

Magda marched through the drafting room, her face flushed. "The plebiscite is cancelled," she said. "Hitler is on the border. Men and tanks up and down the border. He called Schuschnigg with an ultimatum."

As Ernst and the others crowded around Magda, Nick walked toward his drafting table. Someone said, "Seyss-Inquart ordered our army not to fight. He ordered the army to stand down." Someone else said, "Seyss-Inquart. Traitor supreme."

"Be quiet!" Ernst said. "Quiet!"

Nick took his coat from a hook on the wall. The raw scars in his scalp burned, and a steady throbbing below his right eye ran down and along his jawbone. When Ernst saw him, he asked, "Where do you think you're going?"

"Out to join the fun," Nick said. Ernst could no longer fire him because he would not return.

"Still making jokes," Ernst said. "Anyway, you're right. Nobody can work in this . . . earthquake. No more work today. Everybody go home."

Magda stopped Nick. "Be careful, sonny."

"Sure." He walked through the drafting room and into the foyer to the elevators. He rode down with two men who agreed that Adolf Hitler would save Austria.

In the lobby Nick saw the crowd shoulder to shoulder outside, heard them chanting, "Anschluss! Anschluss! Anschluss!" The word assaulted him from every direction. He buttoned his coat. He had to leave fast, before Carly came for him. He had to stay clear of her so she would be safe. He himself had to flee, but he didn't know where. He had no destination. He had been cast adrift. Nick pushed his hand into his coat pocket, wrapping his hand around the cold, comforting Beretta automatic. He had a full magazine, and in his other pocket two boxes of ammunition he had bought the day after leaving the hospital. Nick came out of the lobby to join the mob, to get lost in it while he waited for the night.

As the hours passed, the crowds in the streets increased, became more festive. Swastikas large and small became more numerous. The city changed into a single enormous parade ground that Friday, making Der Chineser's mission more difficult.

He had been assigned six men, all armed and in Nazi uniform like himself. He had been given a dump truck, offered by a contractor who had been an early supporter of Der Führer's. Der Chineser chose one of the six men to drive and sat beside him. "Bear left here."

"That takes us away from Leopoldstadt," said the driver.

"Left again on the next corner," said Der Chineser. "And do not contradict me again. Never question my orders, do you understand? Never."

Long before, Der Chineser had memorized the names and addresses of the communist ringleaders in the Zwischentheatre. Nicholas Gallanz led all the others.

In her kitchen, Lottie Gallanz kept fidgeting, listening for her husband's arrival. She saw Sam in the doorway. "Where is he?"

"The streets are jammed," Sam said. "You can't move out there. He's late. I was late."

They heard a banging on the door. "Nick!" Lottie said. He often forgot his key.

They heard another banging. On his way Sam said, "Oh, shut up!" He opened the door and found himself facing Nazis. "Where . . . ?" he said, and got Der Chineser's fist in his face, driving him into the wall as Lottie pulled at her hair, screaming.

Der Chineser charged inside. "Two men in the kitchen!" He grabbed another man and in the narrow hallway said, "The bathroom!" Gesturing at the two remaining Nazis, he ordered, "Search the closets!"

In a bedroom he said, "Look under the beds!" Der Chineser swung his hand across the curtains, back and forth, like he was slapping someone's face.

One Nazi dropped, raising the bedspread. Der Chineser jumped over him, running through the apartment to the sofa. He swung his leg, kicking under the sofa, and pulled it away from the wall. His men followed, standing in a cluster. Der Chineser saw the open door. "He could have slipped out! Fan out, on the double!"

In District XVIII Dolly Stacker entered her apartment as though escaping from a pack of wolves. She locked the door, a carved slab which her father's architect had copied from a church near Padua. In the bedroom she got into a quilted robe, her favorite. Pulling the sash around her middle, she felt safe for the first time.

When Sepp Wiegend arrived, she bolted the door behind him. "They're like animals out there," she said. "Help me." They cranked down all the steel window shields. "Let's fix some dinner," Dolly said finally.

"After I bathe," Sepp said. "I feel like a pig." As he pulled his sweater over his head, she went to the kitchen and took a brisket from the icebox. She brought vegetables to the sink. "Dolly!"

She walked through the apartment to the bathroom. The thick white curtains used for showers dropped from an oval metal frame over the tub. Dolly could see steam rising above the shower head. "Sepp?"

His hands parted the curtains and he put his head through, his face wet and his hair soaked and dripping. "We missed you," he said, inching forward in the bathtub until Dolly saw the intruder.

"You are a pig. Worse than a pig!" she said. She believed he had insulted her, believed she was revolted, but she began to quiver inside and out. He always excited her, always made her wild. She felt his wet hand.

"Come on in."

"In the shower? Never!" she said, but she didn't back away.

"Come on," he said, putting her hand between the curtains.

She said, "I'm all dressed."

"Drop the robe."

"This is crazy, I'm crazy," she said, letting the robe fall. Neither heard Der Chineser's fist on the carved door. Neither heard him kicking the door. A Nazi said, "Nobody home."

"Maybe," said Der Chineser, opening the flap of his holster. He hated the man for capitulating, hated Nicholas Gallanz for eluding him, hated Dolly Stacker, the communist bitch, for making jokes about the National Socialist Party, laughing at Der Führer. Der Chineser raised his gun and fired into the lock. He rammed the door with his shoulder and it opened. "Follow me!"

He saw lights burning everywhere. "Fan out!" Running down the hallway, Der Chineser heard the shower and stopped. Then he stepped forward silently. He had the treacherous bitch.

Behind him a man said, "No one in here," and Der Chineser raised his hand, beckoning the man forward. The Nazi followed. In front of the bathroom Der Chineser heard her, slobbering like a hog in a trough, and then he heard a man with her, two hogs in a trough. Der

Chineser kicked the door, and as it slammed into the bathroom wall, he followed, using his left hand to seize the shower curtain.

Dolly's scream could be heard all through the apartment, alerting all the Nazis. As she fell against the wall, Sepp grabbed her to keep her from falling, holding her with one arm as he turned off the water. He grabbed the shower curtain, trying to shield them, but Der Chineser raised the gun, slashing Sepp with the gun barrel as Dolly screamed, out of control, defeated, forsaken, hopeless.

"Quiet, you trollop!" shouted Der Chineser. "Quiet, you communist traitor bitch!" Dolly screamed and screamed until Sepp put his arms around her, holding her wet, naked, shaking body against his, covering her body with his.

Sepp faced Der Chineser, hiding Dolly. "Get the hell out of here!" he said.

Der Chineser nodded at every word. "Yes, of course, certainly," he said. "We are going. With you! We're taking you! It's Judgment Day for you, for all of you!"

Now all the Nazis watched the fun, filling the bathroom. One said, "In the toilet?" and another said, "Standing up?" and pointed, grinning. "Not anymore."

Sepp held on to Dolly, feeling her shaking against him as she sobbed without tears. He yanked the shower curtain out of the Nazi's hands, covering himself and Dolly. "Get the hell out of here!" Sepp yelled. "Let us get dressed!"

Der Chineser raised Dolly's robe with his jackboot and kicked it into the bathtub. "Find some clothes for him," he told one of his men.

Sepp picked up the wet, twisted robe and held it for Dolly. "Get her out," said Der Chineser to the Nazis, but Sepp moved between them and Dolly, one arm around her, helping her over the side of the bathtub. A Nazi shoved her. "On your way, slut."

Der Chineser gestured at his men. "Two of you go with her. You're responsible. You're all responsible." Der Chineser didn't intend to let her or anyone else slip away tonight.

The Nazi whom Der Chineser had sent for Sepp's clothes returned and threw trousers and a shirt at him. "Get my shoes," Sepp said.

Der Chineser moved backward, into the hallway, watching Sepp dress. He motioned with his gun. "Out."

"My shoes," Sepp said.

"Just get out there," said Der Chineser. "Out there with her, with your communist whore." He followed the prisoner.

"We haven't done anything," Sepp said. "What crime have we

committed? You're breaking and entering. You're committing the crime," he said. Then he saw Dolly.

She sat in the middle of a sofa, her bare feet dangling. She looked tiny, no longer alive, no longer human. The Nazi invasion of her bathroom, their conquest of her apartment had destroyed Dolly Stacker. Sepp didn't recognize her. And he knew his captors intended to end his life as they had ended hers.

Sepp faced the apartment door, hanging askew. Two Nazis stood between him and the door. He took a step. "I'll get my shoes."

"No," said Der Chineser, pointing at the sofa. "Take her. Get the whore into the truck."

The Nazis in front of Sepp walked to the sofa. He took another step, and as they left the door clear, he ran.

He confounded Der Chineser's untrained, untried squad. One shouted, "Hey!" and another shouted, "Get him!" but they didn't budge. A third yelled, "Hey, you," following Sepp, but Der Chineser was quicker. Shoving the man aside, he leaped forward, raised his gun, and fired. Sepp stumbled and his arms came up, and as his head snapped back and he staggered, Der Chineser shot again. Sepp stopped, his arms dropped, he stood without moving, and then fell forward into the doorway.

Der Chineser felt a detonation of elation. He had been in combat at last. He felt proud, and he felt as well a prickly, ticklish movement within him, a sexual sensation he had only experienced alone or in a shuttered room near his rooming house. He pointed at the sofa. His mission had only begun. "Pick her up."

That Friday made Carly frantic. The apartment became a cage. Helga was a messenger, carrying bulletins from Klaus, at the radio, to her daughter. "Nobody is safe," Helga said.

Carly saw the crowds in the streets. Vienna had turned into an enemy camp, thronged with thousands of Viennese who had declared war on their neighbors. She had to warn Nick. She telephoned the drafting room.

"He's gone," Magda said. "They're all gone. You're too late."

Carly waited for Nick to call and tell her he was safe. As the day ended, she telephoned Max Ingster, but there was no answer. She called again and again that evening. She called Judith Emmerich, but there was no answer. She called Peter Dietrich, Dolly Stacker, then Max again. They had all vanished that Friday night.

She tried to sleep, tried not to think of Nick. She left the bed and

returned, over and over. When she woke, hearing thunder, she turned
on her belly, pulling up the covers. But the sound of thunder persisted.
Carly went, naked, to the windows and spread the drapes. She found
the thunder in the street, a long convoy of tanks flanked by two columns of soldiers marching into Vienna. The tank commanders were in
their turrets, smiling and saluting the crowds. Swastikas flew from the
tanks, and each soldier wore a swastika on his arm.

Four columns of soldiers followed the tanks, and behind the troops
came vehicles of every size, weapons carriers, half-tracks, trucks, and
command and staff cars filled with officers. Everywhere Carly looked
she saw Viennese smiling happily at their conquerors.

She had to find Nick. Carly pulled on a robe and called Max. She
said, "Please answer," listening to the telephone ringing. She said,
"Please—" and heard Max. "Hello?"

"Max!" Carly leaped up. "Max, it's Carly! Is Nick there?"

"No, I can't talk."

"Max! Have you seen him? Have you heard from him? Has anyone?" Carly was so excited she didn't see her father at the end of the
corridor.

Max had been with his girlfriend, Ruth Posner, all night, returning
to the small apartment for clothes. "I can't tell you anything," he said.
"I'm going. I can't stay here."

"Wait! Does Nick know where you'll be? Where *will* you be?"

He almost slammed down the receiver before he remembered how
the girl had sat day after day beside Nick's bed in the hospital. "Ruth
Posner. Good-bye."

So Carly had to wait, again. She had to bathe and dress and greet
her mother and father, had to sit at the table with them while the
maids served breakfast as usual and cleared afterward as usual. She had
to believe Nick was all right, that nothing bad had happened to him.

That afternoon, Carly's father said, "I haven't seen a single man,
woman, or child come out of this building today. I haven't heard the
elevators."

"They hate Adolf Hitler," Carly said.

"Be quiet, Carly," said Helga, gesturing at the kitchen, where the
maids were preparing dinner. "We don't know where they go, whom
they see. They're not married, and Vienna is full of German soldiers.
We must be very careful from now on."

Carly had to get away, could not listen to her mother, to her
father, to the ticking clock. She took her coat from the closet. "I'm
leaving."

"You cannot!" Helga said.

Klaus seconded her concern. "Nobody is safe out there."

"I haven't committed a crime."

"Stop it, Carly," Klaus said. "You're a person with a brain. Think!" He pointed at the windows. "You saw them. Hour after hour after hour, a soldier for each of us. We're at their mercy. A life doesn't mean much to these people."

"I must see him," Carly said.

"You can't see him!" Klaus insisted, terrified for her safety. "If you are with him, the Germans will take you when they take him."

"They won't get him," Carly said. "They won't find him."

"You are deluding yourself," Klaus said. "They almost killed him *before* the Anschluss. Now they'll finish the job."

"No-o-o-o!" Carly's voice rose in horror.

"They won't ask questions of anyone who is with him," Klaus said. "They don't travel with a judge and a jury. Whoever they find with your friend will be squashed like him."

"You're trying to scare me," Carly said. "Well, you scared me, Papa. My heart is pounding, my hands are wet, my forehead is wet. I'm shaking inside, and I feel dizzy, feel sick inside. You're right, Papa. They'll try to finish the job," Carly said. "So I can't sit here hoping he will escape. I have to find him and help him escape. I can help him escape," Carly said, believing what she said.

"It's too late," Klaus said. "He shouldn't have stayed in Austria. He should have taken his chance when he still had one."

"Good-bye, Papa," Carly said.

Klaus said, "Carly!" loud enough to scare the maids in the kitchen. "How can I stop you? I must stop you." He pushed the collar of his suit coat up around his neck. Using his left hand, he folded down the corner of the collar so Carly could see the swastika pinned just beyond the boutonniere notch in the serge.

Carly grimaced as though struck by a sudden sharp pain. The stylish man who had all her life hidden presents, unexpected and delightful, suddenly looked deformed. She felt as though she had caught him filching coins from a grocer's till. Carly hated him for revealing himself. He had changed, forever. "I did it for you," Klaus said.

"And for you," she said.

"For all of us," Klaus said. He knew he was losing her.

Helga went to Klaus's side. "I am proud of your father," she said.

"Yes, good-bye," Carly said.

"Wait, listen," he said desperately. "You are with them or against them, Carly." He touched the swastika. "This proves we are with them. Don't you see? We'll be left in peace."

"Peace," Carly said, looking at the stranger with the swastika in his lapel. She started to leave, but Klaus caught up with her and took her arm. Carly didn't protest, didn't struggle. She looked down at his hand and then at him, and Klaus released her.

"You can't stop me," she said. "I couldn't have stopped you from doing what you did, and you can't stop me."

On the other side of Vienna, in Leopoldstadt, Lottie said, "Maybe I'll make tea. Will you have tea, Sam?"

"Good idea," Sam said. He felt cold. As he walked to the bedroom for a sweater, rolling down his shirtsleeves, he almost bumped into his father.

Boris Gallanz carried a purple velvet bag embroidered with a gold Star of David. The bag contained his tallith, his prayer shawl. Sam actually thought the old man had lost his mind, had buckled under the arrival of the Germans. "What are you doing? What the hell do you think you're doing? Where the hell do you think you're going?" Sam stood in front of his father, his arms spread like a goal tender.

"Today is Saturday," Boris said. He hit Sam's arm and walked into him, and the two moved across the room together, like dance partners.

"You can't go out there," Sam said. "It's dangerous out there."

"I'm going to Saturday services," Boris said.

Sam stood against the door. "Since when do you go to Saturday services? To any services? Where were you this morning for the services? Where were you last Saturday, *every* Saturday? You haven't been in the synagogue since Yom Kippur."

"Now I'm going," Boris said. "Get away from the door."

"Why?" Sam hit the door. "They're here! The Germans are here! Adolf Hitler rules here now!" He grabbed for the velvet bag, but Boris pulled it free.

"Get away," he said.

"You're not walking out of this flat," Sam said.

"Let him go," Lottie said, coming out of the kitchen. "He needs to go."

"You're both crazy!" Sam shouted. "You told me what they did to you in Russia." He sprang at his mother. "You couldn't stop crying when—" He broke off as he heard the door open, and when he swung around, his father was gone.

Boris came out of the building into the fading daylight, turning left and walking the length of the block. At the corner he turned left again, toward the synagogue a half mile beyond. He didn't see the gang.

They were behind him and on the other side of the street, many men, some in their twenties and thirties, some older. They wore armbands and swastikas, and they had been in the saloons and streets all day.

They circled two prisoners, both with beards, whom they had forced to their knees in the street. The gang had beaten and kicked the pair, commanding them to clean the street with their handkerchiefs. Now several of the gang stood with legs apart and flies open, wetting down the street and the hostages.

As one of them finished and buttoned his trousers, he spotted another candidate. "Over there!"

Boris heard something indistinct but didn't look, not wanting to be late for the services. Then he heard men approaching, and above the sound of footsteps: "Hey, Izzy, Abie, Ikey, Kikey!"

Boris started to run, but he hadn't run in forty years. His pursuers spread out as they approached, making a circle and converging on him. "On your way to the bank? Bank's closed."

He knew enough to lie, squeezing the velvet bag against him to hide the Star of David. "To the baker, that's all," Boris said. "To buy some bread, some kaiser rolls."

One of the patriots shoved Boris into a stone building wall. "The kaiser is dead."

Boris's head slammed into the wall. The street seemed to tilt and he thought he would fall. "Excuse me," he said, trying to move, but they had him trapped.

The same patriot got Boris's nose between his thumb and forefinger. "We've got a job for you," he said.

Another partisan grabbed the velvet bag and pulled out the prayer shawl, more than two hundred years old. He swung his arm from side to side, making a tent over his head. "He's going to church," said another of Austria's heroes. "They use this to pray."

Someone said, "Start praying." Another added, "On your knees." A third hissed, "You're gonna lick this sidewalk clean with your tongue."

"Please let me go," Boris said as the first warrior struck him, ripping open his lip with a large ring.

"On your knees," he said. "On your knees!"

A taxi driver seeing his loyal countrymen hit the brake and stopped hard, rocking the cab. "End of the line, lady. Far as I go," he said, opening the door to be rid of her.

Carly had taken money from her purse long before Leopoldstadt. She thrust it at the driver. "Here's your change, lady," he said, but the dame was gone. The driver locked all four doors and turned on his headlights, shifting in reverse to avoid the trouble.

In the glow of the headlights Carly saw two bearded men on their knees, with urine dripping from their hat brims. Her belly rebelled and she gagged, paralyzed, unable to turn away from the degradation, the bestiality of the dedicated Austrian volunteers demonstrating their allegiance to the Greater German Reich and Der Führer. Behind her, the taxi driver turned, shifting gears and speeding forward. And in the sweeping arc made by the headlights, Carly saw Nick's father.

"Stop!" She ran toward Boris, pinned by the patrol of dedicated Austrian stalwarts. "Stop! Stop!"

A few of them paused and saw the woman running to join them. One of the younger recruits whistled and said, "She's gorgeous." His companion nudged him back, clicking his teeth. "Over here, honey." Another said, "I've got something for you." A fourth giggled and said, "He's a horse, baby."

As Carly approached, she saw two men grab Boris's arms, one to an arm, as others started clubbing him on his head and shoulders, driving him down to the sidewalk, while others unbuttoned their flies.

A middle-aged vigilante glanced over his shoulder as Carly swung, hitting him in the face with her purse. She ran past him, swinging, hitting another vigilante. She hit still others, pushing through her steadfast countrymen until she stood over Boris, facing the victorious militiamen. "You monsters!"

The middle-aged man came after her. "Maybe you want some, too."

"Yes!" Carly screamed, wild with rage. "Yes, I want some, you coward! Fight me, you coward!" She swung the purse, hitting two men. "I want some!"

Suddenly none challenged her. A man said, "I need a beer," and pushed his way out of the circle. "Me, too," another said, and soon a straggling line of Austria's defenders marched down the street.

As Boris rose, Carly wiped the blood with her handkerchief. He cried out in pain. "Not brave," he said, apologizing. She pressed the handkerchief against his mouth. "Hold it there," she said, bending for his hat. She saw the velvet bag and took it.

"My prayer shawl," Boris said. Carly ran into the street, where the prayer shawl lay in a heap. Carly gathered up the satin heirloom.

They were less than a mile away from Nick, who at that moment was running down an alley to a fence. He climbed over it, went through a littered rectangle where a building had been razed and through the wooden gate of another fence into another alley. Nick stopped several feet from its mouth. He listened for voices before proceeding slowly, stopping at the street and looking in both directions before sprinting across. Nick stayed in alleys, block after block, protected on right and left by the apartment buildings of Leopoldstadt. In the fifth block he reached a short flight of steps. These led to a neglected courtyard and beyond, an open passageway into the building, used for coal deliveries.

He came through the passageway to a light at the far end of the basement. He went up the delivery entrance to the street level, and through another door to the front entrance. Nick opened his coat so he could reach the Beretta automatic he had pushed into the waistband of his trousers against his belly. He had been on the run since leaving the drafting room the day before. He had bought bread and sausage, living in the streets. He was in pain. The wounds on his head and chest itched and throbbed. He was exhausted, but he could not climb the stairs looking like a helpless vagrant when he faced the helpless band on the third floor.

In the shadows of the building entrance, Nick made himself over, made himself fresh, sparkling, full of juice. Putting the gun into his coat pocket, he clutched the bannister as he started up the stairs.

Above him, Boris sat in Sam's reading chair with everyone around him. Sam heard the key in the lock, and cried, "Nick!" Lottie followed Sam as Nick entered and saw Carly, and stopped running, stopped hurting. After the long night and day in the streets, Carly looked unreal, looked magical. "You finally met my family," he said.

"We met in the hospital," Carly said. "Before you . . . while you—"

Nick put his hand in her hair. "Sure."

Carly had him at last. "You didn't call," she said.

"I'm bad for you," he said. "You're in danger with me." Still she held on to him, pressing against Nick to protect him. "You should not be with me, Carly," he said.

"I can't be without you," she said.

"She saved Papa," Lottie said, intruding on them. Lottie had forgiven the czarina everything.

"She saved me," Boris said. Only then did Nick see his father's split lip, the bruises on his face. He wanted to kill the monsters who had fallen on his father, kill them all. He knelt beside the chair. "We're leaving, Papa," he said. He looked up at Carly. "We're all leaving."

"Nick, they came for you last night," Sam said.

Nick pushed himself erect, wobbly. "I won't be back until we can get out, all of us together," he said. "We'll get out together."

"Where will you be?" Lottie asked. "Where will you sleep?"

Carly held on to him. "He'll be safe," she said.

They came down the stairs arm in arm. "Max is with Ruth Posner," Carly said. "You can stay there."

In the entrance, he said, "This way," taking her into the basement. "Hold on to me."

A gust of wind from the open end of the passageway sent the light bulb over their heads swinging from side to side, making lopsided shadows on the brick walls. Carly stopped, suddenly panic-stricken. "Kiss me, kiss me."

She kissed him hard, held him hard, pulling him to her, wanting to make an impenetrable cloak of her body. Hand in hand they left the building for the shadows in the alley.

Early in the following morning, Sunday morning, March 13, 1938, the day Chancellor Kurt Schuschnigg had chosen for the plebiscite, Der Chineser, in uniform, reported to the Gestapo in the Hotel Metropole. No hunter for enemies of the Greater German Reich could claim more success. Of the twenty-four members in the Zwischentheatre he had taken eighteen, including the dead man, Sepp Wiegend. Der Chineser's prize of prizes, Nicholas Gallanz, eluded him, but he had only begun the hunt.

While Der Chineser submitted his report, a very tall, slender man with thinning blond hair, and with the look of an English squire, paused at the desk. The eavesdropper, who wore flawlessly tailored flannel trousers and a plaid jacket, could detect the fanatic's zeal in the Oriental as the names he cited rang out.

The tall man, Colonel Friedrich Varlingen, had long been on detached service from the Corps of Engineers. He had checked into the Hotel Metropole on Wednesday, giving his address as Peenemunde, an island village on the Baltic. Colonel Varlingen had not asked for an office, nor had any been assigned him. Nor had any office in the Hotel Metropole been closed to him all that week. In a pocket of his flannel trousers he carried a small leather case, smaller than a pocket watch. Inside lay a bronze medallion with the seal of the General Staff. Colonel Varlingen represented the Counter-Intelligence Corps of the General Staff.

As Der Chineser finished his report, Colonel Varlingen said, "You're a wonder, Huebner. You make Sherlock Holmes an amateur. How would you like to work for me?"

Colonel Varlingen expected his Gestapo audience to consider him odd, even absurd. He counted on their estimate of him spreading through Austria. Colonel Varlingen liked to be disparaged and discounted because in that way he avoided scrutiny.

When Der Chineser left the Hotel Metropole, he held the temporary rank of captain in the Military Police. He stopped in front of the hotel, dazed by victory. Colonel Varlingen had given him a handwritten chit for an officer's uniform and another for a captain's insignia. A single shadow marred the greatest day of Der Chineser's life: if only the baron could have seen his triumph. The baron had made everything possible. He had chosen Emil Huebner as the volunteer who would join the Nazis. Der Chineser owed everything to the baron.

6

By MONDAY MORNING, March 14, 1938, the day after the cancelled plebiscite, Austria had become part of Germany. In Vienna the Germans occupied all public and any private buildings they needed. They commanded the police, commanded all civil servants. They controlled the city's utilities, all information facilities, newspapers, magazines, the radio, and all transportation installations.

In the study in the palace Fritz sat beside the radio on the table. For almost all his waking hours since Friday morning, Fritz had been in the study listening to the news from the Germans, their kind of news. Each broadcast ended with instructions, followed by warnings.

His binoculars were on the table beside the radio. Since Saturday morning, Fritz had gone to the roof of the palace time after time, climbing through the window of his nursery to watch men and machines moving into Vienna from the west. Troops continued marching into the city more than forty-eight hours after the first elements of the German army had reached the outskirts of Vienna.

Around noon Monday, Fritz heard a radio report announcing the selection of General Heinz Radecker as commander of all troops in Vienna, including all elements of the SS stationed there.

Fritz wrote "General Heinz Radecker" on a pad. He underlined the three words and looked at the pad, making another line beneath the first, making a third line, filling the page with lines before pushing it aside.

From a drawer Fritz took one of his cards with a matching envelope, both bearing the Von Gottisberg crest. He bent over the desk and wrote, "May I add mine to the keys of the city?" Fritz left the study and returned with a key he had borrowed from Zinn. He slipped the card into the envelope and dropped in the key before sealing it. He wrote "General Heinz Radecker" on the envelope which Zinn would deliver in the Daimler that afternoon.

At breakfast the next morning in Este Platz, Ernst Auerfeld said, "I gave everyone the day off. The drafting room is closed, so everyone can go hear Der Führer, so we can go to hear him."

"We? Not we, Ernst," Magda said.

"No fights today, please."

"I am not fighting," Magda said, layering a roll with butter. "I'm not going, either."

"You must go!" Ernst said. "Everyone will be there. Everyone will notice who is there. The Gestapo will notice. Use your goddamn head!"

"I am not standing in the street to listen to a little bastard from Linz," Magda said, spreading raspberry jam over the butter. "I mean it. He's a real bastard."

Ernst threw his napkin into the plate. He watched Magda devour the roll. "Are you coming or not?"

"You are the boss of your drafting room, Herr Auerfeld," she said. "You are not the boss of me."

He spoke quietly, "You'll be sorry, Magda."

They reached a kind of truce after their breakfast showdown. They spoke with civility and avoided each other until they were in bed. The bed had always been their salvation. They had always made peace under the covers.

Early Saturday morning, Berte knocked on the bedroom door. Neither Magda nor Ernst had heard the telephone. Berte knocked again and opened the door.

Magda lay snuggled up against Ernst's buttocks, her knees in the hollows of his knees. Her right arm lay across him with her hand where she liked it and where he liked it. "Missus?"

Magda glared at Berte, leaving Ernst and the bed, taking the old maid out of the bedroom. "What's your rush?"

"It's Rosa. She called, hysterical," Berte said. Rosa worked for Magda's parents.

"Tell me quickly."

"She said, 'Send the missus! Send the missus!' "

"Send me, why?"

"Nothing, nothing else," Berte said.

Magda hurried to the telephone. She heard Rosa wailing. "Rosa! Rosa! Listen, Rosa, you sonofabitch, stop screaming and listen."

"Missus, hurry, hurry, hurry, hurry!" Rosa cried, and slammed down the telephone receiver.

Magda found Ernst in the bathroom, bent over the sink, brushing his teeth. "It's Rosa," Magda said, pulling her nightgown over her head. She opened her bureau drawers, grabbing lingerie. "They didn't call, she called, so it's bad." Magda started opening her bra to slip it over her shoulders, but threw it aside. She didn't have time for a bra. "Quick, Ernst."

In her closet Magda took the first dress she saw, then dropped it. Too many buttons. She grabbed another. "I'll be ready in a minute."

She sat down, raising her right leg to push her foot into a stocking. She rushed, rising and shoving her feet into her shoes. "Ready, Ernst?"

Magda came out of her dressing room as he lathered his face, naked except for a towel around his middle. "Call me," he said.

He had never been so cruel. He set the brush into the shaving mug and picked up his gold razor, a gift from her father. Magda felt the tears but rubbed her face until she hurt, refusing to cry in front of him. "Thanks, Ernst. Thanks very much."

Berte followed her through the apartment. "Take me."

"If I need you, I'll send for you," Magda said. "Hold my coat."

Although Vienna had become a garrison, thronged with military vehicles, Magda used shortcuts and drove to her parents' apartment without a stop. The doorman said, "You can't park there," but she strode past him.

Magda told herself that Rosa had always been nutty. She would return from a day off with tales of being chased by gypsies and threatened by thugs. A thunderstorm could keep her walking the floor all night. Magda hit the elevator door with her fist. There had been no rain last night.

Rosa opened the apartment door still in her robe. She saw Magda and screeched. Magda grabbed a handful of the maid's hair. "Talk, you! Quickly!"

Rosa tried to talk and couldn't, pointing with her other hand. Magda threw her into the wall. She didn't have Ernst, and she didn't have anyone else. Well, she had never had anyone else in a bad time. "March," she said. "Left, right."

Magda found them in their matching chairs. Her father's arm hung over the arm of his chair. Her mother's left shoe dangled from her toes. "Left, right."

The coffee service from England sat on the table between them. "Left, right." There were cookies and two cups in saucers, with a spoon in each. They had died together.

Her father wore his favorite outfit, a tweed suit with a red waistcoat. His head rested against the wing of the chair. Her mother's head was lowered. Seeing her father's eyes were open, Magda closed her father's eyes and kissed his forehead, cold as stone. She stepped on something, and looking down, she saw an empty vial rolling across the carpet. Magda held on to her father's chair, taking deep breaths. The cowards! The goddamned cowards!

Magda went to the lacquered Chinese chest and took out some scotch and a tumbler. She poured three fingers into the tumbler and drank half. She shuddered as the harsh, smoky, single malt whisky went down. Magda stood before the open cabinet, holding the tumbler and reading labels on her father's bottles until she raised the glass and emptied it. "Rosa!"

The maid came to the doorway, refusing to enter. "Make me some coffee," Magda said. She couldn't get drunk because she had to bury her parents.

She chose an undertaker from the telephone book, and in less than an hour she admitted two men dressed like undertakers.

"Deepest condolences," said one man. "Heartfelt sympathy," said his partner.

They needed Magda every minute. They emptied her father's pockets, then the jewelry from the bodies, giving everything to Magda. She had to sign over the bodies. As she wrote her name, one of the undertakers crossed the room, stopping beside a large menorah Simon Kalbeck had purchased in the Warsaw ghetto. "Apologies, madam, *Juden?*"

"Since a week ago," Magda said. Years before, her parents had converted to Catholicism, baptizing Magda.

"We are not like some in our profession," said his partner. "My advice, madam, don't use a Jewish cemetery now. The Gestapo watches the cemeteries now, arresting mourners."

"Go on, take them," Magda said. She had to watch the pair stuff first her mother and then her father into separate bags, and carry each out of the apartment. In the doorway Rosa raised her hand like a kid asking permission to pee. "What will happen to me?"

"Shut up and clean this place," Magda said.

In the lobby, Magda could see a cop leaning against her car. "I warned you," said the doorman.

The cop saw the well-dressed dame coming. "So you're the one," he said. He wore a brassard with a black swastika. "You know better, but we'll forget it this once." He raised his voice as a truck approached. "Been kind of a hectic week."

In the truck German soldiers with rifles guarded men and women looking out at Magda in terror. The cop grinned. "Jews," he said. "Town smells better already."

In Este Platz, Magda let herself into the apartment. Berte hobbled into the foyer. "Is everything all right?"

"Wonderful," Magda said. "Where is my husband?" She had to tell Ernst what he had missed.

"In the bedroom," Berte said. "He's been in the bedroom."

Magda saw a suitcase in the corridor. What was he doing? They couldn't go anywhere until after the funeral. "Ernst?" He didn't reply. Then she saw him, carrying some shirts. "Ernst? Are you deaf?"

He didn't reply. In the bedroom she saw him putting the shirts into an open suitcase. "You can't leave."

He packed carefully. "I'm going," he said. "I intended to tell you today, but you ran out."

"Ran out," Magda said. "My parents are dead."

Ernst's head snapped up. "Dead?"

"They took a bottle of sleeping pills," Magda said. "Last night, I suppose."

"That's terrible," he said.

"I had to bring an undertaker," Magda said. "Two men came. They put Mama in a bag, Papa in a bag. Carried them out like slabs of beef." She couldn't stop talking. "So you can't leave. Not today."

He closed the suitcase with two clicks, like blows from a sledge. "I am going, Magda. For good. Forever."

"You can't," she said, coming to him. "You can't leave me alone here, Ernst. Ernst!"

"Don't make trouble," he said, rolling down his shirtsleeve. "Don't try to make trouble because you will lose."

"Ernst, please." She had never begged, anywhere. "Ernst. Last night you—we—have you forgotten last night?"

He snapped the cuff link and rolled down his other sleeve. "I won't let you go," Magda said. "You're throwing me aside like a whore, like someone off the streets. You can't leave me," she said, and heard the click of the other cuff link.

She became desperate. "Ernst, wait!" she said. "You can't go today. I've lost my parents. Have mercy. Stay until the funeral."

He took the suitcase. "I'll leave through the dressing room," he said. As Magda darted forward to block the dressing room, he added, "I give you fair warning: if you interfere with me, I'll inform the authorities." He nodded. "The authorities. Do you want to deal with the authorities?" He took a step, watching her, took another. Another. Another. Another, another, another, until Magda could no longer see him.

Carly could not stay away from Nick. She had to see him every day, touch him, prove to herself he had not been harmed. Ruth Posner lived in a two-room apartment in a building owned by her brother. There were shops on the street level and two stories above the shops with three apartments on each floor. Because the building was small, and because of the shops, all secrecy was forfeited.

Carly warned them about how much food they bought. Ruth Posner had always lived alone, and her purchases in the neighborhood had always been for one person. "Nothing can change," Carly said. "Each day each of us buys something for the table. Each goes to a different shop in a different street."

"You t-talk like a spy," Max said.

"I hope so," Carly said. "Spies are smart. That's why they're spies."

So they began to learn stealth. Carly began to wear a disguise. She had never covered her hair, but she began to wear hats borrowed from her mother and the maids. She changed them daily, or wore wool skiing caps.

One afternoon she arrived at Ruth's apartment with potatoes, carrots, and a box of brussels sprouts. She saw Peter Dietrich with Nick and Max. "I hope you b-brought a lot of stuff," Max said. "Peter's eating with us." Steam rose from a pot on the stove, and two packages of noodles lay to one side.

The warm apartment, combined with Peter's and Carly's presence, made the day festive. Everyone talked, bunched around the sink, washing and cleaning vegetables. "Hey, it's like old times," Peter said.

They didn't see Ruth Posner until Max turned to take one of the pots hanging from a row of hooks over the stove. "Just in t-time, honey," Max said. She was older than Max, a neat, slender woman with bobbed hair and a thin face. "We're all set," Max said. "Peter brought fruit for dessert. I'll get the noodles going. Where's the fish?"

"There is no fish," Ruth said.

"You were supposed to bring it," Max said, his stammer abandoned in the crisis. "We decided this morning. Remember, Nick?"

Nick said, "Sure," watching Ruth. "We voted," he said. "Two votes for fish."

"There is no dinner tonight," Ruth said. "No more dinners." The apartment became still, and the only sound came from the bubbling, boiling water.

Nick took the noodles out of Max's hand and dropped the package on the stove. "Is there trouble? Tell me," Max said. "Tell us. Something is wrong, correct? Correct?"

"No trouble," Ruth said. "I'm acting before trouble arrives. You're leaving and you're not coming back."

"These are my friends," Max said. "Your friends. You can't chase them out."

Watching her, Nick said, "You're out, too, Max."

"Exactly," Ruth said. "You, too," she told Max. "You're all going."

"Something scared you, right?" Max said, coming toward her. "Tell me what scared you."

"Correct," Ruth said. "You hit the nail on the head, Max. You scared me, you and your friends. They're after you, they're not after me. Nobody is searching for Ruth Posner. I'm not one of you from the Zwischentheatre, making jokes every night, laughing at the Germans every night. I'm not a communist, a trade unionist, a Catholic agitator. I make nobody trouble, my family makes nobody trouble. We are Austrians, true Austrians. My brother skied in the Olympics. He won a Silver Star in the 1936 Olympics. The Germans have already come for him to join their team." She had to be rid of them. Every minute counted. She could almost hear the boots on the stairs. "Pack up!" she said. "Pack! Pack!"

"We have nothing to pack," Nick said.

"Get out, then!" she said. "Go!" She reached for the door, but

Max pushed her hand aside, facing the woman with whom he had slept for more than two years, in whose arms she had sighed and called out his name in rapture. They were close enough to kiss. "We have nowhere to go."

She looked directly at him without flinching, and Max finally realized she had erased him from her life. He was astonished. "You turned me off like . . ." he stopped, and then said, ". . . like the water in that sink."

Nick took his arm, pulling him. "Correct," Nick said.

In the street, the shops were still open, and lights inside and outside made the street bright. "Maybe she went first to the Nazis," Nick said, looking everywhere. "Leave, Carly. Good night."

"Where will you sleep?"

"Somewhere. Go, now. Go," he said, his right hand in his coat pocket, holding the Beretta. If Ruth had talked to the Gestapo, there could be a shoot-out and he had to send her away, fast. "Go." He made himself smile for her.

She released him. Nick caught up with Max and Peter, his finger around the trigger of the automatic. Carly saw them turn the corner. She pulled the skiing cap over her ears, alone and cold, walking like someone lost.

The following day Carly entered the Hotel Sacher just before one o'clock. Lisl Schott liked to lunch late. Carly waited in the lobby among German army officers until she saw Lisl arrive, ready for a long confidential chat.

They kissed and Lisl said, "I feel like I've been released from prison. It's been a prison since—" she stopped, afraid she had been overheard.

Inside the restaurant, removing her gloves, Lisl said, "I thought you disappeared off the face of the earth. Where have you been anyway?"

"Here," Carly said. "In Vienna, leading my life. Life has changed."

"That's putting it mildly," Lisl said. "All you need to do is look around this room."

When they had ordered lunch, Carly said, "This is my treat."

"Absolutely, positively not," Lisl said.

"I called you."

"Returned my calls," Lisl said. "If you weren't my best friend and I didn't love you, I'd never put up with your—with you!"

"That's why it's my treat," Carly said. "So I can atone." Then she added, "We *are* best friends, Lisl."

Lisl's lips quivered. "You know more about me than any other person in the world."

"You're safe because I have a bad memory," Carly said.

"I don't," Lisl said. She reached across the table to squeeze Carly's hand. Then she fluffed her hair. "The things I've told you."

"I didn't listen," Carly said.

Lisl laughed. "I think we're best friends because we're so different. Be honest. Have we ever agreed?"

"We have and we do," Carly said. "We agree on everything important. Friendship, honesty—"

"You're the honest one," Lisl interrupted. "I know my weaknesses."

"We agree on our weaknesses," Carly said.

"There's another reason I love you," Lisl said. "Your sense of humor. You make me laugh." The headwaiter escorted three German army officers to a table. "Would you date one of them?" Lisl asked, almost whispering.

"No," Carly said. "No, I wouldn't."

"What choice do we have? Like the saying: When in Rome . . ." Lisl said. "Carly, they're here. They're not leaving."

"Aren't you afraid of them?" Carly asked.

"They're just men," Lisl said. "I'm not afraid of men."

Carly had been marking time since the headwaiter had seated them. She had given Lisl a chance to scold her. Lisl was on display, her favorite hobby. "I need your help," Carly said.

"One or two even look interesting," Lisl said.

"Lisl," Carly said, waiting until her oldest friend looked at her. "I need your help."

"What is it?" Lisl's voice was hushed. "Tell me," she said, just as the waiter came with their food.

So Carly had to sit silently with Lisl peering at her while the waiter unloaded his tray. As he left, Lisl whispered, "Tell me. You know I'd do anything for you."

"Who's at home now in your house?" Carly asked.

"Me, my mother, my father, my sister," Lisl said, reciting. "Why?"

"Do you remember when your parents would go out and we would be alone? And your sister would be asleep?" Carly said. "Do you remember we'd wait until she was really asleep and not pretending?"

"She told me later she always pretended," Lisl said. "She told me she would sneak out of her room and peek."

"Remember Paul Hohenstein and Skinny Probst?" Carly asked. Paul had been Lisl's first great love, and had been allowed to lie on top of her with their clothes on.

"What about them?"

"Remember how we would sneak them into the house? We didn't make a sound."

"Carly, I can't stand the suspense."

"I have a friend who—" Carly stopped. Lisl decided Carly had become involved with a German officer. "It's Nick. I've told you about him."

Lisl took her hand from the table. She sat erect, almost afraid to breathe. Someone could be listening to every word.

"They're after him," Carly said.

"Don't tell me," Lisl said, afraid to look at Carly, to be seen looking.

"He needs a place," Carly said, and added quickly, "Just for the night, only at night, Lisl."

Lisl spoke to the tablecloth. "You'd better stop," she whispered. "Right now, and don't use my name." She moved back her chair.

"Lisl . . . I'm sorry. He's in the street."

"Don't tell me," Lisl said. "Anything."

"You could let him in at night and he'd be gone in the morning."

"I have an appointment," Lisl said. "And don't you try to stop me. Don't you talk to me. Ever!" Lisl rose, inching away from the table as though she expected to be captured, until, safe from a sudden attack, she turned. Carly saw Lisl's gloves on the floor and bent to retrieve them. "Lisl!"

Carly held up the gloves, but Lisl didn't stop. A German officer left his chair as Lisl approached. "Fraulein," he said, at attention. "One moment."

He walked to Carly's table, coming to attention once more. "Fraulein," he said, taking the gloves. Carly watched him return them to Lisl, bowing and clicking his heels. Lisl left the restaurant, and Carly sat, desperate, as the officer returned to his companions.

In the wine cellar in the palace, Fritz stopped beside the racks of port and raised a flashlight. Behind him Zinn said, "Baron?"

"Yes?" Fritz selected two bottles for any Anglophiles among the guests, then joined Zinn. "Tell me your troubles."

"There is a woman . . . you have a visitor, Baron," said the butler. "Fraulein Siefermann."

"Siefermann." Fritz set down the bottles of port as though he was releasing a butterfly. "Car—Fraulein Siefermann is here?"

"Yes, sir. I know your orders, sir. I . . . she—"

"I'll suspend punishment," Fritz said. He had not seen her since she had discarded him for the love of her life. He gestured at the bottles. "For tonight."

In the Great Hall, Carly stood beside the piano. Fritz wanted to lock her in the palace. "Hello, Carly." He crossed the chamber as though they had never parted. "Have you had lunch? Would you like coffee? Tea?"

"You haven't asked why I'm here," she said.

"I never look a gift horse in the mouth," Fritz said. He gestured. "Sit down."

"I'm here about Nick."

He grinned. "Surprise."

"I need your help, Fritz," Carly said. "The Nazis are after him— after those from the Zwischentheatre but especially Nick. He needs a place to hide."

Fritz raised his arms and dropped them in a classic gesture of defeat. "Carly . . ." he said.

"He must get out of Austria," Carly said. "We must get out. But for all that—money, the right papers—you need weeks, months, and meanwhile Nick is in the streets. Fritz, he's in the streets."

"Carly, the palace is the worst place for him," Fritz said. "When the Germans came, I opened my doors to them. I had no choice. Already, they've turned the palace into an officers' club."

"You could hide him," Carly said. "Please, Fritz. Help him, help us." She could see Fritz tiring of her. "You can't keep Nick here," she said. "I understand. You explained. But you have friends. You know everyone in Vienna."

"Carly, I'm a marked man, too," Fritz said. "The Nazis don't trust me."

Then neither spoke. Carly knew she had lost, knew everything he told her had been fabricated on the spot. Then Fritz said, "This is unnatural, Carly. You're standing here like a stranger."

"I am a stranger here," she said, raising her hand to stop a rebuttal. "Does that seem cruel? I don't mean it to be. I'm a stranger everywhere now. This afternoon in the Sacher . . ." she said, and did not continue. "I have to go," she said, although she had no destination.

As they crossed the Great Hall, she said, "I'm sorry I bothered you."

"*I'm* sorry," Fritz said. "I wish I could have helped."

"Well . . ." Carly extended her hand. "Good-bye."

He took her hand, ready to shackle her. "Not *auf Wiedersehen?*"

"All right," she said wearily. *Auf Wiedersehen*, Fritz."

As Fritz watched her go, he stood motionless, his face a mask. Zinn saved him. "Would the baron like to examine the table?"

Fritz followed Zinn to the palace's state dining room, almost the length of the Great Hall. General Radecker had accepted Fritz's invitation to dinner, adding, "May I bring my staff, Baron?"

Fritz walked slowly around the table, trying not to think of the Huns who would be slobbering over his linen.

"I hope all is satisfactory, Baron."

"Satisfactory," Fritz said. Maybe the general and his hyenas would be hit by one of their own trucks on the way across town. Maybe Nick would be hit by a truck.

After Carly saw Fritz, she lived in a kind of trance, as though she were holding her breath. She lived fighting despair, fighting defeat, terrified of the Nazis, terrified she would lead them to Nick. When he agreed to meet her, they met only at night, late. Carly left the apartment hours before the rendezvous, zigzagging all over Vienna before going to her destination.

She lost track of the days and during the day lost track of the hours. She became a stranger in the apartment, keeping to herself at home although she was rarely there. One day she returned at dusk and saw her father in pajamas and a robe. "Stay away, Carly. I have the sniffles."

Carly forgot her father's cold but the next morning Klaus remained in bed, and Helga, alarmed, summoned their doctor. He examined Klaus. "You have the flu." The doctor wrote two prescriptions, and Helga sent one of the maids to Rosenbloom, their pharmacist.

The maid returned quickly, infuriating Helga. "Why didn't you wait for the medicine? Go back for it!"

Hearing her mother, Carly came out of the bedroom as the cowering maid said, "Missus, there is no more pharmacy. It's smashed, the pharmacy, everything smashed and broken. Rosenbloom is gone."

Carly almost leaped at the maid to embrace her. The maid had given her another chance, and when Helga said, "Come, I'll find you a pharmacy," and took the young woman's arm, Carly rushed to the bedroom for her clothes.

Rex Mulhall! Why hadn't she thought of him? Egon Berghofer, the pharmacist, had used a stage name, Rex Mulhall, at the Zwischentheatre.

Just over an hour later, in Hernalser Hauptstrasse in District XVII, Carly entered an immaculate pharmacy, full of brilliant colors: paper wrappings, spools of gay ribbons, large, exotic glass jars filled with red or green or orange liquids. A woman in a white coat approached Carly. "May I help you?"

"Heil Hitler!" A Nazi in uniform stood at the prescription counter in the rear, his arm extended in salute. He made an about-face, stomping across the shop to the door. Carly and the woman watched him in silence until the door closed. The woman said, "Now."

"Egon Berghofer," Carly said. "Is he here?"

"Yes, in the pharmacy. I am Martha Berghofer. Can I do something for you?"

"He was in the Zwischentheatre," Carly said. Seeing Martha Berghofer look up in alarm, Carly said to reassure her, "So was I. Not in the company, but I knew most of them."

Martha said, "Here is my husband." Egon Berghofer wore a white coat like his wife. He seemed antiseptic, with cropped hair, scrubbed hands, in a white shirt beneath the white coat. "Egon, she is from the Zwischentheatre."

"Don't use that word!" said the pharmacist.

"I'll be careful," Carly said. "I promise," she added to Martha, deliberately including her because she seemed kind, giving Carly hope.

"Why are you here?" asked the pharmacist, and immediately, "I retract the question. Don't tell me. It's better if you tell me nothing."

"Egon, in God's name!" said his wife. "What is becoming of us? Are we supposed to live in a closet the rest of our lives?"

"We are supposed to *live*!" said the pharmacist. "Live as best we can, as safely as we can." He leaned toward his wife. "As long as we can." The door opened and Egon hissed, "Quiet!" leaving them to approach a man and a woman. "Good afternoon, good afternoon."

He gave Carly her chance. She had Martha Berghofer trapped. "Nick Gallanz is in the streets," Carly said, adding, unable to discard them, "like Max Ingster and Peter Dietrich. Try to imagine how it is for them, on guard twenty-four hours of every day. They must have someplace to sleep. Anyplace. Anyplace with four walls and a roof."

Martha studiously watched her husband wrapping a bottle of cough syrup. "Help me," Carly said.

They heard a clang as the pharmacist opened the cash register and made change. "You don't look like a person who hates people," Carly said.

"My father was a pastor," Martha said. "In my family we were raised to love, not to hate. And I learned early it is hard to hate. You must concentrate to hate, work to hate, and this drains you like physical labor. In the end you are yourself the victim of your hate because each day leaves you exhausted, collapsing to regain your strength for the next day of hatred."

Carly stared at the trim woman in her starched, spotless white linen coat. "You talk like a saint."

Martha smiled. "I am not a saint, and would not wish to be one. I like the pleasures of life too much," she said as they heard the door close. Carly shifted, standing with the pharmacist's wife as he approached. "You can't close your ears, Egon," Martha said. "Or your heart."

The pharmacist stopped in front of them like an officer inspecting his troops. "I am in my place of business, and here I decide who speaks and to whom I listen," he said.

"We're in a crisis, Egon," said his wife. "All of us who are decent. Nick Gallanz, Max—"

"Stop there!" interrupted the pharmacist. He pointed at the door. "There are enough enemies in Vienna, Martha. Are you also my enemy?"

She said, "I am your wife, Egon, not your enemy."

The pharmacist was unable to respond, seemed to be searching for a response. Then he said, "You are my friend, Martha. My best friend."

"As you are mine," she said, leaving Carly to stand with her husband.

"They need a friend, Mr. Berghofer," Carly said.

Martha said, "There is a place." The pharmacist whirled around, staring at his wife. "Do you agree, Egon?" she asked. "Egon?"

Somewhere in the pharmacy a cuckoo came out of a clock and returned while Carly prayed. She didn't see the pharmacist take a key ring from his pocket. "Come," he said.

Carly followed him out of the pharmacy and around the shop, away from Hernalser Hauptstrasse. At the rear a wire fence ran from the pharmacy about thirty feet to a one-story building of red brick without windows. The pharmacist stopped at a gate on which hung a large padlock. He used a key to open the padlock. At the door of the building he said, "Help yourself. Always open. Nothing worth stealing."

Carly stepped into a storeroom. She saw old store counters and worn furniture, rugs rolled and stacked against the wall, an apothecary scale like the justice scale on public buildings. The pharmacist removed the padlock key from the chain and stepped back, startled, as Carly leaped forward, throwing her arms around him.

When they returned to the pharmacy, Martha was with two girls in their teens, and Egon hurried to the prescription counter, where a woman waited. The girls paid and left, and when the woman left, Egon joined Carly and his wife. "They must never enter the shop," he said. "They are strangers to us. If we meet, they must pass us as though we are utter strangers."

"They'll stay out of your way," Carly said. "I promise."

"I promise, too, Egon," Martha said.

"You're both wonderful," Carly said, leaving before her benefactor could think of other hazards. "Thank you," she said.

Carly found a locksmith's shop and made three more keys for the padlock, for Nick, Max, and Peter.

A week later Carly came home early one afternoon, and at the building entrance someone said, "Keep going." She obeyed, looking back, and saw Max Ingster.

She stopped breathing as Max came abreast. "Tell me quickly."

"Nothing has happened. Not yet. I hope nothing has happened," Max said, with no trace of his stammer.

"Tell me!"

"That guy Egon has gone to the Gestapo," Max said.

He paralyzed Carly. "Jesus, come on!" Max said, pulling her.

"Where are we going? Where's Nick? Max!" Carly said.

"Shut up and listen," Max said. "You're his only chance."

She began to nod, her head bobbing, rescuing herself so she could rescue Nick. "I'm ready."

"Nick and Peter went out this morning as usual," Max said. "Peter has had a toothache for the past two days. There is a dentist in District VIII he trusts. I stayed in—I don't know why I stayed. Around nine-thirty the storeroom door opens and there is Martha, you know, the wife. Egon just left the drugstore for the Hotel Metropole, the Gestapo. I found Peter in the dentist's chair. Someone must stop Nick and keep—"

Carly was already running into the street, waving at a taxi.

The sun dropped behind the clouds during the ride, and the day turned dark and dreary. Carly told the driver to leave her two blocks from the pharmacy. After a block, she turned and circled around until she faced the rear of the pharmacy. Between her and the pharmacy lay the small red brick building that Egon Berghofer had made a tomb. Far down the block on the opposite side of the street stood a Mercedes-Benz sedan. Under the blackening sky, the car seemed like a hangman's scaffold.

Carly pushed back her hair and started walking toward the store-room. Suddenly someone came around the corner—a stranger. Carly could see everything—the pharmacy, the wire fence and gate, the store-room. The man coming toward her crossed the street to the car. As he approached, the driver's door opened. The man stopped beside the door, talking to the driver. Behind him on the same side of the street, another man walked toward the sedan.

Carly had never seen the Gestapo. The men looked ordinary, looked like everyone else, but Carly knew if they got Nick, he would die.

The driver closed the sedan door. The man on the far side of the street walked back toward Hernalser Hauptstrasse, and his partner walked toward the gate in the fence in front of Carly.

Just then she saw Nick coming toward her and the Gestapo.

She had to stop him, she had to stop him—the words spun around and around in her head, matching her heartbeat, matching her foot-steps. She had to act now, instantly, before he saw her and waved or spoke, and died. "Christian!" Carly shouted, running toward him, her arm raised. "Christian! Christian!" she shouted, because no Jew except the child of Bethlehem had ever been given that name.

Nick heard her and saw Carly running straight at him. "Chris-tian!"

Nick saw the man behind her, then the other man across the street, then the bright steel circle around three spokes on the hood of the Mercedes-Benz. He ran straight at Carly. "Hi, there!"

She leaped at him. "Hug me, kiss me," she said into his ear, kissing him, hugging him, massaging the back of his neck. "We have to leave immediately," she said into his ear. Nick put his arm around her, and they walked away from the men in the street and the men in the Mercedes-Benz.

As they walked past the pharmacy, Nick asked, "Who did it? Who went to the Gestapo?"

"Your friend, Egon Berghofer," Carly said, overcome with anger.

"Tell me everything," Nick said. "How did you know? How about Max? Peter?"

"They're both safe. Martha saved him, saved us all," Carly said. They walked on until she said, "Nick!"

A squad of German soldiers, all with clubs and guns, came out of a building dragging a man bigger than any of them toward a truck at the curb. The man twisted, kicked, tried to bite, in a desperate effort to escape. "Help me!" the man shouted. "Help me!" People quickly left the sidewalk, pretending to see nothing, walking into the street, making a wide arc around the nothing in front of the building.

"Help me, they'll kill me!" shouted the big man, digging his heels into the concrete sidewalk. "Somebody help me!" he shouted, and wrenched his right arm free. A soldier raised his club, hitting the captive's arm. He cried out in agony, and the soldier who hit him yelled, "Hold him up for me!" Others raised the big man, and the soldier hit him in the face. Blood spurted from the man's nose, and still he fought, squirming, writhing, kicking. He kicked the soldier who had clubbed him.

"Hold him!" yelled the soldier, pulling his gun and coming around the prisoner. He brought the butt of the gun down on the man's head. The man dropped to the pavement as blood spread over his hair. The soldier kicked him. "Throw him in the truck. We're late enough."

Carly couldn't look and had to look. She couldn't bear the sight of the bleeding, crumpled figure, but she could not turn away. She felt Nick's arm. "Keep moving, keep moving." He led her into the street, into traffic, away from the truck. Nick held her firmly. "Faster," he said. Carly could see the big man's eyes.

"We separate at the corner," Nick said. "You're going home. No arguments."

"No arguments," she said. "We'll meet at noon tomorrow in Stephansplatz."

"Stephansplatz," he said. "Why wait until tomorrow? Why don't I just jump into the truck back there?"

"Noon tomorrow," Carly said. "Stephansplatz is jammed at noon. It's safe at noon. Promise," she said. "Nick? I won't leave if you don't promise."

"Promise, promise," Nick said, and she raised her arms, taking his face in her hands to kiss him.

In the palace less than an hour later, Fritz saw Zinn come to the door of the study. "Fraulein Siefermann is here, Baron."

Carly stood in front of the fireplace in the Great Hall. She turned, tossing her head to throw back her hair in the impatient gesture which identified her. "I was afraid to call," she said, "afraid you wouldn't see me."

He joined her, leaning forward to kiss her cheek. Her face was cold and smelled of the outdoors, and Fritz remembered her at the schloss after a day with the horses or a tramp in the forest. "I had to come," Carly said. "There is no other place for me to go."

"There is no other place you should go," he said. Then they were silent until he said, "I don't offer you anything because you are not here for a drink."

"Correct," Carly said. She faced him directly. "It's Nick. If he can't escape from Vienna, he will die. They'll kill him." Fritz clasped his hands behind his back.

"They almost got him today," Carly said. "We were lucky today. If . . ." she said, and broke off. "If, if, if, if, if," she said. "There is only one if, a death sentence if. If he stays, he dies."

"I'm helpless, Carly," Fritz said, as though he were refusing an invitation to dinner. Coming to him regularly, pleading for her paramour. She had made the palace a station stop.

"You've been with the Nazis," she said. "You told me they come for dinner."

"Carly, I'm an Austrian. They have us on our knees."

"Not you," she said. "You're not on your knees, Fritz. You entertain them."

"Exactly," he said. "Entertain. I've become an entertainer. They like the palace, like my food, my wine, my cigars, the service they get. I'm at their service."

"He'll die!" Carly said. Her voice filled the Great Hall. "They will kill him! I can't let them kill him!"

"Perhaps we *should* have a drink," Fritz said. "Give me your coat."

She swung her arm. "Cut it out, Fritz! My coat! There is a man's life here, at stake here, and you're playing the host, the perfect gentleman, the gemütlich lord of the Strauss waltz! Stop! *Stop!* This city is one big firing squad, and you want me to take off my coat!"

She pulled, pulled her arms from the sleeves and tossed the coat aside. "There's my coat, Fritz. We're finished with my coat. No more coat. *No!* I didn't come for whiskey, or for coffee, or for waltzes. I came because I must save Nick or he will die! Will you help?"

"Carly . . ." Fritz bent for her coat.

Carly took a deep breath and let it out slowly, like someone about to perform a daredevil feat. "Fritz."

Fritz looked at her, alerted by an indefinable change in her voice. "Fritz, I have something to offer," Carly said. "I think it's something to offer. A bargain. You can call it a bargain," Carly said. She wanted to shut her eyes so she could keep Nick back, keep him away, keep from seeing him. "Fritz, if you get Nick and his family out . . . out of the country, of Austria, safe, safely out of Austria, I'll marry you," Carly said. "If you still want . . . feel . . . if you still feel . . . you must get them out."

Fritz wanted to turn his back and tell Zinn to be rid of her. He wanted to throw the coat at her as she had thrown it, and warn her not to return, never to return. He wanted to grab her, pull her across the Great Hall and into the street, dump her into the street, and, insanely, he wanted to spit at her because she had just spat at him.

He held Carly's coat folded over his arm like a matador with the muleta. He could have been a matador, as slim, as elegant, as seemingly impervious to flaw and failure. "You are willing to marry me," Fritz said. "True?"

"If you . . ." she said, cold and desolate in front of the crackling fire. "After you—"

"First I perform," Fritz said. "If I perform, you perform. True?"

She nodded, afraid to talk, afraid to try and talk. She was losing Nick, she had lost Nick. She could feel herself losing Nick, losing him inside of her. Her insides seemed to be slipping away, she was being drained. She would never, ever . . . for the rest of her life . . . every day for the rest of her life . . . She couldn't cry now, in front of Fritz. "Carly?"

She had to face Fritz. She would always have to face him. "If I can do it, can you do it?" Fritz asked.

"Let's begin with honesty," Carly said. "You can do it."

"I'm not an *ubermensch*, a superhuman," Fritz said.

"You are . . . you," Carly said. "You can do it."

"So we've settled me," Fritz said, waiting.

She didn't flinch. "I came here," Carly said. "I'm here."

"Are you sure, Carly? Are you sure?"

She refused to cry. "I'm sure."

Fritz came to her, raising her coat and opening it. "I think you would like immediately to go home," he said. She nodded, grateful to him, and Fritz draped the coat over her shoulders without touching her. "I'll take you home."

They crossed the Great Hall, walking through the palace to the courtyard entrance. The stable doors were open, and inside Fritz brought her to the small coupe beside the Daimler. "We'll take the runabout," Fritz said. They heard the peeping of birds in a nest somewhere in the eaves. Fritz gestured at the old hayloft. "The safest creatures in Vienna."

Fritz got into the coupe beside Carly and started the engine. "She needs a moment to warm up."

"You must be cold," Carly said.

"Since this is the hour for truth, yes, I'm cold," Fritz said. He shifted gears and drove through the courtyard. Neither spoke again. Fritz drove rapidly. The day was ending and he turned up the head-lights.

In Kruger Strasse, Fritz followed Carly into the apartment lobby. The doorman had disappeared and they were alone. "Fritz?"

"You've omitted something," he said.

"No, no." She looked at him, so safe and confident. She envied his confidence, his cocksure grace.

"You retract your offer," Fritz said.

"No, I . . ." she broke off as the doorman returned. "Something wrong with the elevator? I've had other complaints today. Let me try," he said, crossing the lobby.

Fritz raised his hand and the doorman stopped. "We'll manage," Fritz said, and to Carly, "We were interrupted."

"You didn't answer," she said. "What is your answer? Do you accept?"

"Your proposal," he said. "My answer to your proposal. I thought we had settled this in the palace. Well, Carly. My proposal? Will you be my wife?"

She nodded. "Yes," she said. "I will. Yes, Fritz." She felt old and withered, felt beaten.

"Now you have your answer," Fritz said. "We are betrothed, Carly." He pressed the elevator button and the door opened. "I believe you would like to be alone," he said, holding back the door. Carly stepped into the elevator, and Fritz moved to his right so they were face to face as the door closed. He watched the needle above the door until it stopped. "Baroness Carlotta Von Gottisberg," he said.

7

CARLY LIVED THROUGH
dinner with her parents, lived through the evening. When she escaped, closing the door of her room, she discovered she was not alone. She heard Fritz: "Will you be my wife?"

She had saved Nick by losing him. Carly took off her clothes and got into bed naked, remembering Nick beside her naked. She remembered his face in her breasts, remembered spreading her thighs to take him captive. She had freed her captive.

In the morning, sharing the newspapers with her husband, Helga heard Carly. "Mama."

Carly wore a robe. "Are you busy?" Klaus Siefermann lowered his newspaper, watching his wife cross the room. They lived with a stranger, an alien who came and went like a tenant.

Carly brought Helga into her bedroom. Helga saw clothes on chairs and on the bed, two of everything. Carly took one of her long, loose coats from the closet, so Helga assumed she needed help deciding what

139

to wear. "It's a problem now in the spring," Helga said. "The day begins cold and ends warm, or exactly the opposite."

Carly dropped the coat over a chair. "I'm finishing with Nick today," she said, and looked at her mother. "I'm breaking off with him. I'll never see him after today. You can help me. Will you help me?"

Helga had to be careful, had to behave like Carly behaved, like a stranger with a stranger. Helga had to sound like Carly, like she spoke to a clerk. "I'll do whatever you ask," Helga said.

Two hours later, as clocks in the Inner City struck eleven, Carly entered Stephansplatz, the giant square in front of St. Stephen's Cathedral. She wore a long tweed coat with a collar and a bright yellow scarf around the collar. The scarf fell over her breasts, and dropped below her shoulders. She had pulled a black ski cap down over her ears. Far ahead, two priests crossed the square, young men, walking fast with short steps, their cassocks billowing in the wind like Carly's coat. She said, "Pray for me."

She could not be still. Carly walked through the square and around the cathedral. She left the cathedral, choosing streets at random, trying not to think, not to think. Then she could stay away no longer, and as she made her way back to Stephansplatz, she began to hurry.

The square had filled. Carly looked for Nick, walking from one side of the square to another. She crossed at a different angle. She walked back and forth, back and forth.

Carly saw him before he saw her. She wanted to throw herself at him, press herself against him, feel his flesh against her flesh. She wanted to make them vanish. But she said, fiercely, "Do it!" and ran toward Nick, waving. Then he saw her and forgot Adolf Hitler, forgot everyone on earth.

Nick held her close, looking into Carly's face as though they had been apart forever. "Hello, beauty," he said, and kissed her. He kissed her again, and said, "Company," as a squad of German soldiers marched through the square.

In another place in that early spring of 1938 Carly and Nick would have been in a convertible or in the rumble seat of a convertible, in a movie balcony, on a porch swing, in a rowboat or a canoe, in a blanket on the grass, in the hay on a hayride, but they were in Vienna, Austria, in the month after Der Führer claimed the country of his birth.

The squad of German soldiers marched past and Nick said, "Maybe now you'll tell me why we're here."

"There is a way out for you and your family," Carly said. "You can get out—"

Nick stopped and stopped her. "Out? *Out*? Really? *Really*, Carly?"

Now that she had started, she had to end it, end it. "Fritz can arrange a way out for all of you."

"All of us," Nick said. "How about you?" The cathedral bells thundered overhead, striking twelve o'clock. "How about you? Carly!" Nick said, and louder, "Carly, how about you?"

"I can't."

She took the wind out of him. "I go and you stay," Nick said. "Is that your message?" Her silence made him angry and he took her arms, holding tight. "You brought me here to say good-bye," he said, shaking her. "Tell me!"

"This is your chance," Carly said.

"Me, me, me," Nick said. "Tell me about you!"

"I can't leave my family," Carly said.

Nick released her. She had come with a miracle and then desecrated it. "You're lying."

"Fritz is waiting for you in the palace," she said. "And people are looking. People will hear us."

Nick put his face against hers, talking into her ear. "Nobody hears me now. Try the truth now."

She had to end it, had to escape while she could. "I can't leave my family," Carly said, and started walking, walking fast.

Nick stayed with her. "You're still lying. Why are you lying?"

She wouldn't look at him, walking as though she were alone. "I can't go!" Carly said. "I can't! I can't! I'm afraid!"

"You're lying!"

"You'll lose Fritz!" Carly said, afraid she would fail, afraid she would buckle under his pounding. "You'll *lose*!"

"Stop lying!" Nick said, grabbing her. She shook him off. He followed and took her wrist. She fought him. "You're drawing attention!" Carly said. "You're molesting a woman! You'll bring the police!" she said, fighting him, breaking free and running, weaving through the people in the square.

She surprised Nick, so she had a big lead and she widened it. Nick ran but couldn't find her. Then he saw the yellow scarf billowing behind her. He followed the scarf, and lost it. And saw it on the left. Nick ran into someone, ran around him, but couldn't find the yellow scarf.

On the edge of the square, Helga stood beside the taxi she had hired, holding the door handle as though she could keep it from moving. She searched the square for Carly, her head high, standing on the balls of her feet. Helga wore one of Carly's floppy coats and a black ski cap, and around her neck a bright yellow scarf exactly like Carly's which she had bought earlier that morning, following Carly's instructions. Helga had hired the taxi, following Carly's instructions. Helga's heart pounded and her belly made flip-flops. Where was she?

In the square Nick saw the billowing yellow scarf again. "Carly!" He felt a stitch in his side. He had not yet fully recovered from the murderous assault in December, from the brass knuckles and the black-jack. "Carly!" The pain in his side increased.

Beside the taxi Helga saw Carly, saw her running, saw her pull off the black ski cap and remove the yellow scarf while she ran. Helga followed instructions, opening the door. Carly ran, ran, reaching the cab, running past Helga, running, running. Helga waited, waited, watching the square, searching the square until she saw Nick. She made sure she saw Nick, made sure Nick saw her before getting into the cab and slamming the door. "Go, go," Helga told the driver. "Go!"

Nick saw the taxi moving, saw it skirting Stephansplatz as he ran, tilted, the pain in his side like knife thrusts. He saw a cab, and stopped, put two fingers in his mouth and whistled, waving at the driver. He could barely see the other cab.

Behind Nick, a block away, Carly ran in the street, dodging traffic, darting into another street, dashing across to the other side, following two men into a café filled for the lunch hour. She shook her head as the headwaiter approached, skirting him, moving toward the rear, toward the door marked, "FRAUEN," women.

A woman came through the door and Carly went around her, pushing back the door, finding a corner, covering her face with her hands. Here, alone, hidden, she succumbed at last, weeping in great, convulsive sobs.

In her taxi, Helga said, "Hasenhauer Strasse. Turkenschanz Park," sending the driver far out to the outskirts of Vienna. As the driver left the Inner City, Helga looked out of the rear window and saw a taxi following. After a mile, she looked again and saw the same taxi. Helga settled back, but her breath came fast, as though she, too, had been running.

Behind her, Nick sat over the driver's seat, watching the cab ahead. The pain beneath his ribs had subsided. "Don't lose him," Nick said.

Near Turkenschanz Park, Helga said, "Stop here, anywhere here." She had followed orders exactly. By the time she paid the fare, Nick opened the rear door of her cab.

"Thanks for the tour of the city," Nick said. He bent, extending his hand, and Helga took it, stepping out of the cab.

When he saw Helga, Nick stepped away. He bit his lip, turning from side to side as though he could find Carly here, miles from Stephansplatz. "Two scarves," he said. "Two caps, two coats. Very good. Excellent. Disguises." He frightened her.

"You won," Nick said. "Today." Fritz waited in the palace. "You're a wonderful mother," he said, returning to his taxi.

That morning Fritz told Zinn he would admit any guests, and he went to the entrance for Nick. "Sorry I'm late," Nick said.

"Haven't you heard? The clock has stopped," Fritz said. "Hitler stopped the clock."

"Joke," Nick said, looking at the ornate entrance.

"Nothing has changed," Fritz said.

"Not here," Nick said.

"I'm dumb." Fritz made a face. "I apologize, Nick. I'm sorry." Nick raised his hand, flicking his wrist.

Taking him into the study, Fritz went to his desk and dropped into a chair. "What did Carly tell you?" Fritz had to eliminate any surprises.

Nick stopped beside a large globe, spinning it and watching continents chase each other. "She said you could get us out." He glanced at Fritz, at the cashmere and the loden cloth and the flannel and the suede Fritz wore. "How did I become so lucky?" He went to the bookcase, raising his hand to trail his fingers across the leather bindings.

"Carly asked if I could help," Fritz said. "I told her I would try."

Nick turned, stopping beside a mahogany humidor with the Von Gottisberg crest above the brass lock. "Carly is not going," Nick said.

"She isn't in danger," Fritz said. "You're in danger. You and your family."

"Me and my family," Nick said, passing the desk and stopping beside a carved chair with a high back and a velvet seat. He ran his hand over the back of the chair, over the crest. "Nobody gets out," he said. "Rothschild had to give Goering his railroad to leave Austria."

"I don't know Goering," Fritz said, watching Nick moving slowly around the study. "Sit down, old boy."

"I lost the habit lately," Nick said. "Lately, in Vienna, if you sit, you can die." He came to the desk, facing Fritz like a prosecutor. "Yesterday I'm a fly in a bottle," Nick said. "Today I'm free. Almost free. I can go. Carly cannot go. But nobody is after Carly. Is anyone after Carly?"

Fritz picked up the letter opener, pointing it at Nick. "You'll have to ask Carly."

"Sure," Nick said. "Why ask you about Carly? I can ask her."

"So we've settled Carly," Fritz said. "Let's settle you." He rose from his chair, looking directly at Nick. "I've volunteered to help." Fritz raised a gold bowl. "I am not offering you a pot of poison," he said. "Do you want to leave Austria?"

"I have no choice," Nick said.

Fritz set down the bowl. "Now we can proceed. I can't get you out, but with luck we'll come close, close enough so you *can* get out. Where is the loosest border? Italy, of course. The problem is not at the border. The problem is between here and the border, between here and Innsbruck. It's one long booby trap because you never know when you'll hit a checkpoint. The Nazis move their checkpoints around like chessmen. Some days you can drive from Vienna to Innsbruck without seeing a barrier. Other days it's one long stretch of high hurdles. And it's hopeless without a Safe Conduct. I told Carly I would try for a Safe Conduct. Pretend I'm successful." Fritz raised the letter opener. "Here is the Safe Conduct, here in the palace. You'll leave from here, from the palace. You'll take the Daimler. You'll have the look of authority in the Daimler. The Nazis like authority. You can drive?"

"Drive, sure," Nick said.

"So you are in the Daimler with a Safe Conduct which brings you to the schloss—to the castle, to the village really," Fritz said. "Deliver the car to Otto Kesselring. He has a garage in the village." Fritz dropped the letter opener and came around the desk. "You'll need a guide for the border. There are men in the village who can take you across. Do you have money?"

"Sure," Nick said. He couldn't take money from Fritz.

They left the study. "You have a lot to do, old friend," Fritz said.

In the circular entrance of the palace Nick stopped, his back to the door. "Fritz—"

Fritz raised his hands, pretending horror. "No speeches. Christ, not that!" He opened the huge door, grinning. "*Wiedersehen.*"

Nick went from the palace to a café with a telephone, and called Carly. "Not home," said the maid.

He had to give his family the news, but he couldn't come to Leopoldstadt in daylight. Nick began to walk, but in less than a mile he entered another café and called Carly again.

She reached the telephone ahead of the maid, standing beside the taboret as it rang a second time. The maid came, rubbing her hands on her apron. "Not home, mister."

The next morning, Fritz drove to General Radecker's headquarters and asked for directions to the Military Police. He entered an office where a woman twice his size sat behind a desk. "Captain Huebner," he said.

"Name," she said, taking a clipboard.

"Fritz Von Gottisberg."

The woman ran her finger down the clipboard. "You have no appointment," she said. "You shouldn't have been allowed in the building."

"Well, as long as I'm here . . ." he said.

"You're leaving," she said. "Or do you want an escort? That can be arranged. The charge is trespassing. The first charge."

"Tell Captain Huebner I'm here," Fritz said.

"Maybe you want to commit suicide," said the rhinoceros. She pulled the telephone cord, bringing the instrument across the desk. "Maybe you're suicidal."

"One of us is," Fritz said. "I'm here for Captain Huebner. I have information involving the Greater German Reich and the Chancellor of the Greater German Reich, Adolf Hitler. Der Führer. My information is a matter of supreme importance and urgency. Call Captain Huebner. If you do not call him, if I do not see him, I can tell you with total confidence you will be executed within twenty-four hours. The Greater German Reich will execute you, and I will witness the proceedings."

She looked up at Fritz, both afraid of and loathing him, and then she raised the telephone receiver and said slowly, "Fritz Von Gottisberg," and by the time she set down the instrument, a door opened and Der Chineser came through it like a projectile.

"Baron! How are you, sir? Please come in, Baron. Please."

The baron's arrival brought back, vividly, Der Chineser's enduring guilt. He remembered every detail of the episode which began that Monday morning in November of the previous year when the baron had delivered the Daimler to Spangenberg for servicing before a hunting trip to the schloss. Alone with Der Chineser, the baron had told him of the pack of communists in the Zwischentheatre, and of Nicholas Gallanz, who led the treasonous band. Der Chineser had failed the baron. Nicholas Gallanz still lived, still roamed Vienna freely. "Since Mahomet won't come to the mountain . . . " Fritz said.

"Just send for me if you want anything, sir," said Der Chineser.

"I'm always at your service. I'll never forget you, sir. I'll *never* forget you, all you've done for me."

"Belay . . ." Fritz said. "I spotted a good man and gave him a chance to prove it. Tell me about yourself."

"Baron, sir, I feel like I'm living a dream, a dream come true," said Der Chineser. "All my life I mourned for our country, our great, wonderful country. All my life I wished I had lived in the years of the empire, of our splendor, our triumphs. Now it has come true! Already Der Führer had changed Austria. Already we are a different country. The Greater German Reich will restore Austria to leadership."

"I'm proud of you, Emil."

"Everything is your doing, sir," Der Chineser said. "Without you, I wouldn't be here. You gave me my chance. Sir, my entire life has changed since the first night I saw you in the drill hall."

"Emil, I want a promise from you," Fritz said. "Give me your word you'll never again, anywhere, to me or anyone, repeat that recital." Der Chineser vowed, solemnly, and Fritz said, "You're probably wondering why I'm here. I need a Safe Conduct."

Der Chineser stared at the baron. Fritz shrugged. "Nothing ventured, nothing gained. *Wiedersehen*," he said.

Der Chineser darted forward. He had disappointed the baron once. Der Chineser had never seen a Safe Conduct, but he could not allow the baron to leave without hope. "I'll try, sir. I'll do whatever I can, Baron, do my best."

"It's not fair to you, comrade." Fritz tried to leave, but Der Chineser was in front of him.

"Sir, it's an honor," said Der Chineser. "I consider it an honor, a great honor, that you came to me, chose me."

"I told my . . . told the individual, the chances were one in a thousand, one in a million," Fritz said. He slapped Der Chineser's shoulder. "Don't be a stranger."

One afternoon later that week, Zinn came to the Great Hall. "Captain Huebner, Baron."

Fritz saw Der Chineser behind the butler. "In here, Captain, in here."

Der Chineser came down the marble steps. "Sir, I have it."

Fritz slapped his thigh. "I held my breath," he said. "You could have come to soften the blow."

Der Chineser gave Fritz an envelope with a black swastika in the lower left-hand corner. "I could not fail you, sir."

When Fritz was alone in his study, he studied the envelope. The

Safe Conduct had been signed by a Colonel Friedrich Varlingen, Military Police, and was valid for ten days. When Nick telephoned, Fritz said, "Your ticket has arrived. You have until a week from Tuesday."

Nick had to tell Carly. He knew the maid would answer the telephone, would say, "Not home, mister." But he raised the receiver. "Not home, mister."

A half hour later Nick walked into Carly's building as though he lived there. He had to see her, had to hear her say, "Nick," say, "Nicki."

The maid opened the door. "Carly? Miss Siefermann," Nick said.

The maid knew his voice. She closed the door and locked it. Nick rang the doorbell, rang and rang the doorbell. He banged on the door, and it opened.

Klaus Siefermann had to protect his daughter. His daughter had become a zombie. Carly had stopped living, eating, sleeping, drifting through the apartment like a wraith. Helga kept Klaus awake, in mourning. "Tell Carly I'm here," Nick said. "Tell her!"

"Do not threaten me and I will not threaten you," Klaus said.

"Tell Carly—" Nick said, and Klaus interrupted:

"Allow me to continue," Klaus said. "Do me the courtesy. Extend me the courtesy I extend you. You're a man, behave like a man. We'll talk man to man. Understand? Man to man. I have nothing against you, any of you, understand? I wish you no harm, any of you. But my daughter comes first, Carly comes first with me. Understand? Of course you understand. She is my daughter. And she will not see you. Think! If she wanted to see you, she would see you. You know Carly. Nothing and no one can stop her, could stop her." In her room Carly could hear every word.

"Therefore you will stop your harassment. I tell you this without anger, without hate. Stop your siege. Go away: And stay away," Klaus said, "or you will force me to take steps. Do not force me to take steps." He closed the door.

Nick almost kicked the door, almost started to kick it down. His family saved him. Lottie and Boris and Sam, waiting dutifully in Leopoldstadt for him to carry them off on his magic carpet, brought him back from lunacy. He had to rescue his family.

A mile away in Este Platz, Magda sat at her vanity, where she had the strongest light, rereading the letter from Dieter Rantzau which had been delivered that morning. She had been forced to buy glasses after Ernst's departure, but she kept the glasses hidden, even from Berte.

Magda put the pages of the letter in order, setting aside the snapshot Dieter had enclosed. She raised the letter to the light.

Dear Good Friends Magda and Ernst:

Never in a thousand years would I have believed I would one day discover and live in the country of which Goethe has written. Remember, "Kennst du das Land, wo die Zitronen bluhn?"

Fanny and I have come to that land. We are among blooming lemons, blooming oranges, grapefruit, avocados, peaches, pears, cherries, grapes, and flowers like carpets everywhere. Everywhere!

To retrace our steps from Vienna to London, from London to New York, and from New York three thousand miles to this paradise would require almost as much time as we needed to make the journey. We are here. Happily. America, California, Hollywood, the sun, the sweet air, the smell of orange blossoms, of jasmine, of honeysuckle, of gardenias, all combine to make life pleasant.

Life is pleasant, dear friends. Here we have already found new friends, new from the old country. After all, we are in Hollywood! Charlie Chaplin, Greta Garbo, Marlene Dietrich, Ernst Lubitsch, Von Stroheim, Gregory Ratoff, all are neighbors. We never see them, but they are neighbors.

We see others, actors, actresses, directors, or those hoping to be actors, actresses, directors. Among these is Dieter Rantzau, who also strives to be an actor.

I can see Magda's face as she reads these lines. Dieter Rantzau an actor? Why not? Can I act? Naturally, I cannot. But I look like an actor, and a European with an accent is a saleable commodity here in Hollywood.

And I need a saleable commodity, dear friends. Why? Forget forever Dieter Rantzau, the artist, the painter of portraits. Here the camera reigns supreme, and those who buy painters buy Picasso, Matisse, Braque, Chagall, Modigliani, Renoir.

This came as a blow. Fanny's inheritance is a modest sum, and we have drawn steadily on it since leaving Austria. Learning I could not paint for profit, I searched for a new trade.

I have one man to thank for my new career. He is Adolf Hitler. In Hollywood Hitler is big business, the biggest. The movies have a ready-made villain. The Nazis are immer the villains.

So far, in my first month, I have already worked in two

motion pictures, or simply pictures, as they say here. Only, if you see my two, you must look carefully. I am in and out like a flash.

Anyway, I could write a book about what has happened, dear friends. Fanny and I think of you often, and are afraid for you. For you Adolf Hitler is not a villain in a motion picture. For you the villain is real. Our thoughts and prayers are with you. Fanny joins me in warmest greetings and encloses a photograph of your two friends from the New World.

Magda folded the letter and raised the snapshot, looking at Dieter and Fanny on horses, facing the camera. "They must have tied her to the saddle," Magda murmured.

She stuffed the picture and letter into the envelope and rose, leaving the dressing room to burn it. Dieter Rantzau could have brought terrible trouble upon her. The Nazis were busting down doors, taking people from their beds. They could as easily open mail. With Ernst, the coward, loose in Vienna, she had enough trouble.

Magda reached the hallway and heard the doorbell. She stopped and began to tear the envelope, pulling it apart, pulling out the letter and the snapshot. She leaped back into the dressing room, tearing at the paper, trying to close the door with her shoulder, trying to give herself time. Then she heard a man say, "Nick Gallanz."

She took a deep breath. Magda stuffed the torn papers into her pocket and returned to the hallway. "Gal-l-l-l-anz!"

In the foyer Berte moved aside to admit Nick. Magda summoned him. "You're sure you're alone? The Gestapo wants you, wants all of you from the Zwischentheatre."

"You have old news," Nick said.

"Everything is old," Magda said. "You're too young for philosophy. We'll have a drink." She took him to the bar and poured herself a tumbler of scotch. "You?"

"Nothing," Nick said. "I didn't come for a drink. This isn't a courtesy call."

"No yelling," Magda said, raising her glass. "Since Ernst left, I'm not accustomed to yelling anymore. I'm now accustomed to silence." She took a big drink of scotch. "Talk softly or don't talk." She looked at Nick. "Don't tell me how you live like an animal, you're hunted like an animal, how your life hangs by a thread, how much danger you're in, how much you've suffered. This isn't a courtesy call," Magda said, and laughed bleakly. "You're here for you, not for me." She walked past him, on her way to her chair beside the winter garden, and Nick followed her.

In her chair she drank again. "Time for your speech," she said.

"I need money," Nick said. "I can't say exactly how much, but a lot."

"What collateral do you offer?"

Nick sprang forward, standing over her. "Stop your clever games. Stop playing the queen. This isn't the drafting room, where you can strut your stuff. This is life and death."

"Really," Magda said. She drained her glass. "I try to fool myself," she said. "I leave the whisky on the other side of the room because by walking to and fro I believe I drink less. Bring me the bottle." Nick glared at her, and she smiled. "Bring me the bottle and grow up."

She watched him stride across the lovely room. At least he had some spine. "Not that one! The square bottle!"

Nick brought her the decanter and she poured another drink. "Tell me your story," Magda said. "I promise nothing, but I have been alone so long I'll listen to anyone." She raised her hand. "Softly, softly."

"We're getting out," Nick said. He told her about Carly, about the meeting with Fritz, about the Safe Conduct Fritz had obtained.

"Fritz?" Magda set down her glass. "He's not a humanitarian. I've known him a long time. He's a nobleman, but noble?" Magda shook her head.

"We're friends," Nick said. "We're all friends," he said, and saw Carly, remembered her here at Magda's party, when they had all been together, when they had left together, squeezed into Fritz's little coupe. "He's giving us his car, the big car, the Daimler," Nick said. He remembered Carly and Fritz at the castle, waving good-bye as Fiegel drove him to the train. "We take the Daimler to the village and there find men who will lead us across the border. But I need money for those men and afterward, for hotels, for food. I can't move without money. I'm paralyzed. There's a car waiting, there's a Safe Conduct. I'm like a man who discovered a tunnel from Vienna to Italy but I can't enter because I don't have the admission fee."

"If you want my money, you take me," Magda said. "You take me with my money."

Nick said, "Fritz—" and Magda interrupted:

"There is room in the Daimler," Magda said. She pushed herself out of the chair. "Me with my money," she said. "This way."

As they walked through the apartment, Magda said, "I must leave Austria. I am in danger here. My husband is a cur. He could cook up

THE JUDAS KISS • 151

a scheme, a cur's scheme. He could go to the Nazis and tell them as a loyal Austrian and supporter of the National Socialist Party of the Greater German Reich, he puts honor, duty, country, before his personal life. He could tell them he left his wife because he discovered she was not only a Jew and a communist but a . . . lesbian or a . . . pickpocket."

They came to the foyer and Magda opened the door. "We'll go to the drafting room," she said. "Berte I trust, but the others, too, are loyal Austrians. You will call Fritz and I will listen. This is your collateral."

In the drafting room Nick telephoned the palace. "We're ready."

"The sooner the better," Fritz said. "How about Saturday?"

"Saturday, yes," Nick said. "Fritz, there will be one more. Magda Auerfeld."

"I'm not counting," Fritz said. "Come early Saturday, alone. Come at first light to the stable entrance in the courtyard."

"First light, stable entrance," Nick said. He set down the telephone. "You heard it all."

Magda looked around the drafting room. The apartment had become a graveyard, and her parents lay side by side in another graveyard. If she remained, Vienna would become her graveyard, and she did not plan on dying to please that ugly little bastard with the Charlie Chaplin mustache.

Magda opened a drawer of Ernst's desk and took out a large leather case. "Ernst's drafting instruments," she said. "My father bought this, so naturally Ernst can't use it now in the Greater German Reich." She shoved the case under Nick's arm. "You'll need to earn a living in Italy," she said, extending her hand. "We'll make a success, sonny."

At dawn Saturday morning Carly stood at her bedroom windows as though she could see the Daimler moving through the empty streets. She was losing Nick, losing him now as she looked out at the gray city in the daybreak silence. She tried to think only of the good times with Nick, the good days and nights, before the Germans, the days roaming through Vienna, the nights at the Zwischentheatre, the nights when they were alone.

There had been no hesitation between them, no fumbling, no shy embarrassment, no awkwardness, from the beginning, from that first day in Max's apartment. She would never have Nick again, never feel him. She had lost Nick, lost everything, and she knew, ashen and desolate, that she would not even be allowed to mourn. Fritz waited. Fritz waited. Fritz.

Fritz came awake long before dawn, and he was ready long before Nick arrived. Alone, Fritz opened the massive courtyard gates, and he remained beside them until he spotted a figure in the distance. "All set," Fritz said as Nick approached.

In the stables Fritz opened the Daimler door. "Your Safe Conduct is in the glove compartment." He stepped aside. "Move it! Move!"

Nick took the door and stepped on the running board. "You're saving lives," he said. "We owe you our lives."

"You have a long road ahead," Fritz said.

Nick got into the car. "If you should see Carly—if you . . . ," he said, and stopped. He started the engine. Fritz followed the Daimler into the courtyard to the open gates. He walked into the street and remained until the limousine turned at the corner.

In Este Platz, Magda waited with Berte. "Repeat what I said," and, sharply, "without tears!"

The old woman said, "When I woke you were gone. You told me nothing. I know nothing. Your clothes are here, in place. Monday morning I go to the other apartment, your parents' apartment." Berte raised the envelope Magda had given her. "Here is my proof." Magda had transferred ownership of the apartment which her parents had willed to her.

"Good, good," Magda said. "Now I leave," she said. "We kiss and I leave. Without tears." She opened her arms and enveloped the old woman she had known all her life. She felt Berte's shoulders shaking. "Enough," she said, and pushed Berte aside. "Without tears!"

Magda left the apartment carrying her purse. Around her middle, against her bare skin, she wore a velvet belt, like a money belt, and in it she had stuffed every ring, bracelet, diamond choker, diamond tiara, and earring she owned, including everything she had taken from her parents' apartment. Magda waited in front of the building, and as she sighted the Daimler, stepped into the curb, ready to go, to go.

She got into the front seat beside Nick and he drove through Este Platz. "Turn here," Magda said. "*Turn!*" Nick obeyed and turned once more, into the Rennweg. "Too slow," Magda said. "Too slow, move, move, move."

Nick stopped the Daimler. "Are you mad?" Magda cried. "Gallanz!"

He set the emergency brake. "Gallanz!" she cried, and Nick said, "Shut up!" turning in the seat. "Quiet!" He put his forefinger to his lips. "Be still. Absolutely still." The only sound in the limousine came from the idling engine.

"Good," Nick said, like a teacher praising a recalcitrant student. "Listen, for your sake. We're starting a long day, a dangerous day, the most dangerous day and night of our lives. We're crossing a country full of enemies. So I will not take enemies with me. I have my load." Nick pointed at the empty rear seat. "Three broken-winged chicks in a coop who cannot fly, who wait for me to carry them. I carry them and there is no room for anyone else. You can fly. You made your conditions for this journey. You and your money, you said. All right. But not your mouth. I'm not driving through Austria under your directions. I know this country, too. So you can stay, you and your money, but silently. Silently. And no arguments, no rebuttals, no debates. No *debates*. We travel under my rules. I make the rules. You accept the rules. You must accept. You came too far already to turn back. You are committed. And remember this, too. You are with me today. I am not with you today." Magda almost kissed him.

Nick swung around, releasing the emergency brake and shifting gears. Magda sat beside him silently as he drove to Leopoldstadt. He parked in the alley, and Sam, who had been standing in the delivery entrance watching for the limousine, said, "Mama, Papa, he's here." He went into the basement for Lottie and Boris Gallanz. "Nick is here."

Nick jumped out of the Daimler, rushing toward them. "Hurry, hurry," he said. He frowned as he saw the small suitcase his mother carried. "I told you, Mama. We bring nothing."

She held it under her chin, squeezing it against her chest. "My mother's silver ladles," she pleaded.

"Nick, it's one little bag," Sam said.

"We're out for a joyride," Nick said. "We're having a day in the country. We're not *fleeing*."

"Nick, it's one little bag," Sam said.

"Get in the car, Sam," Nick said, pushing his brother. "Take Papa." He pushed his father before turning to Lottie. "Give me the bag," he said, tugging at the suitcase. It slipped out of Lottie's hands, and she cried out. Nick flung the suitcase against the building, taking his mother to the Daimler.

That early in the morning Nick had the streets to himself. Nearing the outskirts of the city, Nick was picking up speed, ready for the open road, when he saw the barriers ahead. In the same moment Sam jabbed him in the back. "Nick!"

"Soldiers!" Lottie said.

Boris craned his neck. "Soldiers?"

"Not a word!" Nick said, speaking into the rearview mirror. "Not a goddamn word." He glanced at Magda. "From anyone."

Soldiers on both sides of the road flanked the checkpoint. Nick stepped on the brake, and the soldiers moved on the big sedan.

As Nick rolled down his window, a lieutenant strolled toward the Daimler like he intended to buy it. He stopped beside Nick, looking into the limousine, looking from one occupant to another, slowly. Except for the blonde in the front seat, none of them belonged in a Daimler. "Where did you get the car?"

"It belongs to the Baron Fritz Von Gottisberg," Nick said.

"Sounds right," said the lieutenant. "Why are you in it instead of him? You and yours?"

"The baron is my friend," Nick said, feeling the lieutenant's hatred.

"You wouldn't be dumb enough to steal it," said the lieutenant. "Where do you think you're going?"

"To Innsbruck," Nick said, and leaned across Magda to open the glove compartment. "To visit some relatives."

The lieutenant examined the occupants once more. "Want to bet?"

Nick offered the envelope. "I have this." As the officer took the envelope, Nick pushed in the clutch pedal and inched the gear shift out of neutral. Nick had decided long before that the Nazis would not take him.

The lieutenant read the Safe Conduct and looked at the swine in the Daimler. The swine had been playing with him. "I'll remember you," said the lieutenant.

They were stopped twice more that day, at Steyr, and in midafternoon at Mondsee, beside the lake. They were confronted by the same scorn at each of the checkpoints.

Then their luck changed. A deserted road stretched ahead. When Nick stopped for gasoline, Magda opened her door. "At last a toilet."

They had come through the foothills and were in the Alps, climbing and turning as the road followed the contours of the mountains. Late in April, the first wildflowers were blooming despite patches of snow in the meadows, and they saw small bursts of color in all directions. The mountains were capped with snow, and above the glistening white mantle to the west, an early amber moon was cushioned among the white peaks in the sky.

Nick turned and the schloss lay in his path, high above. He saw the windows glowing red in the last moments of sunlight, saw the towers and turrets they had explored with Fritz. And he saw Carly dressed for a day in the fields and forests. He could see her in the evening in the candlelight.

"Where do we stop?" Magda asked.

He didn't know. "Up ahead. I'll show you," Nick said. Climbing, he caught sight of the castle again and again until he turned onto the crest of a long, sloping hill and drove down into a meadow. As the sun dropped and the shadows moved across the meadow, Nick saw an abandoned, rusting hayfork. "I'll leave you here."

"Why are we stopping here?" Magda asked. Nick ignored her, leaving the Daimler to help his mother and father out of the limousine. Magda turned in the front seat, lowering her feet to the running board, reaching for Nick's hand. "You need a ladder for this car," she said. "I will not miss this car."

Nick held on to her. "I need money for the guides," he said.

Magda reached inside her coat pocket for her father's wallet. "I could say something."

"In Italy," Nick said, folding the money Magda gave him. He got back into the Daimler and turned on the headlights. Although he had been in the village with Carly and Fritz, Nick did not remember it well.

He drove into a hamlet with one street and homes scattered behind the street and in the mountainsides. There were shops on both sides of the street for several hundred feet and then fields once more. Nick passed one garage with open doors but no identifying signs. "Come on, come on, come on," he said.

He could find no other garage, and when he returned to the open doors, he swung the wheel. Inside, the Daimler's headlights lit up a long one-story building lined with cars, some covered with tarpaulins, some in various stages of being cannibalized. As an elderly man in overalls came away from a bench, Nick pushed down the two metal safety teats on the Beretta in his pocket. "Otto Kesselring?"

"Kesselring," said the old man.

"You know this car," Nick said. "Baron Von Gottisberg's car. He told me to leave it with you." Nick stayed clear of the old man, peering into the corners of the garage. He could easily be trapped in the garage. Otto Kesselring could be a Nazi, or he could be dead with a Nazi in overalls substituting for the old man. Nick had been a target since March 12, and all strangers were dangerous. But he had to gamble on the old man. "I'm on a little holiday," Nick said. "I'd like to see the country around here. Do you know someone who could show me the country?" The old man looked past Nick into the street, and Nick whirled around, pushing his finger through the gun's trigger guard.

"Try the hunt club," said Kesselring. "Go left to the top of the street."

"Sure," Nick said. "The top of the street."

Turning left outside, he suddenly noticed a large swastika fluttering overhead. Nick had been searching for the garage and had not seen the Nazi standard. He walked under the swastika like he was scaling a fence. It hung from the *Rathaus*, the city hall.

He walked along the street, passing shops, toward the darkness beyond the village. He passed a cobbler and thought he had left the town but found a chalet set back from the line of stores. Stag horns were mounted over the entrance. Nick climbed wooden steps. The windows were steamed over.

Inside, a large room ran the length of the chalet. More horns were mounted over a long bar. There men stood shoulder to shoulder, facing bartenders who wore Tyrolean hats with feathers. Other men sat at tables drinking, and many of them wore hats as well. A man left the bar with a beer stein in each hand, stopping beside Nick. "This is a private place, *mein herr*."

The voices in the chalet fell, and at the bar the drinkers looked at the stranger. Everyone looked at him. "Otto Kesselring sent me," Nick said. "I have a few days off and I'm looking for someone to show me the area."

A bartender said, "Try the Rathaus. They'll show you the area."

Another man said, "They'll arrange a one-way passage for you," and many of the men laughed.

The man with the beer steins set them down and went to the door. "I'm sorry. Members only."

"Sure," Nick said. In the street, lights burned in the shops, and a spotlight played on the swastika. He thought of his family and Magda standing around the hayfork in the dark. He could hear Magda swearing.

Fritz had told him he would find a guide in the village. Nick hurried back to the garage to get help from Otto Kesselring. The garage doors were locked. Nick heard a piano. He came to a small store with café curtains across the window. Inside, a boy sat at an upright piano and a woman stood over him, her hand moving up and down, keeping the beat. She looked kindly, and Nick decided to take a chance on her.

"Mein herr."

Nick heard a man hail someone. Looking at a car beyond the piano teacher's shop, he saw the driver, a man in a beret, holding the open door. "I'll give you a lift," the man said.

Had he seen a beret among the Tyrolean hats in the chalet? Nick convinced himself he had seen the beret so he could get into the car. "Close the door."

The driver looked older than Nick, in his thirties. "It costs money to see the country around here," the man said.

"I have money," Nick said. They drove out of the village, and once in the darkness the driver stopped the car.

"My name is Paul Grietze," he said to the city boy in the city clothes. "Some tours cost a lot of money," he added. "Do you have a special tour in mind?"

"Name a special tour," Nick said.

"Italy," said Paul Grietze. "Italy costs a lot of money."

"Are we safe sitting here?" Nick asked.

"Where have you been lately? No one is safe any longer, here, there, anywhere," Grietze said. "Money."

"We can pay," Nick said.

"How many are you?"

"There are a few persons with me," Nick said. "What's the difference whether you take one or twenty-one?"

Grietze pulled off his gloves. "You've seen horse races, right?" he said. "Someone is always first and someone is always last. Everyone else is strung out in between. On a tour we can travel only as fast as the slowest among us." He put his gloves together, finger to finger, and set them on the dashboard. "How many? How many men, how many women, and the ages, especially the ages."

"We're five," Nick said. "Three men and two women." Nick told Grietze the ages, guessing at Magda's.

"We're now talking about a whole lot of money," Grietze said. He gave Nick the figure.

"Satisfactory," Nick said, counting from the stack Magda had given him. He extended the bills.

"You're only halfway there," Grietze said.

"When we see Italy, you see the other half," Nick said. He held the money in front of Grietze's face. "I'm taking a chance with you," Nick said. "You're a stranger and I'm in a strange place. You picked me up from the street. You could take this and I'll never see you again."

"*You're* taking a chance?" Grietze said. "You could be a Nazi. There's a law now against leaving the country. What's so funny?"

Here in the Alps, for Nick as mysterious and foreign as the Congo, a smile crossed his face, however fleeting. He took Grietze's hand and shoved the money into it. "Straight ahead," Nick said. "I'll tell you when to stop."

They drove in silence. "Almost," Nick said, pointing. "There. The hayfork." Nick had the door open before the car stopped. "It's me," he said to soothe his chicks. "Everything is fine."

"Not with that moon," Grietze said. The moon had risen above the peaks and lay high overhead, ripe as a peach and burning bright. "Damn moon," Grietze said. "There'll be two of us."

"When do we leave?" Nick asked, and saw Magda walk into the road.

"When we come for you," Grietze said. "Tell her to stay the hell out of sight." He gunned the engine and shot off, drenching Magda in exhaust fumes.

Nick pulled her off the road. "He's the guide. He'll be back with another guide." Nick looked at her in the moonlight. "Now you know what I know," he said to stop an interrogation.

He approached the hayfork like a cheerleader. "We're all set," he said. "We're on the way."

Boris Gallanz said, "I think God is tired of us. I think God said good-bye in Vienna."

Nick pointed at the sky. "We're a lot closer to Him up here, Papa. Give Him another chance." Nick prodded Sam. "Counselor, we're bound for Italy. You'll be drinking espresso tomorrow morning."

"Your voice carries," Sam said.

Nick's mother grabbed him. "It's a bad sign when Papa gives up. He scares us."

"I'll keep you at my side," Nick said. "He doesn't scare me."

They waited for hours. The temperature dropped steadily, and Magda began to pace. "Where are they? Warm in bed with their wives," she said.

Before Nick could confront her, Sam said, "I hear something."

"Quiet!" Magda said. Nobody spoke, nobody moved, until Sam pointed.

"Over there," he said, and they all heard footsteps, boots on sand and pebbles. Nick saw two figures crossing the road.

"Relax, everyone," said Paul Grietze. He and his companion, Felix Nestroy, a tall, sinewy man, were in ski pants and sweaters. Grietze went from one to the other of the five pilgrims, peering at each. "We have fifteen kilometers," he said.

"Let's go, let's go," said Felix Nestroy. He wore gloves and began to clap his hands.

Grietze tapped his chest. "I lead, I'm number one." He pointed at Magda. "Two." He pointed at Lottie. "Three. Four," he said, pointing at Sam.

"I'm four," Nick said.

"You're not in charge," said Nestroy, and to Grietze, "Straighten him out, fast."

"Sure," Nick said. "I'm four." He went to Grietze. "Who's five, my friend?"

"Five," Grietze said, gesturing at Boris. "Six," he said, pointing at Sam. "We're off."

As Grietze crossed the road, Nestroy nudged Sam. "I follow you." Nick held his mother's hand. They dropped down into a deep meadow, but in less than a kilometer they began to climb.

The land rose gradually, but from that point on they climbed steadily. Nick felt the beginnings of a stitch in his side and then a sharp pain in his rib cage where his broken ribs had mended. He bent forward, trying to make it easier, trying not to give himself away. But the pain in his chest persisted, sharper, and he grunted. Grietze looked back. "How is she?"

Nick held on to Lottie. "A mountain goat," he said.

"We'll be in the woods in an hour," Grietze said. "Once we're away from the moon, we're mostly out of danger."

At the tail end of the column, Felix Nestroy joined Boris. "You're doing real good," Nestroy said, hoping he wouldn't need to leave the old man. Even in April they could be in thirty inches of snow within three kilometers.

They continued in silence, climbing beneath the lovely amber moon. Nick tried to count off the seconds, deliberately biting into his lip to forget the pain in his chest and the stabbing stitch across his belly. He began to pant, putting his glove over his mouth to muffle the sound. He needed to rest, but he couldn't stop the caravan. He said, "Can't stop the caravan," to himself, repeating the words slowly, again and again, until Grietze said, "Almost." Nick looked up and saw trees ahead. "We'll take a break there," Grietze said.

The moonlight couldn't penetrate the dense fir and pine. Nick leaned against a tree, breathing deeply, waiting for the pain to subside, making himself jolly for his family. After a while he joined the guides. "How much farther?"

"Less than you think," Nestroy said.

"Between two and three kilometers," Grietze added. "Closer to two." He turned on a flashlight and walked into the woods. The thin beam of light vanished.

"There's a trail," Nestroy said. "Paul will find it. He just did." Nick saw a faint light low to the ground.

Grietze returned. "We'll keep the same order," he said. "We'll hit some ice, so watch for it. We've come too far for an accident this close to the end."

Grietze did not push them, and Nick proceeded without discomfort. Soon they were above the timberline. They rarely spoke. Even Magda fell silent. They approached huge boulders and between the massive rocks were patches of snow and ice. "Careful now," Grietze said. He looked back at Magda. "Stay clear of the ice. Tell them."

They saw water glistening and soon came to a tiny lake. Grietze made a wide turn away from it. Ahead and above them stood an *Alpenheutte*, a small, sturdy hut that was home for cowherds who grazed their cattle in the mountains during the summer months. Grietze stopped and Nick saw Nestroy walk past everyone to join the leader. Nick followed. "Yes?"

Nestroy grinned, nudging Grietze, who smiled and raised his arm, pointing. "Italy. Less than a kilometer."

Nick swung around, spreading his arms. "Italy!"

Magda blew the hair out of her eyes and hit Nick in the behind. "We made it, sonny!"

"Couldn't have done it without you," Nick said.

Sam rushed forward, squinting into the night as though he could see St. Peter's. He hugged his baby brother, his savior. "Where's my espresso?"

Then Boris claimed Nick. "Come here," he said. "Let me kiss you." Nick leaned forward and Boris kissed him on the cheek.

"Let me kiss you, too," Lottie said.

Nick bent over his mother. Grietze watched the celebration. "*Mein herr.*"

"A minute," Nick said. He left his mother, taking money from his pocket. He paid Grietze, who said, "Done and done. Straight down from the Alpenheutte to Italy. Don't stop and don't stop when you cross the border."

"Done and done," Nick said. As he spoke, a Nazi in uniform,

with a gun, ran out of the Alpenheutte above them. "Halt! Don't move! Nobody move!"

Nick pulled the Beretta from his coat, flipping off the safety teats.

Another Nazi came out running, gun raised, and then four more plunged through the Alpenheutte door. They were from the village and outlying farms, new converts since the Anschluss, untrained and undisciplined, all armed and all shouting commands. Lottie screamed and Boris's voice rose in terror, terrorizing the Nazis.

Grietze and Nestroy dropped onto their bellies, crawling, and Sam, trying to escape, stumbled over them. He stayed erect, running, and a Nazi shot him in the back. Nick fired, killing the Nazi. "Get down! Get down!" he yelled. He hit another Nazi and the man spun, clapping his hand to his shoulder and staggering. "Get down!" Nick yelled, shooting.

Magda went to her knees, trying to take Lottie down with her. But Lottie stood over Sam until she was hit. She cried out and as she crumpled, Nick raised the Beretta, looking for another target, and felt a white hot poker dig into his right arm. His gun dropped, and he grabbed his wrist, his hands sticky with the blood pouring from the wound.

One Nazi quit and ran. Another ran. The wounded Nazi yelled, "Don't leave me! Don't leave me!" after them.

Nick fell, pawing for his gun with his left hand. He found it and got his finger through the trigger guard, but his hand was bloody and slippery. He couldn't get a solid grip on the butt to raise the gun. He could see the Nazis escaping, even the wounded Nazi, but he couldn't stop them. His right arm was on fire. He tried to rise and lost the gun, falling hard, unable to stifle a long groan of agony. He put his left hand flat on the gun, curling his fingers around it and raising it. He had to stand, to get to his feet. He came up by inches, sweating in the cold night. He got to his feet, swaying, head bowed down by the torment in his wrist, holding the Beretta in his left hand, a wild figure, an apparition.

Nick saw Sam facedown in the snow turning red with blood, and knew his brother was dead. His mother was a bundle of rags near Sam, and Nick knew she was dead. Nick saw his father standing alone, weeping. Boris had lost his hat, and his hair blew in the wind. Nick took one step, then another, kept going until he was beside his father, but Boris didn't acknowledge him. Boris looked straight at him, weeping, tears falling across his face. "Lottie," Boris said. "Sam. They killed

Lottie and Sam." Nick had to get away because he wanted to hit his father.

Standing near a boulder, Magda saw the gargoyle on his way, the grotesque, moving like he had just learned to walk, a teetering, tottering step at a time. "They were waiting," Nick said, dumbfounded. "They were waiting for us," he said, forced to accept the shattering truth. "They knew we were coming," he said, and louder, "They knew we would come!"

Magda saw his right hand, his wrist. "You're shot!"

He ignored her. "They were sent there! Someone sent the Nazis to trap us and kill us!" Magda was with a wild man. "This was an ambush!" Nick said. "This was a planned ambush!"

"Listen, we must go immediately," Magda said. "If they came once, they can come again." She looked into the wild man's eyes. "They can come again." Her arm shot out. "Italy! Get the old man!"

He ignored her. "They hid in the Alpenheutte for the mice to walk into the trap," Nick said, and then, his voice ringing in the night, "We were betrayed!"

"I know this already," Magda said. "Listen," she said, pointing. "There is Italy. We're going to Italy. You'll have to see a doctor." She took his left arm. "Italy!"

He shook her off. "Who betrayed us? Who sent us here to die? They sent us here to die!" he raved. "But why send us here? They gave me a Safe Conduct. We had a *Safe Conduct*," he said, trapping Magda against the boulder as though he had to convince her. "Fritz gave me his car. Why send us here to kill us? They could have killed us in Vienna." He looked down at the bodies in the snow. "They killed off my family. Sam never hurt a single human being on this earth. My mother never hurt a single human being on this earth." He stopped, staring at Magda. "Did you see where the guides went?" He turned, and as he did so, he started to fall, but Magda grabbed him, keeping him erect. "I don't see any dead guides. I only see my dead family," he said, pulling himself free and leaving Magda, crossing the battlefield, making his wobbly way toward the Alpenheutte.

Magda left the boulder, staying clear of the bodies in the snow. She got to Boris and said, "We're going now." She pushed him. "Come on, we're going."

She could see Nick swaying ahead of her, and as she followed, towing Boris, she saw Nick drop. He rose to his knees and raised his left arm. As she drew closer, she saw a Nazi on the ground, then Nick holding the blunt barrel of the Beretta, hitting the Nazi with the butt, his arm rising and falling until Magda squatted and pulled him away. "He's dead. You cannot kill him twice."

Sometime before dawn they came to Merano, a town in the Italian Alps. A few streetlights burned, and in the glow of one Magda saw the word, "LOCANDA," inn, on a wall. She began to pound on the door. "Open up!"

She continued banging until she heard shutters creaking above her and saw light. Magda stepped back as someone leaned out of the window. "Come back in the morning."

"I've got a sick man," she said. "I can pay."

"In the morning," said the innkeeper, reaching for the shutters.

"You," Nick said, and to Magda, "Hold on to me." Magda put her weight against him, and gasping, his breath coming in fast bursts, Nick pointed the Beretta at the window. "Let us in before I kill you," Nick said. "I'll *kill* you!"

The innkeeper saw the bloody scarecrow holding the gun. "Give me a chance to dress," he said. "Just let me get my clothes."

The shutters closed. Magda got Nick to the wall of the inn, and Boris followed them. They could hear the wind whistling down through the mountain passes. "If he doesn't come soon, I'll kill him myself," Magda said as the door opened.

The owner, a stooped man with a long nose, faced them. His name was Pietro Vincelli. After looking down at the gun in the bloody hand, he pulled his pants on over long underwear. His bare feet were in espadrilles, and he was freezing. "Come in! Come in!" he said, shivering, but nobody moved. Boris didn't hear him, and Magda held up Nick.

"Are you blind? Help me!" Magda said. The Italian took Nick's right arm, and he groaned, a long, expiring croak of agony, and slumped against Magda. Vincelli came out of the locanda, shivering. With him in front and Magda behind Nick, all three sidled into the inn ahead of Boris, who followed the procession.

"Over here," said Vincelli, moving sideways, with Nick between him and Magda. "On the couch there." Pulling and pushing, they crossed the narrow lobby to a sagging sofa, and as they lowered him to the cushions, Nick's head fell back, he lost consciousness, and there, mercifully, the night of the holocaust ended.

Magda pushed her hands into her back, rubbing, while Vincelli shuffled to the entrance and closed the door. When he returned, Magda said, "First, whiskey. Don't worry about money. There is money." She followed Vincelli. "Two, get a doctor." She looked at Nick, on his back on the sofa, his right arm over the side, blood dripping from the wound in his wrist.

Vincelli opened a cabinet. "Wine, Strega, or brandy?" he said.

Magda took the bottle of brandy. "Get the doctor."

"In the morning," Vincelli said.

"A glass," she said, removing the bottle top. She took a long swig from the bottle. Pietro gave her a glass, and she poured three fingers of brandy into it. "Get the doctor or I'll get him. And when he's finished, I'll move across the street with my money." She drank from the glass. "Hurry, man. I don't want him dying on me."

Early the previous evening, in the palace in the Himmelpfortgasse, Colonel Friedrich Varlingen said, "Baron, I have never seen a more attractive home."

"Frankly, Colonel, neither have I," Fritz said.

Varlingen shook his head and laughed. "Neither have I," Varlingen echoed. "Very good, Baron."

They were twelve for dinner. Fritz lingered beside Varlingen, Der Chineser's superior. "Since I'm being honest, I'm not one of the world's best hosts," Fritz said. "This is a bachelor's house."

"You could change that fast enough," Varlingen said. "*I* would," he said, gesturing at Carly, who stood beside the piano with another colonel.

Fritz eyed her in turn. Carly wore a pale blue dress, cut low so that it dropped below her shoulders. She had a bright ribbon in her hair, which lay across her bare back. Although spring had only started, her face had already tanned. She wore a faint shade of lipstick, and she looked like a skier just back from the slopes. "She is a pretty girl," Fritz said.

"She is ravishing, Baron, and you know it," Varlingen said. "She is unmarried or she would not be here with you. Seize her."

Fritz raised his glass, acknowledging Varlingen's suggestion. "It's a thought."

Carly held a glass of vermouth which she had not tasted, afraid she would be ill if she drank. Fritz had surrounded her with men who would kill Nick on sight. She listened to a major beside her talking about his children, loyal daughters of the Third Reich. She listened hard, trying to obliterate the thought of Nick somewhere in the Alps.

Seeing Fritz leave the officer with whom he had been chatting, she excused herself. "Fritz?" When he reached her, she murmured, "I'm going home."

Fritz assumed one of the ten pigs had insulted her. "Tell me exactly what happened."

"I can't stay," she said. "I can't face these . . . people. I tried, but I can't. I'll say I'm sick or something. Anything."

"You shouldn't be alone tonight," Fritz said. "Not tonight, of all nights."

"Anything is better than eating with Nazis."

"Carly." He touched her hand and then took her fingers. "I'm not a Nazi."

She said, "I remember what I've seen them doing to people, to innocent men and women, to children.

Fritz smiled in the event any of his guests were watching them. "This isn't the time, but it must be said, Carly. I've told you before, I entertain them. I won't stop. That means you won't stop because you will be here. They are here, Carly. They are the rulers. So we must live with them. But we will survive them. We'll rid Austria of these . . . vermin."

"When I listen to you, I can almost believe it," Carly said.

"I state this as a fact," Fritz said. "So you can believe it. And you can leave. This time. I'll make the excuses for you. But you won't be able to hide. I won't be able to hide you. They've won, Carly, but in the end we will win."

She looked at the glass in her hand. "You're much braver than I am."

"Carly." When she looked up, Fritz said, "No one is braver than you." He had never been more honest. "Ready?" He took her elbow.

Fritz had seated her at Varlingen's right. "Miss Siefermann," Varlingen said. "Correct?"

"Carly," she said. "Carly is all right." He saw her hands in her lap, saw her knuckles become white as she squeezed her hands.

He said so that only they could hear, "Do you hate us that much?"

Carly raised her head, startled, and immediately looked away, separating her hands. She forced herself to face him. "I feel as though you've been spying on me."

"You are correct," Varlingen said. "I *am* a spy. That is what I do. Even an army needs policemen, and for many years I have been a policeman. If the fates had made me a jeweler, I could tell you the exact worth of the ring you are wearing, of the cuff links in the baron's shirt. But I am a cop. In my trade I index humanity. It becomes a habit."

Because she hated the colonel, Carly forgot to be afraid of him. "So you are always working."

She made him smile. "I said, it becomes a habit. If a woman is squeezing her hands, she is trying not to scream." He shook his head slowly, patiently. "We have not come to Austria with instructions to frighten women and children, Miss Siefermann."

"But you didn't bring toys," Carly said. "You brought guns and tanks."

"I'm not only a cop, I'm a soldier," Varlingen said. "I follow orders."

Just then Fritz rose, holding his glass. "We Austrians are an old, old breed. We have welcomed many guests. Now we welcome the Greater German Reich."

Everyone drank and Carly knew the colonel waited for her to drink. She sipped the wine. "I didn't welcome you, Colonel," Carly said. "I wasn't in the street, throwing flowers at your soldiers."

The colonel wondered if she had more guts than brains. He tapped his glass with his knife. "Gentlemen, gentlemen. Miss Siefermann has told me that when we entered Vienna, she did not rush forward with flowers for our troops. We must convert her. The Reich has a place for someone with Miss Siefermann's candor."

The colonel made dinner and the evening easier for Carly. He didn't act like a soldier or a policeman. He didn't talk about himself like the other guests. When the Nazis were leaving, he bent over her hand. "You are as intelligent as you are beautiful."

As the last guest left, Carly whirled around. "Fritz! Is Nick there? Is he in Italy?"

Fritz pushed back his sleeve to look at his wristwatch, and then he nodded. "They've crossed the border."

Carly clasped her hands. "Thank you, Fritz."

He went for her coat. "You should sleep soundly tonight," he said.

"You've made it possible," Carly said.

They walked through the palace into the courtyard to the coupe. They rode to Kruger Strasse without speaking. Fritz slid across the seat, following Carly out of the car and into the apartment building.

"Well . . ." Fritz said. "Onward."

Carly could not send him away like a stranger. He had saved her as well as Nick. She leaned forward, catching Fritz off guard, and kissed him, her lips warm and moist.

"Good night . . . dear," she said.

Fritz crossed the lobby. He could feel Carly's lips, feel Carly. But in the street, in the lonely night, she slipped away once more, he lost her once more.

8

ONE AFTERNOON IN ROME in late spring that year Magda left the hotel, walking to a small park nearby. She found an empty bench and sat in the center to discourage any uninvited companions. She dug her glasses out of her pocket, setting them low on her nose, and opened her purse to get the letter which had come to the hotel that morning. Carly had written CS and the Kruger Strasse address in the left-hand corner of the big envelope. "*Scheiss,*" Magda said, raising the letter which she had already read twice.

Dear, dear Magda,

I found you! In Rome! I can't believe I am writing to you. I am so happy I can barely write. See how I write? See the letters, slanted and choppy? My hand is shaking, my fingers . . . and I'm crying. Just now I had to stop until I could stop crying. You are safe! And if you are safe, Nick is safe! Now I'm crying again.

Wait . . . Now I'm back. Crybaby. I'm not even ashamed. I'm too happy to be ashamed.

I've just come from seeing Berte at your parents's apartment. And she gave me your address.

She saved me. I've been crazed. It seems like ten years since you left. I haven't counted the days, I have counted the minutes. Not a minute has passed since that Saturday morning in April when I have not thought of you, prayed for you, prayed for me, because if something had happened, I would have been lost, too. If you had not survived, I could not survive.

And since that Saturday, I have been waiting to hear from you. Why hasn't Nick written? I've asked that question a thousand times. Why this silence?

This morning I could no longer bear it. I had come to the limit. I could not live through another day of silence. I went to Este Platz. I could not take a chance on slipping past Ernst coming out of the drafting room, so I paid the doorman to fetch your maid, the young one. And she sent me to Berte with whom you have, blessedly, communicated.

Dear Magda, I can't stop writing. I say the same things over and over. I'm afraid to stop, afraid I will lose you again, lose Nick again . . .

Magda lowered Carly's letter and folded it. She took the small envelope sealed and marked "NICK," from the large envelope. She tore "NICK" first, tearing the letter and then the envelope to bits. She tore the large envelope and her letter. She filled her purse with the shreds of paper and left the bench, walking through the park to a large refuse can. Nick did not need that little bitch back in his life.

When Magda returned to the hotel after a massage, she promised not to have a drink until six o'clock. She could not allow scotch to rule her life. The concierge came out from his station. "*Signora,*" he said, looking up at the ceiling and shaking his head.

Magda knew someone had died. "Which one?" She hit the concierge in the chest. "Quickly! Which one?"

When she left the concierge, she passed the bar as though snubbing someone, choosing a chair facing the doors. She stayed until long after night fell, until she saw him enter the lobby. "Nick."

He carried his right arm across his chest. A thick plaster cast covered his arm from the wrist to the elbow. He had always been lean, but in the last few weeks Nick had become cadaverous. He looked like someone starving. Whenever Magda urged him to eat, he left the hotel dining room. Magda didn't know him. He was alone even when they were together, even when they were in a crowd. He had seceded. The world no longer interested him. As he crossed the lobby, Magda pushed herself out of the chair. "I must tell you. Your father is dead."

He looked at her as though she had killed Boris. "A maid found him on his bed in his clothes," Magda said. "He's still there." Nick walked past her. She caught up with him at the stairs. She had to say something. "At least he didn't suffer."

"Not since the Alps," Nick said. "He's been dead since that night in the Alps."

In the room Nick had shared with his father, he raised the sheet covering the body. Behind him the concierge, who had followed him, stopped in the doorway. "Signor, forgive this intrusion in your time of grief. We wait for your instructions, Signor." Nick glared at him, and the Italian stepped back into the corridor. "Funeral instructions, Signor. We have available to you a list of the finest funeral directors in Rome. I assure you, Signor, the finest."

Nick let the sheet fall as though he had dropped something into a wastebasket. "Take him," Nick said, leaving the bed, passing Magda as though she was invisible. "The medical schools are always short. He can make up the shortage."

Magda pushed Nick, hating him. They would be cutting off Boris's arms, his fingers. They would gouge out his eyes, rip open his belly. She despised Nick Gallanz, despised him!

In the morning, Magda waylaid Nick. "Listen, you. I am not a governess sitting in the park with my baby. I sit here, alone. They shot your wrist, not your tongue. Talk to me."

"They made me an orphan," Nick said as though Magda had asked him for the right time.

"They made me an orphan, too," Magda said. "But I am alive. I'm living! You stopped! You want to die."

When he looked at her, Magda felt like a victim. "I'll never die," Nick said. "They had their chance."

"Ja, ja," Magda said, bored with the melodrama. "We should make plans. This hotel is not cheap, and Italians anyway are not my favorites." She waited. "Say something."

"All right," Nick said. "Sure." He left her, crossing the lobby to the concierge.

"Signor Gallanz!" said the concierge, smiling at the ghoul who had turned his father over to students with knives. "Deepest sympathies, Signor. How can I serve you?"

Nick raised his right arm. "Find me a doctor."

"An orthopedist," said the concierge, setting a telephone book on the counter. "Professor de Lisi. Absolutely the finest in Italy." He leaned over the counter, whispering, "Ciano's doctor."

The concierge telephoned and spoke rapidly. "Ciao," he said, and to Nick, "He can see you in a month, in the . . . ," the concierge broke off, running his pencil along a large calendar pasted to the counter. ". . . in thirty-six days. But this is Rome, Signor. We find another."

Nick closed the telephone book. "Get me a hammer."

The concierge raised his head slowly, looking at the plaster cast, looking at the ghost. "Signor . . ."

"Do it," Nick said. The concierge set aside the telephone book carefully, like someone in terrible danger. "In the repair shop," he said. "In the basement, Signor. This way."

Nick raised his left arm, stopping the concierge. "I'll find the basement."

The repair shop was a brightly lit room lined with steel shelves. Nick saw stacks of light bulbs, window shades, upright lamps in clusters, faucets and doorknobs and doors against a wall. He walked toward a dirty, cluttered desk. Behind him someone said, "Ciao."

A man in overalls carrying an open wooden toolbox walked through the shop. Over his heart was stenciled "ANGELO." "I need a hammer," Nick said.

"Let me help," Angelo said. "Tell me the problem, Signor." Nick raised the cast. Angelo set down the toolbox. "A doctor put that on you," he said. "A doctor should take it off."

"Sure," Nick said, taking a hammer out of the toolbox. Angel put his hand over the hammer head.

"What happened?" he asked.

"I had an accident," Nick said.

"With a hammer you'll have another accident," Angelo said. "Let go." He turned the hammer head counterclockwise. "Let go," he said. "I'm stronger."

Angelo pushed the hammer into his toolbox. "A doctor really should do this," he said. "Sit on the desk." He took a coping saw from the toolbox and tightened the wing nut holding the blade. "Put your arm across your legs."

Angelo began to saw between the wrist and the elbow. A thin

film of white powder rose from the cast. He did not pause, and soon on both sides of the blade, the cast shifted and sagged. Angelo set down the coping saw, pushing his fingers into the slot he had cut in the plaster of paris. He yanked hard and the cast separated. Angelo held up the two sections. "You are free."

Nick looked down at his bare arm, very white, the skin puckered like the skin of someone old and frail. High in his wrist lay a small crater made by the Nazi bullet. The bullet had smashed both bones of the forearm, the ulna and radius, lodging in the compartment above the metacarpals, the long, delicate, and intricate bones of the hands. Nick raised his arm, looking into his palm. He bent his fingers, and when the discomfort prevented further articulation, his hand had become a claw. Nick slipped off the desk. "Thanks."

In Magda's room, if she had been close enough she would have slapped him. Propped up in bed, resting after breakfast, she glared at Nick. "The doctor said eight weeks."

"Don't tell him," Nick said.

"How will you hold a pencil? You are an architect."

Nick sat on the radiator beneath the window, raising his right hand to show her the claw. "I'm an architect no longer," Nick said. "The Nazis finished my career like they finished my family."

"You're finished, too," Magda said.

Nick came up from the radiator, standing over her bed like a scarecrow. His rage, his outrage, the agony which had engulfed him after the slaughter in the Alps, had given way to a kind of longing, a compulsion to conclude the ambush in the mountains. For Nick the night in the Alps had not ended, could not end until he learned who had betrayed him, who had planned his extinction, his family's extinction, who had deliberately set out to eliminate them and him. Nick lived now with a monastic resolve which had become a goad, the single motivating element in his life.

But the Nazis were supreme in Austria, and they had made him a cripple. And he was a Jew. Nick needed time. "I'll find a new career," he said. "In America."

Magda's feet were cold, and she pushed them into the quilt. America was on the other side of the world. "I hate Indians."

"Your friend Dieter Rantzau is in America," Nick said. "The movies use plays for films. I made plays. I am for America."

"America costs money," Magda said.

Nick's face changed. He forgot the stranger in the bed. He rolled his shirtsleeve down over his right arm. "Thanks for everything."

"So it's America," Magda said quickly. She couldn't warm her feet. "I'll tell you, sonny, I don't like you the way I once liked you."

A little over a month later, on a spectacular Saturday in early June, as Vienna lay beneath azure skies punctuated with clouds like white cherubs, Carly stood beside Fritz in the sanctuary of St. Stephen's Cathedral. They faced the primate of Austria, Joseph Cardinal Innitzer, who celebrated the nuptial Mass.

The wedding of Carlotta Siefermann and Baron Fritz Von Gottisberg had become, with her parents' announcement of the betrothal, the ultimate social event of that spring in 1938, the first spring of the German conquest. For weeks the society pages of the newspapers were full of the marriage, and on the day of the wedding the press attended in full force.

Everything Carly wore, from the white gloves to the white lace veil, had been chosen from the chests and armoires and closets of the palace. Fritz had given Carly and her mother a tour, opening all the drawers and doors. "These belonged to your predecessors, Carly. Everything you see is yours."

"I confess to almighty God, and to you, my brothers and sisters, that I have sinned through my own fault."

Carly looked hard at the cardinal, listening hard, trying not to think, trying to follow the Mass which would make her Fritz's wife. She would be Fritz's wife. She felt as though she had been forsaken in a desolate wilderness.

Why hadn't Nick written? Why hadn't he called? Fritz had told her Nick was safe, had made it over the border.

If Nick was afraid of making trouble for her, he could use another name. They had other names. In their lovemaking they had anatomized their bodies with names, Pedro for his, Yvonne for hers. Beneath her veil Carly wanted Pedro.

Centuries of emperors had been crowned in St. Stephen's. Kings had made their brides queens within the rails of the sanctuary. Napoleon Bonaparte had heard the Mass in the cathedral, yet the magnificent church had never been more splendid than on the June day of Carly's wedding. Fritz's invitations had gone to the ranking German army officers and the heads of the Gestapo in Austria, and he had placed them in the front pews.

Colonel Friedrich Varlingen preferred to remain standing near the doors. He could see everything from his corner. So far as Varlingen could determine, the baron had included every man who now ruled his country. He had even invited Der Chineser, the ridiculous zealot whom Varlingen had deliberately chosen for an assistant.

Der Chineser had been one of the first to arrive. He saw everyone come in, every general in particular. Der Chineser looked at the sanctuary, at the choir loft, at the flowers, at the beautiful men and women around him. In his wildest fantasies, Der Chineser could not have imagined himself in St. Stephen's on the day of the baron's wedding. In all his life Der Chineser could not imagine another honor to equal the wedding invitation in the envelope against the lining of his garrison cap.

Ahead of Der Chineser in the first pew, Helga Siefermann sat beside her husband. Her happiness made her light-headed. She felt almost superhuman, as though she could fly through the air like one of the angels in the cathedral. She could not see Carly's face, but she knew Carly's face, the face of the most beautiful woman in the world, the Baroness Carlotta Von Gottisberg.

Helga took Klaus's hand and pressed it between hers. She remembered his amusement when she told him the baby should be named Carlotta: "Look at her, Klaus. She is a queen." Holding her husband's hand, Helga discovered an unexpected twinge within her, an inexplicable feeling of breathlessness. A faint tickling spread from her belly downward. The sensation astonished her. She could not remember the last such visitation. Years had passed. Helga looked into her lap as though a telltale clue on her gown would give her away. She felt the warmth spread, and unaware of her lips parting in longing, Helga put her hand into the palm of Klaus's hand and ever so gently ran her fingernails across his lifeline, a signal she had not used for longer than she could remember. Helga could feel his eyes on her as his head flipped around, but she studied the sanctuary, hiding her smile.

". . . *forgive us our sins, and bring us to everlasting life.*"

Standing beside Fritz, Carly wanted to cry out for the cardinal to chant faster. She wanted to shout, "Finish this!" as though once the wedding ended, she could escape. She listened to the cardinal moving through the Mass until, mercifully, he made his way across the sanctuary to them.

She had to keep thoughts of Nick away now. She closed her eyes, but he leaped into the sanctuary, his hat crumpled in his hand as he remonstrated with her. Carly opened her eyes and saw Nick behind the cardinal, amazed to find her here in the cathedral with Fritz. She looked away and Nick followed her, saying she could not marry Fritz because she did not love Fritz, she loved him, loved Nick.

Carly begged Nick to leave, but he stayed. He roamed through the sanctuary, through the cathedral, refusing to relinquish her. Carly could not lose him. Nick lunged forward, edging himself between her and Fritz. She could feel Nick's body beside her, feel his thigh against hers, feel his hands, his lips, feel him everywhere on her, feel him in her. She wanted to plead for mercy, beg him to release her, to vanish. She said to herself, "Pretend you're not here, pretend you're gone." She said, "Pretend you're in the country. You're running in the country, and Nick can't keep up with you, no one can keep up with you. You're in a field somewhere, alone, and can't be seen. The grass is high, higher than you, so no one can see where you're running. You can't see anyone because you're hidden in the tall grass. You've lost Nick. You've escaped and you're safe," she said to herself as Fritz took her elbow and both faced the cardinal.

To herself Carly said, "You're still in the country, in the grass," but it didn't work. She said, "You're in a secret place, a cave, you're in a *cave,*" but it didn't work. She said, "You're swimming underwater and it's dark all around so no one can see you or find you," but it didn't work. She heard the cardinal blessing the ring. She heard Fritz repeating words after the cardinal's words. She felt the ring on her finger, his mother's and grandmother's and great-grandmother's and great-great-great-great-GREAT-grandmother's ring on her finger. She had to repeat words after the cardinal. She had to look up at Fritz, had to raise her veil, raise her face, raise her lips, feel his lips on hers. "I thee wed."

Although there were no tears, Carly knew she was crying. Fritz didn't know, the cardinal didn't know, the choirboys in the choir loft didn't know, the other priests circling around the cardinal like porters watching the bell captain didn't know that Carly couldn't stop crying, could no longer hide, could not keep Nick away, could not banish him, although she tried, tried, tried, pleading with him to leave, begging him to go away, please, please, please, if you love me, go, go, go, *go!*

"Father, by your plan man and woman are united, and married life has been established."

As the cardinal left them, Nick disappeared, leaving Carly alone with Fritz. She and Fritz were alone and would never be parted. She no longer belonged to Nick or to herself. She had become Fritz's property. She felt his hand on her arm as he whispered, "Let's run for it."

He saved her from Nick. She turned to Fritz nodding, and he grinned. "You would do it, too." She made Fritz happy. Here, in front of all those Nazi swine and the gaggles of geese Carly's mother had invited, Fritz discovered that his spirits soared. He had Carly! The Baroness Von Gottisberg stood beside him.

As they turned to face the guests, the entire cathedral rose. Fritz glanced at Carly. There had never been a more beautiful baroness. "Only six hours to go," he whispered. Fritz had invited everyone in the cathedral to the palace.

Himmelpfortgasse became a theater. The wedding turned into a public event. A crowd gathered in front of the palace to see the bride and groom and guess at the identities of the guests.

Varlingen decided to walk. Vienna glistened on that June day. Only the uniforms, his uniform as well, provided a clue to the German occupation.

In the palace, Varlingen made his way to the Great Hall. There were hundreds of guests. The colonel had always liked the nobility's devotion to tradition.

"Isn't it beautiful, sir?" Varlingen hadn't seen Der Chineser.

"A dream," Varlingen said. "Point me at the baron and baroness, Captain."

Der Chineser obeyed, and Varlingen started for the newlyweds, nodding at officers he recognized. When he reached the baron and his new wife, Varlingen extended his hand. "Best wishes." He turned to the baroness, clicking his heels. Carly saw just another Nazi, a tall, blond officer. This one said something and she said something, but he didn't go away.

"Carly, you've met the colonel," Fritz said. "He was your dinner partner." She didn't remember. "Colonel Friedrich Varlingen," Fritz said.

"The cop," Varlingen said, smiling at the bride. He had never seen a more beautiful woman. She was spectacular. That other time her hair had dropped below her shoulders. Now she carried her hair in coils atop her head with only a few sandy tendrils at the back of her neck. "I'm the cop, Baroness."

Carly remembered then, because he made her afraid as he had that night beside her at dinner. She hated him for frightening her, and herself for allowing him to succeed. "You were angry when I said I didn't throw flowers the day you marched into Vienna," Carly said.

"Not angry, Baroness," Varlingen said. She had guts, all right, dumb guts. "I said we would be determined to win you over." He smiled once more. "But not on your wedding day." The colonel clicked his heels and left them, and Carly had to look happy for the next guest.

The line never ended. Men bowed over Carly's hand, and women kissed her. Feeling trapped, she repeated the same phrases until, mercifully, Fritz said, "That's the lot," and she could escape.

Carly found her mother surrounded by friends. "Mama, I need your help." She held on to her mother, steering her out of the Great Hall and into the study. Closing the door, she fell against it. "Anything from Nick?"

"No, not today," Helga said.

"Why doesn't he write?" Carly cried.

Helga said carefully, "The mail is slow sometimes. Perhaps he has the wrong address." Helga stood beside the door, ready to bolt.

"I've heard nothing!" Carly said. "Nothing!" She looked at her mother, making Helga uncomfortable. "Have you lied to me? Has there been a letter?"

Helga shook her head. "No!"

"If you've been lying . . ."

"No, Carly, I swear!"

Carly opened the study door. "Fritz is waiting for me," she said, following her mother.

Carly did everything the day demanded. She danced with Fritz, the two alone, surrounded by the guests. She danced with her father, with Colonel Varlingen, with other colonels and generals. The guests remained for hours, reluctant to leave the palace. And even when the last couple was shown to the door, her parents lingered. Fritz rescued Carly, rescued them both. "We have an early train."

So Carly came to the end of her wedding day and the beginning of her marriage. Fritz put his arm through hers. "Alone at last."

Carly began to shake all over. Now she had to do what marriage demanded. She and Fritz were on their way to become man and wife. She couldn't stop shaking. They reached the stairs. "Beddy bye," Fritz said.

There were not enough stairs. She saw the corridor, the doors to the rooms, Fritz's bedroom. "This way, Carly."

They were going the wrong way. His bedroom lay behind them. They were married now, so they would occupy their bedroom. To Carly the end of the corridor rushed at them like a locomotive, and as she tried to drain herself of feeling, they stopped. Fritz opened the door. Lights burned within and she saw a bed which had been turned down. "Sleep well."

As Fritz released her and moved away from the door, Carly swayed slightly and thought she would fall. He leaned forward and kissed her. She said, "Fritz—" and stopped in bewilderment.

"I am not a rapist, Carly." He pushed the door wide open and left her there in the corridor. She didn't move as she watched the distance between them widen and widen, leaving her safe and inviolate. She thought he would turn when he came to his bedroom, would wave, would make one of his gallant gestures, say something witty or clever. But he opened his door and vanished, and as Carly entered the haven Fritz had provided for her, she could feel the self-loathing rise in her like a fever.

She had become the Baroness Von Gottisberg, and in the morning she began to learn how Fritz's wife would live. Seconds after Carly woke, a maid who could see through walls knocked on her door and opened it. The maid drew her bath, and Carly, though embarrassed by the woman's presence and preferring to be alone, allowed the stranger to remain, afraid she would injure Fritz whom she had already wounded beyond any possibility of redress.

The maid anticipated everything Carly did that morning. Helga had packed some of Carly's clothes and brought them to the palace, and the maid had unpacked. She asked what Carly would be wearing on the train and laid out the clothes Carly chose.

Fritz came down from his room long before Zinn expected him. He ordered breakfast served in the Petit Salon, going to the entrance again and again, listening for Carly's footsteps. His joy in her very presence in the palace astonished him. He forgot the melancholy night almost as he left his bed. He felt boyish, frisky. He found himself smiling constantly. The woman he had chosen and lost had become his wife, the Baroness Von Gottisberg. Fritz went back to the table, sipping coffee and listening. As he smelled Carly's perfume, he set down the cup with a clatter. "Good morning, Fritz."

Carly had chosen the schloss for their honeymoon. Fritz would have picked any other place on earth except the Alps near the Italian border, where she would be drowning in memories.

They were taking the Innsbruck express to the village near the castle. Fritz drove them to the railroad station in the coupe, leaving it for Zinn to fetch later. In the train they followed a porter to their compartment. Fritz put Carly beside the window facing the engine. "You won't be riding backward," he said, sitting down opposite her.

"Why should you?"

Fritz crossed his legs, unbuttoning his blazer. "I like the view."

As Fritz suggested some excursions around the castle, Carly saw a man and woman stop in front of the open compartment door. They seemed much younger than Carly and uncomfortable. "Fritz."

Fritz looked at the pair, and the man said, "Excuse me, sir, lady, for intruding. I—we apologize for intruding."

"Perish the thought," Fritz said, gesturing, inviting them into the compartment.

The young man shook his head. "Excuse me, thank you . . . are you married?"

"Are we . . . ?" Fritz said, and stopped, and then, gravely, "We are married."

"We, too, sir. Just now. We just got married," said the fresh groom.

"Congratulations!" Fritz said.

"Congratulations," Carly seconded. Although she was no older than the pair, they seemed younger, standing in the corridor, holding on to each other. And Carly knew they were in love.

"Our parents were against us," said the young man. "They said to wait because of . . . recent happenings. Do you agree?"

Fritz wanted to boot the pair all the way down to the vestibule. "You did the right thing," he said. He saw Carly playing with her wedding ring. "Carly?"

"Yes, of course," she said. "Of course you did the right thing."

"It's unanimous," Fritz told the lambs. The groom put his arm around the bride, and she dropped her head onto his shoulder.

"Thank you," he said. "You're both very nice. You see, we didn't intend to hurt our parents, Thelma's parents and mine. It's not the right way to start out our lives together, but we couldn't wait any longer. We couldn't leave each other."

"Charming," Fritz said as they left. Carly tried to smile, unable to look at Fritz, certain he could see into her. "Too big?" he asked. She looked up, puzzled. "The ring," he said. "Is it too big?" Carly dropped her hands, shaking her head. "Too small?"

Fritz saved her, he always saved her. He made her laugh, and he kept up a chatty, nonsensical dialogue until the steward came to announce lunch. Fritz ordered wine and afterward, lulled by the wine and the rocking of the train, Carly leaned against the seat, drawing up her legs and closing her eyes. Fritz felt heavy-lidded, too, but remained awake, watching Carly. After a while, he rose and leaned over her seat, removing her shoes. He took off his blazer and covered her shoulders.

When she woke, the sun had slipped below the Alps. The sky to the west had turned orange. Carly said, "I must have slept for hours," and discovered Fritz's blazer. He picked up her shoes.

"We aim to please," he said as the train began to lose speed.

The train rolled through the village, passing the hunt club, the

Rathaus, to the station at the south end of the single street. The newlyweds paused beside the compartment. "Thank you for everything,"
the groom said.

Behind them the porter said, "I have your bags, Baron." He followed Carly and Fritz. The conductor stood beside the steps, his hand
extended. "Baroness."

Carly came down the steps and stopped, facing the Daimler, facing
Nick. She could see Nick inside, see his family inside. She wanted to
run. She couldn't run.

Otto Kesselring had the trunk open for the luggage. "Fiegel sent
me, Baron."

"Naturally," Fritz said. He tipped the porter. "Many thanks,
Otto."

Kesselring opened the door for the baroness. "You asked about the
downshift cable, Baron. It's perfect. They'll never make anything this
good again."

"I'm in your hands, Otto," Fritz said. He got into the limousine,
driving slowly. "I've walked on this road since I could walk," Fritz said.
"I've ridden my bicycle along this road, my pony, my horse. I've hunted
along this road, and carried my birds back, carried my rabbits. Once
my father and I carried a deer back to the schloss. My father thought
it would develop my character. Another of his mistakes." They rounded
a curve which stretched toward the castle entrance, and Fritz said, "If
Fiegel had chosen the army, he would have been a general long ago."
Carly saw the castle staff lined up with the butler in his frock coat at
one end. "He even brought up the stable boys."

As Fritz introduced Carly, each man bowed and each woman curt-
sied. Fritz gripped Carly's arm gently. "You were perfect," he whispered.

The castle had been transformed. There were flowers everywhere,
vase after vase, bowl after bowl. The breakfast room had been painted.
Fires crackled in all the fireplaces. "I'd like to get out of these city
clothes and into some country clothes," Fritz said. "Agreed?"

At the head of the stairs Fritz said, "One moment," leaving Carly
and opening every door along the corridor. He returned, spreading his
arms. "Take your pick."

He made her ashamed. She was embarrassed, feeling useless, feeling corrupt, taking everything and giving nothing. She said, "Any one
you say."

He stopped directly in front of her, and his manner changed. "*You*
say, Carly. Now and forever, *you* choose. Everything. It is your right

and your duty. You are the Baroness Von Gottisberg," he said, adding quietly, "Class dismissed."

They dined early and afterward Fritz said, "It's been a long day." Carly dreaded the long walk through the castle, dreaded the staircase, the stairs, the bedrooms. She knew he would be kind even before Fritz said, "Sleep well, Carly."

Her guilt enveloped her like something repugnant. She had cheated Fritz, promising a wife and delivering a companion. But her torment had only begun. The night waited for her, the darkness waited, the silence and the solitude waited, poised to ravage her. Alone, she had no defenses, and she capitulated as she drew up the bed covers. In the dark Nick came immediately to haunt her.

The following morning, Fritz said, "I thought we'd drive over to Innsbruck for lunch." He took Carly to the Stag's Head, where the owner welcomed them. "An honor, Baron. An honor, Baroness." He made the lunch a wedding celebration and refused to let Fritz pay.

They stayed in Innsbruck most of the afternoon. Almost everyone recognized Fritz, and everyone had read of the wedding. Everyone made Carly welcome, and she joined in the fun, at ease with the townfolk who seemed to be at ease with her. "They've worn me out," Fritz said, walking to the Daimler.

As they drove to the castle, Carly watched the shadows fall across the mountains, bringing the night and its anguish closer. She sat against the door, legs pulled up, a million miles from Fritz. She saw the castle in her mind, looming over her like a huge net, and in desperation she said, "Fritz?"

"At your command."

"I . . . you . . ." she said, and broke off. She had to say something to atone. "Let's ride tomorrow."

The course of their days developed a pattern. They rode frequently, and here Carly could, for a little while, be free of her ravenous conscience. Fritz drove her through the countryside, introducing Carly to the Tyrol, to the tenants who farmed the castle's land.

Fritz made the castle a haven, made it impregnable, safe from attack by anyone and anything, yet Carly felt imprisoned. She dreaded each morning, when Fritz would offer her a palette of adventures from which to choose. She dreaded the long day which followed, exhausting herself trying to please Fritz because he never ceased trying to please her. And the day's end led inexorably to the torment of the pernicious darkness. She could not call Vienna and ask her mother if there had been word from Nick.

A week after they arrived, Carly said, "Let's go back."

Fritz said, "How early shall we start?" and Carly knew instantly she had disappointed him.

"No, no, we'll stay," she said, retreating.

"This is my favorite place on the planet," Fritz said. "But it's not the schloss which makes me want to remain." He came closer. "We're alone here," he said. "In Vienna we won't be alone. I'm not ready to share you, Carly." The luxury of speaking honestly, of baring himself, was so new that Fritz almost became frivolous. "I'm delighted to see I've made you blush," he said. "Let's go to bed. I feel sleepy. Am I turning into an old married man?"

So they made their way through the castle to end the day with their customary fraudulence. They climbed the stairs and turned, stopping beside Carly's room. She said, "Good night," and Fritz kissed her cheek. "Good night, Carly," he said, leaving her. She opened her door but remained, watching him.

Fritz didn't look back. He went into his room, slipping out of his jacket. He undressed slowly, methodically, sitting down to remove his shoes. He took off one shoe and raised it, pulling back his arm and throwing it at the wall. "No favors!" he said loudly. "No bloody favors!" He rose, limping, wearing one shoe. He wanted Carly, not some sacrificial lamb. He retrieved his shoe, and when he crossed the room once more, his revolt ended. Carly had not lied. She had brought him a proposition, and he had accepted her offer. Fritz reached for the pajamas on the counterpane.

In her bed Carly heard a thump as Fritz's shoe hit the wall of his room. She thought the sound came from below, from something dropped by a servant. The schloss lapsed into its habitual silence. Carly thought of asking for sleeping pills in the morning, but could not provide the lies she would need to answer Fritz's questions. She could not add lies to their charade.

Nor could she return to her bed each night and endure the hours on the rack before she slept. Carly turned up the light on the lamp beside the bed. She threw back the covers, swinging her legs over the bed, hugging herself, her arms across her breasts, rocking from side to side like a mourner in a pew. Carly had become a mourner, grieving for a world where she had been free, where she had not been sentenced to a life of penance. She had reached the very limits of her endurance, and there, on the bed in the chilled Alpine night, she came upon her salvation. She had to remove the past forever. And if the past would not release her, she would exorcise the past.

Fritz was sleeping and did not hear the door open or close, but seconds later woke to a rustling movement and then swift footsteps. He thrust his hand under the pillows for a Beretta automatic, feeling the cold steel as he smelled Carly's perfume. He whispered, "Carly?" but heard no response. He closed his hand around the gun butt, hearing the bed as she joined him. He said, low, "Carly?" and then felt her body against his.

He pushed the gun far back beneath the pillow, turning to welcome her. He felt her lips on his throat and her hands on his body, fingers trailing along his belly, pausing, continuing, as Carly kissed him, neck and chest until she found his breast with her lips. He felt her hand along his thigh as she kissed him, went from one breast to the other, mouth and hands never still. Fritz put his left arm around her to bring her closer, losing his hands in her hair. "Carly?"

She let her busy mouth reply, her lips on his belly, her tongue in his navel. Carly had fled to Fritz's bed mindlessly, and she fell upon him mindlessly, seeking a refuge in his body.

"Wait," he said, but she would not wait, tantalizing him, her hand like burning coals between his thighs as she kissed, her face on his bare body, kissing, kissing. He felt her tongue once more, moving across his belly, across his chest, on his throat, her lips on his and her tongue searching until he welcomed her. She had him everywhere then, her hair covering them. He raised his hand, sweeping back her hair. In the darkness he could not see her, but she was as clearly defined for him as though they lay beneath the sun.

She raised her leg and set if over his, her thigh against his thigh, calf over his calf, ankle over his ankle, foot beside his foot, while her hand continued its delicate exploration, fingers moving in a slow, persistent rhythm which inflamed him.

Fritz took her shoulders, lifting her over him until he could feel her breasts in his face. He felt her firm, extended breasts in his face, in his mouth, in his face and mouth, before she slid away and lay beside him once more. He tried to trap her but she eluded him, kissing, her tongue trickling down, down, down. She would not free him. She lay with her hair spread across his middle, across his thighs as she raised her head to capture him.

He felt her capture him slowly, deliberately, tormenting him with pleasure. She tormented him, her head hidden, and when it seemed as though she would never relinquish him, she suddenly fell back against the pillows, breathing deep as she lay beside him.

Fritz came up and over her, straddling Carly, raising her fingers to his lips. He kissed her fingers, kissed her arms, held her arms high, kissing. He kissed her breasts, and as he felt her hands on his back, a flash of elation such as he had never experienced ripped through him, and he dropped down upon her.

He was no less demanding than Carly. He began a calculated advance, moving ever so slowly toward his goal. He could feel her body responding to his deliberately hesitant journey. He could feel her hips rising to accommodate him. He could feel her hips moving, feel her hands, feel her ankles around his ankles. Then she lowered her arms, her hands flat on her thighs, thumbs extended and touching, providing a wicket through which he could proceed to his goal.

He took everything she offered him. He had been patient, and waiting had made him insatiable. The years in Katharina's Eden, the nights of instruction there, all gifted and some inspired, had made him a virtuoso. He heard Carly utter a hoarse plea, as though she begged to be released, but he would not, could not free her, could not free himself from her. She had reached some primordial chord of passion deep within him, some formless desire unknown even to himself, a demand of almost unbearable intensity, and she had triggered it, robbing him of reason, of thought, leaving him with an overpowering urge so fierce it could not be checked. Fritz could not get enough of her, could neither slake nor quench his need, and only when Carly cried out once more, half scream, half wail, herself beyond reason, did he pause.

Fritz fell on her as though to avenge himself. They were like enemies locked in combat, and Carly welcomed him, abandoning herself to the battle. They were like beasts in the jungle that night in the dark in the castle. They were like animals, scratching and clawing and gnawing and biting. Biting. Now Fritz could delay no longer, and Carly became as desperate, speaking to him for the first time since entering his bed. "Go now," she said. "Hurry and go now," she said. "Hurry now! *Hurry!*" she said, and could not wait, taking him. She took him, had him. She had him. She said, "Now!" raising her buttocks to greet him. "Now!" she said as he took her. He had her. He had her, and yet she never surrendered. She seemed to engulf him. He had her but she had him, and when he said, "Here! Here, then! Here! *Here!*" his voice rising with each word, she demanded more of him.

"Don't stop!" she said, challenging him. "Don't stop now, don't stop now, don't stop!" she said, the madness in her voice matching his, writhing in his arms, like quicksilver in his arms, entangling him within her, uniting them in a convulsive web of their bodies.

Carly took him with her, took him deeper and deeper into the abyss, until Fritz's voice reached an exultant cry of victory atop the summit and they sank slowly back to the sanity both had abandoned.

They lay entwined in silence, without resources, immobilized by the fierceness of their encounter. Fritz had never, ever, anywhere, with anyone . . . ever. He could neither think nor feel, and for a little while he lay ravished with Carly ravished beneath him. She did not feel Fritz's body because she had become part of it. They were united, bound by the lust which had exhausted and drained them. They had not met as lovers, and they lay together now, each wounded by the other until Fritz found his voice. "Carly."

She was still lost, left in some strange land where she had been thrown by the demands of their encounter. She remained beneath him, victor as well as vanquished, drained and alone even before Fritz released her to drop on his belly. She lay without moving until she heard him, asleep, and could leave his bed.

Carly slept far beyond her usual waking hour. She took the clock from the night table, holding it close, as though she had misread the time, and, like a cruel reminder of a terrible deed, was pinioned by the memory of the night before.

When she joined Fritz, Carly wore a skirt and sweater of no particular brilliance. She wore walking shoes and thick stockings. Her hair was still damp from the shower and she had not used makeup, but in these clothes she came into Fritz's day like a meteor. He became another man, dropping the guard he wore to face the world. He offered no witticisms, no cruel irony. Carly brought Fritz what had always eluded him. She made him happy.

They left the castle early, driving miles into the mountains to another schloss. Fritz bought two horses, one for Carly, one for himself, and the seller insisted on toasting their purchases, keeping them until late in the afternoon.

They did not return until early evening. They spoke very little at dinner, and neither then nor once during that day did either mention Carly's appearance in Fritz's room the night before.

For three nights Carly remained resolute, determined to ignore the past, to be, forever, Baroness Von Gottisberg. Then on the fourth night she succumbed to memories and fled once more.

Fritz heard her scurrying to his bed. Carly dropped her leg over his in a rush to begin. But Fritz moved aside, turning up the light. Carly fell back, startled. "If you stay tonight, you must stay with me," Fritz said.

The bedroom was still until a gust of wind rattled the windows, and then silence returned. Still Fritz was not certain of victory, and when he lowered his head to kiss her, he knew she might run. Then she raised her arms to draw him down to her, and at last Fritz claimed his wife.

Afterward, their moist bodies side by side, Fritz wound a strand of Carly's hair around his finger. "Now I am willing to share you," he said. "Now we can go home."

They returned to Vienna in the Daimler. In the palace Carly said, "I should call my mother to tell her we've returned."

She couldn't run to the study or close the study door, couldn't have secrets from her husband. Standing at Fritz's desk, Carly said, "We're back, Mama." She endured a torrent of questions before she could ask, "Any news?"

"From us? Papa and I have no . . . oh . . ." Helga said. "No, Carly, nothing. No news."

Carly raised the telephone, speaking directly into the mouthpiece. "Mama. Anything?"

"Nothing, Carly."

She could not keep calling her mother. The following day Carly waited until late in the afternoon. "I need some clothes," she said.

"Buy some clothes," Fritz said.

"I have clothes at home—I mean at—" she said, and stopped, feeling her face flush. "May I use the coupe?"

"Carly, it's your coupe," he said, grinning as the color rose in her face. She left him, hurrying through the palace. He made everything easy for her.

In Kruger Strasse, Carly used her key to open the apartment door. "Mama!" Carly saw her mother emerge from the living room.

"Nothing," Helga said. "No letter. No telephone. Carly, you are a married woman. The past is the past."

Klaus Siefermann joined his wife. "Hello, daughter." Carly tried not to look at her father, at the swastika in his lapel.

"I came for some clothes," Carly said, going to her bedroom.

Helga followed her. "Take only what you need now," Helga said. She helped Carly fill a suitcase. "Send your servants for the rest, Carly."

Carly's father came into the bedroom. "I'll help you," he said.

"I can do it," Carly said, but he took the suitcase from her.

"I'm going out for cigars anyway," Klaus said. He didn't give her a chance, leaving the apartment ahead of her.

In the street, walking to the coupe, Klaus said, "I have cigars for another month. I almost called the schloss. I am in terrible trouble— not I, a dear friend. I don't know where to go, whom to ask for help."

He placed the suitcase in the coupe. "You're a baroness now, you're important," Klaus said. "Fritz is a powerful man with powerful friends. This woman—" he broke off, and then faced Carly, trying to be brave. "My friend is a woman."

Carly looked at the Nazi stranger who had just announced he had a mistress. "Her name is Sarah Frisch." He nodded. "A Jew, yes, of course. She is a Jew. Innocent. Alone. Childless. She—they never had children. You must help me."

Carly pointed at the swastika in his lapel. "Why don't you ask your friends?"

"There are no longer any friends in Austria," Klaus said. He pulled out his handkerchief. "They took Sarah's husband," he said. "Took him out of his office, a doctor, while he examined a patient. They marched in and marched out with him. She is absolutely alone. Fritz—" he said, and Carly stopped him.

"No!" She could never again ask Fritz for anything.

"I can't let her sink!" Klaus said. "She'll sink! She has had an easy life, a life of luxury. She is a beautiful woman, so life came easy. You should understand, Carly, you more than anyone, beautiful as you are. She is not accustomed to doing anything for herself."

"Not like Mama," Carly said, unable to spare him.

"I didn't hurt her," Klaus said. "You didn't know and Mama didn't know. And you loved someone, too."

She said, "I . . ." and could not continue. Her father had put Nick between them.

"I have a way out for her," Klaus said. "The villa." He had inherited the villa and an orchard on the Danube. "The farmers come from Hungary twice a week to the market. They go back and forth like you and I crossing the Kohlmarkt. You could take her on a market day."

"You could take her," Carly said.

"Even if I tried, I would fail," Klaus said. "I'm afraid. There! You know the truth," he said, relieved to be rid of his secret shame. "Forget me, I'm a coward. This is not about me. This is a person alone. I'll tell her you're coming, to prepare her. You can't say no, Carly."

The following Tuesday, one of the two market days in the town on the Danube, Carly drove through Vienna and parked across the street from a large apartment building. Sarah Frisch saw the coupe from her window and walked through the apartment where she had lived for thirty-four years.

She left everything behind. "Take nothing with you," Klaus had told her. "Set out like you're going for a loaf of bread."

Carly gave her a head start. At the corner Sarah crossed the street, and in the next block she entered a bakery. Carly stopped beyond the entrance.

When Sarah opened the door of the coupe, Carly started the engine. Sarah got in. "This could be your ruin," she said.

"The bread smells good," Carly said, very frightened. She had seen Sarah once, the day after her father had trapped her. Carly came to Sarah's apartment.

"Your father should not have done this," Sarah said. "You're young, you have your whole life. I've lived my life, lived two lives. Run away from me."

"I can't," Carly said. "I've seen you now, so you're real. If I leave you . . . I can't leave you."

In the coupe they rode steadily and neither spoke. Carly knew every mile of the route. Then, beside the Danube, Carly said, "Another ten minutes," and saw the barriers in the distance. "Let me," Carly said, feeling a chill up and down her back. She spoke to herself, issuing warnings: "Don't show them you're afraid. They'll win if they see you are afraid." She rolled down the window, welcoming the thrust of air against her face.

A German army captain walked into the road. Enlisted men with rifles were on both sides of the barriers. Carly stopped, and when the captain saw the bareheaded driver, he bent for a better look. He had drawn a knockout. "Destination?"

"The Villa Siefermann," Carly said, and gave him the location. "My family owns it. I am the Baroness Von Gottisberg."

"Prove it."

"I'm still Siefermann on my papers," she said. "I was married just . . . recently."

"So you can't prove it," the captain said.

Carly raised her hand. "This is my wedding ring, a Von Gottisberg wedding ring for over three hundred years."

"So you say."

"Why would I lie to you?"

"Everybody lies," said the captain. He pointed at Sarah. "Who is that, the Countess Munchausen?"

"She is my cook," Carly said. "We've come down to open the villa for the summer."

The captain squinted at Sarah Frisch. "What's your specialty, cookie?"

"Boar," Sarah said. Her husband had hunted boar. "Roast loin of boar with chestnuts and spatzel."

"Yum yum," said the captain. "Maybe I'll drop in on you." He took a last, long look at the package behind the wheel.

On Wednesday of the following week, Zinn knocked on Carly's open door. "You have a guest, Baroness. Colonel Varlingen."

"Colonel?" Carly came to the door. "To see me?"

"Yes, Baroness." Zinn extended a card reading "COLONEL FRIED-RICH VARLINGEN." Then she remembered the tall blond officer with receding hair and the perfectly tailored uniform who had sat beside her at dinner and teased her. She remembered him at the wedding reception, an elegant man with manners.

"Did you tell him the baron is out?" Carly asked.

"I did, Baroness," Zinn said. "Then he asked for you. I showed him into the Great Hall. It's . . . hard to refuse them, Baroness, but if you want me—"

"I'll go," Carly interrupted, refusing to let Zinn fight her battles. As the butler left, she went into the bathroom to look at herself, and discovered the card in her hand. She dropped it and walked into the corridor to the stairs.

In the Great Hall she saw him at the far end, moving slowly from portrait to portrait, studying Fritz's ancestors. "Colonel Varlingen?"

"Ah, Baroness." He came to her and as they met, he took her hand and bowed over it. "I like Vienna better when you are in residence."

He made Carly uncomfortable, so clever and sure of himself, the master. She said, "Thank you, you're very nice," and while she spoke, he took her arm, bringing her to a cluster of chairs. He was the stranger, uninvited, but he had taken command of the palace like everything else in Austria. "Ah, this is pleasant," he said.

Carly saw Zinn enter and thought he had returned to announce another visitor, but he said, "Would the Baroness like tea?" Carly felt even more stupid and callow.

"May I have sherry, Baroness?" Varlingen raised both arms. "This . . . serenity calls for sherry."

Carly said, "Sherry," and the butler left them. Beside her Varlingen sat back, completely at ease. "Napoleon said an army travels on its stomach, but it helps if the landscape is pleasant," Varlingen said. He talked about Napoleon and Maria Theresa, about the Turks and their assaults on the city, until Zinn returned with a tray with a decanter and glasses. "You'll join me, Baroness," Varlingen said, deciding for her.

Carly almost said no to prove she could actually think for herself, but she did not want to be rude, or even worse, a silly, ignorant girl in above her head. So she took the glass from Zinn, and when Varlingen drank, she sipped the sherry.

"Lovely," Varlingen said, watching the butler leave. He drank again. "Lovely."

He made Carly feel inept and awkward. Sitting with him, Carly felt as though she kept sliding in her chair, and, holding her glass, she remembered how she had dreaded the weekly visit from the piano teacher, how she had hated the round, slippery, piano stool. She believed the colonel enjoyed teasing her, and she remembered clearly how he had demanded everyone's attention at dinner that night so he could repeat her defiant reaction to the Anschluss. Carly set down her glass. "Colonel, are you here for a reason?"

"Naturally," he said, emptying his glass. "May I have another, Baroness?" He rose without waiting and went to the tray with the decanter, and watching him, Carly felt a sudden, almost triumphant tremor. She knew now why he had come, and the knowledge immediately ended all her feelings of inadequacy. He was just another man after a woman.

Carly rose, no longer afraid of him. His urbane sophistication was all a facade. She watched him pouring the sherry, just another lecher. "You'd better leave."

Varlingen dropped the stopper into the decanter. "You're not very hospitable, Baroness."

"Not to you," Carly said. "Not for your purpose."

He drank the sherry. "My purpose?" he said.

"I know why you're here," Carly said. She disliked him even more because he had fooled her. "Conquering armies," she said. "I haven't been conquered. This house hasn't been conquered. You're wasting your time in this house." She wanted to slap him, hard. "My husband could walk in here right now."

"Your husband is in my office," said Varlingen.

Carly said, barely, "In your—" and broke off, as though the wind had been knocked out of her.

Varlingen set down his glass. "I brought him in, Baroness. I told him when to come so I could share this hour with you. I keep reminding you, Baroness, I'm a cop. Your husband will stay where he is until I join him. You don't know why I came because I haven't told you. Sit down." Varlingen returned to his chair, crossing his legs and pointing at the chair Carly should occupy.

She didn't want to obey, but knew she must. She didn't want to be afraid. She faced him, feeling her fear like a dull, heavy weight pressing down on her chest. "Am I here for a reason? In April I signed a Safe Conduct for the Baron Fritz Von Gottisberg," Varlingen said. "He didn't use it. I believe he asked for the Safe Conduct for someone else, for you. I believe you were the mastermind. You were the mastermind last week when you got that woman out."

Carly felt a bright sting, like a needle, along her eye, and she felt trapped, chained, as she faced the colonel, who had not raised his voice, who might have been telling her an interesting anecdote. "I let you get her out," said the colonel. "I sent along an escort in case you encountered any problems with the Gestapo or other agencies of the Greater German Reich."

Carly said silently, "I am going to die." She shut her eyes, trembling, feeling her skin crawling. She opened her eyes, facing her executioner, feeling numb. The Great Hall grew dark, and she felt herself sinking, sinking, falling away into nothing with nothing and no one to rescue her. She needed Nick, but she had lost Nick, sent him away forever. Carly tried to keep Nick with her, tried to see him, but could not, and she remained alone with the colonel who had just condemned her. "The baron is innocent," she said.

"To a cop no one past the age of six is innocent," said Varlingen.

"He didn't do anything," Carly said. "I asked for the Safe Conduct. It was for me . . . for someone." She looked at the colonel. "He's gone, they're gone."

"Are you afraid?"

He was teasing her, enjoying himself. Carly despised him. "Yes," she said, and then, "Yes, I'm afraid." I'm very . . . yes." Talking helped her. "Yes, I'm afraid. Yes!"

"Good," Varlingen said. "If you were not frightened now, you would be a lunatic. If you were terrified, paralyzed, unable to think, to remember your name, your birthday, you would be useless to me. Tell me your birthday."

"January 31," Carly said.

"Good. Very good," Varlingen said. He leaned forward, far forward and took her hand, holding it between his hands. "You are a brave woman. Very brave. I thought so from the beginning, I had a feeling. Mostly I don't trust feelings, I go exactly *against* a feeling, an instinct. The woman convinced me, the woman you saved last week. Not your mother, not your sister . . . a woman. You put yourself in terrible danger for this woman. So now I am in danger, with you. I've put myself in danger with you now. You're young and you say stupid things, but I don't believe you're stupid. I believe you'll learn. I'll teach you, and to stay alive you'll teach yourself."

He released her and moved back in his chair. "I'll stop for a little while and you can start breathing once more, and ask questions, beginning with your first question," Varlingen said. " 'Who are you?' Correct?"

Carly felt the Great Hall spinning and stop, and then rock from side to side like a device in an amusement park. She held on to the seat of the chair, pressing down hard to stop the tilting, and when the Great Hall turned right side up, she looked at the colonel and could only nod at him.

"I am against Adolf Hitler and his pack of sadists," Varlingen said. "I am a traitor to the Greater German Reich, against the real traitor, the monster, who has corrupted Germany, my Germany," Varlingen said. "I am at war with this monster, and I need troops. I've come today to recruit you. But this is not conscription, Baroness. I take only volunteers. So you have a choice. If you refuse—and you can refuse— you will not be harmed. You'll be safe," Varlingen said, tapping his chest, "from me."

Now the Great Hall began to sway. "Are you asking me to spy?"

"I am asking you to risk your life," Varlingen said, "to let me risk your life. I am asking you to change your life, to forfeit"—his gesture took in the Great Hall—"this. I am asking you to wake each morning with the certain knowledge you may be dead before sunset." Varlingen took his gloves out of his garrison cap. "Think seriously, Baroness. Now I'll return to my office and tell the baron where I have been. I have a convincing story for him, for Fritz, my good friend Fritz."

Varlingen rose as though Carly had vanished. He walked past her, pushing his garrison cap under his left arm, bunching his gloves in his right hand. As he went through the Great Hall, the sound of his footsteps on the ancient wooden floor was like the measured beat of a drum before an execution, and he had just reached the marble stairs when he heard her say, "Colonel," and then, after eons, "Wait."

9

LEOPOLD UNGER SAW HIS first customer of the day waiting as he approached the Ringstrasse, his café on Yucca Street in Hollywood. Nick Gallanz leaned against the door, hands in his pockets. Leopold Unger liked to be alone when he opened, to examine the cleaning crew's work alone and brew the first urns of coffee in an empty café. Still, he waved as though Nick had appeared to save him from bankruptcy. "You can't sleep, either."

Leopold unlocked the door, and Nick followed him to the sinks. "Give me a job."

Leopold turned the tap, filling a pot with water. "I don't need an architect."

"I'm no architect," Nick said. "I'll be a waiter."

Leopold emptied the pot of water into an urn. "You're not a waiter," he said. "You'll never be a waiter."

Nick walked around the coffee urns. "I'm not joking."

"I'm not joking, either," Leopold said. "I don't joke about the Ringstrasse." In what had been a five-and-dime, a failed florist's shop, and a burned-out, seven-stool diner, Leopold had created a Viennese café larger, more opulent, grander than anything ever seen in the Imperial City. He named his café after the enormous boulevard which had replaced Vienna's medieval defensive wall in the last century. Leopold admired the work of Adolf Loos, the seminal architect, and on Yucca Street in Hollywood, he set out to build the Austrian innovator a memorial.

He used white and black tile and leather and ebony and cherrywood. He used Thonet chairs and marble for his tabletops. He used wood panels in the walls, and frosted glass, and he specified coffers in the ceiling. In the brilliant California sunshine the Ringstrasse's lights burned brightly from morning to night. Leopold Unger had banished darkness.

He called his Ringstrasse a coffee house and made everyone welcome, with or without money. But he had planned a full-service restaurant, and the patron who asked could eat and drink from a dazzling menu.

From its opening, the Ringstrasse had been Hollywood headquarters for all those who had escaped from Adolf Hitler. They could find their own kind in the Ringstrasse, share their pasts and try to believe in a future. And for show people, all those who in Europe had been in the theater, in film, in orchestras great and small, for all those in the arts, the Ringstrasse became a haven, an enduring link with the past.

Leopold turned the tap to fill another urn. "My friend, I like you," he said. "I like everybody, but you I *like*. A waiter smiles. You can't smile."

"I'll smile," Nick said, and when he did Leopold covered his eyes.

"You look like you're crying," Leopold said.

Nick walked into him, pinning Leopold against the sink. "I need to work."

"Practice smiling," Leopold said, pushing Nick aside. "I'm falling behind."

Nick started to leave the café but stopped. He had nowhere to go. He had crossed countries, an ocean, a continent. *He* had chosen Hollywood. For more than a year he had tried to outrun his bad luck. He stood among the empty tables in the Ringstrasse like a man on a raft.

Magda and Nick had gone from Rome to Lisbon, waiting there almost six months before Nick could find the right man to pay for help in obtaining visas. Magda sold jewelry for the visas and the voyage to America. In New York she sold more jewelry for California.

They left New York on a sleety, slushy night in December. Magda booked them into the same Pullman car. "I'll take the bottom berth," she said. "If I am on the top, maybe we'll both finish on the bottom."

So Nick lay in the upper berth, facing west, listening to the seductive rhythm of the wheels clicking, "California, California, California," taking him farther and farther away from Carly.

On the morning of the third day, they came out of Union Station into a glorious California morning. They found poinciana in bloom around Union Station, and saw flower carts with pots of red and yellow poinciana. They saw men in shirtsleeves and others in sport shirts. The women were bare-legged and bare-armed. The big red trolleys of the Red Line passed Union Station with windows open and passengers leaning out of the windows. They saw convertibles with the tops folded down, with drivers who looked like movie stars, sleek and brown from the sun. They heard a guitar in the Mexican bazaar near the terminal, and saw Mexican girls with flowers in their hair, walking like Aztec royalty. They came upon a Salvation Army Santa Claus, and Magda stuffed dollars into his pot hanging from a tripod. She opened her coat wide, like someone starting a striptease, raising her head to the sky and rubbing her neck as though she could plaster the sun to her skin. "I am through running, sonny."

They chose a hotel on Hollywood Boulevard, and that afternoon, in the bar, Magda said, "Tomorrow we find Dieter and Fanny Rantzau. I have his letter with his address." She drank her scotch. "Have a drink. We are celebrating."

"When I have something to celebrate," Nick said.

"You're breathing," Magda said. "Celebrate because you are breathing."

The following afternoon, Magda found a furnished apartment on Fountain Avenue near Cahuenga Boulevard, and Nick went into the street to learn English. "I cannot work until I can talk."

He bought a German-English dictionary, and all day and into the night he accosted strangers, confronted sales clerks, sat on park benches, studying the dictionary and asking questions of everyone. Magda hired a tutor recommended by Dieter Rantzau, and when Nick returned to Fountain Avenue, they studied together.

Wherever he went and from the time he woke, Nick kept a solid rubber ball in his right hand, squeezing and releasing, squeezing and releasing. On the voyage to America he had gone to the ship's doctor. After examining Nick's arm, the doctor put the ball into his right hand. "It might help if you stick to it."

"I will never quit," Nick said. He went from the doctor to his cabin, locking himself in before taking the Beretta from his luggage. He pushed the automatic into his right hand, pushed his forefinger through the trigger guard. He could hold the Beretta and raise it, but the automatic wobbled. He went to the mirror and, facing it, put his left hand over the right, lifting his arm up, up, up, until the muzzle pointed between his eyes. He kept lowering the gun and raising it, and when the pain stopped him, Nick hid the automatic and put the rubber ball into his right hand.

In Hollywood, as soon as he could ask directions in English, he went to the movie studios for a job. He filled out an application at every studio, and under "EXPERIENCE" he set down his history with the Zwischentheatre: art director, set designer, stage manager, drama coach, assistant director, casting director, play reader. His right hand lay crookedly on the paper and he could barely write legibly.

On the day Leopold Unger admitted him to the Ringstrasse in the summer of 1939, six months after arriving in Hollywood, Nick remained in the café all through the morning, sitting at the corner table he had made his own. The Ringstrasse was a rendezvous for those like Nick. Threats of suicide were commonplace in the café, but Nick ignored those wretched castaways whose resources had been exhausted. Suicide would be his ultimate defeat and the final triumph for those who had robbed him of everything.

He had come to the end. Magda paid the rent for the apartment on Fountain Avenue. She paid for the food in the apartment and in restaurants. She had paid for his coffee that morning. Someone said, "Finally, a friendly face."

Dieter Rantzau walked into Nick's corner. He had been handsome all his life. Now he looked like an aristocrat. But in Hollywood that day thousands of men, young and old, as distinguished and dashing, hoped to become movie stars. "The worst day of my life," Dieter said, adding, "Since yesterday." He pulled out a chair.

"I've heard it all," Nick said.

Dieter grinned. "So I won't surprise you," he said. "I just came from Metro. My agent sent me to read for a bit part—a Nazi general, one day's shooting. He said it's mine, written for me alone. How can I face Fanny?" The week before, a physician had admitted Fanny to the hospital with a failing heart. "Last night I told her I had the part, it was my part," Dieter said. "This hospital is eating me up alive. I needed that walk-on."

Nick had stopped listening. He tried to flatten the ball in his right hand, looking out at Yucca Street and seeing a Viennese *strasse*. "I can get you a part in the picture."

"Didn't you hear—?" Dieter said before Nick interrupted:

"Sure," Nick said, dropping the rubber ball into his pocket, moving his empty cup aside, clearing the table as he had in the café near the Zwischentheatre. "If the story has Nazis, it has Jews. Some of the Jews have lines."

"Do I look like a Jew?"

"Does Magda? Does Baron Rothschild?"

Dieter's face came alive. He hit the table with his fist. "I'll call my agent."

"Your agent didn't tell you about the Jews," Nick said. Both were on their feet. "I told you."

Dieter leaned over the chair. "I don't need two agents."

"Fire him," Nick said.

"Maybe you're cracking up," Dieter said. "Magda thinks you're cracking up. She says you don't talk, don't eat, don't listen. She says you're in and out of the apartment like a thief." Dieter stood erect. "Thank you for your suggestion, my friend. If God is good, I'll repay you." He moved away from the table, but Nick stepped in front of him.

"I'm on my way to Metro," Nick said. "I'll take an actor with me." He gestured. "There are ten sitting here, more than ten. I have my choice. You are my first choice. Are you with me?"

"You would do this?"

"*Wiedersehen*," Nick said. He walked past Dieter, but the big man followed him. "Nick! Nick!"

They drove to Metro-Goldwyn-Mayer in Dieter's car, and on the lot he said, "Over there." Nick saw a mob of men and women and children, each child with a mother who carried diapers, toys, coloring books, bottles with nipples, soft drinks, sandwiches. "A cattle call," Dieter said.

At the casting office, Dieter said, "Wait," but Nick stayed with him, walking into another mob. A woman with a baby wailing in her arms bumped into Nick, and a bearded man holding a monocle snarled, "Tired of living?"

When Nick escaped, he couldn't find Dieter. The throng moved in all directions. "Dieter!"

Someone said, "Pipe down!" and beside him a woman with gray hair said, "What hole did you crawl out of?"

Nick came up on his toes. If he lost Dieter, he was beaten before he began. Nick yelled, "Dieter!" and raised his left hand, extending two fingers to whistle as Dieter spun him around. "I said cattle call, not cattle barn!"

Nick saw the two pages of screenplay in Dieter's hand. "This is your role?"

"They'll call me when it's my turn to read," Dieter said.

Nick snatched the pages from Dieter's hand. He saw the title, *Forgotten*, in the upper right-hand corner. Dieter had been given a scene in a Gestapo headquarters. Nick scanned the two pages. "How can you read when you don't know who you are?"

"Be quiet," Dieter said. "You are marked already." He reached for the pages, but Nick eluded him. "Give me the pages and leave," Dieter said, but Nick was gone, pushing is way through the crowd until he came to a low railing with a gate like that in a courtroom.

A woman at a desk behind it said, "You'll be called."

Nick showed her the pages. "This is for Alpert, the Jew in *Forgotten.*"

"I said you'll be called. Wait your turn." She looked at Nick. "Wait your *turn.*"

Behind her a door opened into a long corridor, and Champ Gallagher, the director of *Forgotten*, came out of an office with a young actress who had read for him.

"While we wait, who is this Alpert?" Nick asked, showing her the pages. "What is Alpert's trade? Is he rich, poor, sick, healthy, a bachelor, a widower, a father, a grandfather?"

Dieter bent over the railing. "I am not responsible for this man."

"Maybe I'll call the guard," said the woman.

"First tell me about Alpert," Nick said. "Tell me about Muller. Who is this man, Muller? Is he a father, a grandfather?"

Walking toward the gate with the actress, Champ Gallagher heard the foreigner at the desk. Gallagher was a handsome Irishman, well into middle age, who always looked and smelled good. He didn't have enough hair left to count, but he started every day in the barber shop. "What time of day is this scene?" Nick asked. "What day, month, year?"

"You had your chance, mister," the woman said. "The guard will take care of you."

"The man asked you legitimate questions," said Gallagher. "The man is entitled to some answers. Give him a script." He nodded at Nick. "Good luck."

"I'm not the actor," Nick said, pulling Dieter to the gate so the friendly American could see him. "Here is the actor." He took the script from the woman at the desk, nudging Dieter. "Find me a quiet place."

Outside, standing beside a forklift, Nick and Dieter leafed through the script. Nick read the two pages once more, memorizing Alpert's lines. "Read from the script," Nick told Dieter. Nick climbed onto the seat of the forklift, facing a band of Indians naked to the waist and riding bareback. Nick listened, closing his eyes to imagine the Gestapo headquarters. "Good, good."

Dieter knew he should never have left the Ringstrasse. "This is good? This is terrible!" he said.

"Sure," Nick said. "All who read for Alpert will be the same: hunched over, scared, shaking in their shoes, wringing their hands, begging for mercy, waiting for the whip." Nick jumped off the fork-lift. "You are a different Alpert, an Alpert the audience will not forget. In this story the Nazis say you are a Jew. Maybe your grandmother was a Jew. The Nazis know, but you never knew. You are a grandee. Your family came from Spain a thousand years ago."

"Four hundred," Dieter said.

"Pretend," Nick said. "You are a German." Nick remembered Dieter *was* a German. "You face Muller like a German, with contempt. He is beneath you. They are all beneath you." Nick slapped the script Dieter held. "Again," he said. "I'll read Muller and you play a German grandee."

Champ Gallagher always cast his own pictures, down to the characters with a single line. He read Dieter for the Jew, Alpert. "Let's try it once more," the director said, and afterward, "I believe you. See the A.D. for your wardrobe date."

Dieter left the office, walking through the gate, through the crowd, lifting Nick off the floor. "You saved my life."

In the Ringstrasse the next morning, Leopold Unger hailed Nick as he came through the door. "Another customer."

Nick saw a plump little man beside the table in the corner. His black hair was cut short, and his face, white as a corpse, was scary. Nick would have willingly carried him through the streets. Dieter Rantzau had been a fluke born of desperation, a fleeting triumph in a life of daily defeats. But the spooky little man with the chalky face had *chosen* Nick. After the months of flight, of loss, of rejection, a human being wanted him. He felt woozy, reaching for the rubber ball like someone groping for a life preserver. "So I can stop smiling," he said, as though Leopold had offered him the waiter's job.

The little man in the corner faced the stranger. "Mr. Gallanz?"

"Nick Gallanz."

"Dieter Rantzau told me of Metro," said the little man. He had wonderful eyes for an actor, big and black and intense. "You made a miracle for him."

"Sure. Me and Moses," Nick said. "We walk on water."

"I'm an actor. Karel Kaminsky. I heard of something at Paramount. Don't sit!" he said as Nick moved a chair. "We can talk on the way to Paramount."

Nick stepped back. "Where is your car?"

"I hoped you had a car."

"Tomorrow," Nick said. "We'll walk. Tell me what you're reading for while we walk."

Karel Kaminsky said the studio had begun casting a comedy set among the Italian wine makers in the Napa Valley. "There is a gatekeeper," said Karel. "Three little scenes, but more than I've found since I came to America. What's worse is that I am a tragedian. *Hamlet*, *Macbeth*, *Othello*, with these I am in command. Make me a comedian."

They were on Gower Street, passing the Columbia lot. Columbia on the north and R.K.O., Radio Keith Orpheum, at Melrose Boulevard, were the big Gower Street studios. Between them lay Majestic Pictures, which Meyer Milgrim had established with one sound stage.

"Say something," the little man pleaded. They crossed the street and as they passed the cemetery where the faithful still brought flowers to Rudolph Valentino's grave, Nick saw Palladian villas and vineyards in the Umbrian hills, peasants bent over the grapes in the fields, dukes and duchesses in finery on spirited horses. "I've been in California almost a year," said Karel. "I've made three hundred dollars. I've sold everything except the gold in my teeth."

"You have something left for an emergency," Nick said.

The little man winced and looked up at Dieter's friend. "I must have this role," said Karel. "My mother is sick, and my father needs an eye operation. They sit in Lisbon waiting for me to send passage money."

"You are a lucky man," Nick said.

"Stop," said the actor. "You hurt me with your jokes."

"I never joke," Nick said. "Remember, ask for the script with the pages they give you."

At Paramount, an exterior staircase led to the casting office on the second floor of a frame building. Nick expected the bedlam he had seen at Metro-Goldwyn-Mayer, but saw only a short line of men and women. The assistant casting director, a former dancer whom everyone called Doug, took the script pages from a small stack. "An Italian gatekeeper named *Karel* Kaminsky?"

"I would also like the entire script," said the actor.

"Nix." The former dancer wore a Hawaiian sport shirt, white duck trousers, and brown and white shoes. "Featured players see the script."

"As a favor," Nick said.

Doug slowly shook his head. "This isn't amateur night."

"Sure," Nick said, and to the actor, "Outside." Below, they stood under the stairs, reading the gate man's three brief appearances. In two scenes he played against the matriarch of the Italian family. In the third he faced a jilted suitor with orders to bar the man. The matriarch despised the gate man, and the suitor outwitted him. "Read me the lines straight," Nick said, closing his eyes.

Nick listened. "Again," he said, "and now I am the old lady." Nick read the matriarch's lines, playing the two scenes with the actor. "Now I am the unlucky lover." Afterward, Nick leaned against the building. "I am funnier than you."

"Help me," Kaminsky said. "You helped Dieter, help me."

"I really don't walk on water," Nick said. "Try your best." He followed Kaminsky up the stairs. Near the top, though, he suddenly pushed the actor into the wall. "Did you ever play Lear?"

"More times than I can count."

Kaminsky saw something like a smile cross Nick's face. "Play Lear," Nick said. "Do it."

In the casting office they sat on creaky folding chairs beside an open window until Doug said, "Karel Kaminsky."

Doug saw Mutt and Jeff coming. He shook his head. "Uh-uh."

"I am with him," Nick said. "I am his agent."

"We're not casting agents today," Doug said.

Nick snatched the pages out of Kaminsky's hand, throwing them at Doug like confetti. He took the actor's arm. "Forget this picture," Nick said, leading Kaminsky toward the staircase. "Take the Columbia picture. You're too good for this cheap little picture."

"How many times have I heard that stale song," Doug said.

Dragging the actor, Nick said, "I will get you another thousand dollars for the Columbia picture."

"Stop," the actor whispered, "you are ruining me. Why did Dieter send me to you?" he whispered.

Behind them Doug said, "Okay."

Nick opened the staircase door and slammed it into the office wall. Doug leaped forward, hoping they would drop dead. "I said, okay-y-y-y!"

The casting director, an actor since childhood, read with Karel Kaminsky, laughing whenever the little man opened his mouth. He told Kaminsky to wait, and on his way to lunch he stopped beside the pair in their folding chairs. "Make your deal."

The actor fell across Nick, trapping him. "You wrought another miracle!" He kissed Nick on both cheeks. "You brought me back to life!" he said before Nick could untangle himself.

They came down the staircase. "Quick, before they close for lunch," Kaminsky said. "Find the man for the deal."

Dieter had agreed to the Screen Extras Guild basic salary for his few lines, and Nick had never negotiated a salary, his or anyone's. He had accepted whatever the world offered. Kaminsky nudged him. "Hurry."

Nick stopped beside Carole Lombard's convertible and stopped the actor. "If Paramount wants you today, Paramount will want you tomorrow, and tomorrow I will know how to make a deal."

Nick returned to the Ringstrasse and cornered Leopold Unger. "I must learn a new trade, fast."

Leopold listened and took Nick through the kitchen to a telephone. "Heinie Kantor," Leopold said. "He works for Republic Pictures in the payroll office."

At Paramount the following morning, Nick made his deal for Karel Kaminsky. Afterward he walked up Vine Street to the Ringstrasse. Inside, two actors confronted him: a leading man from a stock company in Freiburg in the Black Forest and an elderly veteran from Leipzig. "I've done everything," said the veteran, holding on to Nick as they went through the café to the corner table. "And I can read English. I don't require translators." So Nick had two more clients.

Two days later, Leopold gave Nick a pad with the names and telephone numbers of two women and another man. "I need an office," Nick said.

"Wait until you have money," said Leopold.

"I'll have money," Nick said. He left the café and walked to Vine Street. There he rented an office on the second floor of a building, signing his name wherever he was asked to sign. Early in the afternoon Nick bought a seven-year-old car from a used-car dealer on Sunset Boulevard, signing more papers.

"I almost forgot," said the dealer. "You *have* got a driver's license?"

"Tomorrow," Nick said. He drove out of the used-car lot, turning toward Hollywood Hills.

At dusk that day, Magda pushed herself out of a chair in her apartment. She walked to the open glass doors, hoping for a breeze. She fanned herself with both hands and returned to the chair, picking up Berte's letter.

"Hello," Nick said.

Magda had not heard him open the door. She tried to hide the letter, but she was too late. "Money?" Nick asked.

Somehow, from some unknown informer, Magda's address had become available to those refugees who huddled together in Los Angeles. Many were impoverished, and of these many formed a steady procession of mendicants pressing Magda's doorbell. She had stopped opening the door. Many waited in the street, and she could barely leave the apartment without some threadbare stranger cornering her to beg for money. She tried to lie: "I am not Magda Auerfeld." But the informer, her nemesis, had apparently furnished the emigres with a physical description. She yelled at everyone, cursing each shabby castaway who had forsaken pride, forsaken dignity, but she turned no one away empty-handed. "They will ruin me!"

Some too timid to confront Magda wrote letters, so Nick provided her with an escape that day. "Of course, money," she said. "What else?"

"Now there is one less hand in your pocket," Nick said.

"Go slow, sonny. You are only beginning," Magda said.

"Sure." Nick went into his bedroom, giving Magda her chance to push Berte's packet into her bosom. She heard Nick banging around, and when she came to his door, she saw him emptying the closet.

He said, "I rented my own—" and stopped, dumping his clothes on the bed and walking around it to the door. "It's time," he said, "More than time," and then he raised his crooked hand, touching hers. "This is not the end," he said. "Not for us. There is no end for us."

"*Ja, ja,*" she said, her lips trembling. She swung at him. "If you are going, go!"

She stayed watching him pack. He closed the luggage and picked up his coat, and as he threw it over his arm, the Beretta fell out of a pocket. Nick bent for the automatic. "It's time for the gun, too," Magda said. "Get rid of it. You don't need a gun in America."

Nick checked the safety teats before dropping the Beretta into his jacket pocket. "This gun is not for America," Nick said.

"You fool!" she bellowed in disgust. Magda followed him out of the bedroom. "You are beginning a new life." He kept going. "Stop, I say!" She had to stop him. *"Stop!"*

Nick set down his suitcase. Magda's face had turned red, and he could see her chest rising and falling with emotion. She went to her chair, bending for the envelope. "You are finished in Europe," she said. "Forget Europe." Magda extended the newspaper clipping Berte had enclosed.

Nick read, "Baron and Baroness . . ." and below saw Carly, all in white, beside Fritz in the open entrance of St. Stephen's Cathedral. They faced a crowd, and a crowd stood in the cathedral around them. Magda saw Nick shudder as though an electric current shot through him.

Carly and Fritz. Nick looked at the picture of the married man and woman. He let the clipping fall, taking the suitcase, opening the door, and leaving the apartment, descending the stairs like someone making his way through a jungle.

He left the building, crossing the street to the old car. Nick dropped the suitcase on the seat and got in. He felt in his pocket for the key, and as he pushed it into the ignition switch, his hand fell away from the dashboard and his eyes filled uncontrollably. His entire body heaved with great, convulsive sobs. Horrible, incomprehensible sounds filled the car, like the wretched cries of some flawed creature hoping to be understood. The tears gushed from his eyes while he sat helpless, imprisoned by grief, holding on to the steering wheel as though he hung somewhere in space. Tears covered his face, falling from his chin to his shirt and jacket. He cried out of pain, of agony, of rejection, of isolation, out of final and complete loss. He had been cast adrift, and in that dark Hollywood street he gave way, as a dam gives way, crumpling and torn open by the cumulative force of a thousand misfortunes.

The flashlight blinded him. "What's the problem?"

Someone stood beside the car. Nick closed his eyes against the bright beam, rubbing his face with his hands. "Nothing," he said. The beam moved. Nick blinked hard and fast. He rubbed his eyes again, and when he looked up, he saw a police officer. "I had a—" he said, and broke off, ashamed once more.

To himself the cop said, "A broad," but leaned into the car smelling to make certain. "You're not drunk," the cop said. "Can you drive?"

"Sure." Nick started the engine. "Sure, I can drive."

"Take it easy, okay?" The cop stepped back, waving the flashlight. Nick started the engine, driving down Fountain Avenue toward

Doheny, looking at Carly and Fritz in the windshield. He could not dislodge them. Baron and Baroness Von Gottisberg. They had not been satisfied with ridding themselves of him. They had sent the Leopold-stadter and his entire family off to be killed. Why? *Why?* Nick raised his right hand, forgetting his wound, and hit the steering wheel. The pain shot up through his arm, and he raised his hand, looking at the curved fingers. Why? He could hear Carly: "There's a way out for you and your family." He could hear Fritz: "You'll need a Safe Conduct." In the car Nick shouted *"Safe!"*

He turned onto Doheny Drive, crossing Sunset and climbing high into the hills. Far above the city Nick turned into a cul-de-sac. Apartments ringed the shallow street. Nick had rented the first one shown him that afternoon.

All through his first night in his new home, Nick sat in a chair until daylight turned the walls gray. He pushed off his shoes and dropped into bed, but as he closed his eyes, he saw Carly with Fritz in the palace, in the Great Hall, and, mercilessly, in bed. He remembered Carly in his arms in bed. He returned to the chair, remaining for hours facing the hills. Sometime during the day he went into the kitchen thinking he should eat. He had spent all the money he had buying food for the apartment. But he only stood in front of the refrigerator before closing the door and returning to his chair. Nick pulled off his socks, sitting in his bare feet until the combative voices of a man and woman some-where in the building sent him into the bedroom. He pulled the covers over his trousers and slept at last.

He woke late in the day. Nick had abandoned time, dividing the day into light and darkness. In the bathroom he brushed his teeth until the gums throbbed. Nick returned to the kitchen, standing while he ate out of cans. He gorged himself, stuffing cold food into his mouth, stopping as suddenly as he had begun, leaving sardines and sausages in the open cans.

He did not sleep again until deep into the night, awakening in daylight as someone knocked on his door. He went into the kitchen, taking open cans from the refrigerator as the knocking ended. Nick had sealed himself into a hideout, sharing it with Carly and Fritz. He could not avoid them. They went where he did, tormenting him with their happiness, their lust for each other, their endlessly inventive couplings from which Nick could not escape.

Nick knew he would never leave Carly and Fritz behind, would never be free of them. They would be with him always, waiting for their ultimate triumph, the moment when he collapsed and sank, joining his family in oblivion.

He dropped his clothes, wrapping a towel around himself. Alone and exhausted, his resources drained by Carly's treachery, Fritz's treachery, Nick fought a battle with himself, fought to survive, fought for his life, for what remained of his life, fought to remain whole, remain erect, and when he raised his head to the mirror, deserted and discarded, he claimed a victory. Although he had not won, he had not failed. "Clean up," he said, aloud, without pity. He had to go on so he could face them. He owed Carly and Fritz a debt, owed his family a debt.

Nick's departure left Magda isolated. He remained attentive, inviting her to the Ringstrasse, but she could not abide the breast-beating in the café, the hoi polloi telling anyone who would listen their banal biographies.

One Saturday night, in flight from loneliness, Magda went with Dieter to see Fanny in the hospital. They stayed until the desperately ill woman sent them away, exhausted by the effort necessary to talk with her visitors. In the corridor Magda said, "Prepare yourself."

"Fanny says the same," Dieter said. "She is braver than I."

They came out into the soft, sweet night. "A hospital is a terrible place," Magda said.

"It has become my home," Dieter said. "Here I begin and end my day." They walked toward his car. "Sometimes I blame Fanny, and then I want to throw myself on the floor beside the bed and ask forgiveness. Sometimes I hate everything: the hospital, the smell in the hospital, the quiet. In a hospital everyone waits—patients, nurses, doctors, and most of all, the family—guilty because they are not sick instead of the doomed wretch God has selected."

As they crossed the street, Dieter took Magda's elbow. Their footsteps made the only sound in the dark street. "Beautiful," Magda murmured. "So beautiful." Dieter's thigh brushed hers but he did not move aside, and she felt him once more before they reached the car. He opened the door, taking her arm once more to help her into the car.

They drove without speaking. Once Magda glanced at him, driving with both hands on the wheel, his face grim. The car struck a pothole, and Magda came up in the seat and dropped. She held on to the door handle. They stopped for a red light, and when it changed to green, Dieter turned the corner. "This is not the way to my apartment," Magda said.

"This is the way to my apartment," Dieter said. As she turned to him, he looked directly at her and said, "This is the way to my apartment."

Fanny and Dieter had found a building with a garden court off Robertson Boulevard in Beverly Hills. Dieter parked near the building, and they walked through the still, dim street like strangers. The cloying smell of night-blooming jasmine enveloped them, and in the court a tangerine tree in early blossom added to the heady scent.

Dieter unlocked the door. "I keep the lights burning, hoping I won't feel alone when I am inside," he said. Magda entered the past once more. Fanny Rantzau had made something of Biedermeier here in southern California, choosing solid, heavy furniture and bulky drapes for the apartment. "A brandy?" Dieter asked.

Magda stood in the entry of the small room. "I have Metaxa," Dieter said. "You always liked Metaxa." She did not reply, and he came to her, taking her hands in his. "You are trembling."

She did not protest, did not strike back in outrage, in ridicule. She had dropped her guard. She had been on the alert too long, beleaguered by her enemy, the hostile, treacherous world.

He raised his head to look directly at her, and she did not lower her eyes, and when he brought her to him, she raised her arms, enfolding him with the grace of a ballerina. "You must be gentle with me. I am a nun, a virgin."

Later, together and spent, Magda said, "How could you be so sure of me?"

"No man could be sure of you," Dieter said. "I could not come back here alone tonight. Not tonight. If you had turned me away, I would have gone . . . somewhere, a hotel, the park, to the sea."

Dieter turned on his right side, facing Magda, and she turned her back to him. "I have been alone too long," she said. "You proved this to me. I am not living. I have no appetites. I miss my appetites. I will make a big party."

"You don't know anyone in Hollywood," Dieter said.

"I'll meet them at the party," Magda said, solving that dilemma. "No one refuses an invitation to a party. I learned this long ago." Magda reached behind her, searching for Dieter, and remembered searching for Ernst in their bed in Vienna. She evicted thoughts of Ernst, who would only spoil her night. She found Dieter, claimed him, what remained of him.

Dieter felt her hand. "You're not serious?" She ignored him. "You are serious," Dieter said.

Magda persisted until, triumphant, she said, "Now, you, too, are serious."

"And you are relentless," Dieter said.

She turned to him. "Famished," she said. "I am starving."

Dieter rescued Magda from the loneliness she had endured in Hollywood, and in a way Nick's clients saved him, providing him with a kind of family. He needed roles for them, and he ranged through Hollywood like a buccaneer. Because he was alone, he was indefatigable. Nick registered at every studio, from Universal in Universal City, to Warner Brothers and Disney in Burbank, to Metro in Culver City. He quickly learned the names of every casting director, and he called them constantly. When someone hung up on him in annoyance, he called back immediately. When Nick heard another click, he left his office, driving to the studio to give the casting director a last chance.

He read the entertainment sections of every newspaper, read every Hollywood columnist, read *Variety* and *The Hollywood Reporter*, the trade papers. In the Ringstrasse he listened to all the gossip, and believed everything until he confirmed or rebutted what he had heard. He worked all day, every day.

Everything he had done for fun at the Zwischentheatre he now did for profit. Actors had trusted him in Vienna, and they trusted him now in Hollywood. Nick had an eye for matching an actor or actress with a role, however minor, and he had an ear. He could hear the false reading of a line or an entire page, hear the inaccuracy of delivery and interpretation, hear the misplaced emphasis, the unnecessary emotion, and the absent emotion. If an actor resented his critique or bellowed or bawled, insisting Nick was wrong, he tugged at his earlobe. "You cannot fool me."

He managed to achieve a minor success for minor performers. His clients were forced to work with a new language, and many could barely use it. They were like Nick, all survivors, all holding on by their fingertips. And for all his clients Nick provided continuity, however ephemeral and transient, however small the poorly paid bonanza. In the Ringstrasse Leopold Unger sat down at the corner table beside Nick. "You are a hit."

"Sure," Nick said. "The king of the extras."

One afternoon that fall, Nick returned to Vine Street from Fox, where he had taken a client for a reading. Nick shared a receptionist and a common reception room with a dentist, an accountant, and a sales representative for marine equipment.

Southern California sweltered, and Nick carried his jacket over his arm, his collar open and his tie swinging from side to side as he climbed the steps to the second floor. At the head of the stairs, he wiped his face with his shirtsleeve, and when he lowered his arm, he saw Carly.

She sat in a chair directly ahead, her head bent over something in her lap. Nick reached for the stair rail. He said, barely, "How . . ." as she raised her head and he lost her, lost her again. A stranger waited beside the door to his office. The woman's hair was shorter than Carly's and parted on the side. Nick saw the knitting needles in her hands and a square of wool. She took a pale blue ball from her lap, raising a large leather purse from the floor. The receptionist said, "Mr. Gallanz," gesturing at the woman, who dropped her knitting into the bag.

She was almost as tall as Carly. "I am Sigrid Colstad," she said. "Karel Kaminsky swears you are a genius." She spoke with an accent.

Nick opened the door. "In Hollywood a man who can tie his own shoelaces is a genius."

Sigrid smiled. Her teeth were dazzling white and perfect, and her eyes were blue, like the ball of wool she used. Nick followed her into his office, dropping his jacket on the long wooden table he used for a desk. She said, "I have decided to change agents." She sounded like Garbo, but Garbo's voice was always a caress, and Sigrid spoke like a child, openly and frankly.

Nick had more bit players than he wanted. "I have too many clients," he said. "I am only one man with more clients than jobs."

"I have a job," Sigrid said. "I am under contract to Milgrim at Majestic."

Nick dropped his arm, reaching for the rubber ball, then remembered it was in his jacket. He rubbed his right hand with his left. Sigrid thought she saw the beginnings of a smile on Nick's face. "Is that funny?"

"Sure," he said. "You came to the five-and-dime for an agent."

"Shall I leave?"

Nick wanted to represent her more than he had wanted anything since leaving Vienna. "I am not a jailer."

For a little while they faced each other like duelists, and then Sigrid bent to take a script out of the leather bag. Nick saw the Majestic Pictures eagle on the cover and the title *Ricochet*. "My next picture," Sigrid said. "Will you read the script?" She set it down on the table.

"You are testing me," Nick said.

"Are you afraid?"

"Not lately, madame."

"Mademoiselle," Sigrid said. "I am mademoiselle. Will you read it? This is serious with me."

Nick put his hand over the eagle. "Call tomorrow. I'm here early and late," he said. Sigrid watched him leafing through the script, a young man with a starving face. He seemed harmless, completely unimportant, but he made Sigrid uneasy. She had never encountered anyone as isolated.

The following afternoon, Nick saw her from the corridor once more. He crossed the reception room. "I said, call."

"We are doing business," Sigrid said. "When I do business, I like to see a face."

In his office, Nick sat on her side of the table with the script between them. "You are not Zoe, the heroine," he said. "If you had the lead, you would not be looking for a new agent."

"Darragh Delaney is playing Zoe," Sigrid said. "She is the star."

"Then you should play the sister, Sally," Nick said. "The spider. Did I pass the test?"

"They gave me Molly, Zoe's best friend," Sigrid said.

"Molly is nothing," Nick said. "Stands in the corner like a coat rack. Zoe smiles, Molly smiles. Zoe cries, Molly cries. She is not a person. She is glass." Nick rapped on the script as though knocking on a door. "Did your agent read this story?"

"My agent has two actresses at Majestic," Sigrid said, "and he is sleeping with one."

"So she is playing Sally," Nick said. "Are you better? Don't lie. I'll know if you lie."

"If I could learn to lie, maybe I would also be a star," Sigrid said.

"Tell the truth," Nick said. "Tell the studio you will not play Molly."

"I have a contract," Sigrid said. "I belong to the studio."

Nick took the script, dropping it into Sigrid's lap, and came out of his chair. "Good-bye."

His brutal dismissal made her wince. "An actress can't make such conditions," Sigrid said. "You're an agent, you know the rules. Even Bette Davis can't make such conditions." Nick sat on the table. "I'll be on suspension," Sigrid said. "My salary will stop."

"Will you go hungry?"

Sigrid stood up, digging her fingers into the script, ready to throw it at the callous stranger. "I cannot come to the studio with an ultimatum."

"Send me," Nick said.

"You will not be put into the street," Sigrid said. "Thank you for your critique and your time." She pushed the script into her purse. Nick watched her cross the reception room: trim, erect, purposeful, like a nurse. Carly had walked like a schoolgirl.

The studios closed at noon on Saturday, and the casting offices almost never put out a call for actors. Yet Nick went from one lot to the other every Saturday, looking for leads to use the following week. He always began at Metro and ended at Warner Brothers.

At twelve o'clock every Saturday Nick drove from Warner Brothers through Burbank to Ventura Boulevard into the San Fernando Valley. Near the western rim of the valley he turned north, passing orchards and horse farms until the narrow road became narrower, and the ranch houses and fences were behind him, and he was alone in the dry, clear heat.

He continued until the land fell away. Below, the road curved, skirting an arroyo. Live oaks hung over the far side of the arroyo, the branches moving slowly in the mild Santa Ana. Nick parked and left his car, standing beside the open door while he rolled up his sleeves.

He unlocked the trunk of the car and took out a satchel like a carpetbag which Magda had bought for him in Rome. Carrying the satchel, he went down into the arroyo and made his way up the other side to the live oaks. Nick walked into the trees, stopping after a hundred yards or so. He set the satchel down against a tree trunk, squatting beside it. He took out the Beretta automatic and removed the clip from the gun butt. He opened a box of ammunition and pushed thirteen rounds into the clip, filling it. Nick shoved the Beretta into the waistband of his trousers and reached into the satchel for a leather glove. He had cut off the thumb and four fingers below the knuckles. He had then brought the mutilated glove and a length of sturdy elastic to a shoemaker. He asked the shoemaker to make five cylinders of the elastic and stitch them into the truncated fingers of the glove.

Nick pulled the glove over his right hand. The elastic covered the middle joint of his fingers and thumb, helping him curl his fingers and gain the articulation he needed to support the Beretta.

Nick took a carton twelve inches square from the satchel. He carried the carton to a live oak and removed a white target of circles with a bull's-eye, hanging it from a nail he had pounded into the tree weeks earlier.

Nick retraced his steps, stopping in a clearing on a line with the target. He took the automatic from his waistband, moving the safety teats and pushing the butt up and into the meaty palm of his right hand. He needed his left hand to wrap the bent fingers around the butt so he could get his forefinger into the trigger guard.

Facing the target, he raised the Beretta and squeezed off. He paused, then squeezed off again. By the time he emptied the clip, his face was white and covered with sweat, his lips drawn back over his teeth in pain.

Nick walked to the tree. All thirteen rounds had hit the target, and two lay halfway between the edge and the bull's-eye.

At the satchel he filled the clip once more. He took another target from the open carton and hung it over the first.

Nick stopped in the clearing, the Beretta in his left hand. He fired with his left hand, emptying the clip once more, and walked to the target. All thirteen holes lay within the outer ring, and two were in the innermost ring beside the bull's-eye.

He hung another target over the two on the tree and fired two-handed. As he finished, he heard a horse neigh, and as he lowered the gun, two riders rode into the clearing.

They were Nick's age or older, and both were bigger, filling the Western saddles. One said, "This is private property."

"Yours?" Nick walked toward the satchel.

"No, but we're allowed here," said the other rider. "We're friends of the owner."

Nick squatted, releasing the clip and taking a handful of ammunition. He heard the same rider say, "What're you doing here anyhow?"

"I am shooting," Nick said, loading the clip.

The pair looked at each other, and then the rider who had spoken first said, "We're not blind."

The other said, "You're pretty smart, aren't you?"

Nick pushed the loaded clip into the gun butt. "Smarter than you," he said, walking to the clearing, facing the riders, and raising his arm. "I have a gun."

When the intruders were gone, Nick resumed shooting. He emptied clip after clip, alternating between his right hand and left, shooting until the pain in his crooked fingers forced him to stop.

Nick pulled the nail from the tree and took the targets he had used. He could imagine the two riders galloping to file a report with the owner. He would need a new shooting range next Saturday.

Nick drove back through the San Fernando Valley, using Coldwater Canyon to reach his apartment. He left his car in the short street, carrying the satchel and climbing the steps to the building built into a hillside. Walking to the door, he heard a telephone, and when he unlocked it, his phone was still ringing. Nick raised the receiver and heard a woman with an accent say, "This is Sigrid Colstad."

"He's who?" asked Leonard Votrian in his office at Majestic Pictures Monday morning, listening to his secretary. "Herb Mendelsohn is Sigrid Colstad's agent."

At her desk in the reception room his secretary said, "I told him that. He asked me to call Sigrid Colstad. It's—"

Votrian interrupted, "Sigrid Colstad is on Stage Five shooting wardrobe tests for *Ricochet*."

"No, Mr. Votrian. She isn't," said the secretary. "She's—"

"You're telling *me*!" he said, swinging around in his chair to face the blackboard which covered the entire wall behind him. Every Majestic motion picture, whether being written, in pre-production, shooting, or post-production, was on the blackboard. Leonard Votrian was a New Yorker, an accountant raised in the Bronx who had matriculated at City College, where every student had a full academic scholarship. To Votrian all of Hollywood remained a stage set. "*Ricochet*," Votrian said into the telephone. "Wardrobe tests. Stage Five. October 9. Is today October 9, Miss Malamud?"

"You won't let me finish," said Heather Malamud, facing the rude man who had barged into the reception room without an appointment. "I started to say—"

Votrian interrupted, "Go on, finish."

"Sigrid Colstad is at home," said the secretary. "She switched agents. I didn't believe him, either, so he asked me to call. So I called. It's true, Mr. Votrian. She switched agents."

Votrian picked up a pencil, pushing a pad across his desk with his elbow. "Tell me his name again. Wait . . . spell it." Votrian wrote "Nick Gallanz" on the pad. "I got it," he said. "Call the broad back and tell her to get her ass down here."

Votrian stood up, removing his jacket. More than anything he hated starting Monday morning with trouble. It was a bad sign. As he unbuttoned his vest, the door opened and Votrian saw a sloppy, thin guy moving through his office like a shadow. Votrian dropped into his chair, looking at the pad. "Nick Gallanz. You're new, huh?"

"Almost," Nick said. "And new with Sigrid Colstad."

"Yeah, well, take some advice," Votrian said. "When your client has a call, be sure she shows up for it."

"I came instead," Nick said.

Votrian made quotes around Nick Gallanz on the pad. "Go ahead."

"You gave her Molly for *Ricochet*," Nick said. "She should play Sally."

Votrian leaned far back in his chair. "The studio casts the pictures," he said. "Not the actor, not the actress. You know that unless you're deaf, dumb, and blind. We both know that. So why am I telling you? Because you're a refugee. So I'm making an exception. For you, not for her. Listen, you people cost me plenty last night. An arm and a leg." Votrian and his wife had driven all the way in from Malibu the night before, in the middle of Sunday night beach traffic, for the refugee benefit at the Hollywood Bowl. Meyer Milgrim was one of the cochairmen of the benefit. Votrian and his wife were in the box next to Milgrim and his wife, Mavis. When Votrian's wife saw his pledge, he thought she would faint. "Plenty," Votrian continued. "So get that br— your client down to Stage Five fast."

"For Sally," Nick said.

"Okay!" Votrian leaped out of his chair, and it rolled back into the blackboard. "Show's over. Your client is under contract. Right now she's in breach of contract, understand? Maybe you don't. Maybe you're out of your league. And Sigrid Colstad is out of her mind. You must be some kind of Svengali to her. The woman is screwing around with a career, with a future. The woman will be poison in this town."

"Sigrid Colstad is sick," Nick said. "She woke up with a terrible migraine headache. You can call her doctor."

"Fuck you and fuck your doctor," Votrian said. "Who do you think you're playing with? This is Majestic Pictures, you schmuck. I try to be nice and this is how you repay me? Is she coming or isn't she?"

"For Sally," Nick said.

"Okay." Votrian nodded. "You just cut your throat, Mr. Gallanz. Mr. Schmuck. Your client is out and you're out. You're barred from the lot, you greenhorn!"

Nick sprang toward the desk and Votrian, twice as big, jumped back against the blackboard. "From the lot?" Nick said. He picked up a heavy brass triangular nameplate with "LEONARD VOTRIAN" across the surface. Votrian raised his arms instinctively. "Whole countries have barred me, and you decide to scare me with Gower Street. And you cannot do it," Nick said. "R.K.O. is on Gower Street. Columbia is on Gower Street. And I am on Gower Street. And I'll stay on Gower Street." He set down the nameplate, leaving.

The following day, a slim man in tan gabardine trousers and a crisp white shirt sat beside a table on the patio of a large Mediterranean house in the 1000 block of North Roxbury Drive in Beverly Hills. The man, a native of southern California who carefully avoided the sun, sat in the shade beneath a canvas awning with broad green stripes. He had coffee and the morning newspapers, and a lighted cigarette lay in a thick glass ashtray on the table at his elbow. As he picked up the cigarette, he saw What's His Name, the gardener, walk past the pool house, carrying a flat of ranunculus bulbs. " 'Morning, Mr. Pertsick," said the gardener. "Guess it's still morning."

"Yeah, hi," said Hash Pertsick. He dragged on the cigarette, his first. Hash was thirty-three years old, with wiry, russet-colored hair, already gray, yet he looked almost boyish. He looked scrubbed like a lad on the morning of his first communion. Hash spent a long time in the bathroom when he woke—late in the morning or early in the afternoon—and when he came out, he was spick-and-span, he was shiny.

Hash heard someone behind him, Loretta probably, and then she came through the open French doors, a big, good-looking black woman, shiny like Hash or she wouldn't have lasted a day. "How's about something? I bought some real good cantaloupe and there's muffins I made."

"Uh-uh. I'm okay."

"You sure?" When Hash didn't reply, she picked up the coffeepot and filled his cup. She came out on the patio every day, offering him something new. Hash liked it, and he hoped Polly would like Loretta, along with the house itself. The house was a kind of graduation present.

Hash had bought it three months earlier from this doctor, Doctor Carteret. The doctor was retiring with his wife to Hawaii. Hash went through the place one afternoon, once over lightly, and made the deal. He bought the place furnished. Polly could throw out anything she didn't like.

The telephone rang and Hash heard Loretta answer. She came to the French doors. "For you, Mr. Pertsick." Another telephone with a mile of cord lay at Hash's feet. He picked up the instrument and set it on the table. Heather Malamud said, "Mr. Pertsick? Please hold for Mr. Votrian."

In his office, looking up at the blackboard, Votrian said, "Mr. Pertsick, you don't know me." Votrian introduced himself.

Hash watched the gardener on his knees, digging up the ground. "Yeah."

"Maybe you heard of me," Votrian said. "I heard of you. Leo

Whitfield? From Vanguard Productions? Harvey Papermaster? They mentioned you. Harvey said to say hello."

The gardener was a whiz, planting those things as fast as Hash could count. "Yeah."

Votrian said to himself, "Some conversation," and aloud, "You helped Harvey and Leo with certain matters, certain problems. Studio problems which come up here and there in any studio. I'm calling for the same reason. We have a problem here at Majestic. Can you come over?"

"Around the end of the week," Hash said. He had never lived in a house, never had a gardener. He liked to watch the gardener in the garden.

"I'll tell you, Mr. Pertsick, I got a bad problem in the studio. The end of the week is like next year. Mr. Pertsick?"

"Yeah."

"I could drive out, Mr. Pertsick. Suppose I drive out, okay?"

"I'm in my house," Hash said. He picked up the telephone, walking to the end of the patio, watching the gardener. "What's on your mind?"

Around one o'clock that night, Hash sat in his black La Salle sedan in the cul-de-sac off Doheny Drive under a street light. He wore the gabardine jacket to his suit, plus a tie and hat. Hash didn't like surprises, so he had parked the La Salle in the arc of the cul-de-sac facing Doheny, where he could see anything coming. He had been up in the building but no cigar. Hash had been waiting a long time, and the sedan was full of smoke. He was rolling down the window to dump his cigarette, waving his hands around to push out the smoke, when he heard a car. Then he saw headlights on Doheny, and then they shone in his face. Hash left the La Salle and saw the car, something out of a mud bath.

Nick parked, rolling up the window in case it rained, and walked toward the steps.

"Got a match?"

Nick hadn't seen the man near the big car. "I am not a smoker," Nick said.

The man raised his hand, and a flame rose from the cigarette lighter he held. "Nick Gallanz, right? The agent?" Hash said.

Nick decided he had been trapped by an actor, using the matches and lighter for a dramatic entrance. "Find another agent," he said. "I have plenty of clients."

Nick took a step and discovered the man stood between him and the stairs. "Hang around," Hash said. "I came by to talk about one of your clients. Sigrid Colstad."

Nick looked at the stranger, dressed for a party. "Now? One o'clock in the morning?"

"I'm a night owl," Hash said. He took a deep drag on the cigarette and tossed it into the street. "Sigrid is giving them a problem over at Majestic. You're her agent, so I'm not telling you something new. The lady got a contract. She's got a picture, they put her in a picture. They're all set at the studio, but Sigrid has been AWOL for two days." Hash made a face. "She's a big girl, this Sigrid. Staying home is kid stuff. It doesn't do her any good. It doesn't help you any, either. Making movies is a business. Majestic is in business. So is she, so are you. Stop the kid stuff."

Nick looked at the man who drove the big, shiny car. "You didn't come from Majestic," Nick said.

"They asked me in," Hash said. "Call me a third party. I'm not mad at anyone—you, Sigrid, Majestic. I drove up here to settle this thing with nobody getting hurt and no hard feelings. Here's one way. Sigrid says she's sick." Hash put his finger into Nick's chest. "You tell her to get well."

"I told her to be sick," Nick said.

Hash took out his pack of cigarettes and selected one. Votrian had sent him out with only half the story. "*You* told her."

"Sure. They gave her the wrong role," Nick said. "If they give her the right role, she will make this picture."

Hash always tried to duck trouble if he could. He lit his cigarette. "You guessed wrong," he said. "I'm leveling with you now. The studio has a contract. Bring her in tomorrow. Wardrobe tests, they call it."

"Mister, you don't hear," Nick said.

"One of us doesn't," Hash said. "You're kind of new here, new in America, too. In America when you make a deal, you keep it. And Sigrid has to keep her deal. Otherwise she could be in trouble. Lots of things could happen to her, none of them good. And you could be in trouble. You hear me now, right? You could have an accident. You could be walking down Sunset Boulevard in broad daylight, and slip and fall. You could fall without slipping. You could go down and stay down."

Hash could have sworn the man smiled. "You are a gangster."

Hash said, "Hold it," uncomfortable all of a sudden, like he had found dirt in his pants.

"They sent you to make me afraid," Nick said. "Tell them you made me afraid." He walked around Hash, who watched him ambling along like someone out for some air. Hash knew he could have been holding a flamethrower and the guy wouldn't have looked back. The Nazis must've run all the fear out of the dude. Hash had been wasting his time.

A dog somewhere woke Hash around ten o'clock the next morning, so Loretta heard him moving around earlier than usual, and plugged in the electric percolator.

On the patio later, Hash called Leonard Votrian. "I saw that party last night," Hash said.

"Excuse me, but the girl isn't here," Votrian said.

"You didn't tell me she's home because he told her to stay home."

"Nick Gallanz is not my casting director," Votrian said. "My casting director is downstairs on the first floor."

"Yeah," Hash said, inhaling and letting the smoke drift from his nostrils. "He could be wrong, your casting director. Your guy picks up a check every week, win or lose. Nick Gallanz, if he's wrong, he don't eat. But he keeps the girl AWOL. Who do you believe, your guy or him?"

"Excuse me, but I don't take orders from agents," Votrian said.

He made Hash tired. "Hell, make him an ex-agent," Hash said. "Bring him in off the street, and he'll be on your side. You won't need to worry about actors because you'll be paying this dude to worry."

"Thanks very much," Votrian said. "Harvey Papermaster told me you are cash and carry. How much do I owe you?"

"I don't get paid unless I do something," Hash said. "I didn't do nothing."

Votrian pushed the telephone aside, rising and looking at the blackboard, at his death sentence.

The board was lined horizontally and vertically. The last heading was "DELIVERED," and that column was filled top to bottom. Every movie had a delivery date, when the cans of film reached film exchanges for transmittal to exhibitors. Because exhibitors scheduled pictures for showing months in advance, neither Majestic nor any studio broke a delivery date, ever. Leonard Votrian was responsible for the physical production of every Majestic movie.

Seconds after talking with Hash Pertsick, Votrian bent over his desk for the telephone. "Call upstairs. I have to see Milgrim right away. Production." Meyer Milgrim would throw out the pope if he caused a production problem.

Votrian began to button his vest and stopped, grabbing the telephone. "Did you call Milgrim?"

"Mr. Votrian, I only have two hands," said Heather.

"Thank you. Forget Milgrim," Votrian said. "Use your two golden hands to call Nick Gallanz." Votrian finished buttoning his vest, looking at the blackboard. If he told Meyer Milgrim he had trouble with an actress, he and she would both be finished. No actor made the rules in Hollywood. The men who ran the studios had settled with actors long before. When *Ben Hur* had been released, Francis X. Bushman had become the biggest star on earth. And he began to speak indelicately of studio chiefs. And they had a meeting. Soon Bushman was frying hamburgers in his shop in Chicago. He never worked in Hollywood again.

Votrian fell into his chair. He hated agents. Why had he let Herb Mendelsohn talk him into giving that hooker the role of Sally in *Ricochet*? Votrian knew for a fact Mendelsohn's broad had been a hooker, a cheap hooker, too, in New Orleans. What did he owe Herb Mendelsohn besides heartburn? Let the hooker play Molly. She was lucky to get anything. Votrian could not let *Ricochet* fall behind schedule. That hooligan, Hash Pertsick, had made sense. Votrian had been a man alone since his arrival in Hollywood. Now he would have someone downstairs on his side, someone reporting to him and only him. Votrian didn't need Meyer Milgrim's okay to hire an assistant casting director. He grabbed the telephone. "Miss Malamud, how about Nick Gallanz?"

10

ONE MORNING IN THE
first week of March 1940, Carly walked through the Graben, turning
into Kohlmarkt. She wore one of her baggy coats with a long red scarf
around her neck. Carly's hands were in her pockets, and she played
with some coins in her right hand like someone with worry beads. She
walked as though she was lost, feeling abandoned and deserted and
thinking of turning back or running. Carly lived with fear whenever
Varlingen sent for her, a constant, heavy pressure which lay across her
shoulders like a yoke. She reviled herself for being afraid, calling herself
a spineless slacker on her way to Michaeler Platz.

In the square she stopped, shading her eyes with her hand to look
from one end to the other. Michaeler Platz seemed grimy and forsaken
on this gray day. She could not see the organ grinder, and she believed
immediately she had failed, had somehow misread her instructions.
Fighting panic, she forced herself to enter the square. Her coat billowed
in the wind, and she thrust her hair back from her forehead, trying to
locate the organ grinder. She stopped, waiting for an army truck to

pass, and continued slowly, repeating her instructions: Michaeler Platz between ten and eleven in the morning. Carly stopped once more as she heard the waltz from *Der Rosenkavalier.*

On the far side of the square, shielded by three young German soldiers, Carly saw the organ grinder cranking the music box. His monkey was climbing all over the soldiers, pushing the tin can into their faces for money, jabbering impatiently. Carly put her hand into her coat pocket to gather up her coins.

The frenetic little beast, wearing a tiny army garrison cap, saw Carly coming and leaped from a soldier's shoulder to hers, raising the cup and banging on it with his paw. The organ grinder kept the monkey on a long leash clipped to its collar. Carly dropped some coins into the tin cup, and the monkey sprang from her shoulder to her forearm and down to the ground, climbing up the organ grinder's body.

The man tipped his hat. His coat was covered with miniature swastikas attached to long pins. The monkey took one from its master and jumped back to Carly's shoulder, pushing the pin into her coat. Carly dropped more coins into the tin cup, and as she left, she heard one of the soldiers say, "Need company?"

She said, "Yes, yes, yes," to herself, moving briskly, skirting the new Hofburg and leaving Michaeler Platz to enter the Burggarten. Carly stopped, taking the pin from her coat, and tore open the swastika. Carly removed a tiny cylinder of paper which had been wrapped around the pin. She read, "Osterreichische. Judith, 2."

Carly had almost three hours to kill. She couldn't eat, couldn't think of food, couldn't sit in a library reading, couldn't sit in a park, and she could not return to the palace and invent a new reason to leave again.

At one-thirty, Carly entered the Osterreichische Gallerie, unwinding the red scarf from her neck. She moved slowly through the museum, going from room to room, pausing now and then before a painting or sculpture. Once she sat down on a bench, crossing her ankles and looking at the pictures on the wall, but she saw nothing. She was merely waiting for two o'clock.

Finally she stopped before Gustav Klimt's painting of Judith. The woman in the painting stood erect, facing the world, a brunette partially covered with a gold shawl. Carly saw a full-bodied woman, a confident, patrician creature and yet undeniably, frankly sensual. Her left breast and navel were exposed, and that swath of white flesh, lifelike and startling, would draw any man to Klimt's painting. The woman's frank carnality, her seductive eyes, disturbed Carly. For a little while, alone with the painting, Carly forgot time and place.

"She is one of my favorites."

Carly hadn't seen or heard the intruder come in. Beside her, leaning on a cane, was a wizened skeletal man. His cheeks were sunken and the bones of his face protruded as though the mottled skin would burst. He didn't look at Carly. "I've kept you waiting," he said. "If you are ever offered arthritis, refuse the gift. Sometimes it becomes a vise. I need warm winds and sunny skies, but Der Führer has reduced travel. Look at the painting, child, not at me. We are strangers. Good."

Carly heard heavy footsteps. The floor creaked as the footsteps persisted until she saw two men in dark suits, older men who could be Gestapo. They stopped behind and to one side of Carly. Neither spoke, and Carly expected them to remain forever. She thought of sitting down on the bench near the wall, then of finding the ladies' room and staying until the Gestapo had gone, but she wouldn't know when they had. Then the gnome who had joined Carly left her, walking in a kind of shuffle, using the cane with every step. The two men stepped aside and followed him out, leaving Carly alone and abandoned. She couldn't chase the old man, for that would make the Gestapo or anyone suspicious. She wanted to ask for help, wanted Varlingen to arrive with instructions. She hated Varlingen and then herself for hating him. She heard Varlingen, heard him clearly, every word, here in the lovely museum in front of Klimt's voluptuary: "I take only volunteers." Carly pushed her hair back from her forehead, leaving *Judith* to find the old man.

She left the room and entered another. It was empty, and she crossed it to the broad corridor. He had disappeared! Carly hurried toward the staircase, trying not to attract attention, passing several schoolgirls in uniform.

"Young woman."

He stood in a room to her right. She saw him raise the cane and drop it. "Please."

Carly darted into the room, bending for the cane. She said, "I'll help you," taking his arm. She could not lose him again.

Proceeding at his slow pace, they returned to the corridor. "You may look at me now," he said. "You're my angel of mercy now. Saturday morning. Ostbahnhof," he said, directing Carly to the railroad station for the east. "Come just before ten." His face twisted in pain, and he turned pale.

"Rest," Carly said. "We can sit over there."

"Standing or sitting is the same for me," he said. "And do not interrupt. Let me finish while I can." At the stairs Carly held on to him, and he held on to the bannister. "You must remove one of the guards from his post for at least ten minutes," he said. "That is the absolute minimum. Ten minutes. Repeat everything I've said to yourself. Not to me, not aloud, to yourself. Leave me at the foot of these stairs. One of the guards for ten minutes."

Carly emerged from the museum and stopped as though she had lost her way. She had to turn back and question the old man. "You can't," she muttered, angry with herself once more. Her instructions were clear. Everything else came from fear. She began to walk, faster and faster so she couldn't turn back. Carly shoved her hands into her pockets and found the small Nazi flag. As she crossed the street, she took the flag out of her pocket and began to tear it.

Carly didn't see Fritz until he joined her in the study just before dinner. He put his arms around her middle. "One of the rewards of losing you for the day is finding you." Fritz kissed her. He cocked his head, looking into her eyes, and kissed her once more. "I've missed you," he said. "Walther Cnobra called."

"Cnobra?" Carly shook her head. "Called me?"

"He called here," Fritz said. "Zinn took his name, and I don't know the name."

"And I don't know him, either," Carly said.

Whenever they were alone, Fritz insisted on dining at a small table in the Petit Salon so that he could face Carly. "I told you I like the view."

Later, climbing the stairs, Fritz put his arm across Carly's shoulders. "Sleep well."

Carly left him at the door of his bedroom, and she heard it close as she walked through the corridor. Her door was ajar, and as she entered her room, she discovered that all the lights were turned up.

Carly kicked off her shoes, undressing as she went to the closet. She burrowed into a thick, fluffy robe, and in the bathroom she scrubbed her face. At the bed she reached for the covers and stopped, her hand extended like someone posing. On her pillows lay an emerald.

The green gem seemed alien and mysterious. Carly hugged herself. She said, "Fritz," and saw the string which passed through a gold loop set into the emerald.

The string ran across the covers and over the side of the bed. Carly took the emerald, following the string to the door and into the corridor. "Fritz," she said, seeing a diamond on the floor.

She found another emerald near Fritz's door, and when she opened it, he lay high up in bed. "Carly, how nice," he said, as though he stood at the door of the palace welcoming a guest. Carly saw the string wound around his finger. He pulled her to him, hand over hand, like a fisherman landing a catch. Carly laughed, holding on to her end of the string. Fritz took a small bowl from the night table. Carly saw a cluster of diamonds and emeralds.

She said, "Fritz . . ." and broke off. He continued to confound her with his schemes, his surprises, his gifts. She said, "Where . . . ?" and stopped once more, familiar now with his fairy tales. As he waited with the bowl, Carly threw back the covers.

Afterward, looking up at the cherubs in the ceiling, Carly suddenly remembered Walther Cnobra had telephoned that day. He was a shy government clerk in a village, a bachelor living with his widowed mother, the hero of A Stranger to Love, a comedy which the Zwischentheatre had presented.

Carly remembered the rehearsals, remembered Nick's suggestion that in a woman's presence Cnobra should stammer. Lying beside Fritz, Carly could see the Zwischentheatre stage, could see Nick with Max Ingster, could hear Nick, until her memories became intolerable and she slipped out of Fritz's bed.

Carly waited until noon the next day, until there were more cars, more pedestrians, more German soldiers on sightseeing sorties. She drove through the Inner City and into District VIII, and for the first time since the Anschluss, to Josefstadter Strasse. She came out of desperation, propelled by blind hope. She did not know where to find Max Ingster. Since he had used Walther Cnobra to identify himself, Carly prayed he had offered the name as a code and would be waiting for her in the Zwischentheatre.

In November 1938, on a night since called Kristallnacht, Nazis in Germany and Austria, in every city and town and village, had tried to destroy all physical evidence of a Jewish presence, smashing and looting shops, burning synagogues, killing Jews they captured, setting fires which sent flames into the sky from border to border.

At the storefront, Carly stood in front of a skeleton. The two rectangles where the windows had been shattered were like enormous eye sockets. Blackened by smoke and soot, the doorway remained, but there was no door.

Carly entered and stopped, for it was colder inside than on the street, as though an icy wind roamed through the burned and blackened storefront. Daylight fell into the theater, and for several feet Carly could see the small, familiar room where she had been happy. Nothing remained. Der Chineser's troops had poured enough gasoline to burn down a cathedral. Even the ceiling had been burned, and above her Carly saw charred studs and rafters, like the ribs of a shipwreck. She said softly, "Max." Instantly she turned, looking into the street for passersby who might have heard her. A young woman holding a little girl's hand passed, and then an elderly pair clutching each other for support. Carly turned back, peering into the rear, and this time she said, "Walther?"

She proceeded slowly, avoiding the stumps of burned benches which rose from the floor like tree trunks after a forest fire. "Walther?"

Looking up, she found the track which had carried the curtain. The dressing rooms were ashes. On the floor Carly saw two enamel doorknobs. "Walther?" She heard only the sounds of the street and then, without warning, the voices of all those she had loved, here, backstage. She heard Dolly Stacker announcing that she could not continue her role, heard Judith Emmerich's booming declaration of disaster, heard Sepp Wiegend, heard Max, and, above the jabbering, a shrill whistle from Nick, silencing them. She heard the whistle ringing in her ears, heard Nick, serenely confident, promising everyone they had a hit. Carly heard every word, saw the group huddling around Nick, saw Nick. She said, "Please," begging him to stop, to go away, begging them all to go away, but nobody heard, nobody saw Carly. She ran, raising the ashes and dust which covered the burned floor, running into the daylight. She stopped beside the storefront, head bowed, her back to the street as though she had seen someone she hoped to avoid.

Other voices intruded. Carly saw three women approach, and she followed them, straining to hear what they said to escape from the ghosts who had captured her in the storefront.

Trailing the women, Carly almost passed her coupe. She stopped, quivering as she leaned against the car. She had been with the dead, had listened to their voices. Only Nick remained and he, too, was lost to her.

She had forgotten Max! Carly looked up and down the street as though she would find him among the pedestrians in Josefstadter Strasse. She would never find him. She had left him with the other ghosts. Carly opened the door of the coupe. "About t-time," said a voice from inside.

She said, "Where . . . ?" and Max Ingster fell across her to close the door. As he sat back, Carly threw her arms around him. "I didn't know where to look," she said, holding him. "I didn't remember

Walther Cnobra until—" she said, and stopped. "Max," she said, holding him. For the first time since her wedding, Carly was not alone.

"W-will you let go?" Max took her arms, freeing himself, and as Carly sat back in her seat, she began to weep.

"Carly." Max made a face. "Holy . . . Hey, Carly," he said, his stutter gone in the crisis of a woman's tears. "Hey, will you stop?" Max pulled out a large handkerchief and covered Carly's face.

Crying, she began to laugh and grabbed him again, pressing him to her, unaware that she had made the wiry gym teacher a surrogate for Nick. Max freed himself once more. "This is dangerous, Carly. I'm dangerous, and when you're with me, you're in danger. That's the last thing I want. You're safe, you and your baron, so stay safe. So let's make this fast. I called you because there isn't anyone else. They're all dead or they're all Nazis or they work for the Nazis."

She gave him back his handkerchief and opened her purse. "I don't have much today, but I'll get more."

Max took what she gave him. "Money is only half my trouble," he said. "I need a roof over me. I'm in the streets, Carly. The SS patrol all night, every night, with searchlights and dogs. I'm without papers, Carly, and I can't get them. Do you know of a place for me?"

"No," Carly said, and immediately, "Yes! Yes!" She saw Max's face change, become younger. "The stables. Behind the palace."

The stable doors were never locked, and the large upper story, once the hayloft, had been deserted for decades, unused even for storage. "No one goes there," Carly said. "You can come after dark and leave before daylight. Come tonight."

"Carly." Max leaned forward, his shoulder against the dashboard. "Look at me, Carly. You're sure?"

"I'll leave blankets up there, and a pillow," Carly said. "But we'll need somewhere to meet during the day."

"Stay away from me," Max said.

"I can't lose you again," Carly said. She took his arm, holding him with both hands. "Think of somewhere—the Osterreichische Gallerie!" she said. "Two o'clock Saturday," she said, and instantly, "Not Saturday, Monday. Two o'clock next Monday." She shook his arm. "Promise."

He nodded and Carly kissed him. "L-let go," he said, and as Carly released him, he opened the door of the coupe. "S-stay here," he said. "Wait till I disappear."

Carly saw him crossing Josefstadter Strasse. She saw him reach the far side of the street, passing two nuns, and then Carly lost him.

She drove into District XIV where she never shopped. At a large workingmen's store she bought two heavy wool blankets and two pillows. She bought pillowcases, and with the saleswoman's help she pulled them over the pillows. Her purchases made two large, bulging bundles. "I'll carry one," said the saleswoman.

Carly took a bundle in each hand. "I can handle these," she said. She stuffed the bundles in the coupe. The packages filled the seat, and it seemed as though she had a passenger. About a mile from the store, Carly swung over to the curb and stopped. Fritz might return to the palace at the same time, and they would meet in the courtyard.

Carly jammed both packages into the trunk of the coupe and locked it. She could not dislodge the key. A barber spotted the gorgeous woman and emerged from his shop. "You need a man," he said as the key slid free. Carly almost ran around the car, slamming the door and stepping on the starter.

The stables were empty. She had returned before Fritz. She stopped the coupe and sat, trying to think. She could not unlock the trunk. Fritz could return and catch her.

In the palace, she gave Zinn her coat and kept her purse, walking toward the stairs. "Carly?"

She stopped as though she had stepped into a trap. "In here," Fritz said from the study.

Carly ran her hands over her dress, then over her hair, as though she was covered with clues. Fritz sat at the desk with a big checkbook. Carly remembered giving Max all her money. "I didn't see the Daimler," she said.

"I left it with Spangenberg for brakes," Fritz said, closing the checkbook. "I'll need the coupe tomorrow."

"Tomorrow? I—" Carly said, and broke off, afraid she would make him suspicious.

Fritz joined her, leading Carly out of the library. "Why don't I buy you a car? I will buy you a car," he said. "Pick a car and a color."

"I like the coupe," Carly said.

"Maybe I'll buy me one," Fritz said. He put his arm around her. "I'm freezing." They came up the stairs. "I intend to sink into a steaming tub." Fritz released her. "Join me?"

She held on to her purse with both hands as though she could hide behind it. "Perhaps."

In her room she took the keys from her purse and sat on the bed. Following Fritz in her head, she watched him undress, go into the bathroom to turn the taps, test the water with his hand, push the plunger to lower the stopper. Then she could be still no longer. Carly left her room, walking through the corridor, passing Fritz's door.

In the stables, Carly had to turn on the primitive lamps which hung from the rafters. She opened the trunk of the coupe and removed both bundles, leaving one at the foot of the ladder leading to the hayloft. She carried one bundle up to the hayloft and returned for the second. There were dormer windows in the gabled roof, several of which had been open for decades. Using the ignition key as a knife, Carly ripped apart the bundles, pulling out the blankets and pillows to make a bed for Max beneath the moldering harness hanging from wooden pegs in the walls.

Suddenly Carly heard something and sprang up, hitting a wooden pillar with her shoulder. A soft, fluttering whoosh filled the hayloft, and Carly ducked as a bird flew through the murky light and out an open window.

Carly came down the ladder and, rubbing her shoulder, crossed the courtyard. She was almost at the palace door when she remembered to return to the stables and close the trunk lid. Carly walked out of the stables and saw Zinn. "Is there a problem, Baroness?"

She said, "Problem?" and then, "No, not really," returning to the palace as though she was alone.

Zinn beat her to the door and held it for her. "Can I help, Baroness?"

Varlingen had warned Carly never to leave riddles behind. "I misplaced some stockings I bought," she said. "I must have left them in the shop."

"Let me check the coupe once more, Baroness," Zinn said. "I have a flashlight with a powerful beam."

"Thank you, Zinn," she said. "John Muntz and Sons. It's a tan box."

Carly's left arm ached from her shoulder to her wrist. She ignored her arm. For the first time that day she felt neither fear nor apprehension. She felt triumphant, and in the palace, walking up the stairs, she began to unbutton her dress as she made her way toward Fritz in the bathtub.

In the coupe Saturday morning Carly drove from the palace to a prosthetic shop in District III. The shop window was filled with artificial arms and legs and hands and feet, all grouped around a wheelchair in the center of the display. The wheelchair had a hinged wooden seat. Tilted against it on either side were two more chairs, folded flat. Carly sounded her horn, and the owner came out of the shop with a folded chair. Carly had paid for it the previous day.

She drove directly to the Ostbahnhof, the railroad station for the east. She saw soldiers everywhere, all with rifles and full field packs. More soldiers came out of trucks which stopped in the street, blocking intersections. Carly tried to escape, turning left, away from the Ostbahnhof, discovering immediately she had been trapped. Ahead, the street lay clogged with army vehicles, and two huge vans had followed her. She looked at the dashboard clock as the minute hand moved to twenty-three minutes after nine. Carly knew it was the correct time. Everything worked in Fritz's cars.

She opened the door and leaned out of the coupe. She saw a mass of stalled cars, trucks, vans. She fell back in the seat, closing the door and watching the clock through the spokes of the steering wheel. When the minute hand passed nine-thirty, Carly came out of the coupe. The driver of the van behind her, a corporal, leaned against the fender, smoking. "Hope you brought your lunch, lady."

"I must meet my cousin," Carly said. "I can't be late."

"You can't, but you will be," said the corporal.

Only inches separated the coupe and the car ahead. Carly looked back. The van's bumper touched hers. "Give me some room," she said. She thought she heard the dashboard clock. "Please."

"Lady, you're not going anywhere," said the corporal.

Carly came forward as though she intended to hit him. "Move back!" she said.

The corporal opened the door and stepped up on the running board. "You're still not going anywhere," he said as rain began to fall.

Carly ran back to the coupe. She had lost three more minutes, and when she started the engine, the minute hand moved again, to nine thirty-four. She looked into the rearview mirror and as the van moved, she released the clutch, backing away from the car in front of her. The van stopped and Carly bumped into it. She shifted gears, turning the steering wheel until she could turn no more. Then she inched forward, missing the car ahead by a hair. Driving up and over the curb, she swung the wheel in the opposite direction until she felt the right rear tire come up onto the sidewalk. Carly stopped, turning off the engine and raising the emergency brake. She came out of the coupe, running around it, opening the other door so she could get the folded wheelchair.

The clock in the Ostbahnhof stood at nine forty-seven when Carly entered the terminal, stopping to open the wheelchair, pushing down on the hinged wooden seat until it lay flat. Uniformed men filled the terminal, and she heard, somewhere, the waltz from *Der Rosenkavalier*.

Carly pushed the wheelchair toward the railroad tracks. An iron fence higher than a railroad car rose from the terminal floor. A single iron gate provided the only access to the trains. The organ grinder stood beside two sergeants guarding the gate.

His monkey scurried about on its long leather leash, shoving the tin cup at every uniform it encountered, jabbering away like a harridan on her stoop. A squad of armed soldiers commanded by a captain marched toward the gate. The monkey ran to the captain, cup raised, chattering incessantly, and as it reached the Nazi, he lashed out with his boot, sending the animal flying. The monkey rolled across the floor like a ball, squealing and yowling in pain as the captain took his troops through the gate.

Carly saw two long freight trains, each with two locomotives facing the fence on Tracks One and Two. Armed troops at attention ringed the trains, which stretched from the iron fence beyond the open end of the terminal. Carly saw men standing in the open in the rain.

She heard the monkey wailing, its voice a high, rasping screech, as it limped to the organ grinder. The waltz stopped abruptly as the man, wearing a leather pouch hanging from his shoulder, bent to gather up the monkey and cradle the little animal in his arms. "Here, here, baby," he said, reaching into the pouch to feed the animal. "Here's some good stuff for you." As Carly pushed the wheelchair past the organ grinder, she looked at the clock: nine fifty-three. She came to the gate. "I must meet my cousin."

The two sergeants, who had stood reveille at four o'clock that morning before riding almost two hours from their tent barracks in an open truck to reach the Ostbahnhof, looked at the tall beauty with the long hair glistening with rain. Each of the two sergeants simultaneously wondered what she was like beneath the long horse blanket of her coat. "He's on the train from Munich," Carly told the sergeants at the gate. She could hear the monkey whimpering.

"You'll meet him," one of the sergeants told Carly. "You've got"— he looked at the clock—"nine minutes. He's due in at ten-five." The sergeant grinned and pointed at the wheelchair. "Have a seat."

"No, no." Carly shook her head. "He broke his leg in training. Building a bridge. He's in the engineers and they were dynamiting."

"He's one lucky trooper, that cousin of yours."

Carly said, "Lucky . . . ?" and stopped. She had to take one of them with her through the gate. She looked at the sergeant closest to her. She read his nameplate, "P. Herbst," and saw the other name-plate: S. Lodman. "P.," Carly said, touching the nameplate with the tip of her forefinger. "Paul," she said.

"Try Peter," said Sergeant Herbst, grinning.

"Peter," she said, and pushed her forefinger into the S. of the other. "Stefan."

"Correct," said Sergeant Lodman.

"It's a sign," Carly said, looking into his eyes. She put her hand into his, and immediately felt his fingers tightening around hers. "Help me," she said. After the months with Fritz, Stefan was easy.

"Lady, we're posted here," said Herbst. "We can't leave our post." Carly held Stefan's hand. "You'll be here," she said to Herbst.

"We're both stationed here. We're here until we're relieved," Peter said. They could hear the train from Munich, and then the bright beam of the locomotive headlight flowed along the tracks.

Carly moved her hand in Stefan's. "I need you," she said, low, watching him.

"Hell, I'll be right back," Stefan said, and to Carly, pulling her, "Let's go! Let's go!"

"Stefan!" Peter said. "Sergeant!" Stefan pushed the wheelchair through the open gate, holding on to Carly. "You're leaving your post, Sergeant," said Herbst. "I'm not covering for you." Carly hurried to keep up with Stefan and the wheelchair. "Sergeant, I'm not covering for you!" said Herbst. Behind him the organ grinder raised the leather collar from the monkey's neck.

Carly and Stefan reached the Munich tracks. The locomotive seemed to grow and grow as it chugged slowly into the station, blotting out everything else in the Ostbahnhof. "What outfit is he with?" Stefan asked. He yelled into Carly's ear. "What outfit?"

"I don't know," Carly shouted back.

"What's his name?" Stefan said.

"Gustav Flax," Carly said, ready for him. "He's a corporal." The locomotive passed them, inching toward the barrier near the iron fence.

"Corporal Flax," Stefan said. "Start looking, lady." The train shuddered to a complete stop, and soldiers in full field packs poured out of every car.

At the gate, the organ grinder held the monkey in his arms. Sergeant Herbst paced back and forth across the open gate, his right hand on the big Luger revolver on his hip. He didn't see the two infantry majors approaching in cadence, their legs rising and falling as one. Herbst almost walked into them. He jumped back, coming to attention as the heels of his boots clicked. "The train from Munich," said one of the majors.

Herbst looked directly ahead into space. "Track Six, sir," he said. Behind him the organ grinder bent, lowering the monkey. "Just arrived, sir," Herbst said as the two officers swung past him to the right. In that moment the monkey scurried through the gate.

"My baby!" The organ grinder's voice rose in a cry of anguish, like a mother's for her child. "My baby!" He ran through the gate after the monkey.

"Hey, you!" said Herbst, lunging forward to stop the trespasser. One of the majors turned and saw the procession. He poked his colleague and both laughed. In turn, the organ grinder laughed, raising his hat. They went on toward Track Six, and as the organ grinder bent, hand extended to grab the monkey, the tiny animal, ready for fun, scampered away toward the other end of the terminal, toward Track One.

By now the platform beside the Munich train was filled with troops. "Do you see him?" asked Sergeant Lodman, pushing the wheelchair.

Carly said, "I don't see him yet."

"Where the hell is he?" Stefan stopped, facing her. "The train is almost empty." He should never have let the dame talk him into leaving his post. "Listen, I'm going back."

"Wait, please," Carly said. "He's probably inside. He probably can't get out of his seat."

"Look for him, then," Stefan said.

"Stefan," Carly said, moving against the sergeant, her face almost touching his. "He needs a man. So do I."

Stefan shoved the wheelchair into Carly. "Hold on to this," he said, pointing at the locomotive. "You watch the front end. I'll check these last four cars. These last four and that's it, lady."

As Stefan swung aboard the railroad car, the organ grinder trapped the monkey against the wall of the terminal beside Track One. "I've got you, naughty baby." As the monkey darted toward the tracks, the organ grinder fell forward, stretched full length, getting one of the animal's hind legs. The monkey squealed in protest, but his master held on. He came to his knees, gathering up the monkey. Beside him lay the pouch he carried. Still on his knees, hiding the pouch with his body, the organ grinder pushed it off the platform and onto the rail bed below.

Five minutes later, Stefan Lodman caught up with Carly on the platform. "If your cousin is on this train, he's hiding."

"You only saw the rear cars," Carly said. "He's probably up front."

Stefan set his garrison cap squarely on his head, tugging at the visor. "You find him, lady. He's your cousin," he said. He could be shot for leaving his post. He made an about-face and saw two majors coming straight at him. For a moment he believed they had been sent to put him in front of a firing squad. But they didn't even see him until he raised his arm to salute. They returned his salute, passing him. Stefan strode toward the gate, promising to attend Mass for a full year.

Neither his siren nor his red lights could clear a path for Der Chineser that morning. He sent his driver into one shortcut after another trying to reach the Ostbahnhof, but they were blocked in every direction. An hour after leaving his office, Der Chineser said, "Stop here," opening the door of the Mercedes while the car continued to roll.

He had to walk almost a half mile to the railroad station. Der Chineser knew about the two freight trains on Track One and Track Two. He had been in the station every day for ten days.

Inside, Der Chineser stopped at the open gate. He had checked out the two sergeants, Peter Herbst and Stefan Lodman, when they were assigned to the detail posted at the gate around the clock. "Anything?" asked Der Chineser as he saw a woman in a long coat pushing a wheelchair.

One of the sergeants said, "All quiet here, sir." Der Chineser watched the woman, who reminded him of the Baroness Von Gottisberg. Then she passed under a bright light and he saw her clearly.

Der Chineser would never intrude on the baroness. He stayed far behind, ready to help if she needed it. She stopped at the entrance to fold the wheelchair, and Der Chineser turned slightly in case she looked back. He gave her a head start, and when he came out of the terminal, he saw her crossing the street. He smiled when he saw the coupe up on the sidewalk. She and the baron were two of a kind. He stopped behind a large truck while the baroness put the wheelchair into the coupe. Der Chineser saw her stand beside the car, trapped in the jungle of vehicles. He went to the truck cab and raised his opened wallet to show the driver the small bronze medallion pinned inside. "I want this street cleared starting now. Pass the word up and down."

When he returned to the Ostbahnhof, he went to the gate. "Did you see a woman with a wheelchair?"

Lodman looked at Herbst, warning him to remain deaf and dumb. "Oh, her," Stefan said. "She came for her cousin, sir. Her cousin is an engineer who broke his leg in training. She couldn't find him, sir. Guess she picked the wrong train."

Der Chineser went through the gate. How did the baroness expect to get a man with a cast on his leg into the coupe? She should have taken the Daimler.

Shortly after midnight, a deep, reverberating roar woke Fritz. As he reached for the lamp beside his bed, a second detonation, stronger than the first, tore through the palace. Fritz heard the tinkle of breaking glass, and knew the bedroom windows had caved in from the shock. And he knew as well the source of the reverberating thunder. An arms depot was exploding. Troops and armament had been moving into Vienna for weeks.

Fritz rushed out of the bedroom and down the dark corridor to Carly. She lay against several pillows, holding an open book. "Fritz, are you all right?"

He entered her bedroom for the first time in their marriage. "I was worried about you," he said, stopping as another blast ripped through the city, part of a continuing burst, like an artillery barrage.

The sky became bright. Balls of flame shot into the air, and with these, spears and javelins of fire. The bedroom glowed from the massive explosion, and as they looked out at the fire, another explosion filled the sky with more flames. When he could be heard, he said, "Someone has blown up Der Führer's munitions. And broken my windows."

"You'll freeze," Carly said, adding, "Fritz, you're barefoot."

"We're not in the Arctic."

She raised the covers. "Come into—"

"I'll live," Fritz interrupted. "My problem is finding a glazier who can match these windows." He walked to the door on the icy floor. "These windows survived the Turks."

Fritz found no mention of the explosion in the newspapers, nor did he hear of the episode on the radio. Yet when Zinn and Matilda, his wife, returned from church the next morning, the butler said he had been told of a disaster in the Ostbahnhof. "Two trains full of ammunition, Baron."

One afternoon the following week, Matilda looked up from the sink in the kitchen of the palace as a starling flew out of a window in the hayloft of the old stables. Birds had always been residents of the palace, but the starling held Matilda's attention because it swerved and flew back into the hayloft. As she raised a colander of spinach from the sink, the starling flew out of the hayloft and began to circle the open dormer window, diving and climbing. Matilda set down the colander and, wiping her hands, crossed the kitchen to open the door. The starling's shrill, cacophonous chirping filled the courtyard. Matilda saw the bird dart through the open window into the hayloft, and in an instant it zoomed out from the open stable doors and climbed, returning to the window, circling it once more. Matilda went back into the palace looking for Zinn.

She pulled her husband to the windows over the kitchen sink. "See the crazy bird?"

"It's a crazy bird," Zinn said.

"She flies in and out, in and out," said Matilda. "She makes a crazy sound. Why?"

"I'm not a bird," Zinn said. He tried to get away, but Matilda held on to him.

"Maybe she is not crazy," Matilda said, releasing him.

Zinn found the baron in the Great Hall. Zinn could not dismiss Matilda's suspicion. Long before he even remembered the future baroness's name, Matilda had told him the girl was the baron's first choice. "It's a bird, Baron."

Fritz listened as Zinn told him about the starling. "I sound foolish, Baron. I shouldn't disturb you with this."

"She is our bird, Zinn, a member of the household," Fritz said. As Zinn left him, Fritz raised his arms, putting his hands flat against the stone fireplace. Vienna was a war zone. The Greater German Reich had found thousands of enemies in Austria. Those who had not escaped the country and had not been caught by the Gestapo or the SS were still hiding, on the run.

Fritz turned his back to the fire, trying to think clearly. Then he left the fireplace, striding through the Great Hall. He could think on the way. In the study Fritz bent over his desk and opened the bottom left-hand drawer. He took out the Beretta automatic, ejected the clip, and checked it. He pushed the clip back into the gun butt and dropped the Beretta into the pocket of his blazer.

The coupe was gone. Fritz entered the stables, looking up at the hayloft. He moved quietly, stopping beside the Daimler and squatting to unlock the tool kit above the running board. He took out a slender flashlight and a wrench.

He heard the starling continuing to carry on as it circled the dormer windows. Fritz stopped beside the ladder and threw the wrench up into the hayloft. As the wrench hit a rafter and fell to the floor with a loud thud, he took the gun out of his pocket. He heard only the pro-testing bird. Holding the automatic, Fritz climbed the ladder.

Above, he raised the flashlight. He saw the nest on the floor near one of the posts which supported the trusses along the roof.

Fritz stepped around the nest and advanced through the hayloft. He found the blankets almost directly above the Daimler. He picked up a blanket and examined it. The blanket had not come from the palace. He dropped it and paced off the distance to the ladder.

Carly always let Fritz end their evening. She had made her availability part of their bargain. So that night, like every night, it was Fritz who rose, stretching.

In his room, he lay down on the bed in his clothes, eyes open, his mind blank.

Just after one o'clock he rose, removing his shirt and pulling a black wool sweater over his head. He removed his shoes and put on après-ski boots. With their supple leather and soft leather soles, he was assured of silence when he moved. He pushed the sweater into his trousers and took the blazer from the bed.

He walked to Carly's bedroom, opening her door slowly. He saw nothing in the darkness, but soon he heard the measured beat of her breathing.

He emerged from the palace into a night of bitter cold. A harsh wind tore through the courtyard in spurts, raising and scattering dirt and pebbles like buckshot. Fritz turned his head and raised his arm in front of him to protect his face.

In the dark stables, he paused, listening. He heard only the sibi-lant, sorrowful wind spinning eddies in the courtyard. He walked di-rectly to the ladder.

When his head came level with the hayloft floor, he stopped, straining to see, or hear something, *anything*. As he listened, his body coiled, he heard the heavy, guttural sound of snoring. He had drawn an obliging guest. Fritz climbed to the hayloft and took out the Beretta, pushing off both safety teats. He took the flashlight with his left hand and stepped forward, pacing and counting. He stopped and then inched ahead until his après-ski boot pushed into a thick mass.

He came down on his right knee, raising the Beretta and the flashlight. He switched on the flashlight, and in the beam he saw shoes sticking out of the bunched blankets. Fritz swung both hands to the left until he saw a man's head. He raised the automatic.

Max Ingster came awake blinking hard, seeing only bright flashes.

A keen pain shot through his belly. They had blinded him with their searchlights. They had him surrounded and he couldn't see. Max raised his hand to shade his eyes. In turn he saw a gun in his face, saw a hand, an arm holding the gun, a flashlight, and above that flashlight the familiar face of the Baron Fritz Von Gottisberg. "Welcome to the palace," Fritz said.

He came up off his knee, squatting and moving away like a duck. "Sit up," he said, gesturing with the gun.

Max pushed himself away from the pillows. Fritz said, "More," and "Enough," as Max sat up, the blankets scattered over and around him. "My name is Fritz. What's yours?"

Max's hands lay flat on the blankets. He didn't have a chance. The baron had moved out of reach. Fritz raised the gun. "The Italians put two safeties on this piece," Fritz said. "See? One on each side of the muzzle to make it easier for the shooter. He only needs to move one safety, either one. Tell me your name or I'll blow off your head. And get a medal. You have no papers, or you wouldn't be up here with the rats."

Max had to keep Carly out of it, even if he died. "I'm Gregory Alter," Max said. "I passed your open gate one day and saw the garage. I needed a place."

"So you came back that night with your blankets and pillows," Fritz said.

"Not that night," Max said, watching the flashlight. If he could grab it, he had a chance. "I came two nights later. I brought the blankets that night, and later the pillows."

Fritz moved away, out of reach. "Later the pillows," he said. "And you're Gregory Alter. And I am Little Red Riding Hood. And you're dumb, friend. Because you think I'm dumb." Fritz coughed. "Maybe I won't kill you. I'll march you over to the Gestapo and let them have the pleasure." Fritz rose. "On your feet and no tricks with that blanket. This is an automatic I'm holding with thirteen rounds in the clip."

Max came to his feet. "You'll make me a hero with the Gestapo," Fritz said.

He gave Max a wide lead. At the ladder Fritz said, "At the bottom take five steps and stop. Five steps, friend."

He kept Max in the flashlight beam. Below, Max stepped backward, stopping after five paces. "Bravo," Fritz said. He sat down in the hayloft, his legs dangling over the ladder, descended one rung at a time, watching his prisoner.

Max looked at the handsome young man in the beautiful blazer.

Carly had married a monster, a smooth specimen with a friendly smile and thirteen slugs to put into your heart. "Let me go."

"We've got a long walk ahead of us," Fritz said, waving the flashlight. "On your way."

They came into the courtyard. Max said, "I haven't done anything to you. I'm not a thief."

Fritz shoved Max hard. Max lurched forward, stumbling, and then righted himself. "Finish it, goddamn you!" he said. "Come on, finish it, you sadistic sonofabitch!" When Max saw Fritz raise the gun, though, he cried, "My name is Max Ingster."

"Not Gustav Alter," Fritz said. "Max Ingster. Good night, Max." Fritz gestured with the flashlight, making slashing streaks of light across the courtyard and on the gate. "Good-bye."

Watching Fritz, Max stepped back, facing the gun pointed at his belly. He backed into the gate, reaching behind him to grope for the latch. He raised the latch, opened the gate wide, and darted out of the courtyard into the night.

Fritz returned to the stables. He had to remove the blankets and pillows, had to remove the evidence. He thought of burning the bedding, but abandoned the idea of a fire. There would be a smell, and Matilda or Zinn would look for the source.

Fritz opened the trunk of the Daimler before climbing the ladder to the hayloft. Using his feet, Fritz pushed the blankets and pillows over the edge. He stuffed the bedding into the trunk and locked it.

He felt dirty all over, and when he returned to his bedroom, he stripped off his clothes, leaving everything in a pile for Zinn. He took a hot shower to make himself sleepy, but in bed he lay wide awake and alert. He heard the wind whistling at the window, accompanied by the creaks and groans and sighs of the old palace, and when the room fell silent, he heard the ticking of his wristwatch on the night table beside him. His body ached with tension.

In the morning, Carly sent Zinn upstairs. "He's never late," she said.

The butler returned almost immediately. "The baron is on his way."

Carly heard Fritz coming. He stopped in the doorway. A narrow shaft of light fell across Carly's hair and shoulders, and when she saw Fritz, she smiled in welcome. Despite himself, he felt the longing she provoked, and hated his vulnerability. "Come into the study."

She said, "Don't you want any—?" and rose, stopped by something in Fritz's face, something awful. Walking through the palace, she said,

"Fritz . . . ?" and couldn't go on, could barely keep up with him, could barely stand. She was certain he had news of Nick, bad news. Her letters had been unanswered because Nick was dead. She put her hand against her mouth, screaming inside.

Fritz closed the door of the study. "I found Max Ingster in the hayloft last night."

Carly felt a crushing weight on her chest and leaned against the desk. "Who?"

She infuriated him. Fritz very nearly hit her. "Stop it, Carly. Acting like a fool makes you a fool."

She had to know. "Where is he?" she asked, almost in a whisper.

"Gone," Fritz said. "Your friend, Max Ingster, is gone. He's not my friend, and Zinn didn't provide him with lodging because Zinn knows I would geld him. You did it. You put a man without papers, a fugitive wanted by the Gestapo, in our stables." Fritz stopped, fighting the anger which threatened the logic he revered. When he could control himself, Fritz said, "If the Gestapo had tracked him down, they would have taken us with him."

"He's innocent," Carly said, holding the desk to keep herself from falling. "Fritz, he is innocent."

"So are we," Fritz said. "But we don't decide who is innocent or guilty. The Nazis decide, without any help from you or me."

"He didn't do anything wrong," Carly said. "He acted in plays."

Fritz cursed himself for his stupidity in not solving the puzzle. He walked around the desk, around Carly, his enemy, the Baroness Von Gottisberg. "Naturally, he would be from the Zwischentheatre," Fritz said.

Although he had closed the door, they were no longer alone in the study. Both knew another player had entered. Nick stood between them. "I'm sorry," Carly said. "I want to apologize, Fritz. I didn't think . . . I put you in danger. I didn't mean to put you in danger."

"And yourself," he said.

"I couldn't forsake him," Carly said. "He's alone, Fritz."

"We are alone," Fritz said. "In Austria for two years already, everyone is alone. Everyone is a target. Everyone's life turns on someone's whim, someone's displeasure, someone's urge for excitement, The Nazis murder for fun, Carly. They hunt for the joy of the chase, for the thrill of the kill. The Nazis are the only animals on this bloodied earth who destroy without hunger. Their only appetite is lust."

She clung to the desk, begging for understanding. But he had left her. He stood beside her, but he seemed far in the distance. "You risked everything to save . . . someone," she said, refusing to use Nick's name.

"We were playing for higher stakes than friendship," Fritz said. "The stakes were higher, or have you forgotten?"

She said, "No," in an undertone, and then, raising her head, said distinctly, "No, I have not forgotten."

On the following Saturday afternoon Carly drove out of the Inner City and through District II, continuing until she came to the Prater, the vast park on the edge of Vienna. Carly parked and walked into the crowds, passing the carousel and beyond, the looming Ferris wheel which towered over the park. She walked through a giant gazebo serving beer and sausages and goulash, filled with Nazi uniforms. She skirted a café with an orchestra, and chose another, almost empty. Carly picked a table apart from the few patrons, and when the waiter appeared, she ordered chocolate.

She had to wait more than an hour before she saw the familiar lean figure of Colonel Friedrich Varlingen. He wore a black raincoat over his uniform, the belt twisted around his middle so the buckle hung loose. He carried a folded newspaper, which he dropped on a table to Carly's left. He set his garrison cap on the table and got out of the raincoat, and when he sat down, unfolded the newspaper and raised it.

Carly said, "I need identity papers for—" and stopped as she saw the waiter. Varlingen asked for beer, and when he and Carly were alone, he raised the newspaper once more. Carly told him about Max Ingster.

"This rendezvous is dangerous," Varlingen said, talking into the newspaper. "All rendezvous are dangerous. I am wary, I am clever, but I learned my wariness and cleverness from the Nazis. The Gestapo are unhappy now in Vienna. Berlin wants Domino, and they cannot oblige Berlin. Domino remains . . . loose."

Varlingen had given Carly her code name, remembering his wife in a black cloak and half mask at a masquerade. "The Gestapo have become desperate," he said. "It could be they have decided Friedrich Varlingen should be watched. The waiter could be Gestapo. The man with the two little girls eating hot chocolate could be Gestapo."

The waiter returned. Varlingen drank his beer, and Carly waited until the waiter returned to the service bar. "This is an emergency," she said.

"Correction. This is *kinderspiel*, child's play," Varlingen said. "You have exposed us here for Herr X, for a cipher in the crowd."

Carly tried not to look at Varlingen, following his rules. "He is on his own," she said. "He has no one but me. He needs papers or he'll die."

"You can make the same identical speech every day of the year, every hour of every day," Varlingen said. "We are not the Red Cross. We play for high stakes, as you know. You know everything. I've told you everything. We risk everything because we believe the stakes are worth our lives. You are not Florence Nightingale. You are a soldier, a saboteur, a guerilla." Varlingen lowered the newspaper and folded it.

"He will join us," Carly said. "He could have run but he didn't. He loves Austria. I can vouch for him."

"I am not leading a recruiting drive," Varlingen said, reaching for his raincoat.

"Wait," Carly hissed. She eyed the man with the two little girls before going on. "If I don't get those papers, I'm quitting." Her hands were shaking and, hating herself, she hid her hands so Varlingen would not think she would falter. "I am finished," Carly said. "This is the end of us."

Varlingen rose and opened his raincoat, pushing his right arm through its sleeve. The man with the two little girls took a napkin and wiped their mouths. Carly began to count to herself, willing him to respond, and when she reached twenty-one, she heard him. "Max Ingster."

"Yes—no," Carly said. "Cnobra. Walther Cnobra. C-n-o-b-r-a," she said, spelling the last name. "Make the papers for Walther Cnobra."

"Walther Cnobra," Varlingen said.

Varlingen paused when he came out of the café, and two hundred yards away, beside the shed for the ponies at the pony ride, Fritz raised his opera glasses to focus on the man in uniform folding a newspaper. Fritz had seen Varlingen enter the café, and now he watched the tall, elegant man leave.

The stench from the pony shed, a lean-to with one long, sagging wall, almost made Fritz retch. He stepped behind a discarded cart with one wheel, resting on the axle. Fritz crouched slightly so he was hidden by the seat.

Ten minutes after Varlingen left, someone wearing a pink scarf over a long coat came through the doors of the café. Fritz had followed Carly to the Prater, but he raised the opera glasses. Carly would never turn her lodger over to the Nazis. She had come to the Prater to save Max Ingster. That meant Colonel Varlingen was a traitor to his uniform. Fritz watched the other traitor, the one he had installed in the palace, her long scarf billowing in the breeze as she strode to the parking area.

One Sunday morning in the summer of 1941, Dieter Rantzau walked through a hacienda in Bel Air. He crossed the long gallery which looked out on a swimming pool and cabana, and turned into the master suite. The bedroom had a sloping ceiling with exposed hand-hewn beams bleached almost white running down from the ridge pole. In bed Magda watched him rubbing his damp hair with a large towel. "You would feel better if you swam with me," Dieter said.

"I'll feel better when we are married," Magda said. "Fanny has been dead more than six months. When will you ask me to marry you?"

Dieter dropped the towel across his shoulders. "I think about it every day."

"Stop thinking and speak!"

"Magda, you are already married," he said.

"I divorced Ernst."

"You divorced . . . when?"

"Since a long time ago," Magda said. She touched her forehead. "Here," she said, and put her hand over her heart. "And here. You are paying rent for an empty apartment. For a closet. This house is full of closets."

"I have never been happier than with you," he said. "Fanny . . . I lived with a sick woman from the beginning."

"Here is your chance for a new life," she said.

"Magda, I am a bit player in Hollywood. I have a line here, five lines there. I have no money."

"Dieter, look at me," Magda said. When he obeyed, she went on, "Marry me and you will have more money than you ever dreamed would be yours."

He sat on the bed. "Even if this means the end for us, I cannot take your money," he said.

"You will not need my money," Magda said. "You will have yours because you will not be a bit player for long, believe me." She put their hands under the covers. "I am divorced here, too."

Their eyes met and Dieter kissed her. "I will try not to disappoint you," he said.

"I will not permit you to disappoint me."

Two weeks later Nick walked through the Majestic lot to Stage Six. A studio guard stood beside the door, and over it a red light blinked constantly, a signal that a scene was being shot. A large sign with the word "CLOSED" in bright red letters had been tacked to the door. "Closed set," the guard said.

Nick watched the red light until it stopped blinking. "Sigrid Colstad called me," he said.

The guard put his hand on "CLOSED." Maybe you can't read," he said. "Closed means closed."

"I work in casting," Nick said. He reached for the door handle and felt the guard's hand.

"Here's what you do," the guard said. "Get lost fast, or they'll put you together in the hospital."

"Hospital," Nick said, remembering a white metal bed in a white room, remembering the days and nights and weeks of agony. Nick saw the name etched into the metal nameplate over the guard's shirt pocket. "Schmidt," Nick said. "Come on, Herr Schmidt, put me in the hospital."

The guard looked at the skinny drink of water. "Go on in." They didn't pay him enough to dirty his uniform on the kike.

On the stage, Nick stopped until his eyes adjusted to the cavernous darkness. At one end of the stage, under spotlights, Nick saw the day's set, a powder room in a country club. Like all rooms on a set, it had no ceiling and only three walls, called wild walls, any of which could be moved in minutes. Nick asked a grip for the assistant director. The grip pointed at a man drinking juice from a can. "That's him."

Nick walked through the powder room to the A.D. "Where is Sigrid Colstad?"

The A.D. finished the juice and crumpled the can in his hand. "You're on a closed set."

"You, too," Nick said. "Where is Sigrid?"

The A.D. studied the gate-crasher. "Who wants to know?"

"Meyer Milgrim," Nick said.

"In a pig's ear."

Nick stopped a grip carrying an apple box, a crate used extensively on sound stages. "Tell me—" he said before the A.D. grabbed him.

"Back there," he said, pointing. "Behind the ticket booth." Nick walked toward a deserted kiosk which had been used in a scene the previous day.

"Nick!" Dieter wore evening clothes and had tissue paper tucked under his wing collar so the makeup wouldn't smudge. Nick had managed to cast him as a rich widower.

"Do you know your lines?"

"What a joke," Dieter said. "Hello, good luck, good-bye. I need a role, Nick."

When Dieter left him, Nick spied a miniature Cape Cod cottage with spotlights making a path from the door. The occupant had added flower boxes below the windows. There were fresh geraniums and petunias in clay pots in the window boxes, and on the door Nick saw two D's back to back, for Darragh Delaney, the star of *The Secret of Mrs. Savage.*

Against a cluttered wall behind the cottage Nick came upon two portable dressing rooms with wooden steps. He knocked on a door and heard a woman's voice. "Yeah?"

"I'm looking for Sigrid Colstad," Nick said.

"Keep looking," said the woman as a runner of light fell across the dirty cement floor.

"Nick!" Sigrid Colstad, in a bridesmaid's gown, stood in the doorway.

She pulled him into her dressing room. "I am lost, Nick, alone in the wilderness. This is the sixth day of shooting. How many times has the director spoken to me?"

"Zero," Nick said.

"Zero," Sigrid said. "Zero to me, zero to everyone. Hugh Callender does not talk. He says, 'Action,' 'Cut,' 'Print,' or maybe, 'Again, please.' And he marches to his dressing room. You cannot talk with Mr. Callender. If you have a question, you must give the question to the A.D. He speaks to His Highness. If you ask the A.D. to ask His Highness how he likes your work, the answer comes, 'You will know when I am disappointed.' Nick, he thinks because he is English, he is Alfred Hitchcock. Hitchcock does not speak to actors, so Hugh Callender won't, either." Sigrid's lips trembled. "Now I'm ruining my makeup."

Nick had been hoping for tears, and when she hid her head, he gave her a huck towel from the dressing table. Sigrid covered her face, and soon Nick heard her sniffling. "I am too old for these childish eruptions."

"Sure," Nick said.

They heard a knock, and someone said, "Ready, Miss Colstad."

Sigrid looked trapped. Nick went to the door. "Five minutes," he said, looking down at the A.D. Nick closed the door and stood behind Sigrid, massaging her shoulders as she applied makeup. "Play to me," he said. He knew every word in the script. "This is the scene where you try to poison Lois against Henry Savage. Poison *me.*"

Hugh Callender was a vegetarian, a middle-aged man who wore a business suit on the set. He had brought his own script girl from London. Miss Mahoney sat on a low three-legged stool beside the camera. Callender stood behind her and spoke to no other member of the company.

Crossing the stage to the set, Sigrid said, "I'm still afraid, even with you."

"Good," Nick said. "You are a terrible woman who makes terrible trouble. If you are exposed, you will pay a terrible price. You should be afraid."

"Thank you," she said, furious with him. "I need a friend, not a drama coach."

Nick stopped her. "Let me go," Sigrid whispered. "I'm late."

"Maybe you're not ready for this role," Nick said. "Maybe you will never be ready for such a role."

Sigrid gasped, hating him. Nick would have been delighted if she had struck him. She spun around, heading for the spotlights over the powder room.

Nick found a place clear of everyone while Sigrid joined another actress in the powder room, standing on her mark, a chalk line on the floor. "This is a take," said the A.D. "Settle, everyone." Someone cleared his throat, and then the stage fell quiet.

"Action," said Hugh Callender. Nearby, alone, Nick delivered both Sigrid's and Lois's lines as they did. The two actresses were playing a crucial scene, almost four pages long, and the anger, envy, fear, contempt, each brought to the set inflamed the performance. When Callender said, "Cut," and after a pause, "Print," the stage remained silent for a little while, the crew captivated by the power and conviction of the two actresses.

Sigrid left the powder room, passing the camera as though Callender wasn't there. She stopped in front of Nick, and although she said nothing, he knew she was thanking him.

Then Callender left the set, Miss Mahoney stood up, holding her stool, the camera crew pushed the camera out of the powder room, and the cinematographer walked into the lights, cupping his mouth with one hand. "Varsity!" he said, summoning the grips. Callender had his master shot, and the cinematographer had to light the set for the first of the close-ups.

The A.D. followed Callender but at a distance, and when the director entered the dressing room provided for him, his assistant continued to the Cape Cod cottage. After he knocked, he put his ear against the door. "Miss Delaney? Got a sec?"

In her cottage the A.D. was surrounded by Darragh Delaney, her wardrobe mistress, her personal makeup man, her personal publicity man, and a man named Mel who came from her hometown of Gary, Indiana, and had been expelled from Notre Dame after three years even though he had never failed to make the dean's list. "You said you wanted a closed set, Miss Delaney."

She looked at him in the mirror above her dressing table. "You're here to tell me it isn't."

She listened to the A.D. without interruption. "Wait," she said, and to Mel, "Get Milgrim on the horn. And tell him he can't call me back because I won't be on the lot." Darragh spoke briefly to the head of Majestic and handed the telephone receiver to Mel. She rose, facing the A.D. "Tell the bitch to get in here."

Hardly anyone left the studio later than Nick. When he drove through the Majestic gates that day, he turned south, away from the Hollywood Hills. He continued through Culver City, and beyond Sepulveda Boulevard he saw the glow of lights brightening the sky. Nick had learned of a carnival near the dry canals of Venice, and as he approached, he heard the brittle music of a carousel and saw the circling Ferris wheel.

The carnival, sited in an empty lot, was a seedy collection of tents and booths. Barkers in spiffy suits and straw boaters pointed canes at the people who passed. Nick found the shooting gallery, an open booth behind a counter stacked with air rifles. A row of small wooden ducks moved continually from right to left across the back wall of the booth. Below the ducks stood a line of cheap dolls. "Here's a gunslinger," said the operator, a man with an enormous belly wearing a grey gabardine shirt and a broad necktie full of ducks. He thrust an air rifle in Nick's face. "Take a doll home for your sweetie. All you need's a quarter, two bits." Nick dropped the coins into the fat man's hand. "This here's a pump gun," said the fat man. "It's primed. You shoot and you pump," he said.

Nick pushed the air rifle into his left shoulder. "All you need are five little ducks," said the fat man. Nick squeezed off and a duck fell. "One."

Nick pushed his right hand against the wooden cylinder under the barrel and pumped. He fired and another duck fell. He pumped and fired, pumped and fired, pumped and fired, hitting three more ducks.

The fat man came to the counter, squinting as though he recognized Nick. He turned and brought back a doll. He spoke so only Nick could hear. "Here's your doll. Get lost."

Nick put a dollar on the counter. "I came to shoot."

"I'll bet," said the fat man. "Hey, you, there's only one pro around here and I'm him. Beat it, or should I call my friends?"

Nick pushed the dollar into the fat man's shirt pocket. "Keep your prize and keep the money. Someone will watch me and think he, too, is a shooter." Nick raised the air rifle.

He shot with his right hand, pushing his forefinger through the trigger guard, shooting slower, dropping five ducks. Two teenage boys stopped, whispering to each other. Nick alternated, shooting with his left hand. A man who wore a sweatshirt with "LIFEGUARD" across the front saw Nick shoot with his left hand, dropping five ducks. "Me, too," he said, paying for five shots.

As the lifeguard shot, the fat man joined Nick. "Where'd you learn to shoot like that?"

"I'm still learning," Nick said.

The lifeguard missed all his shots. Nick gave the fat man more money. Whenever he hit five ducks, someone who watched him picked up a rifle. So Nick had to wait his turn. Once, when Nick took his place, pumping the air rifle, the fat man said, "You owe me." Nick gave him a dollar. The fat man wrapped the bill around a roll. "I like your money, pal, but why? You can't get any better."

"I could get worse," Nick said, raising the air rifle. He shot until the pain in his right hand made him quit. Nick walked among the carnival attractions, listening to the barkers. For dinner he bought a hot dog and a soft drink, eating beside the carousel. He was safe in a crowd.

Alone in his car, especially after he had been shooting, Nick became an easy prey to the past. He could not escape the memories of treachery. Why had Carly sent him to Fritz? Why had Fritz given him a Safe Conduct? Why had they sent him into the Alps if they intended to kill him and his family? They could have killed his family in Leopoldstadt. Nick lowered his window as though to clear the car of his demons, and shivering in the chill of the night, he turned toward Doheny Drive and his apartment.

He never left the studio without scripts, and in his apartment he dropped them on the bed as the telephone rang. "Nick? It's Sigrid. I am with Darragh Delaney, Nick, in her house in Holmby. She is on Baroda Drive in Holmby. I told her how you saved me today. You must come immediately, Nick. She needs you," Sigrid said, adding, "Hold on." Nick heard her laughing. "Darragh says if you do not come over, she will kill herself."

One day in August, Leopold Unger drove to Magda's hacienda in Bel Air. Dieter admitted him, leading the owner of the Ringstrasse to the cabana. Magda lay on a chaise in a robe waiting for her masseur. "Tell her," Dieter said.

Leopold couldn't face Magda. "Lion Feuchtwanger is giving a party for two hundred on the day of your wedding."

"That snake," Magda said. "I invited that snake in the grass to my wedding." She raised her hands and Dieter took them, helping her up from the chaise.

"An unhappy coincidence," Leopold said.

She walked along the swimming pool into the long gallery, followed by Dieter and Leopold. "I never liked his books, never," Magda said. She stopped beside a large painting of herself. She had sat for a young Alsatian, a penniless newcomer, determined to get some return for the money she had given him. "The wedding will have to be postponed until September."

Dieter said, "Impossible!" and Leopold, whom Magda had retained for the food and the bar, darted forward.

"Everyone is hired," Leopold said. "I have the best pastry chef in the world. I had to beg him!"

"Beg him twice," Magda said.

Dieter chimed in, "Magda, this cannot be."

She counted on her fingers, her lips moving silently. "September fourteenth," she said. "Sunday the fourteenth."

"I'm sorry," Leopold said, "but all my people must still be paid."

"Yes, yes," Magda said, bearing down on him. "They will be paid, paid, paid, paid. Call me with the amount, and book them for the fourteenth of September."

When they were alone, Dieter said, "All this for an audience, Magda?"

She looked at her handsome, virile, obliging stud. She walked toward him, gathering up her hair. "You are not a pimply bridegroom counting the days," she said. "You can wait." She stopped, coiling her hair atop her head. "But if you cannot—" She broke off, facing him candidly, ready for his suggestions.

Magda divided her wedding day into two parts, both of which she controlled, beginning to end. A small, select group would witness the marriage ceremony. A vastly larger number were invited to the reception which followed. Magda told Nick to come early. "You are the best man."

At the hacienda on September fourteenth, Magda took Nick onto the patio. It had been transformed. A dance floor covered the swimming pool. Leopold Unger had moved a bar into the cabana. On the far side of the pool, waiters prepared long tables of food. Nick looked up at the sky and squinted. "God gave you a perfect day."

"He owes me plenty," Magda said, and, shouting, "Over here! This way!"

Nick saw two young men in black suits carrying four round, varnished poles. A large square of brocade hung from one end. The bearers, dressed like undertakers, thrust Nick back to his childhood in the Leopoldstadt, to the synagogue where his father and mother dragged him, to the huddled group of men rocking and keening in the dank, dark interior, to the women separated by ritual from their husbands. Nick had hated it from the first and hated it now, in Bel Air beside the swimming pool. His parents and Sam had died for their religion. The sepulchral pair joined them. "Show me," Magda said.

The young men set the four posts on end. "Nick," Magda said, enlisting his help. She took a post and Nick took the fourth. Above them the large square of brocade rippled in the air. The four held a chupah, the canopy prescribed by Hebrew law for the marriage. "You'll stand here," Magda told the two.

"Impossible," one said. "The sun will be in the rabbi's eyes."

"Instead of mine," Magda said. "Four-thirty sharp." She pointed. "Leave it there."

They rested the chupah against a jacaranda tree. Magda nudged Nick. "Do you have cramps?"

"I didn't expect this hocus-pocus from you."

"Hitler made me a Jew," she said.

"Dieter isn't a Jew. A rabbi won't marry him."

"My rabbi made an exception," Magda said. "He put the exception into his pocket."

A hairdresser in a white smock came out of the master suite. "Madam."

"She promises to make me beautiful," Magda told Nick. "Come, I'll give you the wedding ring."

Magda wore gray for her wedding, a stylish dress, simple in design, without frills. Her rings lay in the bedroom safe. She chose pearl earrings and around her neck a narrow band of gold. Her golden hair gleamed. Magda picked a tan summer suit for Dieter, which he wore with a blue shirt and a maroon tie she selected. Standing together in the chupah, they were a smashing couple.

Rabbi George Aaron, an American younger than either the bride or groom, understood the motion-picture community. His flock liked their religion short and sweet, and Rabbi Aaron obliged. Magda added a footnote when she interviewed him. "No speeches."

Magda and Dieter were married in less than ten minutes. He put his arms around her. "You will need patience with me," Magda said.

She went directly to the waiting hairdresser. The gray dress had been a surrender to decorum. Magda was giving a party.

Her gown had been sewn to her instructions, a sparkling blue, cut low, and sweeping the floor. She wore a diamond on each hand. She changed her earrings to emeralds, and she discarded the gold necklace for another encrusted with jade. She went to her mirror as Leopold knocked and opened the door. "They're coming."

She could not continue without Leopold. Although she had chosen her guests, she could identify only a few. In the week before the wedding she had rehearsed with Leopold. "Say both names," Magda demanded. "First and last."

In the long gallery, Magda heard the strains of music from the orchestra she had hired. "Do you have enough food?"

"For an army," Leopold said just before he whispered, "Bruno Walter." Magda forgot Leopold, extending her hand to the great conductor.

"An honor, maestro," she said. "You flatter us." She looked over her shoulder at Leopold and mouthed the word "Dieter." Magda remained with Bruno Walter until Dieter came to relieve her so she could return to Leopold.

When he opened the door, Magda recognized the rumpled, pudgy little man before Leopold said, "Peter Lorre."

"Welcome to this house," Magda said, giving her hand to the actor who had been born Lazlo Lowenstein. Dieter returned to greet Peter Lorre as Magda heard the doorbell.

"Heinrich Mann," Leopold said. Magda pushed Leopold aside, hand extended. "Herr Mann. In your presence America becomes almost tolerable." She took the author into the patio.

As she returned, Leopold clapped his hands in homage. "Heinrich Mann," Leopold said, "is the real recluse."

"Pure luck," Magda said, lying. A month earlier she had purchased *The Blue Angel*, Mann's most famous novel. She had written to him asking if he would autograph her copy. He replied, suggesting Magda send him the book. Magda came to his house, and the following day she mailed him an invitation to her wedding.

Magda remained at her door with Leopold until he said, "Whoever is coming, came." As she appeared on the patio, the orchestra trumpets, following orders, sounded a fanfare. Those guests who had been dancing left the dance floor to Magda and Dieter. The orchestra began a waltz, and Magda raised her gown as Dieter took her into his arms.

No one watching the handsome pair was unmoved. The guests were hushed until Sigrid Colstad, teary, began to clap her hands. Other guests joined her, and soon all who had come to the wedding were applauding.

Dieter had asked Magda to invite actors and actresses with whom he had worked, and he danced with each actress, starting with Sigrid. Afterward, sipping champagne, she wandered around the patio until she found Nick. "Stay with me," she said. "I am alone."

Like all Scandinavians who escape from the long months of darkness, Sigrid could not get enough of the sun. She seemed almost bronzed in the fading daylight. "You will not be alone long," Nick said.

Later, as the shadows lengthened, Sigrid returned. "Nick, you haven't danced with me."

"I am not a dancer."

She put her left arm over his shoulder and took his hand. "Try." Sigrid snuggled close, her head in his chest. "You can dance."

"How would you know?"

Sigrid raised her head, but Nick seemed lopsided and she closed her eyes. "Take me home," she said. "You, not a taxi like you would send a tramp."

In Nick's car, she said, "I should not drink at parties. I am vulnerable." She gave him directions and toppled over, lying against him as he drove through Bel Air and down toward the San Fernando Valley. Nick was starting to think she had fallen asleep when she sat erect. "Slow, we are coming to my turn," she said. "There, Winifred Way. The fifth house."

Nick helped her out of the car. In her home, Sigrid said, "Welcome to my castle," and stepped forward, stopping in front of Nick. "You've never asked to see my castle."

"You have a nice castle," Nick said.

"Wait." Sigrid turned, swaying, leaving him. He could see her handiwork everywhere: antimacassars, doilies, chair seats, the curtain, even the hooked rug on which he stood.

"Take off your clothes."

Sigrid came through swinging louvered doors, a white terry robe over each arm. "Let's go into the sauna," she said. "The sauna cures everything."

"I didn't drink," Nick said.

She threw a robe at him. "You are safe with me." She watched him. "Quit running."

"We are alone," Nick said. "Stop playing for the camera."

"You are still running," she said.

He threw the robe over his shoulder. "Where can I undress?" She brought him to her sewing room. Nick got into the robe and opened the door. "Sigrid?"

He saw her come out of a bedroom wrapped in her robe. She wore paper slippers and she carried a pair for Nick. "Follow me."

An offshore breeze swept across the mountains, bending the crowns of the trees flanking the garden. Sigrid took Nick's hand. Built against the back of the garage he saw a small, square building of cinder block. "My second castle," Sigrid said.

Inside, the walls were sheathed in cedar. Facing the door and running the length of the wall were three tiers of benches rising to a low ceiling. Sigrid went to a metal box resembling a fuse box and opened it to raise the heat. "Ready."

She climbed to the top bench. "This is the best spot."

"You mean the hottest," Nick said. He stepped over the lowest bench and sat down on the second. "Ten minutes," he said.

"Always running," Sigrid said dreamily. "Nick Gallanz, the mystery man." She let her robe fall below her shoulders, holding it together over her bare breasts. "Who are you, mystery man?"

"Maybe you shouldn't drink."

"Stop hiding," Sigrid said. He turned away, hunched forward. "Who are you?" she asked. "Where do you come from? Yes, Vienna, but who were you in Vienna? What kind of life did you have? What kind of boy were you? Happy, sad, fat, thin? Were you a bully, a hero, an athlete, a bookworm? Were you teacher's pet, teacher's hate? Were you rich, were you poor?"

Nick did not reply, and Sigrid pushed herself along the bench until she sat directly behind him. "What did you do with your days in Vienna? With your nights in Vienna? What did you like to do? Whom did you like? Whom did you love?"

He saw Carly, saw her running, waving as she ran. "Yourself? Only yourself?" Sigrid asked.

Nick lowered his head so Carly would disappear. "Play another game, Sigrid."

She raised her leg, removing her paper slipper to push her foot into Nick's neck. He moved aside. "I've had enough here."

"Afraid, Nicki?"

He looked up at her. "You are drunk."

"No, not now," she said. Sigrid sat over him, her shoulders bare and her robe lying below the cleavage of her breasts. Her skin was shiny with perspiration, and in the faint, misted light of the sauna she seemed almost unreal, seemed like a nymph, a goddess. Nick could feel her bare foot on his hip. He turned his head as though he could dismiss her, but her touch left him quivering. "I think I lied," Sigrid said. "You are not safe with me."

She bent far forward, dropping her arms over Nick's shoulders and putting her face against his, kissing. Nick felt her wet hands against his wet chest, her bare breasts on his wet back. Behind him, Sigrid moved her hands down from his chest across his belly, across his thighs. She would not release him, and kissing, she slid from her bench to his. Her robe fell to her hips, and as she bent over him, she pulled his robe from his shoulders. "I have wanted this from the first," she said.

Late in the fall of that year, on a dark and blustery morning, Leonard Votrian called Nick. "Let's have lunch."

"I use lunch for working with actors," Nick said.

"They'll make it without you," Votrian said.

"Another time."

"Mr. Gallanz, excuse me. We're having lunch today, you and me. Mr. Milgrim thinks we should have lunch. The head of the studio. So twelve-thirty at my car."

Around twelve-thirty, in his Cadillac, Votrian said, "We'll go off the lot for a change. Do us both good." At the guard's booth Chuck, the guard, saw him coming and raised the bar.

"Did you see the Germans are almost in Moscow?" Votrian said. "Thank your lucky stars you're in America, kiddo."

"Yes," Nick said. "I am in America."

When Votrian swung onto Pico Boulevard, he said, "You didn't ask where we're going."

"Are you lost?"

Votrian glanced at the greenhorn sitting in the big sedan like he was alone. What did the actors see that was so great about the green-horn? "Hugh Callender might come back on the lot," Votrian said.

"He might do another picture for us. How about him, the Englishman?"

"Knows the camera," Nick said.

"How about Victor Gross?" Votrian said. He waited. "Victor Gross."

"You hired me for casting, not directing," Nick said.

"Thank you very much," Votrian said. They came to the outskirts of Beverly Hills. Ahead, rising above the palms, they could see the sound stages of Twentieth Century-Fox, the arched roofs of the cream-colored buildings continuing in a line like the folds of a hill. "Almost there," Votrian said.

Just before the entrance to Fox on the right, Votrian turned left. "You know where you are?" Votrian said. "Hillcrest Country Club." He stopped at the clubhouse entrance, and an attendant opened the Cadillac door. The movie men of Hollywood, denied membership anywhere in Los Angeles, had established their own country club.

Inside, Votrian said, "Take a good look, kiddo. Crème de la crème." Votrian's voice fell to a whisper. "Adolph Zukor," he said, gesturing at the aged founder of Paramount Pictures.

At their table, Votrian waved the menu at Nick. "If you want something and it isn't on here, they'll make it for you. There's Jolson."

Nick saw the bouncy showman, the star of The Jazz Singer, Hollywood's first talking picture. Al Jolson paused to chat with Clark Gable, and at the next table he kneeled beside Lionel Barrymore's wheelchair. "Jolson is on his way to the barber," Votrian said. "The barber shaves his chest. His chest. Would you do that for a dame?"

"I don't have a dame," Nick said.

"Excuse me, girlfriend. Lady friend," Votrian said.

"Why did you bring me to this place?"

"Before we eat? Have it your way," Votrian said. "Back there in the car you said, 'Are you lost?' Remember? The answer is, not me. But I think you are." He gestured. "Ty Power," he said. Votrian raised the linen napkin covering the bread tray and took a roll.

"You said something else back there," Votrian continued. "You were hired in the casting office. Actors. Actresses. Casting them in the picture. That's your job. Directing them is the director's job. You're not the director. You don't belong on the stage." Votrian fell back into his chair. "Say something!"

"They call me for help with the lines," Nick said. "What do the lines mean? What is her attitude in the scene, his attitude? 'Who am I? Why am I doing this?' "

"Send the person to the director," Votrian said. "That's his job."

"Hugh Callender will not talk to actors," Nick said.

Votrian smiled warmly, raising his hand. "How are you, Bob?" Robert Taylor stopped, and Votrian introduced the handsome leading man to Nick. Votrian watched Taylor walk through the dining room. "Nice guy," he said. "Victor Gross talks to actors. Are you listening?"

"Sure."

"Pat Metcalfe talks to actors," Votrian said. "Try to shut him up, Pat. Mitchell Faricy talks to actors. Jeff Coleman talks to actors. And every one of them comes upstairs to Milgrim complaining about guess who?"

The waiter returned with their food. "Starting today, now, stay away from the actors," Votrian said.

"They will find me," Nick said.

"Stop." Votrian set down his knife and fork. "Listen to me. Meyer Milgrim decided Hugh Callender is coming back on the lot, and in his contract will be a certain clause. If you walk on the set, he walks off. In his contract." Votrian took his knife and pointed at Nick's plate. "Your food will get cold."

"I am not a director," Nick said. "I am a . . ." he said, searching for a description of his work with actors.

"A Svengali! You're a Svengali. Were. That's over and done with," Votrian said, attacking his grilled salmon.

Nick looked at the big man hunched over the table. "Do you like actors?"

Votrian chewed and swallowed. "There's no like or dislike," he said. "We're in a business, the movie business. Actors are part of the business."

"Actors are babies," Nick said, trying to make Votrian understand. "Not children, babies. Without mothers, they will die. Not a mother. Mothers. The whole world must love an actor." Votrian astonished him. "You didn't learn this?"

"Not my job, kiddo."

"My job," Nick said. "At Majestic I am the actor's world. If they cannot come to me, where will they go?"

"To the producers," Votrian said. "Let the producers hold their hands."

Nick raised the metal hood covering his plate, looking at the goulash he had ordered. He put his right hand into his pocket for the rubber ball, and when he raised his head, Votrian saw the suggestion of a smile on the greenhorn's face. "I'll be a producer," Nick said.

"I'll settle that one, too," Votrian said. "We're full up."

"Fire someone," Nick said. "Take your pick, they are all amateurs at Majestic."

Votrian had to remind himself that Meyer Milgrim expected a happy ending to the Hillcrest outing. "Maybe you forgot something," Votrian said. "This is a town with short memories for anything good, long memories for anything bad. I got you this job, correct?"

"Have I hurt you?"

"Wise guy," Votrian said. "Just now you did. You're goddamn right you did. I bring you to Hillcrest, treat you like a man, and you make jokes."

"I am not being funny," Nick said.

"And you're not going to be a producer, either," Votrian said. "You're an assistant casting director. Listen, there's a future for you at Majestic."

"My future is already here," Nick said. "You brought me to the studio, so I'll give you the first chance. Make me a producer, because somebody will make me one."

Votrian raised his arm for the check. "Adios."

They left the clubhouse without speaking, and Votrian swung the Cadillac onto Pico Boulevard as though he was being chased. They rode back to the studio in silence, and as Votrian stopped in his parking space, he said, "Finish the week. You're through Friday."

That night, from Sigrid's house, Nick talked with Darragh Delaney, who had been given the script of the picture Hugh Callender would direct. "This is not good-bye, but I will not be on the lot," Nick said.

Afterward, Sigrid took the telephone from him. "My turn," she said. Leaving the stars at Majestic to Darragh, Sigrid began calling featured players under contract to the studio.

Friday morning, his last morning at Majestic, Nick drove to the studio, and as he entered his office, he saw Votrian sitting behind the desk. "Shut the door."

Meyer Milgrim had listened to a full report of the Hillcrest lunch and hired the mutineer. So Nick Gallanz had become dangerous. "Mr. Milgrim has been working on a slate of low-budget pictures," Votrian said. "We'll need producers for the program." Votrian came around Nick's desk. "Your agent can call the business office."

"I am the agent."

"Yeah, you're a whole Olympic team," Votrian said. "You start

Monday. Room one-eleven in the administration building. You'll have a girl. She'll be in there Monday."

"I choose the stories for my pictures," Nick said.

"I'll tell Mr. Milgrim," Votrian said.

Nick watched him clomping across the office. "Shut the door," Nick said.

11

IN VIENNA ONE AFTERNOON
in January 1943, Colonel Varlingen's private telephone rang. "Why aren't
you at lunch, Friedrich?" Varlingen recognized General Probst in Berlin.

"An M.P. shouldn't eat lunch, General," Varlingen said. "It
makes him loggy. How are you, sir?"

"As always, Friedrich," said the general. "Come on over. Today."

"Yes, sir, General," Varlingen said. "Is it something urgent, sir?"

"Come directly to headquarters."

From his desk Emil Huebner saw Colonel Varlingen using the
private telephone. Der Chineser reviewed every hour of every day for
the last month. He took a ledger from his desk to check his diary. Der
Chineser had logged every order he had received, every one he had
executed, time and place. He slipped the diary into the desk drawer.
Der Chineser dreaded error, and in the last month he had been ob-
sessed with perfection.

Der Chineser remembered every detail of an episode a month earlier. "I apologize, Emil," the colonel had said. "This is long overdue."

The colonel set a black velvet box on Der Chineser's desk. "It isn't locked." Der Chineser opened the box and caught his breath, dazzled by the brass insignia. "Compliments of Der Führer, Major," said the Colonel.

Der Chineser said, "Thank you," but the words weren't enough. He said, "I know where this . . . who is responsible. I'll try to be worthy, sir."

"Major, for you it will be easy," Varlingen said.

Now, at his desk, Der Chineser saw the colonel coming and sprang to attention. "Emil, I am ordered to Berlin. I'll pick up some clothes. Call Schwechat and book me on the first aircraft out, civilian or military. Priority booking. I'll deliver the priority at Schwechat." Der Chineser bent for the telephone, and Varlingen said, "Wait. Stay close while I'm gone. You're in command. You're not as lucky as I am because you don't have you."

Der Chineser accompanied the colonel to the corridor. "Make it three or four days," said Varlingen. "I should be back during the weekend."

All that week Der Chineser was at his desk earlier than usual, and he stayed later than usual. Late Saturday he saw Varlingen's secretary fasten the clasp on a large manila envelope. "What is that?" He left his desk. "What do you have there?"

"These are for Colonel Varlingen," she said. "This week's ID renewals. They come over every week from the Hotel Metropole."

"I'll take it."

"It's marked 'EYES ONLY,' " said the secretary, showing Der Chineser the large letters.

"I am the colonel's eyes," he said. The secretary looked at him, paralyzed by indecision. He snatched the large envelope out of her hand. "You can go."

Alone, Der Chineser opened the ledger and set down the days' events, including the secretary's admirable reluctance to relinquish the colonel's envelope.

The ID renewals were routine. Der Chineser locked the manila envelope in his desk with the ledger. He would have little enough to occupy him the next day.

Der Chineser liked Sunday, liked being in the abandoned offices, liked the hollow sound of his footsteps in the empty corridors. He used only a single light on Sunday, a gooseneck lamp on his desk.

He followed his daily schedule that Sunday, beginning with a call to Military Police headquarters for the night's report from the duty officer. Afterward, Der Chineser read again the day logs during the colonel's absence and clipped them for the secretary. He dropped the reports in his Out basket and unlocked his desk to remove the manila envelope. He opened the clasp and held the envelope upside down, making a pile in front of him.

Each ID was a small paper book. Inside on the left was a passport-sized photograph and below, the name and address of the man or woman. The facing page, a printed form, carried a physical description: hair color, eye color, age, height, weight, scars, birthmarks, any other anatomic distinctions, religion, occupation, including housewife and student, and finally, national origin. On the back of that page and on several others were spaces for renewal dates and endorsements. Each endorsement included the name and initials of the endorsing official. Der Chineser made several orderly stacks of the pile on his desk and opened the top one of the nearest stack.

He had chosen Olga Lujack, a woman with black hair cut short, a domestic, forty-seven years old, born in Hungary. Der Chineser examined the entire ID before surrendering the paper book and taking another. He continued, methodical and thorough, learning everything about every man and woman whose ID he examined. He finished two of the three stacks on his desk, and as he took the top ID from the third, Der Chineser yawned. He shifted in his chair, squaring his shoulders, holding the ID like a playing card and opening it with his thumb. He said, "Walther Cnobra," to himself, reading the name below the man's photograph, and then, aloud, "Walther . . ."

Der Chineser raised the ID to eye level. "Max Ingster," he exclaimed, looking at the enemy of the Third Reich. He flipped over the facing page to see the renewal endorsements. There were two endorsements, identical signatures with identical initials: Friedrich Varlingen, F.V., Col., M.P.

The ID fell from Der Chineser's hand and lay on the desk like a tent at a crazy angle. Der Chineser winced and shook his head to make the problem disappear. He cursed himself for his cowardly impulse and sat erect once more, unable to shirk his duty. He raised the ID, looking at the face from the Zwischentheatre he had memorized long ago. Holding the paper book, Der Chineser's heart leaped. The colonel was not an Austrian! He had come from Germany after the Anschluss, after the gang from the Zwischentheatre had been decimated. Der Chineser had found only one enemy, not two.

He copied the address, Sauter Gasse 46, on a pad before chiding himself. Max Ingster had used a false name, so the address was false.

Der Chineser continued his examination of the ID's, but could not dismiss Max Ingster. He had to be sure. He called Military Police headquarters. "I need six men and a driver."

Leading his squad, Der Chineser searched every apartment in the four-story building at Sauter Gasse 46. Sitting beside the driver of the truck on the ride back to his office, Der Chineser felt almost comfortable.

Before leaving that Sunday, he set down everything he had done in his ledger, omitting Colonel Varlingen's mistake. The colonel had never seen any of the Zwischentheatre troupe. Later, over a solitary dinner, Der Chineser tried to forget about the colonel's signature on the ID. But he knew he would be forced to prove the colonel was innocent, as he had proven Max Ingster did not live in Sauter Gasse.

Early Monday morning, Der Chineser climbed the slate steps to the second floor, taking his keys from his pocket to open the offices. In the corridor he saw light falling across the floor where some early bird had managed finally to arrive ahead of him. Der Chineser welcomed the winner. He knew the secretaries reported stories of his devotion to duty to Colonel Varlingen. Just then Der Chineser stopped in the center of the corridor. The light ahead came from the open door to their offices.

Inside, he heard a chair creaking, and a few feet beyond, he found the colonel in his familiar position, feet on his desk and ankles crossed. "Ah, Emil. At last a familiar face."

Varlingen said he had boarded an airplane in Berlin at ten o'clock the night before. "They booked me on an elevator, Emil." Varlingen's hand rose and fell. "Up and down, up and down. In Munich we had to wait almost two hours for an SS general. We landed at Schwechat at dawn. I shaved and bathed, changed uniforms, and came to work. How *is* work?"

"As you left us, sir," Der Chineser said.

"Good, good," Varlingen said. "It's good to be home."

Der Chineser had to settle the issue of Max Ingster before he could start the day. He took nine ID's from the manila envelope, none endorsed by Varlingen. Der Chineser slipped Walther Cnobra among the nine. Shoving the envelope under his arm, he took five paper books in each hand and walked to Varlingen's door. "Sir, these came in Saturday from the Gestapo."

Varlingen saw the manila envelope, saw the "EYES ONLY" in boldface across the top, saw the handfuls of ID's the Chinaman carried.

Varlingen uncrossed his ankles and lowered his legs. "Come across any enemies, Emil?"

"No, sir." Der Chineser set down the envelope and beside it the two stacks of ID's. "I thought the colonel would look through these, sir."

Varlingen spread the nine paper books across his desk like someone playing solitaire. "No enemies," he said. "Communists? Homosexuals? Freemasons?" Varlingen opened an ID at random. "Traitors?"

"I've never done this job, sir," said Der Chineser. "I would appreciate the colonel's opinion."

"Let me have yours," Varlingen said. "Why did you choose these nine?"

"So I could learn from you, sir," said Der Chineser.

"Am I a better bloodhound, Emil?" Varlingen flipped through an ID and opened another. "Never laid eyes on her," Varlingen said. He opened another book. The fourth belonged to Max Ingster, and Varlingen knew Der Chineser had seen the renewal endorsements. "Ah, the Czech," Varlingen said. He raised the open ID "Walther Cnobra, the man with the flying fingers. Best cobbler east of London, Emil. Next time you need boots." Varlingen tossed the ID aside and took another.

"Oscar Zelinka," he said. "Dentist." He raised the ID to show Der Chineser the photograph. "Looks like a greyhound." Varlingen read aloud the dentist's physical description. He took a long time with this and the remaining ID's Der Chineser had selected. "In the clear," Varlingen said. He opened the manila envelope and pushed the nine books into it. "Much obliged, Emil."

Der Chineser walked back to his desk slowly. "Czech cobbler," he said to himself. He had been wrong the previous day. There were two traitors, not one.

On the other side of the suite, Varlingen put the manila envelope into his attaché case. He glanced at his private telephone, then rose from his chair. The Gestapo did not believe in private telephones. Varlingen took his garrison cap and left the office.

At noon that day, Carly walked into Stephansplatz. The square was beginning to fill with lunchtime crowds. She had avoided the square for more than five years because of Nick, but now she was trapped by her memories. Carly remembered every minute of that day, remembered his face, could see his face after more than five years. And she could hear his questions, his protests, his pleas. She walked faster, faster, but could not escape. He was at her side, and Carly, fleeing, began to run.

She came out of the sunlight into the hushed silence of the great cathedral where she had walked down the aisle to Fritz on her wedding day. She could hear Cardinal Innitzer celebrating her marriage Mass, could still feel herself shriveling, losing all hope. She crossed the cathedral to the far side, making her way to one of the chapels.

"You're late," Varlingen said.

"Why did you choose this place? There are a thousand other places," Carly said. "I'll never come here again."

"Never say never," Varlingen said, unbuttoning the breast pocket of his blouse. "There is a problem, and there is also a problem of time. Time is forever a problem." Taking Max's ID from his pocket, he told Carly about the meeting with Der Chineser. "Take this to Kurtz, a printer in Sonnenfelsgasse," Varlingen said. "He's short, with spectacles of which one is black. Kurtz will make a new man of Max: new name, new profession—a geologist, or an oceanographer, or a lion tamer."

Varlingen made her very frightened. "Stop your jokes!"

He smiled at her and ran his forefinger along her cheekbone. "Domino, my brave baroness."

She took his hand in her icy hands and raised it, kissing his knuckles. "When will I know?"

"When you see me," he said. "Otherwise, you have Max, you have the organ grinder. He has others, good ones. You won't be an orphan." He bent for the briefcase between his legs. "Light a candle for me, Carly."

Varlingen returned to his office. He sat with his feet on the desk, thinking of his youth, of his college years, of his daughters, of all the girls before his wife, of his wife, of his daughters.

His secretary left for the day. Varlingen knew Der Chineser would remain as long as he stayed. Varlingen lowered his legs. He went to the windows, watching the sky turn pink with the setting sun, watching the first streetlights brighten while he waited for darkness.

As night came, Varlingen returned to his desk and opened the attaché case. He removed the manila envelope, leaving an American revolver, the .38-caliber Police Positive he had always favored. Varlingen carried the envelope into Der Chineser's office. "Sit down, Emil, sit down. We're alone." Varlingen dropped the envelope in front of Der Chineser. "We can stop the playacting. You haven't been to the Gestapo or I wouldn't be here. I gave Max Ingster an ID and you found it. You may stand now, Major. I am still in command, and I've given you a direct order."

Der Chineser rose and came to attention. "We are fellow officers,

Major," Varlingen said. "We are men who live by a code. I am asking you to remember that code. It is over for me now." Varlingen tapped the envelope with his fingers. "Max Ingster—" he said, and broke off.

"Give me a gun," Varlingen said. "One gun with one round. I've lived as a gentleman, let me die with some dignity." He came to attention, clicking his heels. "I would as much for you."

In his entire life only two men and no woman had earned Der Chineser's devotion. The colonel reminded Der Chineser of the baron. He had the same authority, same confident manner, same ease with language, with dress, with superiors and inferiors. "Major?"

Der Chineser remembered that the colonel had picked him out of a crowd, had brought him the major's insignia he wore. Der Chineser raised the flap of his holster, removing the revolver. He released the cylinder and emptied it, setting six bullets on his desk. Der Chineser slipped one into the cylinder. Holding the gun by the muzzle, he extended it. "Sir."

Varlingen took the weapon. He said, "Thank you, Major," leaving Der Chineser and walking to his office. Der Chineser followed slowly, like someone in mud. He saw the colonel's door close and he sagged against the wall, closing his eyes as though he could hide.

In his office Varlingen put Der Chineser's revolver on the desk and opened the attaché case. He took his own gun and turned down the lights. Varlingen crossed the darkened office to the closed door, which opened inward, to the visitor's left. Varlingen stood to the right of the door and squeezed the trigger, shooting into the floor.

As Der Chineser heard the shot, he watched the door as though he expected Varlingen to return, teasing him for working late. Then he heard Varlingen fall.

In his office Varlingen leaped to his feet. He felt for the wall, standing to the right of the door in the darkness.

Varlingen heard movement, heard Der Chineser cough. Varlingen held the gun like a duelist waiting for the judge's command. As the door opened and he saw the uniform in the light from the corridor, Varlingen fired.

Der Chineser felt a flame over his right ear and dived to the floor. He heard a second shot as he rolled to escape the broad band of light. Varlingen came after him, firing again as Der Chineser rolled into the desk.

He heard Varlingen behind him and extended both hands, snaring an ankle with his left hand and yanking with all his strength.

Varlingen fell, and as he dropped, Der Chineser jumped to his feet, lashing out with his boot to kick the gun out of the colonel's hand. The weapon slid across the floor and caromed off the wall. Der Chineser saw it and dived past Varlingen, who pushed himself erect, stumbling and falling against the desk. As Der Chineser grabbed the gun on the floor, Varlingen snatched up the revolver. Der Chineser fired an instant before his superior.

The gun fell from Varlingen's hand. He swayed and staggered, falling into the light. Der Chineser saw the bright red stain over the colonel's blouse.

As Der Chineser came to his feet, holding the American gun, Varlingen's head rose slowly, like an infant's, and he tried to move but fell back. Der Chineser pressed the light switch. Varlingen lay on his back, his eyes open as blood spread across his uniform. Der Chineser stepped over him and went to the desk, using the colonel's telephone to call the Hotel Metropole so he could make a full report to the Gestapo.

Early one morning that same month Carly slipped out of the palace before Matilda and Zinn stirred. Carly came and went at will because Fritz was rarely in Vienna. He lived mainly in the schloss in the Tyrol. "The Nazis need my crops, Carly," he said. "When I am not in attendance, supervising, the crops suffer."

Ever since he had found Carly in the Prater with Varlingen, Fritz had contrived to be absent from the palace. He submitted required reports to Nazi officials. He rode in the convoy which delivered the crops to Nazi depots. He made himself a necessary element in the Nazi war machine. The Baron Von Gottisberg maintained a defensible distance between himself and the baroness, Colonel Varlingen's crony.

Although Fritz's absence gave Carly a freedom she prized when Varlingen alerted her, she could not dismiss her guilt. Fritz deserved his wife at his side. Whenever he was in Vienna, Carly offered to return to the schloss with him. "I'm in the fields from dawn to dark," Fritz said, and then, smiling, "and after dark I'm a dead man. You would be living with a corpse." His considerate reply made Carly more guilty.

In the Westbahnhof that morning, Carly took the train to Linz, a hundred miles from Vienna. When she walked out of the station there, she saw Max in a small car. He wore a German navy uniform, dress blue with a white cap. Carly proceeded to a park in the distance.

She walked through it until she faced a school. Carly could see the flagpole at one end of the playing field, the swastika fluttering in the breeze. She heard a car, and as it passed, she saw the bright white of Max's cap.

The school bell sounded. As it rang, the doors opened and the children raced out, on their way home for lunch. Carly walked out of the park, crossing the street as boys and girls raced by her. The building emptied quickly.

Where was he? She began to count. A woman closed the school doors. Carly looked over her shoulder at the small car, and when she turned back to the school, she saw a man whose right leg was lame. He stopped beside her. "Have you seen the gypsies?" Carly asked.

"All the gypsies are in Hungary," he said. He had not shaved for several days, and his stubble of beard was flecked with gray.

"Except me," Carly said.

"And me," the man said.

"Where can we go?" Carly asked.

His mouth opened. His teeth were mottled, with large gaps where he had lost teeth. "Go? I'm working."

"We have an audience," Carly said. She had exhausted her instructions and now followed her own. "The school is full of teachers, perhaps at the windows behind us. How many are Nazis? How many will see the woman with the janitor who came and went, poof, like a gust of wind? Take me to a café, any café. I'm a visiting niece, and you are my favorite uncle." Carly put her arm through his. "A café, Uncle."

"I have only an hour," he said.

"Se we cannot dawdle," Carly said, leading him away from the school. She made herself smile. "Uncle who?"

"I am Manfred," he said. "This way."

They crossed the street, walking through the park and across another street. They passed a church and beside it, a large apartment. "The café, Uncle Manfred," Carly said.

"Over the bridge," he said. The bridge spanned a large web of railroad tracks running through a gully.

On the far end of the bridge, Carly stopped. "In here," she said, beside a *bierstube*.

"It's a saloon!" he said.

"You are showing me the lower depths," Carly said. "Open the door, Uncle."

They went to a table. A waiter followed them. "Beer," Carly said, and to the janitor, "Beer, Uncle?" He nodded, watching the waiter, pulling his chair up to the table beside Carly.

"Pass it over," said the janitor. Carly saw Max enter and go to the bar.

"After he brings the beer," Carly said.

"Where the hell is he?" The janitor looked back as the bartender set a stein of beer in front of Max. The waiter crossed the saloon carrying a tray with two steins of beer to the table. The janitor put money in the tray.

"Drink your beer," Carly said.

He drank and set down the stein. "I'll be late," he said.

Carly took a wallet from her purse. From it she removed a small sealed envelope, like a jeweler's envelope. "Is that it?" asked the janitor.

The previous day, in front of the Votiv Kirche, Carly had taken the envelope from the tin cup which the organ grinder's monkey shoved at her. The janitor covered the envelope with his hand. "Finally," he said. He took his hat from the chair between them.

"Wait," Carly said. "Wait, damn you!" Where had they found this crybaby? "Act like a man. Come on, finish your beer."

He raised his stein and Carly drank with him. The janitor paused, holding the stein in the air, and then drank once more, emptying it. "Satisfied?"

He pushed back his chair, and as he stood up, Max took his change from the bar. Carly joined the janitor. As they passed Max, Carly stopped and almost cried out. The janitor was limping with his left leg instead of his right.

She looked at Max and followed the janitor, her heart pounding. "Uncle Manfred, wait for me," she said. Where was Max?

She caught up with the janitor at the door. "Ladies first, Uncle Manfred," she said. He had to open the door, and as she left the saloon, she raised her purse, holding it against her chest.

Carly turned abruptly in front of the saloon door, advancing on the janitor and pushing the Beretta automatic into his belly. "Don't move and don't talk."

She saw Max coming. "The car, quick," she said. Max put his shoulder into the janitor. "This way," Max said.

"Who the hell are you?" he asked, looking at Max. "Are you crazy?" He looked from Carly to Max. "Are you both crazy?" The janitor couldn't stop. "Who brought you into the organization?"

Carly bit her lip, hurting herself to retain her self-control. Keeping the muzzle of the Beretta in the janitor's ribs, she cried, "Where's the car? Where is the *car*?"

"In front of you," Max said. He stopped the janitor beside the small car.

"Open it," Carly said. "I've got him. Don't worry about him." She detested the false janitor because he was her prisoner. She had to deal with her prisoner.

Max opened the rear door of the car. "Inside," he said, using both hands to knock the janitor off balance so he fell into the backseat. "In front, quick," Max told Carly.

She dropped to her knees on the front seat, facing the man in the rear with her loaded automatic. Beside her Max turned the car into the street. "Let's hear it," he said.

"He's lame in both legs," Carly said. "First he had a bad right leg, then a bad left leg."

"I mixed up my instructions," said the prisoner. "They told me to limp. I forgot which leg. Anyone can forget. I'm not a machine."

"No, you're not," Carly said. "You're a liar."

"We're running against the clock," Max said. "Whoever put him in the school is waiting, and they won't wait long. They'll come after him."

"That's right," said the prisoner. "You'd better drop me fast, while they will still let you get away."

"Shut up!" Carly said.

"Forget him," Max said. "He's past tense, Carly."

She almost hit Max. "No names!"

"No names, correct," Max said. A bus turned into the street in front of the small car, and Max slammed on the brakes.

"I can't breathe in here," said the man in the backseat. "I need some air in here."

"So you can yell for the cops," Max said. "Touch that window and you'll need a whole lot more than cops."

"You're stopping," Carly said. "Why are you stopping?"

"I'm in traffic and *you* shut up," Max said, adding immediately, "Amateur night, Carly. We're playing like amateurs."

"Names!" she said, hating him, hating the prisoner, hating the small car, the tomb.

"I'm losing you!" Max said to the bus, swinging out to pass. "Now we're clear," he said, turning at the corner. In the empty street he jammed the accelerator to the floorboard.

"Where are you taking me?" the man said, wiping his mouth with the back of his hand. "Tell me where you're taking me. You're taking me out of Linz!'' he said, his voice filling the small car. He went for the door behind Max, grabbing the handle.

Carly fell over the front seat, raising the automatic and slashing the man with the short barrel. Blood rose in a jagged line from the man's eye to his ear. He covered his eye, falling into the corner. "You've blinded me!"

"Open your eyes," Carly said, not wanting to believe him. "You can see. Look!"

"*You* look," Max said. "Over there. That's where we'll go, that barn."

Carly saw the skeleton of a barn in a field near the road. The barn doors were gone, and parts of the roof had fallen in, but the four walls remained, paint peeling, the wood bleached by the sun. Max turned off the road into the field, shifting down through the gears until he drove into the barn.

He jumped out, opening the car door. "Out," he said, reaching in for the prisoner. "Out, I said!"

Carly joined Max, the Beretta aimed at the prisoner. He stood with his hand against his face, blood seeping through his fingers. "Do it, Carly," Max said. "Stop worrying about names. This guy won't be telling anyone your name or anything else."

"Give me the envelope," Carly said.

"I don't have it," the man said.

"We'll get the envelope," Max said. "Do it."

"I left the envelope," the man said. "We'll have to go back for the envelope to where I hid it."

"We've got to get out of here," Max said. "He's right. His people are waiting! Do it!"

"Listen, please," the man said. "Please, listen. I didn't touch the real janitor. I didn't participate, didn't join in that part."

Carly hated him for the janitor's death, hated Max for prodding her, hated Varlingen for abandoning her. "Carly!" Max said.

"I'm just like you," said the prisoner. "Just taking orders like both of you."

"Give me the gun!" Max said. "Give me the goddamn gun!"

She wanted to throw the gun at him and leave them in the barn, but she couldn't. She was the leader of the mission.

"Look, here it is," the man said. "Right here." He put his hand in his pocket and held up the white jeweler's envelope.

"Drop it," Carly said.

"Shoot him!" Max said.

"Look," the man said, raising his hand with the envelope, like a magician completing a trick. The envelope fell to the ground.

"Back," Max said, waving. The man stepped back, and Max bent, scooping up the envelope and springing to his feet. "Carly!"

She had to squeeze the trigger. She could not. She had never killed anyone, killed anything. Her eyes smarted and she felt dizzy. "Carly!"

"No, please," the man said. He raised his hands, lacing his fingers. "Please, I'm married, too, like you. Three children. Please."

"Give me the goddamn gun!" Max said.

"Please," the man said, stepping back. "Don't . . . please," he said. Max raised his arm to take the gun just as Carly fired.

The man grunted and grimaced. He said, "You . . ." and his legs buckled and he sank slowly to the dirt.

Carly's insides revolted. She held her breath, leaving the barn and walking through the field. She heard the car behind her but kept moving. The car stopped, and then a shadow fell across hers as Max caught up with her. He put his hand over the hand holding the Beretta. "Your safety is off," Max said, pushing down the two metal tabs to lock the trigger.

She saw neither Max nor the road which curved toward Linz nor the birch trees on the far side of the road. She said, "Three children."

Max put his arm around Carly, leading her to the car. "Think of what the N-Nazis are doing, what you've s-seen them do," he said. "S-stop feeling—" he said, but could not continue. They had made orphans somewhere. "Y-your train."

In the Westbahnhof in Vienna, Carly shambled through the terminal like a derelict. She went to a telephone booth and called her parents' apartment, as she did every afternoon except Sundays. "Mama? Did the mail come?"

Helga Siefermann said, "You're late. Yes—" and Carly interrupted.

"Anything?"

Helga said, "Something came, Carly. Your—" she said, but Carly interrupted:

"From California?"

"California, yes, but—"

"Good-bye!" Carly came out of the telephone booth running. She ran into the street. Sometimes there was a taxi. She saw an empty cab and ran faster, believing it was a sign of good luck. Carly opened the taxi door. "Kruger Strasse! Hurry! Hurry!"

Helga remained in the corridor beside the telephone. She heard the elevator, then Carly's footsteps, and when the door opened, Helga said, "You didn't let me finish."

Carly said, empty inside, "Now you're finished," taking the envelope.

She had retained the taxi, too weary to walk to the palace. "Stadt Park," she told the driver. When he stopped, she took money from her purse, giving the bills to the driver without looking either at the amount or at him.

She crossed Reisner Strasse. The doorman recognized the baroness who came to see the old woman on the fourth floor. "Elevator broken, Baroness. Sorry. Almost two weeks already. Every day they say they are coming."

Carly raced up the four flights of stairs, fighting for breath as she knocked on the apartment door. As she knocked again, the door opened. "Oh, Baroness," said Berte. "All those steps," she said, following Carly.

"Look," Carly said, raising the envelope she had taken from her mother, facing the old woman to whom Magda had given her parents' apartment. "Here is my letter," Carly said. Beside Nick's name were the words "NOT AT THIS ADDRESS," and below, someone in the Vienna post office had stamped, "ADDRESSE UNBEKANNT." "You told me he was in California," Carly said. "He and Magda."

"California, yes," Berte said. "I showed you, Baroness. You saw the address."

"You must have made a mistake," Carly said. "Let me see Magda's letter."

"Burned," Berte said. "If the Nazis—" She broke off, then added, "Let me show you, Baroness." The old woman went to a highboy, opened a drawer. "I, too," she said, taking out an envelope. Carly saw Magda's name and flanking it, "ADDRESSE UNBEKANNT." Maybe another letter will come," Berte said. "We'll wait."

Carly said, barely, "Wait," and walked to the door. She had waited years, waited centuries for word from Nick. She had written everywhere, letter after letter, begging for a reply.

Berte locked the door after the baroness. Then she went into the kitchen. In a cabinet, between plates, she had hidden a letter from Magda. Berte brought a writing tablet and a pen with an inkwell to the kitchen table. Berte opened the tablet and wrote, "Just now came the baroness with a letter stamped Addresse Unbekannt. I said everything you told me. I showed her my letter with your false address. I think she will stop now. But she is young . . ."

When Carly reached the palace, she wanted to sneak upstairs and hide, but the rooms were ablaze with lights. "Zinn?"

Carly walked through the palace. "Zinn?" she repeated, but heard Fritz answer: "Carly?"

He stood on the steps of the Great Hall. "In here, Carly."

"When did you get back?" she asked. "You didn't tell me you were coming. I'm sorry I wasn't here."

"I have a surprise," Fritz said. He kissed her as though she was his mother. "Let me show you."

He took her into the Great Hall, stopping before an enormous poster pasted to the wall opposite the fireplace. An enormous swastika covered a map of Europe. "I had it done in Innsbruck," Fritz said. The woman artist had worked on the poster in the nude while Fritz, nude, watched her.

"The Russians have broken the siege at Stalingrad," Fritz said. "Operation Barbarossa is kaput, Carly! Hitler has lost Mother Russia!" Carly could not remember Fritz so gleeful. He seemed boyish. "We're having a party!"

Carly sat down, hands in her lap, like a child being reprimanded. "Another party."

"We're honoring Der Führer's genius," Fritz said. "The greatest genius since Napoleon. Get a new dress, Carly. Buy something smashing." He stopped beside her. "We are loyal citizens of the Third Reich," he said. "I like to remind the Nazis of my devotion. Our devotion. The baroness and I."

Fritz transformed the Great Hall. He hung swastikas everywhere and placed collection boxes for Nazi charities all through the palace. One afternoon he telephoned the schloss. "Fiegel, you're being drafted. I'm giving a party, and I can't bring it off without you."

Fritz sent Zinn to deliver the invitations. Der Chineser returned to his office late one day, and saw on the desk a square white envelope with his name. He turned it over and found the Von Gottisberg crest.

Saturday night, Der Chineser dressed like a boy on his first date. Standing in front of the mirror, he held another mirror in his hand, examining himself front and back, looking for a blemish. He pushed back the sleeve of his blouse to look at his wristwatch. He had hours to endure.

Der Chineser sat down to wait. The invitation said, "Supper and Sport." Supper made him apprehensive. Der Chineser always ate alone. Sport upset him. He had never entered a sporting event. Der Chineser thought of walking. He lived miles from the palace and could use up the long wait. Der Chineser rose but remained beside the chair. He could be caught in a sudden rain or splattered by a speeding car. Der Chineser squeezed the back of the chair. Himmelpfortgasse confronted him like a battlefield. For the baron's wedding everyone in Vienna had squeezed into the palace. Tonight he would be one of a favored few. Supper and Sport. After a while he removed his blouse. Der Chineser needed a remedy. He got out of his uniform.

He walked through Ottakring. Within a mile of his boardinghouse, Der Chineser entered an apartment building and climbed three flights of stairs. He knocked on the last door.

It barely opened, trapped by a chain. A woman inside, in a negligee, said, "Honey, you're a week early."

"Let me in," he said, putting his hand against the door.

"Honey, shshsh," she whispered. She had very bright dyed blond hair and told men to call her Zee Zee. "I'm expecting someone." She shook her head, reproving him. "Naughty boy. I can't disappoint my regular. I wouldn't disappoint you," Zee Zee said. Der Chineser came every other Saturday night.

"Open up and let me in," he said.

"Little monkey. Can't get enough, can you?" Zee Zee slipped the chain, stepping back to admit Der Chineser. She bolted the door and trapped the chain in the slot. "Just for a little bit," she said, "because you're so faithful to Zee Zee. But it will cost, honey. I know you. I need a rest after you. I'll have to turn someone away," she said, lying.

Der Chineser knew she lied. "Let's go," he said, walking ahead of her.

The overstuffed apartment had small carpets atop big carpets and chairs and sofas everywhere. The rooms were dimly lit by lamps covered with milky and colored glass. Zee Zee followed him into her bedroom with a high bed and a headboard almost reaching the ceiling. She stopped, extending her hand palm up. "Double the usual, honey."

He paid and began to pull off his clothes, avoiding her.

Zee Zee removed her negligee, naked except for her brassiere, which she did not remove. Her upright, firm breasts were her pride and remained her personal property. She got into bed. "My my," she said. "You must be having some hot dreams. Let me see . . . oh, honey, it's beautiful. Honey, it's so big-g-g-g. I've never seen you like this, honey. Oh, come on, come on." She raised her arms. "Hurry."

Two hours after Zee Zee, Der Chineser walked into Himmelpfortgasse, moving briskly until he saw the solid line of Mercedes-Benz staff cars on both sides of the street. Drivers leaning against the cars came to attention, saluting as Der Chineser went by, and his arm rose and fell steadily. He followed an officer with a woman, staying close behind, waiting to slip into the palace unnoticed.

Zinn opened the palace doors but Fiegel was greeting the guests, and escorting them to the Great Hall. Der Chineser looked at his wrist-watch: ten minutes after nine. He could leave in an hour, slip out unnoticed. But the baron might be insulted. An hour and a half, Der Chineser decided.

Fiegel learned each guest's name before reaching the baron and the baroness. "Major Huebner."

"Emil!" Fritz shook hands and presented Der Chineser to Carly. She watched the strange major making his way among the guests, avoiding everyone.

Fritz had established a gambling casino in the Great Hall. Tables of roulette, baccarat, and chemin de fer filled the lofty room. Fritz hired the croupiers and established the evening's rules. "The house will take ten percent of all winnings for war relief," he told his guests. "We need medical supplies for our wounded. Austrian soldiers bleed, too, ladies and gentlemen."

He caught up with Der Chineser. "You're here to have fun, Emil," he said, putting a thick wad of money into Der Chineser's hand.

"Sir . . . Baron . . . I can't take this from you," said Der Chineser.

"You can and you will," Fritz said. "Good luck, Emil."

Der Chineser had never gambled in his life, but he considered the baron's invitation a direct order. He went to the nearest table, a rou-lette table. "I wish to play."

Nearby a general held up a fistful of money. "Baron, my lucky night!"

"Bravo," Fritz said as a woman with the general stopped him. "Make him quit, Baron."

"Madam, he outranks me," Fritz said, slipping around the table to escape.

Around ten o'clock, Fritz went to the entrance. "Have they stopped coming, Fiegel?"

"I think so, Baron."

"You've earned a break," Fritz said. "You, too, Zinn." Fritz re-turned to the Great Hall, going from table to table. He found Der Chineser playing roulette. "Quit while you're ahead."

"I'm losing, sir."

"Try another game," Fritz said. "This way, Emil." Fritz stopped at one end of the bar, away from the drinkers and tables. "I miss Colonel Varlingen," Fritz said. "Is he sick?"

"Sick? Colonel Varlingen?"

"You are quoting me," Fritz said. "I invited Colonel Varlingen to the party. He is absent. Therefore he could be ill. Is he? Is he out of town? Is his absence permanent?" Der Chineser looked straight ahead. "Emil?"

"Baron, sir . . . Colonel Varlingen is gone," said Der Chineser.

Fritz had to hear the rest. "Friedrich would have sent his regrets," Fritz said. "He didn't send any. Emil?"

"Yes, sir."

Fritz shifted, trapping Der Chineser against the bar. "Do you trust me, old comrade?"

"With my life, sir, Baron," said Der Chineser.

"Thank you for that," Fritz said. "Emil, the subject is Colonel Friedrich Varlingen. I wish to learn the facts explaining his absence here tonight. So far you have responded to my questions with evasion. Since you trust me with your life, Emil, let me say I trust you with mine. Where is Colonel Varlingen?"

Der Chineser could not defy the baron. He tried to whisper. "The colonel won't be back, sir."

"Emil, you are not a witness, and I am not a prosecutor," Fritz said. "Tell me the rest."

Slowly, whispering, Der Chineser obeyed the baron, and while Fritz listened, he felt a noose lowering over his head. "I submitted a full report to the Gestapo, Baron," said Der Chineser.

"Bravo," Fritz said, hitting the bar with the flat of his hand. "Bartender, bring the major a beer!" He jabbed Der Chineser in the ribs. "Try the baccarat, Emil."

Because Fritz wanted a drink badly, he turned away from the bar toward his guests, including those from the Gestapo. He felt as though guns were trained on him. Varlingen could have left files, documents, could have left names. By now the Gestapo had stripped his office and quarters, had swarmed over the house in Peenemunde, had brought his wife and children in for questioning. If the Gestapo learned the Baroness Von Gottisberg had been involved with Colonel Varlingen, the baron would be coupled with her. Carly had made the palace a bunker.

At ten thirty-five, Der Chineser stopped beside Carly, beneath the giant poster on the wall. "I wish to express my thanks, Baroness, for this honor."

He seemed so uncomfortable Carly felt like shielding him from the other guests. "You can't leave, not with all this food," she said.

Der Chineser had obeyed the baron, gambling until he lost the money, and he had remained a reasonable length of time. "I'm on duty early."

"Early tomorrow," she said. "It's still early tonight."

"Well," he said, running out of conversation. "Not early," he said, raising his arm and pushing back the sleeve of his blouse. "After ten-thirty."

Carly caught a glimpse of the oversized wristwatch with its heavily scored case and a thick band. She frowned, pricked by some dimly familiar but elusive memory. Then, as Der Chineser pushed down his sleeve, her memory was triggered. She had to be sure. "Is it that late, Major? Look again."

Fifteen feet away, near the piano, where Fritz had been pinioned by a beanpole of a woman with red hair, he spotted Carly and Der Chineser. "You can't leave, Baron," said the beanpole, hugging him. "You've brought me luck."

"I've promised another," Fritz said, jostling her in his rush. Carly looked like wax.

Der Chineser raised his arm to show Carly the baroque wristwatch which had belonged to Sam Gallanz. Der Chineser said, "Ten thirty-six now, Baroness," as the baron grabbed him.

"Duty calls, eh, Major?" The baron raised his hand. "Fiegel!" he said. "Fiegel will fetch your cap, Emil."

He had Sam's watch! "Fritz, you're chasing away our guests," Carly said.

"No, no," said Der Chineser. "I was leaving." He saw the baron's butler. "I . . . good-night," he said.

Fritz had Carly's arm, holding her firmly, raising his other hand in farewell. "Good night, Major."

"He's wearing Sam's wristwatch," Carly hissed. "Where did he get it? Where's Sam? Where's Nick? Let me go." Fritz was hurting her. "Let me go!"

Fritz would not release her. "You are the hostess, the mistress of this house. Behave like the mistress of this house."

Der Chineser and Fiegel crossed the Great Hall. She was losing him. "Where did he get that watch?" She faced Fritz in a fury. "I have to know! I'll make him tell me! Let . . . me . . . go!"

"That man is connected to the Gestapo," Fritz said.

Fiegel and Der Chineser climbed the steps, leaving the Great Hall.

"I don't care about the Gestapo," Carly said. "If they want you, they get you, so don't try to scare me with the Gestapo. I'm too scared for you to scare me." She wrenched her arm free, striding through the Great Hall with Fritz beside her. "I want to know where he got that wristwatch," Carly said. She needed her Beretta. "I'll make him tell me."

Their bodies brushing, Fritz said, "He will tell you nothing. He will die gladly before opening his mouth." They came to the steps and at the top Fritz swung her around. They faced each other like enemies. "But he will tell me," Fritz said. "Let him go, Carly, and I'll bring you the answers."

She saw Der Chineser standing near the door of the study. Fiegel emerged with the garrison cap and escorted him to the entrance, Zinn ahead of them. "I'll bring you the answers," Fritz said.

Carly lived through Sunday. Fritz could not locate Der Chineser Sunday. She lived through most of Monday. Fritz found her in the study late Monday afternoon. "About the wristwatch."

She came out of her chair, came to him as though they were being reunited. "You remember Colonel Varlingen," Fritz said. "The fellow with the tailored uniforms."

"I think so," Carly said. "The man who enjoyed teasing me."

"He had the wristwatch," Fritz said. "Der Chineser found the wristwatch in Varlingen's desk."

The light seemed to fail and Carly thought she would fall. Fritz saw her turn waxen once more. "Found?"

"Der Chineser has taken Varlingen's place and his desk," Fritz said.

Carly thought of Friedrich, his hand against her face. He would not have harmed Sam or Nick. Where had he got the watch? How? When? She had a thousand questions but only one mattered: where was Nick? She stepped back against the bookcase, putting her hands behind her to hold on. "So we'll never know," she said.

"You could ask Varlingen."

"Where is he, Fritz? Your friend the major must know," Carly said.

Fritz smiled, bestowing the accolade on her performance. He remembered the romantic, gushing fawn in Salzburg, ready to be hanged for her independence. His wife had become a master of deceit, the most dangerous threat to his life. She had cheated him from the beginning. He had expected nothing but honesty, and she had countered with treachery. "The Nazis never publish itineraries," he said, and added, as an afterthought, "Oh, I have a personal announcement. I am leaving for the Ruhr."

In factories all through the Greater German Reich, slave labor, mainly Jews, worked at the machines. The SS guarded them, both in the factories and in the barracks, and civilian managers supervised the work, delivering the quota assigned to each installation. "I'm leaving tomorrow," Fritz said. He could not be the Baroness Von Gottisberg's accomplice in treason surrounded by Jews in a mill near some godforsaken hamlet halfway across Europe.

Carly raised her hand as if to deflect a blow. "Tomorrow? Oh, Fritz!" First she had lost Varlingen, who had kept her erect, kept her mobile, praising and censuring, coaxing and cajoling, and always present, always *there*. And now Fritz was deserting her. And Nick? She could not cry in front of Fritz.

Fritz summoned Matilda and Zinn. "I am leaving the baroness in your care, and if I do not see her smiling face when I return, I will not be seeing your smiling faces, nor will you."

During dinner, Matilda hung around the table, and Zinn made reasons to return constantly. "Out!" Fritz said. "You are banished. This is *auf Wiedersehen*, not a wake."

Carly and Fritz went from the Petit Salon to the stairs. At his door he brushed her cheek with his lips. "Good night."

"Not good night," Carly said, taking his hand. She had only herself to give him. "Not tonight."

"Especially tonight," Fritz said. "I have miles of instructions to set down for Zinn." He closed the door of his bedroom and locked it. If Carly reached his bed, naked, she had him. Fritz could not resist. And he did not intend to discover an heir when he returned to claim the palace.

—— ◄ 12 ►——

IN JUNE OF THE SAME
year, 1943, Leonard Votrian turned off Gower Street into the Majestic
lot. At the gate wooden arms extended from either side of the guard's
booth across the studio street. Chuck, the guard, wore a navy blue
policeman's uniform with a shield on his garrison cap and another over
his heart. He had William Powell's slender mustache. "Miss Lerner
called. He's looking for you, Mr. Votrian. She said go straight up."

Meyer Milgrim's initials were all over his offices. The two letters,
coupled as in a cattle brand, had three vertical strokes instead of four.
When Miss Lerner, the senior of Milgrim's three secretaries, saw Votrian, she stepped on the buzzer under her desk. "Careful."

Milgram had copied Mussolini's office, adding more space. His
desk, big as a ship, stood at an angle in a far corner. Milgram was a
solid man of medium size with a big chest. He wore a fresh white shirt
every day of the year. As Votrian came through the door, he said, "I'm
still waiting to hear from that genius of yours."

"He's not a guy you can rush, this Gallanz. He's a guy who is very devoted, very dedicated."

"*Domino* is the best story I've read in ten years," Milgrim said. "I'm offering him the best picture in Hollywood today."

"He's like a surgeon, Gallanz," said Votrian. "Every line is dissected, torn apart."

"He's had the treatment three days," Milgrim said. "How long does it take to read eighty-three pages?"

"You want him to be honest," Votrian said. "You want him to tell you whether he likes the story."

"Whether he likes the story? I like the story," Milgrim said. "My name will be on this picture. This is my personal production for the year."

"Why do you think he's taking so long? He wants to be sure for your sake," Votrian said.

Milgrim came out of his chair. He put his thumbs into the waistband of his trousers and moved them from side to side. Meyer Milgrim's father had peddled ties and socks out of a suitcase on the docks in Boston. He had found his son a job with the longshoremen, but after two years on the docks, a cousin who owned a neighborhood movie house in Dorchester hired the boy and exploited him. The boy did everything in the theater, and every night when it closed, he had to run for it, through the gangs of Irish in the streets. He held his own, and when they knocked him down, he always got up. "Go downstairs and tell Nick Gallanz to pick a writer. I want a screenplay of *Domino*."

Milgrim looked down at a large framed photograph on his desk. A stunning blond woman sat in a chair flanked by three children, two girls and a boy. "Mavis walks the floor all night finding ways to knock me," Milgrim said. "My worst enemy, and she loves *Domino*."

Votrian crossed the long office. As he closed the door, Miss Lerner said, "I haven't seen him like this in I can't remember how many years."

"Thanks." Votrian hoped she drowned. He passed the elevators so he wouldn't meet anyone. He felt as though his clothes were too tight. Votrian came down the stairwell, holding on to the railing. "My genius," he muttered.

On the first floor, in the producer's wing, Nick Gallanz's secretary, Carole, saw Votrian coming. "He's not in."

Votrian wanted to drown her as well. "What time does he get in?"

Carole held a pencil with both hands as though she could protect herself with it. "He won't be here today, Mr. Votrian."

Votrian raised the telephone and set it in front of her. "Get him on the phone."

She grimaced. "He won't answer."

"Try," he said, and grabbed the receiver, thrusting it into her face. Carole took the instrument and dialed. She heard a ring, then several others, and raised the receiver so he could listen.

Votrian went straight through the building to the executive parking lot. In his Cadillac he rolled down the front windows to keep from choking, and as he swung into the studio street, he blew the horn. Chuck said, "Yeah, yeah," pushing the switch to raise the wooden arm. Votrian drove out of the lot and into Hollywood, his left elbow on the open window, telling himself to calm down and make a battle plan.

Benedict Canyon slices through the western end of Beverly Hills and runs into and across the Santa Monica Mountains to the San Fernando Valley. Mulholland Drive crosses the crest of the mountains east to west. Just below Mulholland, Votrian turned left into a narrow dirt lane, a corniche barely wide enough for two cars.

A half mile from Benedict he reached a brick drive flanked by open iron gates. The drive twisted, leading to a large arc with a four-car garage. He saw Nick Gallanz's car and parked behind it.

Directly ahead lay a pebbled lane bordered on both sides with white oleander forming a bower. Votrian walked into the lane stretching ahead of him like a chute. He could hear the stones grinding beneath his feet.

He came out of the oleander and stopped, blinded by the glare of the sun which seemed closer here, above the city. Overhead, rising from three ascending levels of broad stone steps, stood a Mediterranean villa, its white walls gleaming. The villa towered over Votrian, dwarfing him, dwarfing the oak trees, the pine, the sycamore, and the eucalyptus reaching for the clouds, which looked like giant puffs of candy in the blue sky. The villa was enormous, more fortress than home, stretching in all directions, with battlements and shutters thick as planks on the narrow leaded windows.

The door, like the gates below, was open. Votrian said, "Hello," crossing a foyer suitable for a public building. The foyer rose the height of the villa and was empty except for a chair and a coat tree beneath a curving staircase. "Hello." Votrian stopped, listening, and heard movement. He followed the sound to a drawing room which seemed designed for royalty, seemed like a cathedral, and, like the entrance, was almost barren, as though the furnishings were being systematically removed. Votrian heard a dull thump and saw a figure near the distant wall of the drawing room. "Nick?"

Votrian heard a second thump as he came out of the foyer. "Nick?"

Nick stood beside a large basket filled with darts. He held a dart in each hand, and he threw first with his left and then with his right in a smooth, fluid motion, like a bird in flight. "Nick, can't you answer?"

The darts Nick had thrown were bunched together in the center of the dart board hanging on the wall. He threw again, left and right. "Next time, knock," he said.

Votrian pointed at the foyer. "The door is open."

"You can knock on an open door," Nick said. He walked forward to pull the darts from the dart board.

"Why is it open to start with?"

Nick walked past Votrian, dropping the darts into the basket and taking one in each hand. "So I can escape," he said, throwing.

"You have escaped," Votrian said. "You're here, in America."

"Sure," Nick said, throwing with his right hand and reaching for two more darts.

"You and your stale jokes," Votrian said. "I'm tired of your stale jokes, and of you, boychik. Hey, stop your fucking games, okay?" Votrian leaped forward, standing between Nick and the dart board. "I'm talking to you. Guess why I'm here," Votrian said. "You've got a job. You're a producer at Majestic. Today is a working day. You're supposed to be in the studio."

"I am between pictures," Nick said.

"Not since Monday," Votrian said. "*Domino* is your next picture."

"I told you Monday she is not for me," Nick said.

"I gave you the treatment to read," Votrian said. "Did you read the treatment?"

Nick pointed at a table, and Votrian saw the pale blue Majestic script jacket. "I cannot believe her," Nick said.

"You'll pick a writer and you'll do a script so you *will* believe her," Votrian said. "This Domino is perfect for you. They call her a miracle woman. Nobody knows how many people she has saved from the Nazis, this mysterious woman."

"I make comedies," Nick said.

"It's time for a change," Votrian said, and louder, "I just left Milgrim. I lied from beginning to end to buy time for you. Here's a story everyone in Hollywood would give his arm for. Meyer Milgrim stole it away from everyone. The newspaperman who wrote the treatment *met* Domino. And even he doesn't know her. Nobody knows her. She comes and goes like a shadow, crossing whole countries without a trace. Nobody has a clue. Some say she's a nun, some say she's a countess, a princess, a teacher in Vienna. *You're* from Vienna. This is your picture."

"Find someone else," Nick said. He reached into the basket, but Votrian stopped him.

"Look, schmuck, it's showdown time," Votrian said. "Milgrim is on my ass. I brought you into the studio. You owe me."

Nick came closer as though he couldn't identify his guest. Votrian thought he would smile. "I owe you?" Nick asked. "I've made three pictures for Majestic in two years. Even Milgrim never made a picture as cheap. I had the three biggest grossers on the lot, and I made three stars for the studio. Philip Sanborne is a star now. Sally Monk, Jefferson Barrett are stars. All with seven-year contracts, and so far all three make less than a grip. And I owe you? Without me you would still be opening celery tonic for Milgrim." Nick put his forearm into Votrian's chest, pushing him aside. "I talk too much. Get out of here."

"Tough guy," Votrian said. "I know someone tougher. Meyer Milgrim puts his name on one picture a year. Sometimes he skips a year if he doesn't find the right one. This year he found the picture: *Domino*. He found the producer: you. Right now, *now*, he's waiting for an answer."

Nick lunged forward. He snatched the script from the table and pulled a pen from a mug. Nick spun around, shoving the script against Votrian's chest. Across the blue cover he printed a large, black "NO!!!" "Deliver the answer."

Long after darkness fell on that lovely June night, Nick turned on all the outdoor lights and walked down the stone steps to his car. He drove through the canyon and through Beverly Hills into Hollywood, to the Ringstrasse.

As Nick made his way through the café, Leopold Unger slipped between tables to intercept him. "I almost didn't recognize you, it's been so long," Leopold said. "I'll apologize if you tell me what I did wrong."

Nick headed for the table in the far corner. "I forgot."

"You joke," Leopold said. "I know you joke. I know you." Men and women alone, or sitting in pairs or in groups, welcomed and hailed Nick. He nodded or raised his left hand to make a kind of half twist of his wrist in acknowledgment, but he never paused. At his table Nick ordered dinner and told Leopold to send him coffee. Soon a waiter came with a pot and a pitcher of cream. Nick poured the coffee and cream simultaneously, and after his first sip, he poured more cream.

He didn't see Magda enter. She stood in the doorway, a regal and commanding figure. Leopold came running. "An honor!" He bowed. "A real honor!"

"Is he here?" Magda looked from side to side. She refused to wear glasses in public, and except for the tables nearby, she could not identify the patrons.

"Of course he is here," Leopold said. "Everybody is here." He stepped aside so Magda could precede him. "Everybody is always here."

Nick saw her coming. He pushed back the table for leg room, rising to leave, but Magda took a long step, blocking him. "If you are lucky, you can still save yourself."

So Nick knew she knew everything. He had learned early how fast news travels in Hollywood, and bad news traveled fastest. "Dieter," he said. Nick had found him a supporting role at Majestic, playing a famous surgeon in a movie about the fall of France.

"Lucky for you," Magda said. "Sit," she said, taking a chair facing him. A waiter appeared to set down a tumbler with three fingers of scotch. Magda raised the glass and sniffed it, and then drank half the whisky. "Dieter said your Milgrim went home early, the first time in history. Why? You are why. Listen to me and remember every word."

"I'll pay for the whisky," Nick said. "Drink your drink and drive carefully."

"You are young," Magda said, as though Nick had not spoken. "You made a mistake. Apologize. Ask forgiveness."

"Like you would."

"I don't work for a living," Magda said.

"You're here, so I'll tell you, too," Nick said. "I do not believe in this woman, this Domino."

"You are not a priest," Magda said. "Nobody asks you to believe." She sipped the whisky. "You made a good beginning with Milgrim, and you must not spoil it. I sent Dieter to bring me Milgrim's address. Go to him now, tonight." She set a three-by-five-inch pad on the table between them, pushing it across the marble top to Nick. He brushed the pad aside like someone cleaning crumbs.

The pad dropped onto a chair, and Magda said, "I am finished with you. Forever. I've had enough." She drained the glass, raising herself from the chair.

The next morning, Nick had an appointment with a writer who

had a premise for a comedy. He swung into the Majestic street, stopping beside the guard's booth. "Chuck?" The guard appeared, hating what he would have to do. "Press the button," Nick said.

Chuck couldn't look at the guy. "My orders are you can't come on the lot," he said. "You're suspended." He gestured. "They cleaned out the office. I'll get your stuff."

The news of his expulsion galvanized Nick. He opened the car door, slamming it into the guard's shins. "Hey!"

"Leave my stuff," Nick said. He came out of the car. "I take my stuff."

Several bulging manila envelopes were piled on a shelf in the booth. Nick heard one car horn and then another, and saw three cars behind him. Nick ignored them, refusing to be hurried, tossing the envelopes into the front seat like someone throwing horseshoes. When he had emptied the shelf, he returned to his car. He drove past the booth, making a wide turn to face the street. Nick saw Leonard Votrian in his Cadillac in line. Votrian looked through him.

Nick drove directly back to the villa in the Santa Monica Mountains, the front seat piled high with the bulging manila envelopes. He made two trips into the villa, dumping the envelopes in a pile near the dart board. He dropped to the floor, opening an envelope and emptying it. He went through the contents quickly, making a pile of scripts, letters, newspaper clippings and magazine articles which might make a movie. He opened several more envelopes before he found the script he was looking for. In the upper right-hand corner of the title page Nick read, "Moses Serlin," and below, a telephone number.

Moses Serlin, a Hungarian émigré, wrote comedies influenced by his idol, Ferenc Molnar, the author of *Liliom*. One of Serlin's plays had been produced in Budapest, and Molnar had come to the theater, congratulating the young man. "I see talent on this stage."

In Hollywood Serlin could not find a movie job. He worked nights in an all-night liquor store. He had mailed Nick a play with a long autobiographical letter which included the Molnar incident.

The hero of the Hungarian's play was a young man who courts a wealthy girl but falls in love with her sister. Serlin's plot failed to sustain the play, but Nick knew how to fix the story while retaining the delicious premise. Serlin's dialogue was superior, amusing, racy, and constantly suggestive without slipping into vulgarity. Nick had gone to Votrian. "I found a story I like."

"The studio is choking with stories."

"This could be something special," Nick said. "A big, funny picture."

"You and Milgrim signed a contract," Votrian said. "The contract says you'll make pictures from stories owned by Meyer Milgrim."

In the villa Nick took Serlin's play, and in crossing the drawing room, he saw the *Domino* script cover on a chair were Votrian had dropped it the day before. Nick grabbed the story of the Austrian heroine and threw it at the pile on the floor for the cleaning woman to remove.

Nick took Serlin's play into the sun, reading from page one, making notes all over the pages. He read the play again and again. Around five o'clock he dialed Serlin's number. "This is Nick Gallanz."

Early that evening Nick drove to Pico Boulevard and turned east. He parked near Vermont and walked to the liquor store on the corner, Serlin's play under his arm.

Inside, a man Nick's age, neat and orderly, wearing rimless spectacles, left the cash register at the far end of the counter. Nick held up the play. Moses Serlin said, "You are Mr. Gallanz. I recognize you from your pictures, and once in the Ringstrasse my wife and I saw you."

"Nick. You cannot collaborate with a Mr.," Nick said. "I told you I like your play. I didn't tell you I'm suspended." Serlin looked at the floor, and when he raised his head, he seemed older.

"Before you kill yourself, listen to the rest," Nick said. "Your play needs work, much work. I will work with you. When we finish, we will have a shooting script. And I will make a picture."

They began the following afternoon in the villa. "Your hero, Eric, does not fall in love with the sister," Nick said. "Falling in love with the sister is not a comedy. Falling in love with the maid is a comedy."

Serlin looked at the floor. "The maid?"

"Your way or my way? Decide now," Nick said. "If the story must go your way, good-bye. If it goes my way, it must go my way all the way. Beginning to end. We will also have a picture."

The little man opened his copy of the script, trying to smile. "Your way."

"We begin with the people," Nick said. "The audience will not believe your story if they do not believe your people."

They continued until Serlin had to leave for the liquor store. "Tomorrow," Nick said.

Eleven days later, as Nick waited for Serlin to arrive at the villa, Votrian called. "You got more luck than brains. Come on in, boychik. Milgrim said, 'Give him another chance.'"

"Milgrim barred me from the lot," Nick said.

"He changed his mind."

"He did not change my mind," Nick said.

Late the following afternoon, Nick walked to Serlin's car with the Hungarian. "We have the people now," Nick said. "Tomorrow we begin on page one with the play."

Serlin started his car, and as he circled the entry, he had to stop for a mail truck. A postman left the truck, holding an envelope. "Mr. Gallanz?" Nick raised his hand. "Need your signature for registered mail," said the postman.

Nick saw the Majestic eagle on the envelope. He carried the envelope into the villa and took out the letter.

Dear Mr. Gallanz,

You have ignored repeated requests from Majestic Pictures Corporation to resume your services with the Corporation to whom you are under exclusive contract.

Unless you report to the Corporation studio within twenty-four hours after receipt of this notice, you will be in breach of contract.

Paragraph Two, Page Five of your contract with the Corporation stipulates that your services with and for the Corporation will continue for the term of your contract, ending midnight, November 30, 1945.

Until midnight, November 30, 1945, you are prohibited from performing any services involving the creation and production of motion pictures exclusive of such creative and production services performed for Majestic Pictures Corporation.

Any performances of such services by you will place you in breach of contract. The Corporation will immediately institute legal proceedings to prohibit such services. In addition, the Corporation will seek financial redress for loss of revenues caused by your absence.

Nick dropped the letter on a table. He turned on the spotlight over the dart board and for an hour threw darts, using both hands. Afterward, he sat in a big chair with Serlin's script. Later, he took the script into the kitchen, reading while he ate crackers and cheese. He took the script upstairs with him and read in bed, often reading the actors' lines aloud, listening to the spoken words. He remained awake for hours, and not once did the registered letter and Milgrim's threat leave him.

Nick called Votrian's office early. "Nick Gallanz. You're alone?"

Heather Malamud said, "Yes, but he'll be here any minute. We all miss you, Mr. Gallanz."

"I, too," Nick said. "I need a name. This man is a gangster."

"A gangster!" Heather thought she had heard everything until that moment.

"Votrian sent him after me," Nick said, telling her of the man who had accosted him in front of the apartment off Doheny Drive.

"Oh, him," Heather said. "Now I remember—" Her voice changed abruptly. "Gotta run, hon. Bye."

So Nick knew Votrian had walked into the office. He waited more than an hour. Heather called at nine o'clock. "Sorry, Mr. Gallanz. First chance I've had. His name is Pertsick," she said, and spelled it. "There's an address and a phone number."

Hash Pertsick had set the alarm the night before. He also told Muley Rose, whom he had known all his life, to call him at six sharp, and he told Loretta to come into the bedroom at six. Hash had never been awake at six o'clock in his whole life.

When Nick telephoned, Hash was in the Santa Fe railroad depot in Pasadena, waiting for the Super Chief, which they told him was never late except that day. "Christ."

There were always movie stars on the Super Chief. Although the journey ended in Los Angeles, the stars got off in Pasadena so they could avoid reporters. But the studio press agents called the newspapers to make sure their clients had a reception. Hash saw a couple of reporters with their photographers, drinking coffee out of paper cups. "Relax."

He couldn't stay in one spot, so he started pacing up and down the platform. He was looking at his wristwatch for the twentieth time when he finally saw the train. The redcap to whom Hash had slipped a fin came after him. "Won't be long now."

The train stopped. The conductors came out with their stools. The passengers were right behind. Hash didn't see her. He headed for the tail end of the train, all the way to the last car before coming back. She had to be in there. She had called from the station in Chicago. Hash couldn't find her, and then she was right in front of him, waving and running.

One of the photographers glanced at the girl, a good-looking dame, a kid, with reddish hair and freckles, and she had great legs. The photographer saw the sport with the cream-colored hat grab her.

Polly Pertsick held on to her brother as though she might lose him. "Oh, Hash!"

She made him feel special. His kid sister graduating from college. At least he had done something with his life. He said, "Hello, angel," and cocked his head to look at her. "Hey!" She was crying. "Polly!" He pulled out his handkerchief. "Uh-uh," he said, although his own eyes were moist.

Polly took the handkerchief. "How about you?" she said, laughing and crying. "I'm so happy!"

"That makes two of us," Hash said. He finally got a good look at her. She had green eyes, Ma's eyes. She had Ma's high cheekbones. Hash always figured some Russian must have sneaked in on somebody one night back there somewhere. Christ, she was beautiful.

Polly wasn't beautiful, but she was an attractive young woman of twenty-two with a marked physical resemblance to her brother. She folded his handkerchief and pushed it back into his pocket. "I can't believe I'm home," she said. "Home to stay."

"You're home, angel," he said, holding on to her. "Let's get your bags, right?" He signaled the redcap.

In the parking lot, Polly made a beeline for a black La Salle sedan. Hash stopped her. "Uh-uh."

"It's exactly like yours," Polly said. "Did you sell it? You didn't have an accident?"

"Relax," Hash said. The redcap followed them. "Over there," Hash said, showing Polly a convertible.

"You've got a new car!" Polly said. Hash let the redcap stow the bags, waiting until he was on his way.

"*You've* got a new car," Hash said. She started crying again. Hash had to keep a straight face, reaching for the handkerchief again. She covered her face with the handkerchief, digging her head into his shoulder as she had been doing ever since he could remember. "Hey, where's the funeral?"

"Hash, it's beautiful." She ran her fingers over the hood. "I love it."

"Hop in," he said, holding the driver's door.

Polly backed away. "I can't," she said. "Not yet. I'm too shaky. You drive."

In the convertible Polly snuggled up close, like old times. Hash sneaked a peek at her. He lowered his head to kiss her hair, and she smiled and put her arm through his. Hash remembered when she would hold on to his hand with all her might. He remembered when she was born. The family was half-starving when she was born.

Hash's mother had always worked because his father wouldn't. The old man sat in the park. For a while after Polly was born, Hash's mother couldn't work, and she kept sending him out with stuff to hock. Hash still couldn't pass a pawnshop without wanting to duck.

Prohibition saved them. Hash's mother began making moonshine in the kitchen. She sold it out of the kitchen, pints and half pints, and she also delivered. At twelve years old, Hash was her delivery boy.

When Hash was fifteen, their mother died. Hash's old man remarried as fast as he could, a rich widow with real estate. Hash and Polly and the old man moved in with the widow, who had three kids of her own. She hated Polly and Hash. She fed them scraps. *Scraps.* A couple of weeks later Hash left. He took Polly with him. She was seven years old.

When he left, he had a job with another bootlegger, a big operator. Hash was good at his job. He followed orders, he wasn't afraid of trouble, and he was dependable. In Boyle Heights in east Los Angeles, they all knew about Hash's line of work, and he couldn't let Polly suffer for it. He furnished an apartment in Hollywood which could have been a million miles from the old bailiwick. He was only twenty-four when Prohibition was repealed, but Hash couldn't wait. "If whiskey becomes legit, we become legit."

After Repeal, Hash became single-O and he stayed single-O. He became available for certain people around town. He listened to propositions. Some he liked, some he didn't. He didn't like anyone nosing around. When anyone asked, Hash said, "I got a few things going."

In Beverly Hills the following day, a Saturday, Nick turned off Sunset into Roxbury Drive, and in the second block he stopped across the street from a big white frame house with blue awnings over the windows. He came up the curving flagstone walk and rang the buzzer. He heard chimes inside, and soon the door opened. He faced a black woman in a crisp white uniform. "Mr. Pertsick," Nick said.

"Who's calling?" Loretta asked.

"Say Nick Gallanz. He knows me." Loretta closed the door. A sputtering rumble filled the street, and a low foreign runabout hurtled through Roxbury with a roar.

Loretta returned. "You better call on the telephone first."

"So he's home."

"He says—hey, you!" Loretta swung and missed.

Inside, Nick said, loud, "Mr. Pertsick!" He stopped beside a wide, curving staircase, trying to find the gangster. "Mr. Pertsick, I—"

"Out here," Hash said, interrupting from the patio. He wore a white shirt and gray summer slacks with faint, narrow stripes. "It's okay, Loretta."

"He just come zipping through," Loretta said, glaring at the bum.

"It's okay," Hash said, returning to the table with his coffee and newspaper. "You always bust into people's houses?"

Nick faced the slim man, bathed and shaved and glistening in his expensive clothes. He saw the silver coffeepot on the silver tray, and the bowl of muffins. Beyond Hash, Nick saw the dappled sunlight on the rhododendron and the azalea, the double rows of rose bushes, the forsythia draped along the rain gutters circling the garage, and at the rear, the bougainvillea covering the entire wall at the alley like a crimson standard. He heard the insolent demands of a blue jay in the jacaranda, like the raucous crows at the schloss circling overhead as Fritz led an adventure. For a moment Nick imagined Fritz and Carly arm in arm. Hash rescued him. "Loretta told you to call," Hash said. "You're breaking and entering."

"I called all day yesterday," Nick said.

"This is my house," Hash said. "I don't do business in my house."

"I'll remember next time," Nick said, extending the registered letter with the Majestic eagle on the envelope.

"Listen, you've had a hard time, Hitler and all that," Hash said. "That buys you just so much. So long, pal."

A door opened and closed. "Hash? Why didn't you wake me?"

Polly came through the open French doors. "I prayed you would still be home," she said, and stopped, finding the man with Hash. "Oh, hi . . ." she said. The man looked directly at her as though they were alone.

Polly felt Hash's arm around her, warm and safe. "Hello, angel."

"I'm interrupting," she said. The man with Hash was like a hypnotist. She couldn't turn away. "I'm sorry."

"For nothing," Nick said. His voice made goose flesh rise along Polly's arms. She kissed Hash and entered the house, stopping behind a chair, leaning this way and that for a glimpse of the strange man. She had never encountered anyone like Hash's guest, anyone as . . . different.

On the patio Nick took the letter from the envelope. "While I'm here."

Polly saved the guy. Hash read the letter fast, read it again, and folded the sheet of paper along the creases. He had not forgotten the guy that night in the dead end of Doheny Drive. Hash gave him back the letter, waiting. He had never gone broke keeping his mouth shut.

Nick said, "First they fire me, and now they say I cannot quit."

"You bust into my house to tell *me?*"

"I'm through with a boss," Nick said.

Hash took a cigarette from his pack and lit it. He moved a chair to sit down. So Nick knew he had finally been asked to stay. "Keep Milgrim out of my life," Nick said.

"Just like that," Hash said.

"I'll go now," Nick said.

"Yeah," Hash said. He was one cocky wetback.

Hash had kept the weekend open so he would have Polly all to himself. He made her drive the convertible. He took her to a pair of nifty restaurants. She loved the house and everything in it, even her room. By Sunday night Hash felt as though she had never been away.

After he came downstairs Monday, he sat on the patio watching Mr. Magic, the gardener, doing his tricks. When he began to roll up his hoses, Hash called Leonard Votrian at Majestic. "Fix it for me to talk with your boss."

"Tell me the subject," Votrian said.

"You're not the boss."

"I'm the boss for people like you," Votrian said. "Why do you— hello?" Votrian listened. "Hello?"

After lunch with Polly, Hash drove to Majestic, and in the administration building he rode the elevator to the fourth floor. He opened the door with Milgrim's name on it, removing his hat when he saw the three dames sitting at desks under all the diplomas on the walls. "Yes?" said Miss Lerner.

"I'm here to see Mr. Milgrim," Hash said, taking out a leather card case.

"Mr. Milgrim has no appointments scheduled for this afternoon," said Miss Lerner.

"Police," Hash said, opening and closing the card case.

"We didn't call the police," said Miss Lerner. Hash walked to the double doors. "Who are you?"

The doors were locked. Hash turned. "You gonna open this or should I?" He watched the skinny dame until he heard the click.

Hash came into a funeral parlor. He saw Milgrim a mile away with Votrian standing beside the raised desk. Milgrim was on the phone yelling, "Next time, ask first!" Milgrim banged down the telephone receiver. "Who are you? I know Chief—"

"He's no cop," Votrian interrupted. Hash grinned shamefacedly. "Maybe *I'll* call the cops."

As he moved toward the telephone, Hash said flatly, "Don't try it," and Votrian stopped.

Milgrim hit the desk with both fists, raging at Votrian. "Who is this . . . person?"

"I heard about him from Leo Whitfield and Papermaster," Votrian said. "They've used him for certain matters and we—I had a problem."

"I'll settle your problem," Milgrim said. He lifted the telephone receiver. "I have my own police."

Milgrim had dialed only one number before Hash said, "Don't," shaking his head. He dropped his hat on the desk. "If I go, I'll only come back. I got in once, I can get in again. Maybe I'll have a stomachache next time, or it'll be raining and I'll be wet. That doesn't make anyone feel great. Forget the phone," Hash said. Milgrim replaced the telephone receiver. Hash saw the framed photograph beside Milgrim, the good-looking dame with the three kids. Hash gestured at Votrian. "Take a walk, pal."

Votrian started for the doors. Milgrim said, "Leonard!" but Votrian didn't stop. Hash moved a chair and took an ashtray from a table. He heard the door open as he sat down, crossing his legs. "Who the hell are you, breaking into my studio?"

"Votrian told you," Hash said, taking out a cigarette. "I help out people." He lit the cigarette, raising his head to watch the smoke. "Today I'm helping Nick Gallanz."

"You're not talking now with Leonard Votrian, mister. You're talking now with Meyer Milgrim. All your tricks are for nothing. A wild goose chase."

"How d'ya know? I haven't said nothing yet." Hash set the cigarette in the ashtray. "Listen, this is your place, Majestic. You made this place." He looked up at the man in the chair on the platform. "Here's what I figure. I figure we're sensible people."

Milgrim leaned over the desk as though he intended to vault over it. "Like your friend, Nick Gallanz? The snake in the grass?" Milgrim raised a script with a pale blue cover. Hash could see the slanted title, *Domino*, across a masked figure in a sweeping cloak. "Here is how he repays me for making him a mensch. I offer him the best picture of the year, of the war. My personal production." Milgrim slammed down the script. "And he spits on me."

"You don't want a guy like that around," Hash said.

"Nick Gallanz is right now in breach of contract," Milgrim said. He hit the script with both fists., "Nick Gallanz is looking at a lawsuit right now while we're talking. Your friend thinks he had trouble over there!" Milgrim's arm shot up, pointing at the windows facing west over Gower Street as though Europe lay across the Pacific. "Now he will first find out the meaning of trouble."

"That's a two-way street, trouble," Hash said.

"My lawyers get paid fifty-two weeks a year," Milgrim said.

"Yeah." Hash looked at the cigarette in the ashtray and took another from his pack. "Your lawyers won't bring him back," Hash said. "You can't bring him back if he won't come."

"I'll teach him a lesson," Milgrim said. "I'll teach them all a lesson."

Hash lit the fresh cigarette. "Last week you barred this guy from the lot, you didn't want this guy."

"I changed my mind."

"So did he," Hash said. "What good is someone if he's not on your side?"

"He is under contract," Milgrim said. "A contract is the foundation of this industry."

Hash uncrossed his legs and rose. He took his hat from the desk. "You're a smart guy, be smart," Hash said. "He's no good to you this way. Tear up the contract."

"I told you," Milgrim said. "I'm not Leonard Votrian. I'm not Leo Whitfield. I didn't build a studio hiding in the bushes, afraid of my shadow."

Early that evening, Hash parked on Ocean Avenue, above the sea in Santa Monica. He walked back from his car until he came to a black Buick Limited. There were two men in the Buick. The driver, Muley Rose, was about Hash's age. The other man looked old enough to be their father. Hash stopped beside the driver. "Wait until later. Midnight, around there."

He returned to the La Salle and drove south, toward Santa Monica Pier. The Buick Limited remained at the curb long after the occupants were alone on Ocean Avenue. They spoke rarely and only of boxing or horse racing. Sometime after midnight, Muley Rose drove from Santa Monica into Beverly Hills.

Meyer Milgrim lived on four acres on Summit Drive. A high iron fence enclosed the land, and the entrance and service gates were always locked. A cabana separated the tennis court and swimming pool. A miniature Mount Vernon faced the cabana, a two-story playhouse built to scale, with a kitchen where the two girls could reach everything, and a gym in which all the equipment had been made especially for their brother, Jed.

Muley parked in the block beyond the estate. When he and his companion left the Buick, the older man carried a black leather bag resembling a doctor's bag. They stopped at the service gate, where Muley took a flat kit, like a wallet, out of his jacket pocket. The older man raised a flashlight until the beam caught the rectangular brass lock set into the gate. Muley opened the lock as though he had a key. They crossed the lawn to the playhouse, which had never been locked, a precaution against fire or an earthquake. The trespassers were in Mount Vernon for less than five minutes. They left the playhouse, crouching to get through the door. The older man had his black bag. Muley stopped at the gate to lock it. In the Buick Muley drove without headlights until they came abreast of the Beverly Hills Hotel on Sunset.

The explosion thirty minutes later rattled the windows of the hotel. People five miles from the Milgrim estate heard the blast. Lights came up in homes all around Summit Drive.

The playhouse erupted: brick, tile, glass, wooden framing flying a mile high. The smoke blacked out the moon. Pieces of Jed's gym equipment were found the next day in Benedict Canyon.

Beverly Hills firemen called Los Angeles for reinforcements, and units responded from as far east as La Brea Boulevard. There were firemen on the grounds most of the night saving the main house, cabana, and garage.

Five days after the disaster, on Saturday afternoon, Votrian played in his weekly foursome at Hillcrest. Votrian never drank there, determined to keep his wits in the clubhouse. Votrian didn't see Hash until he opened the door of his Cadillac. "Get in."

Hash sat in the front seat, his hat tipped to keep out the sun. Votrian dropped down behind the wheel. "Relax, you're in broad daylight," Hash said. "Monday morning you tell Milgrim to send Nick Gallanz a release from his contract. You and Milgrim like registered letters. Do that."

Hash opened the door and Votrian saw him walk to a Buick Limited. The driver turned the Buick carefully, moving slowly. Votrian wanted a drink, but he stayed in the Cadillac, remembering the newspaper photographs of the rubble which remained of Mount Vernon.

* * *

In the villa the following Tuesday a postman came to the open door. "Nicholas Gallanz?"

Nick saw the envelope in the postman's hand, and closer, the Majestic eagle in the corner of the envelope. Minutes later Nick called Hash Pertsick. "You like the telephone, so I am on the telephone."

"Who's I?"

"Nick Gallanz. The mailman brought me a registered letter."

"What'ya know?"

"You made me free," Nick said.

"Me and Abraham Lincoln," Hash said.

"Tell me what I owe."

Hash watched Polly in the pool cutting through the water in a fluid streak. Hash could always slip the dude a tab to pay, but he had a hunch. "I'll think of something."

In the villa Nick pushed a dart through the letter from Milgrim and threw it into the bull's-eye. He took Serlin's play into the sun. When he heard the Hungarian on the steps, Nick went to meet him. "You're late."

One afternoon four weeks after Nick and Serlin began rewriting, Nick pushed the pages of the manuscript together like a dealer with a deck of cards. "We made a screenplay." He took a pencil. "One Moses is enough. I'll make you Michael."

Nick said, "I have a new title," writing "MAIDEN VOYAGE" across the manuscript. He said, "By Michael Serlin and Nick Gallanz," writing the names below the title.

The Hungarian sat rigidly, like a plebe being hazed. "Why is your name on this play?" Serlin said. "I wrote this play. I sat with blank pages and wrote this play."

"You wrote a play," Nick said. He slapped the manuscript. "We wrote this play."

"It's my play," Serlin said. "The people in this story are mine." He tapped his forehead. "They came from here."

Nick made a gun of his left hand and put his forefinger against his temple. "And here."

"You're not being fair with me," Serlin said, frightened.

The beginning of a smile crossed Nick's face. "Correct," he said. He took forty of the one hundred and twenty pages. "I brought the maid to your play, so everything with the maid belongs to me." He made two stacks, pushing the larger stack at Serlin.

"No, I don't . . . Don't," he said, shaking his head. "I want both our names." Serlin replaced the forty pages.

Nick had already forgotten Serlin's outburst. "You'll be late for work."

He found a typist in the yellow pages. "Bring your typewriter," Nick said.

"I work at home," said the typist.

"Stay home," Nick said, turning the yellow pages.

"Wait, wait," the typist said.

She came to the villa the following morning. Nick carried her typewriter. "Don't you trust me?" she asked.

"Sure," Nick said. He watched her type *Maiden Voyage*, taking each page as she completed it. She was never alone. When he had a clean manuscript, Nick mimeographed several copies.

One morning he drove down from the villa, leaving his car near the Beverly Wilshire Hotel. Inside, he went to the barber shop in the basement, standing by the doors.

A half hour later, Champ Gallagher came out of the barber shop. The dapper, natty director had intervened for Nick at Metro the first day with Dieter.

They walked to the stairs and Champ Gallagher came up the middle like any star. "Mr. Gallagher, I very much liked your picture, *Forgotten*, the Nazi picture," Nick said.

Champ grinned and winked. "Tell you a secret, bucko. I liked it, too."

They walked through the lobby. "I believed your people," Nick said. "One director in a hundred gives you real people."

Champ stopped at the entrance. "I ought to start every day with you," he said. Nick followed him out of the hotel onto Rodeo Drive.

"I have a story for such a director," Nick said. "My story needs Champ Gallagher."

Champ stopped. His lips tightened, and he was no longer an affable Irishman. "You're hustling me," he said, pointing at the manuscript under Nick's arm. "You just happen to have a copy. Get lost."

"Before you spit, I, too, have made a few pictures," Nick said. *"Dare to Love, One Magic Moment, Forever Faithful."*

Champ said, *"One Magic Moment,"* and finally took a good look at the bloke with the accent.

"You would have made my pictures better pictures," Nick said.

"You're cute," Champ said. He turned toward Charleville. "Working the street like some hooker. But you're wasting your time, sport. Meyer Milgrim doesn't like me and I don't like him."

"And I don't like him," Nick said. He raised the manuscript.

"You must give me an answer by four o'clock." He had to establish his primacy now, at the outset.

Champ's face reddened. "You're not that cute, sport. Nice knowing you."

"You can finish by four o'clock," Nick said. "You can finish by ten. Your day belongs to you. Last week you refused that musical with Betty Grable." Champ Gallagher no longer accepted a term contract from a studio, choosing his own pictures. "Four o'clock," Nick said. "Bring the script. The address is on the cover."

They stood facing each other in the shaded street, safely clear of a sprinkler which cast a spray of water across one hundred and eighty degrees of a flawless lawn. The street was deserted, and the only sound came from the click, click, click of the sprinkler. Champ pulled the manuscript out of Nick's hand. Nick watched him walking toward Charleville, moving with quick little steps, like Chaplin. Nick had almost eight hours to endure.

Around two o'clock that day, Nick went to the basket of darts, throwing with both hands. He didn't hear Champ until the director said, "Anybody home?"

Champ wore a blazer with a club patch over his heart. He stopped behind a sofa, facing Nick. "Answer one question, sport. Where are you putting this story?"

"If I make a Western, I use America," Nick said. "For bedrooms I use Hungary."

Champ dropped the script onto the sofa. "Keep any whiskey in the place?"

The next morning, Nick drove to Pleiades Pictures, around the corner from Chaplin's studio on Cahuenga. Pleiades Pictures, begun in 1916, had changed owners and names more often than anyone could count. The lot grew to four stages, all decrepit and ramshackle, like the rest of the studio.

There were no studio police at Pleiades. The stages needed paint. Nick drove along a studio street, dust rising behind his car. He stopped a man carrying a screen door. "Point me at the office, please."

"Number seven," the man said. "First left and it's on your left."

Nick parked beside a building which seemed slanted. Inside, his footsteps on the bare wood floor reverberated like an echo. He heard voices and followed them to an open door on the second floor. A gray-haired woman wearing too much eye shadow sat beside an open window near a desk. In a doorway to her left, Nick saw a plump man in a scivvy shirt wiping his face with a huck towel. "This heat is killing me."

"Nate Butwinick?" Nick asked, asking for the owner of the studio.

"Do I look like that dried-up old fart? If you're here for Butwinick, get lost," said Augie Mikva.

"Who rents stages here?"

The plump man grinned. "Hey, a customer." Augie Mikva wiped his face, bowing and swinging his arm. "After you, Alphonse."

In his office Augie had fans going in all directions. "So you're making a picture," he said. "We got it all, cutting rooms, music stage, the works."

"Today I need a production office," Nick said.

"Comes with the deal," Augie said, facing a fan.

"I am not ready for photography," Nick said.

Augie walked around his desk. "Screw," he said, wiggling his thumb.

Nick took a checkbook from his pocket. "Yes or no? I am hot, too."

Augie grinned, pulling Nick to the chair behind the desk. "There's a pen." He watched Nick writing. "You *are* lost," Augie said. "You're looking for a phone booth."

Nick tore out the check. "This is what I have today."

The check disappeared in Augie's hand. "Four weeks," he said. "You got two rooms downstairs." He grinned. "Don't mess up the place."

Augie's secretary took Nick to his offices. The gray-haired woman bounced along like a coed. "He's Nate Butwinick's son-in-law," she said. "Fire and water. I'm Grace Sudeith. I come with the place. I'm the oldest thing on the lot." She smiled, showing dentures like a tiger's canines. On the first floor near the staircase, she stopped, using both hands to push two flanking doors. "Headquarters."

Nick saw two identical, square cracker boxes. The drawn window shades were cracked. Each room had a desk and a wooden swivel chair, a glazed light fixture in the ceiling, and a long, rectangular gas wall heater behind the desk. Nick opened the door connecting the two rooms and raised the windows in the room he chose. He stayed until after dark, and by the time he left Pleiades, he had arranged for a second mortgage on the villa.

In the Los Angeles business district later that week, Nick entered the Midway National Bank on Flower Street a few minutes after it opened. He carried a copy of *Maiden Voyage* under his arm.

A row of desks, each with a nameplate, ran along one side of the bank. Nick read each name, stopping when he came to Luther Gustafson. A big man in terrible clothes watched Nick. "The gate opens both ways, friend."

Luther Gustafson had been an All-American two years running at the University of Southern California. He graduated in 1936, in the worst years of the Depression. He ignored the offers to play professional football. "No more bumps," he said. He asked for a job at the bank and began at the bottom.

"Mr. Gustafson, my name is Nick Gallanz. I've heard of you."

"Gus. Everyone calls me Gus. I've heard of you, too."

The big man was the bank's loan officer for the motion picture studios. He knew everyone in Hollywood, and he knew everything that happened when it happened. He dressed and spoke like the master of ceremonies at a service club meeting in the boondocks, but he could add and subtract in his head faster than anyone with whom he did business. "I liked your films," Gus said. "My mother liked them, and she's tougher on Hollywood than I am."

"I have another one for her," Nick said. He showed Gus the script. "And I have a director. Champ Gallagher."

"One of the best," Gus said.

"I have money," Nick said. "I need another hundred thousand dollars to start casting. I know you read the script before you loan money." Nick set the script on Gus's desk.

"True," Gus said. "But I'm not reading your script. I wouldn't come near you with a ten-foot pole, friend. You're poison and you're poison for me. Meyer Milgrim is a client, and even if he wasn't, there's the rest of Hollywood. You shoved their noses into it, Nick. They'll never forgive you, and they would never forgive me if I gave you a dime."

"I won't tell them," Nick said.

"They'd know before you got back to Beverly Hills," said the big man. "Thanks but no thanks."

Nick rolled up the script, standing against the desk, facing the All-American. "You let me talk," Nick said. "Why did you let me talk?"

"I'll answer that one, and I don't give a good hoot in hell who hears what I said. I let you talk because I'm jealous," Gus said. The big man came out of his chair. "Good luck, friend."

His candor, his warmth, were an echo of Fritz in the palace, delivering the Safe Conduct and the Daimler, sending Nick off to die with his family in the mountains in the snow.

When Nick returned to the villa, he saw a telegram under the door knocker. He opened the yellow envelope and read, "READY WILL-

ING AND ABLE DIRECT MAIDEN VOYAGE PROVIDED YOU SET START DATE
PRINCIPAL PHOTOGRAPHY WITHIN FORTY-EIGHT HOURS. REGARDS. CHAMP
GALLAGHER."

Holding the telegram Nick walked through the villa, as though he
was lost, going from room to room. He couldn't ask Magda for money.
He owed her too much. He had no one else. He stopped beside the
basket of darts, dropping the telegram. He took a dart in each hand.
Nick believed that if he lost, Carly and Fritz won. He threw with his
left hand, hitting the very edge of the bull's-eye. He threw with his
right, missing the bull's-eye completely. Nick took two more darts. He
had to find a hundred thousand dollars in two days. He could not lose,
could not let Carly and Fritz finish him. He threw rapidly with both
hands, following the darts to the board. Both were in the bull's-eye.
Nick cleared the board and dropped the darts in the basket. He took
the Beretta and several boxes of ammunition from the armoire in his
bedroom, and left the villa on his way to a new range he had found in
the San Fernando Valley.

Around nine o'clock the following night, Nick drove down Los Feliz
Boulevard and turned at the entrance to Griffith Park. He followed the
signs to the observatory, climbing constantly until he reached the top.
Nick left his car in the parking area, walking past the circular building
with the giant telescope to a parapet. All Los Angeles lay below him.
The lights extended for miles. He heard a car and looked back at the
parking area as a convertible filled with boys and girls vanished.

Nearby a woman said, "Look, sweetie. No, the other way. There.
The bunch of lights all together. See?"

"Yeah, yeah," said the man with her. "I see."

"Carthay Circle, I'll bet," the woman said. "Probably having a
premiere."

Her companion said, "I didn't hear nothing about a premiere."

She said, "Pardon me. Darryl Zanuck must've slipped up," and
laughed. She laughed like a child, in gleeful, convulsive bursts.

Behind Nick, Leonard Votrian said, "I must really be nuts listening to you." Votrian wore a dark hat with a wide brim.

"You're smart," Nick said.

"Always the wise guy," Votrian said. "Now what, wise guy? Going
to blow up the temple?" The Wilshire Boulevard Temple, an imposing
Byzantine synagogue, had the most important congregation in Los Angeles.

"I shouldn't come within a mile of you," Votrian said. "I'm taking a chance with my whole career. Meyer Milgrim has one ambition left in his life: to destroy you. Milgrim's children are like the air he breathes. Right now there's a wall around his property with spikes on top. Touch the spikes and it's like the electric chair. You burn." They heard footsteps and Votrian, startled, pulled down on his hat brim. "I could be a dead man in this town tomorrow."

"You're dead already, standing behind Milgrim with toilet paper," Nick said. "You came because you want to live."

"Sigmund Freud," Votrian said. "What have you got? I got five minutes."

"I have a story," Nick said. "I have Champ Gallagher. I need two young actors, fresh faces, a girl and a boy. I can make this picture in fourteen days without leaving the stage. I'm short one hundred thousand dollars."

"You brought me up here to tell me that?"

"You brought me," Nick said. "You told me the observatory in Griffith Park."

"Still the wise guy," Votrian said. "I'm a working man, wise guy. With a family. The lessons alone make me poor. Piano, tennis, horseback riding, ballet dancing, summer camp, skiing camp."

"People know Leonard Votrian," Nick said. "The banks know you. You have friends in Hillcrest."

"Friends in Hillcrest," Votrian said. "You talk like your pictures. A hundred thousand dollars isn't a fairy tale, it's a fortune."

"Leonard Votrian can find the money."

"Because you looked in your crystal ball," Votrian said.

"Because you are still here, still telling me you cannot bring me the money," Nick said. "But you can bring me the money."

"I have to drive all the way back to Malibu," Votrian said.

"I'll make you a producer," Nick said. "We'll produce this picture. Without me you'll live your life bowing to Milgrim or the Milgrim after this Milgrim. We'll be partners. Fifty-fifty."

Votrian tugged at his brim hat. "I'll check around," he said, leaving the parapet. Nick stayed with him.

"The deadline with Champ Gallagher is tomorrow."

"Tomorrow? Come on-n-n-n," Votrian said. "You couldn't *print* the money by tomorrow."

"No start date tomorrow, no Champ Gallagher," Nick said. They stopped beside the Cadillac. "I'll tell him Leonard Votrian has the money."

"Not my *name!*" Votrian waved his hands. "I have to do this in a cave. You can't use my name."

"Your kids are waiting in Malibu," Nick said.

Votrian watched him. "Tell Gallagher if he talks, we're in the sewer."

"I'm at home or at Pleiades."

"Wait," Votrian said, and grabbed Nick. "Give me five or ten minutes before you start down."

He saw a kind of smile on the greenhorn's face. "God is the only witness," Nick said. "He has no one to tell."

"Wise guy," Votrian said. He unlocked the door and bent to enter the Cadillac.

One morning at Pleiades two weeks later, Nick's telephone rang. "It's Grace Sudeith. Can you come up?"

Nick climbed the sagging staircase to the second floor. Grace had an open purse in her lap, holding a lipstick and looking into a hand mirror. "You can go in."

Nick opened the door to Augie Mikva's office. The fans were gone. A man in a white shirt and vest was bent over a cardboard box on the desk. "Close the door."

Nick closed the door, and when he turned to the desk, he was facing Leonard Votrian. "I bought the studio."

Nick looked at his new enemy, an enemy he could identify, unlike those who had cut down his family. "Congratulations."

"I'll bet," Votrian said. "Did you think I'd sit out there in Malibu signing checks? I don't sign until I see the merchandise, starting with pencils and paper. Everything comes through me."

"Except film," Nick said. Votrian bent over the desk, so he didn't see Nick grab the carton and fling it aside. The carton slid across the desk and over the side, emptying as it dropped.

"*Except film,*" Nick repeated, standing between Votrian and the desk. "You don't touch film. You don't see film. No dailies, no first assemblage, no rough cut, no answer print. You see a picture for distribution when I deliver the picture. Say yes or no now, *now,* or I'll tell Champ Gallagher good-bye. I'll find another director and I'll find another hundred thousand dollars." Nick raised his left hand, pushing Votrian. "Yes or no?"

"Yes," Votrian said. "You heard me, yes," he said, and stronger, "You better deliver, wise guy. I'm not alone in this. People are depending on me, understand?"

"Sure," Nick said.

"Close the door."

"Sure," Nick said, leaving.

That afternoon Hash Pertsick sat beside Polly as she drove them into Hollywood. Hash hadn't figured on the sun when he bought the convertible. The sun gave her freckles. Hash loved her with the freckles. "Where are we going?" she asked.

"See a fella," Hash said. "He's a producer in the movies. I figured you might get a kick out of being in a studio."

Hash played with the hair at the back of Polly's neck. He didn't believe in luck, but he believed in lucky breaks if you recognized one when it came along, like that call from Nick Gallanz around noon: "We didn't finish," Nick said. "You told me, 'I will think of something.' Did you think?"

"I'm in no rush," Hash said.

"I am," Nick said. "I am making a picture. Why don't you help me with it?"

So Hash's hunch had paid off. He took a deep drag on his cigarette. "What's on your mind?"

"Nothing like before," Nick said. "Come to Pleiades. When?"

"How's this afternoon?"

In the convertible Hash watched Polly turn onto Fountain Avenue. The guy had lifted a ton off Hash's chest. For a long time he had been trying to figure what to tell Polly to explain the house on Roxbury, her tuition and clothes, and items like the Super Chief. She had been away at one school after another since her twelfth birthday. Summers she had been at camp, and later, when the counselor said she was old enough, to Mexico or somewheres. Now she had come home to stay. He couldn't tell her about the dog track in Tijuana, or the ship out of Vera Cruz and what it carried. "Turn after Cahuenga, angel."

Nick heard them in the corridor and came out of the office. "Welcome," he said, and saw the girl, the sister. "Welcome."

Polly faced the strange man who had come to Roxbury Drive, feeling his eyes looking through her. She said, "Oh . . . hello," her voice suddenly squeaky.

Nick brought them into his office. "The chairs are clean," he said. "I cleaned them." He moved one for Polly. "Please."

He waited, close enough to touch. Polly felt clammy and queasy and hollow inside. "I, uh, thank you," she said stupidly.

Hash listened while Nick told them about Pleiades, about his picture. Then Hash took a handful of change from his pocket. "Get us something to drink, angel, will you do that?"

Polly scooped up the money. Hash had saved her. She needed fresh air, to look decent, to get away for a few minutes, but as she crossed the corridor, she wanted to return, wanted to be with Hash's friend.

In the office Nick said, "I'm not thirsty, either."

"Yeah," Hash said. "Say it. We haven't got all day."

"Leonard Votrian is upstairs," Nick said. "He bought the studio."

"What'ya know?"

"He has many partners," Nick said. "I need one." He went to the open connecting door. "You can come and go. Hello, good-bye. Votrian will know you are here." He watched Hash take a cigarette from a pack. "I already have a bill with you."

"You won't get hurt," Hash said. "I'm not Votrian."

"I'll clean up your office."

"You mean burn it," Hash said. Christ, the setup was perfect. Polly could fix up the place. Give her something to do. "We'll start from scratch." Hash lit the cigarette. "Fix up your dump, too. You're supposed to be a producer." Hash heard Polly say, "Thanks," to someone. "Come on in, angel. I got a job for you."

13

ONE AFTERNOON A YEAR
later, in the spring of 1944, Der Chineser was summoned to the Hotel
Metropole, Gestapo headquarters, for a meeting. He came early and
was directed to room 300.

Rows of wooden chairs lined the room. Der Chineser found a place
in the first row. The room filled quickly with men in and out of uniform. Latecomers stood along the walls and in the rear. At two o'clock
the talking subsided. Der Chineser heard footsteps. A man in a trench-
coat carrying a weather-beaten hat passed him, stopping at a table facing the audience. He was young, younger than every man in the room.
He looked like someone who organized his college classmates in protest
crusades. His name was Arndt Bol, and for a time, facing his audience,
he seemed to be alone, holding his hat, running his forefinger carefully
along the crease in the crown. Then he dropped the hat on the table
and hooked his thumbs into the pockets of his trousers. "Some of you
know me, some of you don't," said Bol. "I'm from Berlin. I just flew
in from Berlin. I'll be around awhile. The subject is pilots, our pilots,

the Luftwaffe, and their pilots, the English, the Americans, the French, the Poles, the Russians.

"Our pilots are good," Bol said. "Our anti-aircraft is good. We're shooting down a lot of their pilots, but the trouble is they don't stay down. We pick up a few but not enough. Their pilots move around the Greater German Reich like they were on dress parade. For a whole lot of them the parade ends in Vienna. These pilots get on a magic carpet in Vienna, and, zip, they're back in England, back in Africa, back in Italy, back in Moscow, Kiev, Omsk, Minsk, Pinsk, Finsk, Dinsk, Ginsk . . . ," said the young man who looked like a collegian.

"Long ago we interrupted one of those parades," Bol said, "and we learned a woman here in Vienna keeps the magic carpet flying. Domino. They call her Domino. She sends the pilots whom the Luftwaffe has shot down home to shoot down the Luftwaffe." The young man paused, and when he resumed, he seemed to be speaking directly to each man in the room. "I told you I came in from Berlin, came to this hotel directly from Schwechat. Obergruppenführer Himmler sent me. My orders are from Obergruppenführer Himmler. He told me to get the woman, Domino, the heavenly angel, and I am going to get her. You and I are going to get her." Bol picked up his hat and perfected the crease. "We'd better get her."

In Poland that same afternoon Fritz's plane, a converted Junkers JU 290, originally used for reconnaissance, landed at an airport in the middle of a prairie with farms on three sides and a long border of sycamore trees on the fourth. "Baron Fritz Von Gottisberg?"

Fritz raised his arm. "Baron?" A lumpy man trotted across the runway. He wore a uniform no part of which fit, topped with a woolen overseas cap falling to his ears. "Oscar Lemski, your highness."

"Not your highness," Fritz said. "Never use those words. Where is your car?"

"No car, Baron, sir." Lemski led Fritz to a flatbed truck. "The window on my side is broken, Baron."

Fritz dumped his luggage onto the flatbed and stepped onto the short running board, swinging himself into the truck cab. Lemski climbed in beside him, grunting. "How far?" Fritz said.

"Twenty kilometers, Baron," Lemski said. They were on a two-lane dirt road studded with potholes. The sun lay on the horizon behind them.

"Your lights," Fritz said. Lemski yanked at a knob on the dashboard. They were completely alone on the road. The day ended abruptly, and they drove into an inky night. Fritz had not slept in thirty-six hours. He had been roused two nights earlier in his quarters at the foundry in the Ruhr. The call came from the chief of army procurement in Berlin. "We have an emergency."

Fritz had been flown to Frankfurt, where he waited until noon of the next day for a plane to Prague. He waited again, through the night, until he found a seat on a flight to Cracow, where he transferred to the Junkers. He had not bathed. He had eaten odious food. He had a new job in Poland, near the Russians. He swayed from side to side in the cold, uncomfortable truck cab. "There, Baron. The factory," Lemski said.

Fritz saw two rows of lights, and at an angle, more lights. "Home," Lemski said. The Germans had built a fence around the factory. Fritz could see spaced wooden towers for searchlights and machine guns.

A long two-story building lay ahead. There were windows up high. The factory made an L, each arm longer than a city block. Lemski drove past the building to an open gate, stopping between two guards. "Here is the new commandant."

Lemski parked behind a Mercedes-Benz sedan. "The office, Baron."

There were two men inside in business suits, each at a desk covered with file folders and ledgers. Fritz said, "Fritz Von Gottisberg."

Someone growled, "In here." Fritz walked between the desks to an open door and into another, smaller office. A man sat on an iron cot beside the door, writing on a pad, and another man watched Fritz from behind an oversized desk. Neither man rose to greet the new factory manager. "Edvard Hohendorff," said the man behind the desk. "Gestapo, Warsaw."

Hohendorff held an enormous green fountain pen, and he put it together, screwing the top onto the bottom. He had been a railroad accountant when he joined the Nazi party in 1925, the first man in his family, in the company, in his church, to join. He looked at the slim, handsome stud in the lovely coat with the beaver collar. "Whose wife made you a favorite with Berlin?"

Fritz could not stop the twitching in his legs. He had come halfway across Europe to stand before an executioner.

"Baron Fritz Von Gottisberg," said Hohendorff. "I wouldn't have picked you for factory manager. I had my own man, but Berlin didn't like him. Berlin likes you. I checked on you. The Von Gottisbergs haven't done anything except fish, hunt, and dance in three hundred years. And fornicate." Fritz felt pinioned, as though he had been thrust into a straitjacket. "You are the boy wonder, the wizard," Hohendorff said. "We'll see."

He patted the ledgers on the desk like someone stroking a cat. "You've been told what went on here. A disaster. Your predecessor stole enough shoes to outfit China. There were more shoes leaving this factory than sausages coming out of Frankfurt, only we never saw any. Your predecessor, Herr Spriester, was selling them somewhere. I'll find out where."

Hohendorff left his chair, shoving the green fountain pen into his pocket. He had to look up at Fritz. "I am responsible for production in this factory, and you now are responsible to me," Hohendorff said. "Use your wizardry, Baron, or you will never sleep in your castle again. You can believe me, Berlin or no Berlin." Hohendorff went to the man on the cot. "Get up, you sloth!"

Hohendorff pulled his hat and coat from a wooden rack. "We're taking your car," he told Fritz. "You'll be too busy for a car."

The two men in the outer office saw Hohendorff coming and rose to attention. "They're staying," he said. "They'll be sending me a daily production report."

Lemski stood in a corner, trying to be invisible. Fritz watched Hohendorff and his gang fill the Mercedes, watched the red taillights until the sedan went through the gates. "Where do I sleep?"

"You have your own place, Baron," Lemski said. "Your own chalet."

In the truck beside Lemski, Fritz tried to forget his interview with the Gestapo chief. Dead tired and cold and hungry, Fritz let himself sink into a rare moment of fantasy. He thought of running, as though he could slip through the gates, elude the guards, elude the army, the SS and the Gestapo, could move, unseen, through Poland, through Germany, through the Alps and Italy, could make his way, unharmed, across the Mediterranean, could be rid of the Nazis, of the war, reaching safety before dawn, safety forever.

"Baron."

Fritz saw a small square house beside the guard barracks. Lemski opened the door. "Home sweet home, Baron."

Fritz walked into the bedroom. He heard Lemski set down the suitcases. "Tomorrow morning strip everything and take it to the laundry," Fritz said. He removed his coat and sat on the bed to push off his shoes. Fritz stretched out, pulling the coat over himself.

A deep, throaty horn, like a tuba, woke him. Fritz swung his legs over the bed, bending for his shoes.

He left the house in a rush. He saw the rows of men in striped prisoner uniforms, their shaved heads like matted poles in the cold, gray, misty morning. Fritz didn't know how many he had, but he needed every living pair of hands that could produce shoes for him. "Good morning, sir."

A man with a cane, in a fresh uniform and a raincoat, limped toward Fritz. He was young, trying to look older with a thick mustache. "Lieutenant Jurgen Kuhl, sir. Commander of the guard." Kuhl tapped his left leg with the cane. "Souvenir of El-Alamein, sir. I have coffee."

"Later," Fritz said, walking toward the rows of striped uniforms. On his left, the first prisoner in each row was a *Kapo*, a foreman. All Kapos had minor privileges, and all were more fit, physically stronger than the others.

Fritz stopped beside the prisoners, revolted by them because they had allowed themselves to become prisoners, to be caught, to be herded like sheep, splattered like vermin, like cockroaches, to be shackled, to be humiliated and humbled, to be shorn of their hair, to be tattooed, branded like cattle, to submit, submit without protest, to the cruelty, the savagery, the venom, the thousand daily assaults on their bodies, their minds, their sanity, by the thugs of the Greater German Reich. The compliant Jews had infuriated Fritz from the first weeks of the Anschluss, from the days when he had seen grown men dressed for business on their knees in the streets of Vienna, scrubbing manure from cobblestones. They should never have surrendered. They should have resisted, schemed, bribed, should have tried to escape, should have fought, should have died fighting.

Fritz moved slowly to his left, from one prisoner to another, examining each scabrous specimen he passed. He could see the sunken cheeks of starvation in every one. He passed a man with one eye and one empty socket. The next had open, festering sores on his face and neck. He passed another whose lips moved constantly, silently, a big bruiser who might have been a circus strong man. He passed another with only the thumb remaining on his right hand, then one with no teeth, whose mouth hung open like a skull's mouth. He passed another, taller than himself, who had eyes but didn't see anything, didn't see Fritz.

With Jurgen Kuhl limping behind him, Fritz inspected every prisoner in every row, and when he finished, he watched them filing across the compound and into the factory. They dragged their feet. They were starting the day completely exhausted. These skeletons were Fritz's work force, the only force which could save him. "When do they eat?"

"They've eaten," Kuhl said. "They have breakfast and dinner in their barracks. We give them lunch here."

Fritz watched them file into the factory. "I'm ready for your coffee."

The guard commander's post was beside the gates. Fritz drank a mug of coffee fast, like a drunk with his first belt of whiskey. Kuhl refilled the mug and Fritz sipped it slowly, thinking of the zombies in the factory. He emptied the mug and came out into the compound, walking to the office.

Hohendorff's men were at the desk. "Gentlemen," Fritz said, "we haven't been introduced."

They stayed in their chairs. One said, "Otto Schuss." The other man raised his head. "George Quartzlehd." Fritz smiled, anxious to shoot them.

"Fritz Von Gottisberg," he said, walking between the desks to the smaller officer behind the pair.

At noon, the rumbling sound of the horn filled the office. The two Gestapo left to eat with the guards, and Fritz crossed the compound to the factory. Inside at the entrance were three metal barrels. The prisoners, each with a bowl, formed three lines, and two prisoners at each barrel ladled out a dark liquid. "Save some for me," Fritz said.

When the last three men were fed, Fritz took a ladle and dipped it into the barrel. He swished the liquid around. "What is it?"

"Gruel," said a prisoner. "Lunch is always gruel."

Fritz raised the ladle and wet his lips. The ladle had a vinegary smell, and what he tasted felt like mud on his tongue. He extended the ladle. "Delicious."

He moved slowly through the factory while the prisoners, at their machines and benches, emptied their bowls. The starving men were not getting enough nourishment to blink their eyes. Fritz left the factory, welcoming the dull, overcast day as though he had come out of a cemetery. Spriester, the thief he had succeeded, had been hung, and Fritz easily imagined his own gallows above the compound.

He returned to his office, a prisoner like those in the factory. He sat waiting for the workday to end. The afternoon seemed to last a year, and when, mercifully, Fritz heard the horn, he went to the windows, looking for Kuhl.

He saw the prisoners emerge from the factory, lining up in formation. He saw the guards surrounding them, heard the muffled sound of commands. The prisoners plodded and stumbled past the windows. Behind them, limping, Kuhl followed, holding long white strips of tally sheets. Fritz left the windows and stopped, trapped and unable to escape. He heard the door open, then the tap, tap, tap of Kuhl's cane, and made himself cheerful. "Give me the good news, Lieutenant."

"Not so good, sir," Kuhl said. "They dropped below the quota."

"They're getting lazy," Fritz said. "Wake them thirty minutes earlier."

The next morning, Fritz stood at his office windows as the prisoners arrived. He saw Kuhl and Gerd Kellerman, the factory doctor, arrive. Fritz carried a chair outside and stood on it, facing his work force. "If any of you cannot hear me, speak up, because you will be held accountable for everything I say here today." Fritz paused. "You all know what occurred in this factory. Your commandant deceived the Greater German Reich, the brave soldiers in the field. He was a thief and a traitor, and we, you and I, must repay the Reich for this treason. You're starting a half hour early today. You'll work a half hour later. This is our new schedule. We have a production quota to maintain. Not the *old* production quota." Fritz paused once more. "I said, 'our.' I said, 'we.' I am also starting earlier. We are in this together. If a man cannot work, if he claims illness, Doctor Kellerman and I will not protest. Auschwitz is just over the hill."

Now Fritz could only wait as he had waited the day before. He saw Schuss and Quartzlehd, the two Gestapo, arrive, heard the scratching of their pens. He heard the noon whistle, welcoming the solitude when the pair left for lunch.

That afternoon Fritz sat through another eternity. The day ended and searchlights brightened the compound, and finally Fritz heard the hoarse factory horn. He waited for Kuhl, and when he saw the guard commander holding the tally sheets with the day's production figures, Fritz knew he had lost. "We didn't fall behind, Commandant."

"Wake them an hour early tomorrow," Fritz said.

That night Fritz woke intermittently, and in the dark he pictured long, neat rows of numbers on tally sheets which wound around him like a shroud.

On the following afternoon, the figures were no higher than the previous day's total. The prisoners were working two hours longer without increasing production. As Fritz looked through the long tally sheets, Kuhl said, "Let's drive into town, Commandant. We can have some dinner somewhere nice and forget this place for a little while."

Fritz made himself smile. "Some other time, Lieutenant. I need to lose weight."

For the next week Fritz stayed in his office every day and late into the night. He stacked the tally sheets in front of him. He failed every day, but he could not think of surrender. He needed a goad which would energize the prisoners, transform his crop of clods into whirl-winds. When Fritz ate, he schemed. When he shaved, showered, dressed and undressed, when he lay in bed, he plotted and failed, and plotted anew.

One morning early, at his desk, Fritz raised his head as though he had been taken by surprise. His body tensed and he stared at the barren wall, his face grim. He didn't move, listening to the horn, to the prisoners' footsteps entering the compound, to the muted whirring sounds of the machines in the factory. Schuss and Quartzlehd arrived. Once Fritz patted the desk with his hand. Later, he moved his forefinger like someone keeping time, and later he said quietly, "Maybe."

The day ended with another disaster on the tally sheets. Fritz remained at his desk until after nine o'clock, when he strode through the office and into the compound to rouse Dr. Kellerman.

Fritz was ready before daylight. In the dirt in front of his office stood a wooden table with a large pot of water. A tin cup dangled from the pot. Kuhl and Dr. Kellerman, in his white coat, were with him. "Does spring ever come to this tundra?" Fritz asked.

Dr. Kellerman rubbed his hands. "We are too far north for spring."

The sound of the horn filled the compound. Soon the prisoners shuffled through the gates and lined up in formation. The night before, Fritz had asked Kuhl for a list of the Kapos. Now he unfolded a sheet of paper. "Those whose names I read will remain."

"Hurwitz," Fritz said. "Rosenbloom, Gleckman, Steiner, Cardozo, Schuneman, Pasternak, Cohen, Lazer, Shapiro, Jacob, Pfeffer, Kaplan, Lapidus, Bomberg, Polansky, Heller, Singer, Schreiber, Applebaum, Shapiro, Eli, Wiener, Danovsky, Bachrach, Liebfeld, Alpern, Bercovitz, Kessel."

The Kapos stood in their tracks, each distanced from the others, like players in a pageant. Fritz let them stand and worry, let them face their commandant and guard commander and doctor, let the bitter wind tear at the rags they wore. Then he said, "Danovsky . . . Lazer . . . Alpern . . . the two Shapiros . . . you twenty-seven Kapos are lucky men. You're eating regularly, sleeping in beds, under a roof. You're safe. Germans are dying in the east and the west. Austrians are dying. There are millions of brave men in the Wehrmacht who would give anything to be in your place. You could say it's the luck of the draw. You were dealt better cards. Maybe you've been spoiled. I think you've been spoiled. We have a production goal in this factory. On my arrival

I asked you to share it with me. You haven't come near it. This must change because the Wehrmacht needs shoes. So you must change. You must be at the top of your form, eager, alert, competitive, demanding more of yourselves and your men." Fritz gestured. "Dr. Kellerman can provide this extra spark. He has a pill which increases physical capability, raises individual performance and achievement. Every morning each of you will be given one of these pills. All right, Doctor."

Dr. Kellerman set his medical bag on the table. As he opened the bag, Kuhl said, "Fall in! Single file!" The Kapos formed a line. The doctor took a large orange bottle from his bag and spilled some white pellets into his hand. Fritz faced the first Kapo. "You're . . . who?"

"Pfeffer . . . Solomon Pfeffer."

"Solomon Pfeffer, you are inaugurating a historic event," Fritz said. "Together we advance on a new frontier, extending the horizons of science. Doctor."

Dr. Kellerman gave Mannheimer a pill. Fritz dipped the tin cup into the water and raised it. "Bottoms up!" The Kapo put the pill into his mouth and drank. Fritz slapped him on the back. "Next!"

"Over here," Kuhl told Mannheimer, pointing to his right. The next man stepped forward.

Standing beside Dr. Kellerman, Fritz watched all twenty-seven prisoners take pills. "Well done," Fritz said. "A final word." He stepped out into the compound, facing the Kapos. "You have just been poisoned."

Someone made a choking sound. Someone gasped, sucking in his breath. Someone said, barely, "Poisoned . . . ?"

"You have fourteen hours to live," Fritz said. "Just over fourteen hours, say the end of the working day. Then you will die unless—" Fritz broke off. "Doctor."

Dr. Kellerman took a large blue glass bottle from his bag. "Here is the antidote," Fritz said. "You can live or die. The choice is yours. You are the Kapos, the leaders. Fill your production quota and you live. Fail to fill your production quota . . ." Fritz spoke as though a stranger had asked for directions. "We've done our part. We have provided the incentive you lacked. You have a reason for meeting your quota." Fritz gestured, dismissing them. "The doctor and I will be waiting here."

Not one of the twenty-seven men moved. They could feel the poison coursing through their bodies. Fritz took one step forward, spreading his arms. "Go!" he shouted, as though driving a flock of chickens. "Go! Go!"

Fritz broke through the terror which had immobilized the Kapos, turning it into fear. They were afraid of dying. Fritz took another step, pointing at the factory. "Shapiro, Jacob!" he shouted. "Go! Gleckman, go!" He clapped his hands rhythmically. "Move! Move!" He pushed the nearest Kapos, using both hands, shoving them toward the factory. He was as desperate as they.

Less than ten minutes later Fritz rode through the gates in the truck, sitting beside Lemski. "Take me to the richest farmer," Fritz said.

"They are all poor, Baron," Lemski said. "They are starving. The Germans demand everything."

"Drive carefully," Fritz said. Lemski tried to avoid the ruts and potholes of the country lanes. They rode through the planted fields as Fritz looked for signs of new life breaking through the tilled soil. They passed a farmhouse, and within a mile, two others on opposite sides of the road. The wooden houses seemed deserted. "Where are the farmers?" Fritz asked.

"In the fields, Baron."

"Thank you," Fritz said. "Where are their wives?"

"There also," Lemski said. "The Germans took the children, Baron. The boys they didn't kill are in the army. The girls try to hide, Baron. Even little girls."

In the distance Fritz saw a ribbon of smoke rising in a crooked trajectory. "Over there."

Lemski drove on for more than a mile until they came to another road. Fritz could see a roof, see birch trees, see the smoke. "Turn."

As they approached, Fritz saw a large barn, and beyond the birch trees a farmhouse from which the smoke rose. "Do you know the people?"

"I've seen him, the farmer," Lemski said. "He came to the market. His name is Wojcik or Klokzsa."

"Pick one," Fritz said. He could smell the smell from the barn now, and he sat up, trying to see more. When Lemski stopped near the farmhouse, they heard the milk cows in the barn. Fritz stepped down from the truck, raising his head to the clean, crisp air. He opened his coat. He could see his breath when he exhaled. He tried to forget the factory, tried to shield himself, to keep the Kapos and the quotas out of his mind. "Lemski, introduce me."

They walked to the rear of the farmhouse, through a shed to a door. Lemski knocked and a heavy woman with gray hair opened it. Immediately she shrank back, bowing, her hands in her apron. "Mister is in the fields," she said in Polish. Behind her an aged wisp of a woman huddled over a large stove with two baking ovens. "My mother and I are alone here," said the younger woman. "There is nobody else." She shook her head. "Nobody."

The kitchen was more than Fritz had hoped for: scrubbed and spotless and warm, with a worn floor of burnished wood. A large table, scarred and pitted, stood in the center of the kitchen with a mound of cabbages and another of turnips at one end. "Tell her I want to buy some bread," Fritz said.

Lemski spoke to the woman, who answered in a torrent and opened a cabinet. She took out a large, square loaf of rye bread. "She gives you a gift, Baron," Lemski said.

Fritz entered the kitchen and Lemski followed. "I would like a slice of bread and butter," Fritz said.

"Oh, there's no butter," Lemski said. "The Germans take all the dairy products."

"Tell her I am not a German," Fritz said. He stood beside the table. He had bounced across Poland in Lemski's open-air tank to get away from the factory. At the castle in his boyhood, he had been given breakfast in the kitchen. The cook always had fresh bread and new butter churned the same morning. Fritz moved a chair so he could sit at the table with a plate and a thick slab of bread covered with butter.

"Baron, she—" Lemski said before Fritz raised his hand, stopping the Pole.

Fritz took off his coat, pushing the Beretta down into the pocket. He hoped he would not be forced to show them the automatic, to sit at the table while two illiterate crones hugged each other saying their prayers. Fritz took out some money and put it on the table. "Bread and butter," Fritz said. "You may have a slice, Lemski."

They were served with plates, knives and forks, and napkins bigger than towels. The slice of bread covered the plate and the butter, in a bowl, was icy cold, yellow as an egg yolk. Fritz spread a thick layer of butter on the bread and set down the knife to tear off a chunk as he had long ago in the kitchen in the castle. "Good, eh, Baron?" Lemski said, but Fritz didn't hear him because he saw Carly.

Carly faced him across the table, fresh from her morning bath, with her hair combed back from her forehead and held by a bright ribbon. Her forehead was shiny and her cheeks were pink, and her lips were pink. She said, "What shall we do today?" ready for adventure, and Fritz looked down, to lose her. He could not lose her. She followed him, caught up with him, slung her arm through his, matching strides with him.

"Baron?"

Lemski leaned over the table. His plate was clean. "Something wrong with the bread, Baron? With the butter?"

Fritz stuffed bread into his mouth. He ate rapidly, breaking off another chunk, facing Lemski so he would not see Carly. He could feel his longing for her all through him.

Fritz put more money on the table, and stuffed money into the aged woman's apron. "Moment, Baron," Lemski said, crossing the kitchen for the loaf of bread. "It's our bread."

Fritz took his coat and in the truck beside Lemski, said, "Slowly. I am in no rush."

They rode through the gates long before Fritz wanted to see the factory. Lemski stopped at the office. "Am I through for the day, Baron?"

Fritz didn't answer. He didn't greet the two Gestapo at their ledgers. In his office he heard the ticking of the clock but didn't look at it, didn't look at his wristwatch. He thought of running out of the office, into the factory to yell at the prisoners, badgering them to work faster, work harder, longer. He thought of calling Kuhl, calling *someone*, talking with someone, anyone. But he had never asked for help, never admitted he needed help, and he sat in his chair as though he had been strapped into it, waiting to win or lose.

"Baron?"

Dr. Kellerman stood in the doorway with his medical bag. "Almost time, Baron." As he spoke they heard the horn ending the day. Fritz's mouth was dry. He wet his lips. Dr. Kellerman said, "We'll soon know," as the outer door opened, slamming into the wall.

"Commandant!" Kuhl yelled. "Commandant!"

Fritz heard Kuhl's cane, tap, tap, tap, but couldn't see him. He waved the doctor aside, and as Kellerman stepped back, Kuhl appeared, waving the tally sheets. "They made it!" Kuhl yelled. "Every one of those twenty-seven Kapos came in with the quota!"

Fritz had the tally sheets, reading swiftly, leafing through the stack, adding, adding again to be certain.

"Unbelievable," said Dr. Kellerman. "Really unbelievable."

Fritz had a crazy impulse to drape the tally sheets around his neck like a wreath, but he dropped the papers on his desk. "Line them up, Lieutenant," Fritz said. He followed Kuhl and Dr. Kellerman into the compound. The Kapos were waiting. Fritz joined Kuhl and Dr. Kellerman at the table with the pot of water.

"Congratulations," Fritz said. "You have proven Doctor Kellerman's pill works. It's another magic bullet. Nobody dies tonight. Nobody will die tomorrow if you meet your quota. Doctor, distribute the antidote."

Fritz had been lying since dawn. In Dr. Kellerman's office the previous night, Fritz had said, "Is there a poison which won't kill you for a while, for twelve hours, say, before you need to take an antidote?"

"I'm not God," said Kellerman. So Fritz had been forced to improvise.

While the Kapos swallowed the fake pills in the compound, Fritz returned to his office. His luck had turned, but the Kapos were luckier. Fritz had lied about the poison, but not about their fate. If the Kapos had not produced their quota of shoes, Fritz would have completed the hoax to save himself. He had prepared for failure. He would announce that he couldn't spare the guards to dispose of the twenty-seven bodies. Fritz would have marched the Kapos into Lemski's truck and driven them to Auschwitz.

At his desk, reading the day's production totals, Fritz heard Kuhl's cane. "With permission, Commandant. Doesn't this call for a celebration? Would the commandant do me the honor of being my guest for dinner in the city?"

"It will be my honor," Fritz said.

They came out into the compound and walked toward the gates. "I'm familiar with the town," Kuhl said. "Does the commandant have a preference?"

"Young meat," Fritz said. "Something fresh and unspoiled, something around twenty, say. Do I ask for the impossible?"

"Rely on me, Commandant," Kuhl said. Fritz had never accepted a companion on his forays, but the evening demanded a celebration, and Fritz, too, needed an antidote.

In northern Yugoslavia that same night, far south of the shoe factory, Carly and her three flyers moved through the mountains above the Adriatic. Carly had taken so many of them out of Austria that she had long ago begun giving them names. On this journey the Frenchman was Frenchman, and the elder of the two Americans was Navigator. She kept the other American, Orville, the only one whose name she remembered, at her side. She had been worried about Orville since the first night out of Leoben in the Alps in Styria. Orville, a tail gunner, and Navigator, were from the same B-17, a bomber from England. Like Frenchman, they had parachuted after their aircraft was hit. Carly had a moment alone with Navigator after an hour on the trail. "He's been that way ever since we were shot down," said Navigator. "Like he's out of gas."

Now, less than twenty-four hours from the end, they had a night without a moon, the best kind of night. "You'll sleep in England tomorrow," Carly told Orville, but he was gone. She said sharply, "Wait!" stopping the others, turning back to find Orville. He moved slowly, in a wobbly circle, like someone dazed, and Carly, afraid of losing him, ran toward the young American. "Orville," she said, hugging him. "We're on the last lap, Orville."

She heard him say, "Can't," like someone confessing to a crime. "I—" he said, and broke off, surrendering to the nightmare which had claimed him a month earlier when the big bomber began to burn over Germany.

She had him, holding on to keep him erect. "We, not I," she said. "We're together, Orville."

Navigator joined them. "Can't quit now, Orville."

"There," Carly said. "You heard him, Orville. He gave you an order." Carly and Navigator flanked the boy, taking him along.

"We should leave him," Frenchman said. He stood directly ahead.

Frenchman had been a mutineer from the beginning, sniping at Carly all the way. "Remember D'Artagnan," she said. "One for all and all for one." They went past Frenchman, who walked apart and a little behind the other three.

Soon they reached the lip of a canyon. "This is a kind of reward," Carly said. "Downhill." She went ahead to lead, but Orville stopped.

Navigator went back for him, but Frenchman was closer and faster. He took Orville's wrist with both hands, spinning like they were playing crack the whip. When Frenchman let go, Orville toppled and dropped hard. He lay on his side, motionless, welcoming the cold, damp ground. "This time we leave him," Frenchman said. He looked at Navigator. "He'll sink us. We must leave him."

When Navigator didn't protest, Carly knew he had joined the Frenchman. She needed Max now, not tomorrow night. "I don't leave men for the Germans."

"Look at him," Frenchman said. He prodded Orville with his boot. The tail gunner didn't move. "I'm not dying for this . . . lump."

"Help me, Navigator," Carly said, bending over the tail gunner. She heard a click, and when she looked up, Frenchman stood over her with an open knife.

"I said leave him," Frenchman said. "We're losing time. We must move out."

The knife looked longer than a bayonet. Carly rose very slowly. "Move out, then," she said.

"Hey, wait a minute," said Navigator. "What the hell is this?"

Carly watched the knife, pointed at her throat. "Move out," she repeated.

"You'll take us," Frenchman said. "You're not here to die. You're too young to die. You'll take us."

"With Orville," Carly said. "Where I go, Orville goes."

"You and Orville," said Frenchman. "You love Orville, stay with him. You told us we reach a town tonight, by the end of the night. We sleep there and tomorrow we proceed due west. I can find west. I know where the sun sets. Three hours out we come to a road and follow it to a telephone pole. Not very complicated. We'll tell your people the Germans jumped us." Frenchman pointed at Navigator. "We escaped." Navigator wouldn't look at Carly.

"West," Carly said. "Road. Pole. And the code word," she said.

"She's bluffing," Frenchman said. "Can't you see she's bluffing?" He closed his knife, nudging Navigator.

"Good-bye," Carly said.

Frenchman wanted to kill her. He shoved Navigator. "Are you coming?"

Navigator raised his fists. "Try it again, Frenchman. We're always fighting your fucking battles!"

"You're all a pack of—" Frenchman said, and stopped. He knew the bitch was lying. She was an arrogant, lying bitch, swinging those buttocks around, but why should he gamble now, with the end coming? "Take him!" Frenchman said.

So the mutiny was over, but Carly didn't want another. "How about you, Navigator? Do we take Orville?"

"Hell, yes," Navigator said. "Remember, I'm the guy who hid him out. I pulled him through Germany, remember."

"You're a hero," Carly said to the turncoat, an officer willing to abandon one of his men.

"We're wasting time," said Frenchman.

"You . . . man!" Carly said. "I hear you in my sleep. Barking at me, mile after mile after mile. I've never answered you. I understood your position. You were a soldier without his weapon, in enemy territory, on the run, without the language. You were delivered to a woman, taking orders from a woman. You could have been kind, Frenchman, and if not kind, you could have tried to understand my position. So from here on, you don't talk. You follow and tomorrow night you'll be on your way to your squadron, your comrades, your language. You'll be able to lie to your grandchildren." Carly raised her hand. "The knife."

"You're not getting it."

"You'll never see your countrymen," Carly said.

"Because you'll leave me? You can't," said the Frenchman. "I'll follow you." He gestured. "Your partners are waiting."

"Not partners," Carly said. "Partner. One. He's a Jew from a big family. They had to hire a hall for their birthday parties," Carly said, lying. "The Nazis needed a battalion to shoot and hang and gas his family. I'm his family now, and if I tell him about you and your kindnesses, he will kill you. He might use your knife," she said, and took it out of Frenchman's hand. "Come on, help Orville."

The two flyers pulled the boy to his feet. "Poor Orville," Carly said. "He wants to die and we won't let him."

Orville had cost them time, and Carly had to push them to reach the town before daylight. The town had been a supply depot for Yugoslav partisans until the Germans bombed and strafed it. The few survivors were evacuated, and no living thing remained.

Carly brought them to the railroad station in the center of the ghostly city. "One more night," she said, pulling off her black wool cap, like a navy watch cap. She shook her head as her hair fell, digging her fingers into her scalp. Navigator watched her. Every morning when he closed his eyes, he thought of her without clothes.

From the beginning they had slept in pairs while the other two stood guard. "Good night," she said to Frenchman. "You're tired. There are benches in the stationmaster's office. What's left of it. Good night, Navigator." She stuffed her cap into a pocket. As the older men crossed the depot, she hugged Orville. "Alone again."

"You should have shot me," he said. Carly smiled to keep from crying.

"North or south," she said, gesturing. "You choose. Which side will you take?"

"Oh . . ." he said, and now Carly thought he would cry. "North."

"*Wiedersehen*," Carly said. "We'll meet again, Orville." The bombs had left big holes in the station. Carly crossed the depot to the open south wall, stopping beside a wooden beam which hung from the battered roof, dropping to the floor like a playground slide. She listened for footsteps behind her, and when the depot became still, she looked over her shoulder. The young American in his heavy flying pants and leather jacket stood behind a rain barrel, his arms at his sides. He seemed frail, about to fall once more. "Orville," she murmured.

Hours later, when the sun lay overhead, Carly said, "Our turn," taking Orville to the stationmaster's office. Frenchman and Navigator lay on benches facing each other. "Time."

Frenchman came awake instantly. Carly shook Navigator, who said something and tried to turn over, but Carly shook him again. He opened his eyes, sitting up on the bench. "Some navigator," Frenchman said. "Doesn't know where he is."

"Neither do you," Carly said. "You can get a drink from the sink in the men's room."

As the two flyers left the stationmaster's office, Carly closed the door to bar Frenchman's voice. Orville stood between the benches like someone who had lost his way. "Take one," Carly said.

She curled up on a bench, using her right arm for a pillow. Orville sat facing her. "Supposed to be a man," he said.

"Good night." She saw his eyes fill.

"Some man," he said. His face crumpled, and the tears fell. "Oh, Jesus . . ."

Carly dropped down beside him, her arm across his shoulders. He rubbed his eyes, trying to stop crying. "I'm sorry," he said. He huddled against her, and she began to rock from side to side like a mother with her baby.

"Something happened," he said. "Don't know what happened. I'm . . . zero."

"Stop," she said, holding him. "Stop." She could feel his face against her breasts, and then his arm fell across her thighs. She felt as though he was sinking and would slip away unless she saved him. She moved aside, looking at him, his lashes wet with tears. She had to save him. "You are not a blank," Carly said, lowering her head to kiss him. She kissed him again and again, until she felt his arms around her, felt his hands against her, felt him breathing hard and fast. "Orville," she murmured. "Here, Orville," she said, pulling at her zipper to help him.

Later, in his arms, Carly saw him looking at her, his eyes wide, as though he had never seen anyone like her, as though she had appeared at that instant from another planet. "You're wonderful," he said.

"You are wonderful," she said. "Promise you will remember." He nodded, embarrassed. "Say it."

"I promise," he said.

"Good. Remember you are wonderful," Carly said. "We must sleep." She went to the other bench and stretched out, facing Orville. "Sleep," she said.

He closed his eyes and soon she heard the American's measured breathing as he slept. She watched the boy, thinking of him in her arms. She thought of Fritz's lovemaking: elegant, sophisticated, end-lessly stimulating, thoughtful, and considerate of her. She felt neither remorse nor guilt, nor did she believe she had been unfaithful. Her infidelity had occurred long ago, in the schloss, when she had gone the first time to Fritz's room on her own. She had become an accomplished adulteress. Looking at the young American asleep on the bench, Carly thought of Nick and turned, closing her eyes. She needed to sleep, and she fought as she always did to banish Nick so she could continue to live.

She woke in the last moments of daylight, leaving the bench im-mediately, pulling down on her sweater. The stationmaster's office had grown dark. She could barely see Orville, sleeping with his legs drawn up and his face in his folded hands. He made Carly smile. She bent to kiss him, but he did not waken. "Orville." Carly shook him until his eyes opened. "Time," she said.

He looked up at the beauty, the fairy queen with her long hair and face burned by the sun and wind. She made his heart stop and start. "I'm ready," he said, and Carly, very moved, took his hand, bringing him up from the bench.

"Tell me again."

He said, "Tell me . . . ?"

"Repeat what you said when you woke." She tugged his hand.

"I'm ready? Is that what you mean?" He didn't understand. "I'm ready."

She whacked him across the shoulders. "Now we go," she said.

As they came out of the stationmaster's office, Frenchman said, "Let's get started."

"We'll wait," Carly said.

The bitch blocked every suggestion he made. He had encountered other bitches like this one, hating men because they were, in actuality, afraid of them. "We face a long night," he said.

"Night," Carly said. "We move at night." She walked across the station to the beam which had dropped from the roof. "We go when we cannot see this," she said, slapping the beam.

Navigator circled Orville. "You okay?"

"Yeah, I'm okay," Orville said.

"You feel okay? I mean . . . upstairs," said the Navigator, tapping his head.

"Yeah, I guess."

"Okay, then," Navigator said. "No slipups tonight, Orville. No, uh, combat fatigue, huh?"

"I heard you, Lieutenant," Orville said. "Honest." He didn't look at Carly.

Frenchman couldn't stop moving. He paced from one end of the station to the other, glaring at Carly as he passed. Almost an hour after she and Orville had come out of the stationmaster's office, Frenchman stopped in front of her, raising his arm. "I can't see my hand in front of my face. Is that dark enough for you?"

"We can go," she said. "Orville?"

"Yo," he said somewhere behind her.

"Navigator?"

"Yes, yes!"

"Good boy, Navigator," Carly said. She pulled on her gloves. "The sun dropped behind the church," she said. "We stay on a line with the church."

They left the shattered railroad station, crossing the road to a hill which rose from the center of the bombed town. "We don't push," Carly said. "We have a long, long night. So we take a stroll in the country."

They climbed the hill, walking abreast, Orville on Carly's right. They were together, and on their left, several feet apart, Navigator and Frenchman walked side by side. "Germans," said Frenchman. "Only the Germans would bomb a church."

Beyond the church they came to open country, and within a mile they reached a forest which rose in front of them like a black wall. "We could be in there a month looking for a way out," said Frenchman.

"I've made it in two hours," Carly said. "Orville?"

"Yo!"

"Stay close," Carly said. "Everyone close." She raised her left arm. "Navigator, let me touch you."

Carly kept them bunched together as they approached the first line of trees. "Now comes the easy part," Carly said. "We drop our guard here. We are all by ourselves here."

She stopped twice in the forest, insisting on rest periods despite the objections from Frenchman. Even Navigator turned on him. "Hey, stuff it, okay?"

Overhead, a gray moon, a slender crescent, slid free of the clouds, making their passage easier. They were deep into the mountains, and when Carly brought them out of the forest, they began to climb, spread out once more, with Orville beside Carly. He came closer. "Could I ask you something? Could I write to you? I mean, afterward. When the war is over?"

She could see the boy beside her. He seemed even younger in the pale light of the moon. "Is there no one in America?" she said.

"Kind of," Orville said. "There was in high school, the last two years. This girl and me were . . . steady. But it's not . . . I didn't promise anything."

"Well, there is a boy," Carly said. "And I did promise." She touched him. "We have what we have. We have this . . . secret."

As they came to a plateau, Carly stopped them. "The road is there," she said, pointing.

She took her flyers across the plateau and down, through more trees and into a gorge. Within minutes they came to the road. "Stay back," she said. "There are Nazi troops around here."

She went ahead. The road ran between wide dirt shoulders. She could not hide. She saw the road make a long, lazy curve in the distance. Where was the telephone pole? She hurried, and when she came to the curve, she saw the pole on her left.

She crossed the road, running along the shoulder to the pole. She reached up to push some tendrils of hair under her wool cap. She turned in a circle looking for Max. She was on time and he was never late.

"Carly."

She stopped breathing, moving her right hand down toward the Beretta in her pocket. Anyone could call her name. "Upstairs, Carly."

Twenty feet above her, Max stood on the steel rungs set into the pole for the linemen. He came down like a monkey. Carly remembered him at the Zwischentheatre, doing front and back flips to loosen up before a performance. She raised her arms as he dropped to the ground. "Max, Max, Max," she said, holding him.

"T-take it easy," Max said. "We're in good shape."

She released him, looking into the darkness. "Where are your people?" she asked. Max had started from Furstenfeld near the border of Hungary.

Max whistled once, low. Carly heard a racket, the noise mounting till she saw two flyers come out of the darkness. "Too loud," she said, annoyed with the Englishmen. "You are not in London on parade."

The two Englishmen were hulks, and in their quilted flying suits they dwarfed Carly and Max. One of the pair pointed at her. "Who's he?"

"She," Max said. "N-not male, female. You'll be taking orders from her."

"From us," Carly said. "This way." She walked toward the road. "Come on, stay close."

She heard one of the Englishmen whisper, "How old is she?"

Carly pulled up the zipper, sealing the Beretta in her pocket. "One hundred and two," she said, low, and louder, "Let's cross here."

They ran across the road and dirt shoulder until they were beyond the range of any headlights. Carly kept them running all the way to the mouth of the gorge. "Orville!"

"Yo!" He made Carly smile. The American was like a younger brother. She said, "Some brother," to herself, and aloud, "We are seven." She joined Max. "We follow him. Single file. Stay close." In the hills Max, the gym teacher, was a mountain goat.

They went through the gorge and turned into a canyon. Max took them through it and across a narrow valley full of rocks. He turned to Frenchman. "Slowly here. Take handholds where you can." His diction had become precise. "Do what I do. We're on a schedule now. We can't wait for anyone. Pass the word."

They continued without a break, climbing and descending. The ashen moon slid in and out of the clouds, but even in the darkness Max kept up the pace, moving through the hills as though he was crossing the street. "How much longer?" asked Frenchman.

"Much," Max said without pausing.

The flyers were all puffing. Even for Orville, the baby of the bunch, it was hard going. "I thought you said—" he began, and Carly interrupted:

"Save your breath."

Ahead, Navigator said, "Jesus, let's take five, okay?"

Max ignored him. He brought them through another canyon to another hill and began to climb. Carly heard the flyers fighting for breath. Then Navigator said, "I can't make it," and ahead of him Max stopped.

"You made it," he said. The flyers were grouped around him. "Carly?"

"Yo!" she said, smiling at Orville. "Look down."

They stood on a narrow shelf in the hill which rose high above them. Below lay another valley, a ribbon, longer than any they had crossed. "We wait," Max said.

"You're going to land a plane in there?" said Navigator.

"No more rocks," Max said. "The partisans took them away."

"The hell with the rocks," said Navigator. "You can't get a plane out of there. You need ground speed. You need a runway."

"The partisans made a runway," Max said.

On the far side of the valley, beside an oil barrel, a Nazi lieutenant faced the leader of the Partisan squad which cared for the valley. The Partisan, Dobrin, stood among four Nazi soldiers with rifles. Lieutenant Wex Bruckner commanded three full platoons of an infantry company based fifty miles from the valley. An informer had given the Nazis the valley location and the date of the next airlift. Lieutenant Bruckner had stationed his men in the valley twenty-four hours before the partisans arrived. He positioned his machine guns and mortars on the high ground on either side of the valley so that he would have the maximum benefits of cross fire. He had three staff sergeants to whom he would entrust his life for his three platoons. "No shooting," he had told his sergeants early that day. "I want prisoners, not corpses." Lieutenant Bruckner's younger brother had died fighting the Russians. He had been wounded and died. Lieutenant Bruckner believed the Russians killed the wounded. "These Slavs in this valley come to tend their airfield. I need them to tend their airfield."

Beside the oil barrel Bruckner said to the partisan, "Tell me again what you do."

"I light a fire when I hear the airplane," said Dobrin.

"Show me," said Bruckner. "Don't do it, but show me how you do it."

Dobrin, a former history professor, raised a thick branch with rags wrapped around one end. "I light the rags and drop this into the barrel."

"You hear the aircraft, you light the rags, you drop the torch into the barrel," Bruckner said. "You men," he said to the four soldiers, "will watch him do this. If he doesn't, you kill him."

Bruckner left the men guarding the partisan and walked along the valley perimeter to the next barrel, where the next partisan was surrounded by four more soldiers.

Above them Carly slapped her thighs, hopping from one leg to the other to keep warm. "You can have my flight jacket," Orville said.

"You're a flyer, you need your jacket," Carly said.

"Maybe you have the wrong night," said Frenchman. "Maybe it's tomorrow night."

"You talk too much," Max said. "You, too," he said to Navigator.

"Show me the airfield and I'll shut up," Navigator said.

One of the Englishmen said, "I suppose you have a contingency plan."

"The aircraft has never disappointed us," Carly said. "But if there is no aircraft, we return tomorrow night."

Frenchman confronted her. "And the night after that, and the night after that."

"Yes," Carly said. She almost hit him. "Yes, yes, yes. These are the instructions." She could not control her anger. "We did not shoot you down. The Germans shot you down. We saved you." In her rage she punched Max. "He and I saved you! He and I and others!" She pointed into the valley. "And those partisans. And we die, too. Try to remember that. We die, too!"

Max grabbed her. "We'll never hear the plane if we don't shut up," he said.

Carly twisted free, sick of him as well, sick of *men*. She felt as though she had been locked up in a cage with these . . . crybabies.

"Still cold?" Orville asked.

She wanted to hate him with the others, but the American was too young, too callow, too . . . silly. "I'm hot now."

Below them, Lieutenant Bruckner continued his methodical inspection of the valley. "Wait for my flare," he told his sergeants. "Let them believe they are alone until then."

He returned to Dobrin and the soldiers guarding him. Bruckner said, "When . . . ?" and stopped, cocking his head as he heard the first distant sound of engines. He felt the excitement rising within him as the aircraft approached. "Now!" Bruckner said.

Dobrin struck a match, touching the flame to the soaked rags wrapped around the branch. Bruckner saw the bright flames from other soaked rags burning. The valley lighted up as Dobrin dropped the burning branch into the oil barrel.

Fire erupted from the barrel, driving everyone back. Fires circled the valley, showing the pilot every foot of the landing strip.

In the hills Max said, "Single file and spaced out. If I fall, only I fall. If you fall, the same."

"I hear four engines," said Navigator. "He'll need more runway."

Carly let them all pass, following Orville. They came down fast. The aircraft dropped out of the night, a transport, enormous and unreal, descending into the ring of fire, landing gear extended, the red stars on the wing a blur as it zoomed past them.

Lieutenant Bruckner raised his flare gun. He watched the aircraft touch down, heard the growl as the pilot reversed engines and the transport lost speed.

Still it hurtled forward. The pilot veered to the right, the wing passing over the fires from the barrels, to complete his landing and make the turn so he could take off as he had landed, into the wind. Bruckner held his flare gun, waiting. Max reached the valley floor, using the flyers' language to keep them together. "Bunch up! Bunch up!"

In the big Russian aircraft the pilot cut his ground speed. "See anyone?"

"No one," said the copilot. "Nothing."

Behind them the two crewmen unlocked the hatch which opened into the cabin. One of them set a metal ladder on its side against the fuselage. "Do you see them?" he asked.

Across the valley Max said, "We go now," shoving Frenchman, then Navigator.

Carly shoved Orville, then the Englishmen. "Go, go."

In the cockpit the copilot said, "Here they come!" The pilot didn't stop, allowing the transport to crawl along the valley. On their knees the crewmen lowered the ladder, hooking it into the fuselage and holding it.

Bruckner saw the figures running toward the plane. He let them come so they would make one target with those aboard the transport. He didn't see Dobrin break and run. One of the four soldiers guarding the prisoner fired at him and missed. "Lieutenant!" Dobrin reached the barrel and took the burning branch.

Bruckner shouted, "Shoot him!" Raising the flare gun, he fired. "Shoot him! Kill him!"

The four soldiers guarding the partisan fired, and all over the valley and in the hills, Nazi soldiers saw the white comet rising and bursting over them.

In the transport, the pilot saw someone with a burning torch running toward the aircraft. The partisan was hit but kept coming. "Get them on! Get them on!" the pilot shouted. The copilot couldn't hear him above the machine-gun fire. The partisan was hit again and again, spinning from side to side with the force of the rifle bullets, but he kept coming. He tried to shout, but his mouth filled with blood, and as the torch dropped, he fell forward, beneath the red star on the aircraft wing.

Frenchman and Navigator were already in the moving transport. The two crewmen pulled an Englishman up the ladder. "Come on, come on!" yelled the crewmen. Below, Carly, Max, Orville, and the second Englishman ran beside the moving airplane. As the crewmen reached for the Englishman, Max pushed him aside and grabbed Carly.

"Go, Carly, go!" Max said, pushing her onto the ladder and yelling at the crewmen, "Take her!"

The crewmen bent over the fuselage, and Carly felt their hands on her arms and shoulders, yanking her off the ladder and throwing her past them into the airplane.

Running, Max pushed the second Englishman into the ladder. "Climb, you! Climb, climb!"

Across the valley, Bruckner saw mortars landing behind and in front of the moving aircraft, saw puffs of dust from the machine gun and rifle bullets hitting the ground. He ran forward, firing his revolver. "You're missing!" he shouted as though he could be heard. "Are you blind? You're missing an elephant!"

In the cabin, a crewman on his knees over the ladder got a bullet in his head. He released the second Englishman, who dropped onto the cabin floor, his bare hands scraping the floor for purchase. Below, one foot on the ladder and one dragging as the aircraft lumbered forward, Max shoved Orville, using his hands, his head, his shoulders. "Get in! Get in!"

Carly was on her knees pulling Orville, and beside her the second crewman pulled. "We'll lose Max!"

They got Orville into the aircraft. Carly lay on the floor, arms out for Max. The pilot continued to pick up speed. One of the loops on the ladder worked loose, and Max, trying to climb the rungs, swung like a pendulum. Carly got Max's hand but couldn't raise him. The crewman tried and couldn't raise him. Orville dropped down, lying atop the dead crewman, shouting, "Help us! Goddammit, help us!"

An Englishman fell on them, reaching out to get Max's arm with both hands. He held on, and Max, kicking, managed to get one foot through a rung. Carly and Orville clamped on as well. As the pilot reached the end of the valley and turned into the wind at full throttle, Max crawled into the cabin.

A mortar shell dropped directly onto the runway a few yards ahead, and the transport shuddered and rocked. The crewman, talking Russian and gesturing, asked for help with the heavy hatch, and both Englishmen and Orville helped him. There were bullet holes all over the fuselage, and many windows were shot out. When the hatch had been sealed, the crewman dropped flat, gesturing at the others until everyone lay below the windows. They lay on their bellies, listening to the gunfire and the exploding mortar shells above the roar of the engines.

Carly believed the aircraft would be hit and burst into flame. She couldn't see. "Max? Max!"

"I'm here." Carly pawed the air, searching for him.

"Where are you?" she asked, and finally felt him beside her. "Why did you put us on this plane? We don't belong here." She was close to her emotional limit, close to the end of her resources.

"We would be dead on the ground," Max said. "The Germans ambushed the partisans. They almost had us, Carly."

Somewhere nearby, Navigator said, "He'll never make it. He hasn't got enough runway for this tank." As he spoke, the pilot pulled back the wheel, and the nose of the transport rose as the plane lifted off.

One of the Englishmen crawled to the cabin wall, looking through a shattered window. By that time the transport had climbed beyond the range of the German rifles and machine guns. The Englishman let out a whoop and the cabin filled with cheers. The crewman put a square flashlight on the cabin floor and took a tarpaulin from a rack, dropping it over his dead comrade. Carly fell into a seat. "Max." He squatted beside her, holding the seat for balance. "We're going to Russia," Carly said. "How do we get to Austria?"

"Ask me in Russia," he said, adding, "We're alive, Carly. We're not down below, starting to fertilize the fields." He pointed at the tarp. "We're not like him."

"Max!" She wanted to hit him. "There'll be pilots waiting in Austria, depending on us. They're lost without us."

Max rose and bent over her. "Even Saint Joan rested between battles," he said, and left her, going forward into the cockpit.

The pilot flew north and slightly east, still climbing over the Yugoslav mountains. Max knelt between him and the copilot. "We'll be stranded in Russia," he said. "Or England if we go there."

The pilot answered in Russian, and the copilot nudged Max. "I have some German," he said in German.

Max could see the copilot in the glow from the instrument panel. Max spoke slowly, clearly. "Do you carry parachutes?"

"We are not airborne without parachutes," said the copilot.

"Take us to Austria," Max said.

"Take . . . ?" The copilot peered at Max. "Austria?"

"Tell him," Max said, pointing at the pilot.

The copilot frowned. "Tell him?"

"Hey!" Max took the copilot's wrist. After the years on the par-

allel bars, Max could tear telephone books with his hands. "Stop repeating everything. Tell him to turn for Austria."

The copilot spoke in Russian. The pilot glanced at the man on
the floor and spoke briefly. "He says leave the cockpit or he will kill
you or I will kill you," said the copilot.

Max rose slightly, hunched over in the cockpit. "When we land
in Russia, I'm going from this aircraft to the commanding general," he
said. "I'll tell him my comrade and I take Allied flyers through Austria
to planes like this one, or to boats on the Adriatic. We take Russian
flyers. I'll tell him that for the rest of the war Russian flyers will have
nobody on the ground to save them."

The transport hit an air pocket and dropped several hundred feet.
Although Max managed to grab the seats and keep his footing, he
banged his head on the cockpit ceiling. The pilot laughed and when
he stopped, Max said, "Tell him."

The copilot leaned over the seat. The pilot looked at the intruder,
shouting until Max cut in: "What does he say?"

"Look at the wing," said the copilot. Max bent low, watching the
wing rise as the pilot began his turn.

In the cabin Max saw Carly in his path in the aisle. "Max, I'm
sorry," she said. "I behave like a tyrant. How do you stand me?"

"Not easy," he said gravely. "We're going home."

Carly followed him. "Home? But how? He can't land in Austria."

"We can," Max said. He went to the crewman. "Parachutes," he
said, moving his hands as though pulling on the shrouds.

"Parachutes," Carly said, falling through the sky. Parachutes failed
to open.

Max took the crewman to the hatch, backed off until he stood
against the cabin wall and leaped across the aisle, pulling at an imagi-
nary ripcord. "Parachutes," Max said, making a V with his fingers.
"Two parachutes."

The crewman nodded, talking fast, leaving Max and going to a
curtain behind the cockpit. "You'll sleep in your own bed tonight,
Carly," Max said.

She wanted to stop the Russian crewman. She said silently, "I
can't." She imagined herself plummeting through the sky feet first,
spread-eagled, helpless, falling to her death.

The crewman brought them the parachutes, the lady first, pushing
it into her belly. Carly let it fall, and Max came close, looking into her
face. "Carly, this is easy," he said. "You played hopscotch. You jumped
off a fence."

Carly said, barely, "Yes." She didn't see Orville coming.

"He's right," Orville said. The crewman nodded, agreeing with the American and instructing the beautiful woman in Russian. The crewman saw the fear in the beautiful woman's face.

"It's like a small jump," Orville said, taking her parachute. "You bend your legs," he said, bending, "and plop, you're down and it's over."

"Take the parachute," Max said. "Take it, Carly."

"Get the feel of it," Orville said. He raised Carly's right arm and put it over the parachute. The crewman took her left arm.

Frenchman enjoyed the show. "You must be careful landing," he said. He used his hand like an ax, hitting his leg below the knee. "You can crack it wide open."

"Maybe I'll disappoint you." She turned to the crewman. "Hook me up," she said, screaming inside. The crewman, who didn't understand, understood courage.

He hooked up the parachute, pulling it snug against her belly. He tried to amuse her, tried to take the beautiful woman away from her fear. He puffed out his cheeks, holding his hand in front of him, waddling back and forth, showing her she looked like a pregnant woman.

He hooked up Max. "All set," Orville said. "Better sit down." He took her to a seat, and Max sat beside her. "You'll be good," Orville said. He would have jumped with her. "You'll be great."

Carly's eyes felt wet, as though she had been weeping. She could feel the fear coursing through her, wave after wave of cold, numbing, paralyzing dread. She heard Max talking to her, making promises she knew were lies.

Navigator knelt beside her. "Thanks for what you did," he said. "Forget the Frenchman. I fly with some real tough Frenchmen, real good guys."

She couldn't reply or even look at him. The aircraft flew to Austria, bringing her to her end over Austria. Carly felt as though she was melting from the seat and sliding across the floor. Orville stood over her. "Getting close," he said, and ahead, Carly saw the crewman come out of the cockpit, gesturing with both hands for them to rise. The two Englishmen helped the crewman open the hatch.

Max took Carly's hand in his. "We go together," he said. He took his ripcord with his left hand. "We count one, two, three, four, five," he said, and released her. "When I drop your hand, you pull." The crewman beckoned.

Max took her hand. She could not move. The crewman wiggled

his fingers, summoning them. She had to move. She took one step, then another, wanting to hide.

They came to the open hatch. The wind tore at her. Max held on to her hand. The crewman waved them out, kept waving. They came to the very edge of the cabin floor. Then Max jumped, taking her with him, and they dropped from the airplane into nothing. One . . . dying . . . two . . . dying faster . . . three . . . dying faster . . . four . . . faster . . . five, Max! . . . He released her and she pulled.

Something jerked her hard, and she saw white over her head, a billowing umbrella which swelled to a canopy as she slowly floated down through the dark night.

She had stopped dying. She returned from a void into which blind terror had thrust her. She saw the other parachute, then Max hanging in the air. Far, far below she saw pinheads of light. She was light-headed, unable to think. The escape from paralyzing fear had come with such swiftness, was so overpowering, that Carly could not yet accept her rescue from oblivion.

In Sopron, a town near the Hungarian border about forty miles from Vienna, a squad of soldiers with binoculars were on the roof of the post office, the city's highest building. The squad, one of three, had been on duty for two hours when they were relieved, returning in four hours. "Sergeant!"

A soldier stationed above the swastika over the post office entrance had his arm in the air. "Two of them!"

A sergeant sprinted across the roof. "I see them! Corporal, take over!" The sergeant ran to the field telephone. He had orders to report any parachute sightings to the officer of the day at battalion headquarters, who would relay the information directly to Major Huebner's command in Vienna.

High above the post office, Carly saw the lights growing. All at once the ground rushed up at her—fields, trees, farmhouses, barns—and remembering, she bent her knees.

Carly dropped into soft earth among shoots of wheat and fell forward. Her parachute crumpled and then filled as a gust of wind took it across the field, dragging Carly. She ran after it, gathering up the shrouds until she could fall on the silk. She said, insanely, "Got you!" smiling in the darkness. She came erect, holding the big white ball of silk in her arms. But where was Max?

She found a patch of white far across the field but did not see him. Then a figure rose from the ground, moved, and fell. She saw the figure rise again and fall again. Max?

She found him on his side. He tried to smile. "You made it," Max said.

"You're hurt." Carly dropped beside him. "Where?"

"My ankle," he said. "The gymnast broke something in his left ankle."

"We'll fix you," Carly said, as though she had a team beside her. She came up on one knee. "First let's get you out of the harness," she said. She gathered up his parachute.

Max raised his hands. "Help me."

Carly tried to lift him. "No good," he said. "Get behind me." He came up on his right hand. "Under my arms, Carly," he said. "Lock your hands around my middle." He waited and said, "Now," pushing hard as Carly lifted him. He fell against her, and she teetered but stayed on her feet, holding him as he hopped around on his right leg.

They came across the plowed field with Max using Carly for a crutch, his left leg bent at the knee so his foot was raised. "Easy," he said as she stepped into a furrow, stumbling and losing him, who fell, bringing her down with him. "Aiieee!" He shook with the pain.

On her knees Carly began to weep and stopped, furious with herself for playing the crybaby. She tasted the salt of her tears. "I'll help you," she said. "I remember."

But they fell again. Max dug his hands into the cold earth, gasping from the pain. "You'd better go, Carly." She didn't acknowledge him. "Carly, I can't make it." She remained silent. "Carly, get out!"

"Shut up." She put her face in his. "I mean it, shut up." She dropped down to lift him.

The dawn saved them. They saw trees ahead. "Stop there," Max said. They reached the trees as the first, foggy gray haze brightened the horizon. Carly saw a road and on the other side, in a grove, a large brick house.

Inside the house Nestor Konrad, Sopron's postmaster, left his bedroom for breakfast. His wife, Hannah, had woken an hour before, adding wood to the stove as she made breakfast. Halfway down the stairs, he heard the heavy knocking on the door.

Konrad stopped, pulling the sash of his robe tight around his belly. The Nazis had come once, searching for weapons. He heard his wife and cried, "I will go."

They didn't knock a second time. They were too sure of themselves. Konrad walked through the parlor of the house his wife had inherited from her father. He opened the door, finding a pair of filthy derelicts arm in arm. Konrad knew they were fugitives. "Get out!"

One fell across the threshold and into the vestibule, sending Konrad backward into a clothes tree. When he righted it, both were inside. "Get out!"

Carly helped Max to his feet. She saw the woman stop behind the man in the robe. "Get out!" Konrad said. "The army is all around this house!"

"Around, not in," Carly said, helping Max. Konrad and his wife followed them into the parlor.

Max lowered himself into a sofa. "Bring a chair." Hannah Konrad carried a chair to the sofa. Max lifted his left leg and lowered it. He sighed as the pain eased. "My ankle is broken."

Carly pulled off her black cap, shaking her head. "You cannot stay," Konrad said.

"For a few hours," Carly said, talking to the woman. "I'll come back with a car. You are good people. So are we. My friend and I are—"

Konrad sprang forward, interrupting, "Don't tell us, we don't want to know! We're not involved! We're not Nazis, we're not anti-Nazis. I'm a postmaster, the postmaster! I followed my father, my grandfather, all postmasters, servants of the state! You must leave this house!" Konrad pointed at Max. "Take him and—" Konrad stopped because Carly had the Beretta in her hand.

"I hate this gun," Carly said. "Whenever I carry it, I pray I will not use it. Don't make me use it, mein herr."

"Or me," Max said, holding his gun.

"Nestor!" Konrad's wife moved fast, shielding his body with hers. "He can stay," she told Carly. "You're hungry. I will bring you breakfast." She looked at her husband. "You can have breakfast with Nestor."

"Sit down," Max said. "Both of you sit. There. Facing me. We'll skip the breakfast."

The pair obeyed, sitting side by side like strangers. Carly pushed the Beretta into her pocket and closed the zipper. She went to Max, whispering into his ear, "I'll take the train and bring back the Daimler."

Carly walked toward the vestibule. "Jesus, I forgot about the parachutes," Max said.

Carly looked back into the parlor. "I didn't."

She left the brick house, crossing the road to the field. Within a hundred yards she saw a white carpet of silk rippling over the field.

Carly gathered up the yards and yards of silk, looking for a hiding place. She walked through the field, flat as a skating rink. She had to catch a train for Vienna, had to drive back to Sopron, had to care for Max. She stopped, ready to discard the parachutes. In the distance she saw a steeple. Carly started running.

At eleven minutes of eight that morning, Carly boarded a train for Vienna. Three hundred yards from the railroad station Der Chineser came out of the Sopron post office. He had been on the roof with the soldier who had reported the sighting. With Der Chineser were three military police officers, and in front of the post office, behind the staff car, stood a lorry with twenty M.P.s he had brought with him from Vienna. "We follow the road past the soccer field," he said.

In the staff car with the driver, Der Chineser saw the steeple before an officer behind him said, "Major, the church!" The Nazis had dragged whole populations of enemies out of churches. Der Chineser had to stop although Domino would never gamble on such a dangerous refuge.

An enlisted man found the parachutes behind the altar. Der Chineser knew the young man from Berlin in room 300 of the Hotel Metropole had not come to Vienna for parachutes.

Der Chineser lost time at the church, time his quarry gained. Ahead on the left Der Chineser saw the field. He leaned forward to look past the driver. A mouse couldn't hide in that field. He dropped back into his seat as the driver came up on the large brick house. "Off the road," said Der Chineser.

The lorry followed the staff car. Der Chineser kept ten of the enlisted men and gave the other ten to an officer. "Spread out," he told him. "One of them could be a woman. Keep to this side of the road. You'll waste time in the field."

Der Chineser took five of the remaining enlisted men, assigning the other five to Captain Truppe, the ranking officer accompanying him.

In the parlor of the house, Nestor Konrad said, "I must use the bathroom."

The pain in Max's ankle coursed all through his leg as Konrad came out of his chair. "No," Max said.

"You must allow me to relieve myself."

"Do it," Max said. "But you stay." Max saw the woman put her hand over her husband's hand. Max decided the Nazis had made him a Nazi. "Go ahead," he said, waving the gun as they heard the knock on the door.

A sheet of pain burned through Max's leg. They heard more

knocking. "Get rid of whoever is there," Max said. "Remember, I've got your wife."

At the door Captain Truppe pushed Konrad into the parlor, following the postmaster with five enlisted men following him.

Max saw the Nazis with Konrad. Hannah screamed, "Nestor!" throwing herself at him. Behind him, Der Chineser, who had come in from the back of the house, put the muzzle of his gun into Max's ear. "Drop it."

Max let his gun fall, and Der Chineser kicked it. A soldier bent for the weapon, and another soldier with Truppe searched the postmaster. A third searched Hannah.

Der Chineser walked around the man with his left leg on a chair. "You've had an accident."

"Stupid," Max said, grinning. "I think I'm still a kid. I was on the roof checking the postmaster's gutters. Instead of using the ladder, I jumped."

"Papers." Max rolled onto his side to get his papers. Examining them, Der Chineser said, "Albrecht Kimmel. From Wiener Neustadt. You're a long way from home, Herr Kimmel."

"We're friends," Max said. "I come up and do odd jobs around here.

"And you broke your leg," said Der Chineser.

"My ankle," Max said. As he pointed and said, "My left ankle," Der Chineser raised his gun and swung, bringing the butt down on the fracture. Max twitched, his head snapped back, and his voice rose in a cry of unbearable agony.

Der Chineser said, "Let's try the truth. The truth is you broke your ankle in that field when you landed in your parachute. You and your friend." Der Chineser stood over Max. "Where is your friend?"

Max said, "I'm alone," and Der Chineser swung the gun, slamming the butt into the broken ankle. Max made a horrible, retching sound, shoving his hand into his mouth, biting down viciously to handle the pain.

"Albrecht Kimmel," said Der Chineser. "Any relation to Max Ingster?"

Max's head drooped as he waited to be hit. "I . . . uh, right . . . Max Ingster."

"That's your name," said Der Chineser. "I need your friend's name."

In the parlor the sound of Max's breathing seemed thunderous. "Your friend's name," said Der Chineser, counting to three before raising the gun and swinging with all his strength, shattering the bones in the damaged ankle.

"Stop!" Hannah's voice drowned out Max's moans. "Stop! He came with a woman! A young woman dressed in man's clothes! A man's cap!" Hannah passed her hand over her head. "She removed her cap. Long hair, hair below her shoulders."

A surge of feeling more intense than sexual frenzy shot through Der Chineser. "What color hair?"

Hannah said, "Not light, not dark. Between blond and brown." She thought the Oriental would strike her. "Between blond and brown."

"Like sand," said Der Chineser.

"Like sand, like sand," said the postmaster's wife.

Der Chineser looked past the woman. He no longer saw her. He saw the baroness, saw her clearly, saw her with the baron in the Great Hall of the palace, and then, magically, with Colonel Varlingen in the Great Hall. *Colonel Varlingen.* And *Max Ingster* from the Zwischentheatre. And *Nick Gallanz* from the Zwischentheatre. The baroness had gone daily to the Prinz Eugen Hospital while Nick Gallanz was a patient.

Domino! Der Chineser had the identity of *Domino*, the invisible woman, the wonder woman, the goddess who had eluded the entire Gestapo, even Heinrich Himmler. Der Chineser felt immense. He felt huge, felt as though he towered over everyone in the house. "Truppe, round up the detail. Bring every officer and enlisted man into this house. Remove the vehicles. Bury them. When you have done that, fetch me so you can prove it." Der Chineser knew Domino would return. Domino would not forsake a comrade.

The telephone rang late that afternoon. The sound paralyzed everyone except Der Chineser, who put his gun into the postmaster's ear. "Answer."

Der Chineser raised the telephone. "Say you can't hear. Say, 'Louder, speak louder.'" Der Chineser stood head to head with the postmaster as he said, "Hello."

Twenty miles south in a country store, Carly said, "Who is this?"

The postmaster could feel the gun in his head. "Louder," he said. "I can't hear."

"Who is this?"

"Speak louder."

"*Who . . . is . . . this?*"

"Nestor Konrad. The postmaster of Sopron," he said.

"You have a guest," Carly said. "Let me speak to him."

Der Chineser nudged the postmaster, nodding. "Bring your guest to the telephone," Carly said.

Der Chineser stepped aside, trying to whisper. "Truppe! Bring him! Quick! Quick!"

They raised Max from the chair, carrying him through the parlor. Der Chineser said, "If you want to live, tell her to hurry."

The postmaster gave Max the telephone. Der Chineser raised his gun, holding it between Max's eyes. Carly said, "Hello! *Hello!*"

Max saw the gun muzzle, big as a cannon. "I'm here."

"Max? Are you all right?"

Der Chineser's lips moved. "Hurry."

"Max?"

Max saw the gun muzzle, saw the murderer behind the gun, saw Carly in the stables behind the palace with pillows and blankets for him, saw her in the forest with the flyers, in the mountains with flyers, in Vienna at night with flyers. Max saw her stretched out on the deck of the fuselage in the aircraft, pulling him into the cabin, and he saw the partisan, full of bullets, warning the Russian pilot. Max shouted, "Run, run, run, run, run!" and rammed the telephone into Der Chineser's face as he dove forward, wrenching free of his captors.

Der Chineser fell back into the door, losing his gun. As Max fell, Der Chineser yelled, "Don't shoot! Don't shoot!" but two soldiers were already firing.

Der Chineser came erect, standing over the dead traitor, holding himself in check to keep from strangling the soldiers. Truppe picked up the Luger. Der Chineser slipped the gun into his holster.

He had lost Domino, lost his prize before he had her. He could not march into the palace to arrest the baroness. He needed proof, and Max Ingster had cheated him out of it. And even if he delivered the baroness to the Gestapo, even if the young man from Berlin took her on Der Chineser's say-so, he could be wrong. The real Domino could surface later. And Der Chineser would be delivered to the Hotel Metropole.

The next afternoon in Himmelpfortgasse, Der Chineser posted two Gestapo across the street from the palace and two others on the street behind the palace. "Where she goes, you go," he told the Gestapo. Der Chineser walked to the staff car, where Truppe waited beside the open door. "Kruger Strasse," Der Chineser said.

They waited for hours. The day ended. A square of light from the lobby of a nearby apartment building fell across the sidewalk. As Truppe shifted in the seat, Der Chineser saw a trim man crossing Kruger Strasse. The man entered the apartment building, and then the doorman appeared, nodding at the staff car, following Truppe's instructions. Der Chineser lowered the window. "Soon," he said. An hour later he opened the car door.

On the eighth floor a maid greeted them, stepping back and opening the door wide when she saw the uniforms. "Herr Siefermann," said Der Chineser. He gave the maid a card.

Carly's father hurried down the long corridor, holding the card. Behind him, at the entrance to the living room, Helga stood against the arch. Klaus's mouth was dry. "Major Huebner?" One of them seemed Oriental.

"I am Major Huebner," said Der Chineser. "Captain Truppe."

Klaus looked at the card as though he had not read it. "Military police," he said. "Aren't they for the army?"

Der Chineser saw the flecks of red in the man's eyes, the color of his face. Der Chineser had given him an hour to drink. "Could you spare us a few minutes?"

"Certainly." Klaus made a little bow. "Gentlemen."

Helga saw them coming and returned to her chair, trying not to seem afraid. "Helga!" Klaus went to her. "Major Huebner, Captain Truppe," Klaus said. "My wife, gentlemen."

Helga greeted them and excused herself. Klaus went to the bar. "Please join me." He made two drinks and refilled his own glass. "To the Reich," Klaus said. He escorted them to the sofa. "At your service, gentlemen."

"Spoken like a loyal citizen of the Reich, Herr Siefermann," said Der Chineser. "You *are* a loyal citizen, a member of the party since nineteen thirty-seven. It took courage for a man to declare himself in those days. You are one who fought the communists in the homeland. You proved your courage long ago."

Klaus raised his glass and drank. "Thank you, Major," he said. "I am always ready to serve the Reich. Alas, war is for young men."

"There are many ways to serve the Reich," said Der Chineser. He set down his glass, so Truppe had to forget about drinking. "We have enemies everywhere, Herr Siefermann, even here in Vienna, even in our own homes."

Klaus crossed his legs. "Our two servants are simple women, Major. They came to us straight from the farm. They aren't involved in politics. I can vouch for them."

"And your family?" asked Der Chineser. "Can you vouch for your family?"

Thirty feet away in the serving pantry, Helga did not hear her husband reply. Klaus said, "My family," like someone choking. The two fiends on the sofa had discovered somehow that Carly had driven Sarah Frisch out of the country. The Nazis settled every account. The monsters wanted him to give them Carly. All over the Greater German Reich children betrayed parents, mothers delivered sons to the army, fathers led the Gestapo to their daughters in the Underground. The Oriental and his helper needed Klaus's testimony to hang Carly. They would take him to some barred tomb where Klaus knew he would provide the testimony they demanded. They knew everything, so they knew Klaus Siefermann was a coward.

Klaus had to get up even if he fell. He showed the monsters his empty glass. "Excuse me," he said, wiggling out of the chair like a timorous child sliding into a pool. "A moment," he said. He had forced Carly to save Sarah while he hid here near the whiskey. At the bar Klaus filled his glass. His fear made him dizzy.

"You can help us, Herr Siefermann," said Der Chineser.

Klaus repeated the words to himself as he walked to the windows. He could feel them reaching for him, feel their talons in his back, demanding his beautiful Carly, his beautiful, brave, magnificent child. At the windows he said, "I understand." Holding his drink, he leaped forward.

Helga heard the brittle sound of breaking glass. She came out of the serving pantry to clear the mess they had made and saw, across the room, the curtains billowing in the wind, over the hole high above Kruger Strasse.

— 14 —

I N SANTA BARBARA ONE
night that fall, a small group of men and women stood under a movie
theater marquee. They seemed out of place, like tourists, and in a sense
they were. All had driven north from Los Angeles late in the day, and
they flanked the theater doors, bunched together like tourists waiting
for their guide.

At the curb Votrian leaned against his Cadillac in a no-parking
zone. A fat man wearing a Hawaiian shirt and smoking a cigar sat in
the front seat. "Won't be long now, Milt," Votrian said. He left the
fat man and walked under a white sign with the words, "SNEAK PRE-
VIEW," hanging from the marquee.

Ahead of him, Champ Gallagher joined Nick. "Ready for fame
and fortune, laddy buck?" The director looked like an actor in a blue
blazer and blue shirt with a yellow polka-dot tie. He released Nick and
introduced a stunning blonde in her thirties or early forties, statuesque
and confident.

"Nick?" Votrian took Nick aside. "Are you nuts altogether?" he said, trying to keep his voice down. "Shapiro isn't blind. He sees you. Can't you come over and talk to him?"

"We talked," Nick said. "He picked Santa Barbara."

"You're not the distributor," Votrian said. "Milt Shapiro is the distributor. He says they're all critics in Los Angeles."

"Sure," Nick said.

Behind them, Earl Flavin, the young theater manager, opened the doors. "Our regular feature is over, folks," he said. "We can seat you now."

Votrian waved at the Cadillac. "Milt!"

Ahead of them, Magda and Dieter led those from Los Angeles. Many in the audience were in the lobby buying refreshments and staring at the movie people from Hollywood. In the center of the lobby, standing end to end, were two long, chest-high tables, like those in a bank. On the tables were glasses filled with short, sharpened yellow pencils and stacks of three-by-five cards.

Inside the theater, the last three rows to the right of the aisle had a red velvet cord around the seats. The manager lowered it. "Mr. Shapiro."

The distributor took the first seat in the last row and Votrian sat beside him. Polly tried to catch up with Nick, but Champ Gallagher had him, and she and Hash sat in the row behind him.

Earl Flavin stayed in the aisle until all the Hollywood people were sitting. "Let's get going," Shapiro said.

Polly felt like she was suffocating. "Do you think they'll like it, Hash?" she whispered.

"Soon find out," he said.

Nick heard the two of them. The lights dimmed and for a little while the theater was black. Nick went through the movie in his head, looking for mistakes, for bad scenes, for dull scenes. He saw only great scenes, perfect characterizations, and then the words *Maiden Voyage* appeared on the screen, riding little waves like those in a child's drawing. "Oh, gosh," Polly whispered, crossing her fingers on both hands.

Ninety-three minutes later, as "THE END" rode across the same little waves, the lights glowed and the audience came alive, seats creaking and murmurs rising in the theater.

In the lobby, Earl Flavin used wooden wedges to pin the doors against the wall. The lights from the lobby, plus those in the ceiling and on the walls of the theater, seemed to catch everyone off guard. Everyone looked guilty. Without the darkness, the theater, unimaginative and neglected, seemed tawdry and illicit. The audience, anxious to leave, moved steadily to the aisle and toward the lobby.

Polly tried to keep her mind blank. She didn't expect everyone to adore Nick's picture. She didn't expect people up here in Santa Barbara to react as she had. She came from one environment, they came from another, from churches and Sunday schools and family picnics. Still, even they could not resist the charm of the story.

Those in the last three rows remained in their seats, silent until Magda said, "They are writing books in the lobby." Someone else said, "This is their big night." Because so many were talking, only Milt Shapiro and Votrian heard Earl say, "We're about ready."

Shapiro rolled out of his seat, coming into the aisle like a football lineman. Earl slipped past him. "Almost," he said.

Nick climbed over his seat into the empty row ahead. In the aisle he saw two women at one of the tables in the lobby, and when he came out of the theater, another man and a woman were still writing. All the doors to the sidewalk were open, and the theater manager stood to one side, holding the stack of cards he had collected. Votrian and Shapiro were at the tables facing Earl. As the last two women dropped their pencils and crossed the lobby, Earl took their cards, leaving the door to join the pair at the table. "Good luck," the man said, giving Earl his card. "Me, too," said the woman, surrounded by all the people from Hollywood. "I mean . . . you know what I mean."

Earl said, "Thank you, folks." He didn't see the fat man in the Hawaiian shirt.

"Gimme," Shapiro said, pulling the cards out of his hands. Several cards fell to the floor. "All of them," Shapiro said. Earl bent to retrieve the cards, and when he came erect, Nick stood between him and the fat man. Nick took the cards Earl held, nudging the theater manager aside to face Shapiro.

"All of them," Nick said, bumping into the big belly, driving the fat man back against a table.

"Animal!" Votrian took a step and stopped dead because Hash was in his way.

Nick kept Shapiro pinioned against the table. "Give me the cards," Nick said. "*Maiden Voyage* is my picture, not yours."

Champ Gallagher left his date to arbitrate the problem, but Nick put an elbow in his ribs. "Stay out!" Nick saw Hash coming. "You, too!" He turned to the fat man. "Now, you," he said, trying not to explode, "give me the cards," he said, raising his hand. "Quick, while I still like you."

Shapiro set the cards into Nick's hands. "Get away," Nick said. He faced the others, alone at the table.

"So read them, already," Votrian said.

"Sure," Nick said, raising the top card. He read aloud, "Is this a love story or a comedy or a mystery or what?" A car backfired somewhere, and when Earl closed the doors, he sealed them off from the world.

Nick read the second card: "Who loves who and why?"

Polly said, "Whom," under her breath.

"Lose your voice?" Votrian said.

Champ said, "Let's hear it, laddy. We can take it. We're big boys." He smiled at the blond woman. "And girls."

Nick said, "Is this a love story or a comedy or a mystery or what?" He read, "Who loves who and why?" and set that card atop the first.

Nick raised a third card and read, "I liked the ending but didn't understand the story."

Polly heard Nick go on, "You should have dumped the movie and stuck with the music." She wanted to leave, wanted to disappear, wanted him to stop.

Nick continued, "Better luck next time," and "Terrible!"

One person wrote, "Why don't you creeps go back where you came from?"

"Nazi bastards," Votrian said.

Nick picked up the next card. "I'm a mother and I would never treat my son the way she treated Eric. Neither would any other mother I ever met, including my own."

He picked up the next card. "Strike three, you're out."

He picked up the next card. "No woman would put up with Eric and his shenanigans, so Karen doesn't make sense."

He picked up the next card. "Wonderful! Sidesplitting all the way. And wise."

"Some college professor who got lost," said Shapiro.

Nick picked up the next card. "Are you trying to hint at something between Eric and his mother? Boy, that's sick."

"Balls," Champ said, and his date said, "Whoever wrote that card is a sick one."

Nick picked up the next card. "What's funny about measles?"

"He didn't have measles," Polly said. "He pretended!"

Hash said, "You fooled them, angel."

Nick picked up the next card. "Too long!" He picked up the next one. "Why does Eric act like he has another girl, and why does his mother go along with him?"

He picked up the next card. "The finest film this year. I loved every moment."

"The professor's wife," Votrian said.

Nick picked up the next card. "The best part of the movie is the music, and the best music comes before the movie. So keep the screen dark." He picked up the next card. "Even your title is screwed up. If anyone is the maiden, it's Eric."

"At last," Dieter said, "a civilized man."

"Or woman," Magda said.

"Man or woman," Votrian said, "he didn't like the picture."

"He's wrong," Champ said, tired of taking a beating. "They're all wrong."

"They're never wrong," said Shapiro. "It's their money. They're buying the tickets."

Nick picked up the next card as Magda said, "No more. I've heard enough. Dieter," she said, giving him an order.

He took some car keys from his pocket and put them in her hand. "I didn't hear enough," he said.

Magda stayed. Everyone stayed. Everyone heard Nick read every card. Nobody spoke when he finished. Votrian turned to Shapiro. "Milt? Say something, for God's sake!"

"We'll wait for Riverside," said the fat man, who had scheduled a second preview in the desert town east of Los Angeles.

The group dispersed for the long drive back to Los Angeles. In the villa hours later, Nick's telephone rang. "Did I wake you?"

"Sigrid?"

"No, this is Polly," she said, walking in a tight circle and winding the telephone cord around her wrist. "I know it's late, but I couldn't sleep so I took a chance."

"You won," Nick said.

"Those people in Santa Barbara are wrong," Polly said. "Dead wrong!"

Below on the patio, Hash doused his cigarette. The hours in the convertible had made him stiff all over. At the head of the stairs he saw light under Polly's door, and then he heard her. "You made a wonderful movie. Maiden Voyage is wonderful," she said, so Hash knew who was on the other end of the line.

"Most movies are fairy tales," Polly said. "They take place in never-never land. Maiden Voyage is about everyone . . . the people next door. And you make a moral judgment," Polly said, quoting her English professor. "You fulfill the primary obligation of any art form."

"Tell them in Riverside," Nick said.

She wanted to hold him and comfort him. "Don't be sad."

"I'm happy," Nick said.

"And don't tease," she pleaded.

"Promise," Nick said.

In Riverside the following week, in the lobby of the Red Mill theater, Nick finished reading the preview cards around eleven-thirty. Someone said, "It's worse than Santa Barbara." Another said, "They hate us out here."

An usher said, "Wow!" and opened a door at one end of the lobby to take out a vacuum cleaner.

Polly said, "It's not fair."

"They didn't bust any rules," Hash said.

"We're dead," said Shapiro, wearing a different Hawaiian shirt. He pulled a cigar out of his shirt pocket, unwrapping the cellophane as he left the theatre.

In the lobby all those who had come from Los Angeles avoided each other. Votrian raised the stack of preview cards. "Here, burn these. Anything, only get them out of my sight." The theater manager took the cards as Votrian leaned against a table, looking as though he might sink to the floor. He stared ahead. "If I could find a lunatic with one hundred thousand dollars, I'd sell him this picture tonight."

"I'm a lunatic," Nick said.

"Hero," Votrian said, "you don't have a hundred dollars, forget a hundred thousand."

"The banks are closed," Nick said, eyeing Polly beside the table.

"I still have to drive home," Votrian said. "Let's go." He started for the doors. "I feel like I'm at my own funeral." He stopped. "Are you coming?"

"It's not my funeral," Nick said.

"Choke," Votrian said, and outside, "Milt? Where are you, Milt?"

In the lobby Nick joined Polly and Hash. "I need a ride." So Hash knew why he had dumped Votrian.

"You can come with us," Polly said. "We're across the street."

At the convertible she added, "We can all fit in the front."

"Hop in," Hash said, standing back. He wasn't sitting in the middle and messing up his clothes.

They were squeezed together in the convertible. When Polly

turned the ignition key, she jabbed Nick with her elbow. She said, "I'm sorry." She felt her face flush and rolled down the window.

Hash pointed. "The light, angel."

Polly came down on the brake so hard the convertible rocked. "I'm sorry," she said, and to herself, "Can't you say anything except 'I'm sorry'?"

"Polly is still mad at the audience," Nick said.

"I am mad," she said. "Especially at Leonard Votrian. He's a . . . traitor."

On the sign reading, "Los Angeles," Nick noticed the arrow pointing to the highway. "Votrian is a fool if he sells this picture," he said.

"If I had the money, I would buy it," Polly said. She glanced at Nick. "That's not fair. It would be like stealing the movie from you."

"You and me are the same," Nick said. "All we need is the money."

Hash listened to the greenhorn trying to hustle a hustler. "The light," he said as red changed to green.

They encountered few cars on the road to Los Angeles, and the deserted highway, the silent night, and the steady hum of the engine combined to stifle conversation. In less than an hour they could see the first lights of the city. "My car is at the studio," Nick said.

Polly drove to Pleiades. Nick thanked her and followed Hash out of the convertible. "If someone buys *Maiden Voyage* from Votrian, he becomes my partner for life," Nick said.

Hash listened. He was cute, all right, saving it for the last. "Good luck," Hash said.

Driving through the lot, Polly said, "He worked so hard."

"Yeah," Hash said, finally able to stretch his legs. "Getting late."

On Roxbury Drive, he followed Polly out of the garage. "I'll grab a smoke," he said. "Night, angel." He watched her go up the stairs.

Hash lit a cigarette and went out on the patio, finding a dry chair. Christ, nobody liked the picture except the people who had made it. They couldn't all be nuts in Santa Barbara and Riverside. Hash got out of the chair. One hundred grand.

Stick to your own racket. How many times have you made that speech? "That's the trouble," he muttered. "My racket *is* the rackets." And with Polly home, he had to be hiding that fact from *her* all the time. Sooner or later she'd figure out he was only taking up space at Pleiades. But one hundred big ones!

Votrian was no schmuck. You needed something upstairs just to stay afloat in Hollywood. And Fatso, the distributor, didn't look like they were holding benefits for him. Okay, forget it, Hash told himself. You're not taking the food out of Polly's mouth if you pass on this. He lit another cigarette. He had seen Nick's other pictures. Polly had asked to see them, and one afternoon in a screening room at Pleiades, they watched *One Magic Moment*, *Forever Faithful*, and *Dare to Love*. Hash had to admit, he didn't think of leaving.

Around noon the next day, Hash found Polly on the patio. "You still like that picture, angel?"

"I love it . . . Hash!" She wrapped her arms around him. "You're wonderful!"

"I'm something," he said.

Polly kissed Hash and slung her arm through his, walking to the garage with him. "Would you like to take my car?"

"I'm too old for your car." Hash touched the tip of her nose. "You're starting to peel."

At Pleiades, Hash opened the door between his office and Nick's. "Have you ever seen a hundred grand?"

Nick came out of his chair. "You will soon be very rich."

"I am rich," Hash said. "Hanging around you could make me very poor." He tossed his hat on the desk. "I'll go up and see Votrian."

Twelve days after the Riverside review, *Maiden Voyage* opened at a neighborhood theater in New York. Around nine o'clock that night— midnight in the East—Nick's telephone rang. He felt a fluttering in his leg, and his flawed hand ached. "Ace?"

"Here it is," said Ace Redding in Manhattan. He held a folded newspaper in a drugstore telephone booth on Broadway and Fiftieth Street. Redding was a free-lance press agent who had worked on *Forever Faithful*. "This is Wesley Alton Greer," Ace said. "The dean's review for tomorrow's paper. Nick?"

"Read it."

Redding plastered the newspaper against the wall of the telephone booth. "Here we go," he said, and read aloud:

> Now and then but never, alas, often enough, a fresh and original film appears to cancel out the hundreds—over five hundred last year—of repetitive, predictable, lackluster motion pictures which Hollywood issues week after dull week. The welcome arrival is Maiden Voyage.
>
> It docked in New York yesterday, and is the most sophisti-

cated, witty comedy to escape the California abattoirs in longer than a weary skeptic can be expected to remember.

Escape is the decisive word. The preview cards for Maiden Voyage were almost unanimously negative. Nobody liked the film. Nobody liked the people or approved of what they did. Predictably, the savage indictment raced through Hollywood like one of California's flash fires. Maiden Voyage was pronounced dead on arrival.

The distributors, legally contracted to show the picture, were obviously determined to let it sink without a trace. Why else would they open Maiden Voyage at the Riviera, a tiny art house so far north in Manhattan one expects to meet Commodore Perry taking shelter in the lobby? The distributors hoped to bury their turkey quickly. Some turkey.

They might have succeeded if the name Nick Gallanz had not been on the picture. He is, with a newcomer, Leonard Votrian, the producer of Maiden Voyage, and he also collaborated on the screenplay. Gallanz is a young Austrian who escaped from the Master Race.

This is his fourth film. The first three were made at Majestic Pictures, and despite the penny-pinching pincers Meyer Milgrim keeps around his productions, Gallanz's movies were distinctive and unique. He had flair.

Free of Milgrim, all which lay implicit in Gallanz's previous films now appears on the screen. Maiden Voyage is a gem.

The story is a treat. Eric is a mama's boy. Far from denying the indictment, he revels in it. So does Mama. They adore each other. Eric adores all women, including some of his friends' mamas. And she is very proud of her son. She regards his conquests much as the mother of an Olympic champion basks in her boy's achievements.

But Mama is no fool. She won't be around forever, and someone will need to look after Eric and provide for him. So she scouts around for a rich, eligible young woman, in that order.

Eric is no fool, either. Mama doesn't have to convince him. They descend on Karen, their prey, like Attila and his mother. Karen doesn't have a chance. Even her sister falls for Eric. Karen's mother succumbs. Her father welcomes the son he never had.

Divulging more of the plot would be criminal. Nick Gallanz and his accomplices deserve your uninformed attention.

Chief among them is Champ Gallagher, the director. He is an old hand who has been one of Hollywood's better directors for a long time. Maiden Voyage makes him one of the best.

Gallagher allows Paul Darcy to play Eric with just enough aplomb. He lets Gladys Loring sail through Mama without losing her verve. You believe her, believe her outlandish schemes.

Dieter Rantzau, another émigré, heretofore limited to bit parts, will be a walk-on no longer. Rantzau is a handsome fellow with the perfect posture for uniforms and dinner jackets. Gallanz saw something more than a clothes horse. Playing Karen's father, Rantzau displays a splendid comedic instinct, and in a touching scene where he comforts his daughter, he taps a dramatic lode worth future exploitation.

In his pictures Nick Gallanz pleads a single, self-same case. He asks us to remember the world will not always be at war, that the killing will cease. He abjures the battlefield to remind us of man's humanity, his insatiable zest, his celebration of life.

Redding kicked open the folding door of the telephone booth. "Nick? Hey, did you pass out on me?" Ace laughed and said, "I didn't want to tip my mitt, so I just said I had the review. Hey, maybe I ought to go into pictures. I'm pretty good, right? Nick?"

"I'm here," Nick said, standing. His eyes smarted. "I'm here."

"Bet on it, buddy boy," Ace said. "From now on you're right there on top." He waved the newspaper and cried, "Wait, I saved the best part for last! Here's the headline on the review: 'MOVE OVER, MOLNAR. YOU TOO, LUBITSCH!' " Ace giggled. "You, too, Lubitsch. How do you like them apples?"

"I like the apples," Nick said quietly, as though he did not want to be overheard. "Send me that review," he said. "Buy ten, twenty papers and send them air mail."

"First thing in the morning," Ace said.

"Tonight," Nick said. "Go to the post office right now."

"On my way," Ace said.

Nick put down the telephone, then called Hash. Loretta answered. "Him and Miss Polly are both out."

Nick called Magda, but there was no answer. He called Sigrid, listening to ring after ring. He had no one to tell. Nick walked through the villa, bright with lights, listening to his footsteps, and stopped beside the basket of darts. "Sam."

He wanted to tell Sam, to see his kind, gentle face. He wanted to empty bookstores for his brother and bury him in books. He wanted to tell his mother and father, send them out to buy furs and diamonds. He wanted to drive them through Beverly Hills urging them to choose a house, any house. He wanted Sam to choose a house for the books. He wanted them at one table in the Ringstrasse, eating and drinking.

Carly and Fritz had even turned his triumph into defeat.

Nick took a dart in each hand, throwing at the board, right, left. He threw again and again before he finally whirled around in a rush. In the entrance he grabbed a satchel on the closet floor, carrying it out of the villa, hurrying down the flights of steps as though he was late.

At the garage Nick turned up the lights inside and out. He pasted a target to the garage door and returned to the satchel on the rim of the driveway. Nick raised the Beretta and squeezed off, shooting fast. He emptied the clip, filled it, and raised the automatic again. He did not pause to examine the bull's-eye. He shot like someone in battle, shooting until he had used up all the ammunition in the satchel.

In Malibu that night Votrian listened as his brother Sheldon, a New York physician on Central Park West, finished reading Wesley Alton Greer's review. "Len, you're a smash hit!"

"Yeah, thanks," Votrian said. He hit his chest with his fist. He could feel his whole dinner coming up.

"I'll send this to you, Len," his brother said.

"Sure, thanks." Votrian heard his wife calling.

"It's just now sinking in on me," said his brother. "Do you realize what you've got, Len? You've got a gold mine. This is Wesley Alton Greer. In New York he's the be-all and end-all."

"It's great," Votrian said. "I appreciate your calling, Sheldon."

"It's terrific!" said his brother. "You should see Naomi. She's prancing around like this is her picture. Len, I'm proud of you! It's almost one o'clock here. I'm making rounds six hours from now and I'm not even sleepy." Votrian's wife called him again.

"Get some sleep," Votrian said. He left the telephone, walking to the deck.

"Len, come to bed, you'll be dead tomorrow," his wife said.

"Will you for God's sake stop yelling!" Votrian yelled. "And don't come downstairs with your goddamn recipe for hot chocolate!"

On the deck Votrian stood against the wooden rail, facing the Pacific. Moonlight flickered on the waves. He had made a deal with that hoodlum, and Pertsick would be coming to take *Maiden Voyage* away from him. Sheldon had read him one review. Votrian counted the newspapers in New York: the *Trib*, the *New York Herald Tribune*, the *New York Times*, the *Mirror*, the *News*. Those were just the morning papers. The *Sun*, *Journal-American* . . .

At Pleiades early the next morning, Ace Redding called from New York. "Nick? You won't believe this! *Maiden Voyage* opens on Broadway Thursday!"

"You're sure?"

"I got my sources, kiddo," Ace said. "The day after tomorrow. You haven't seen the other reviews. Wesley Alton Greer is mild compared to some of the other notices. Don't say it, they're on the way. Boy, do I ever wish I was working on this picture."

"You are working on this picture," Nick said. "You begin now, today."

"Hey, great," Ace said. "Listen, I don't want you thinking I did this to hit you for a job."

"You are wasting time," Nick said, and heard Fritz saying the same four words in the palace in Vienna as he gave Nick the Safe Conduct.

That afternoon, Hash stopped in the doorway between his office and Nick's. "You're buying a movie today."

"You know nothing?" Nick left his desk.

"Like what?" Hash had never seen him smile.

"Last night . . ." Nick began. Hash didn't interrupt. "Thursday the picture comes to Broadway," Nick said. "I won't make you poor."

"Too early to start counting," Hash said.

Votrian had been practicing all day just in case the hoodlum showed up. He couldn't come across like a dope, and he couldn't treat the hoodlum like a dope. When Grace buzzed and said, "It's Mr. Pertsick," Votrian was prepared. He didn't jump up from the desk to welcome the man with open arms. He didn't look happy, he didn't look sad. "I'm glad you came by."

Hash dropped his hat on Votrian's desk. "We got some unfinished business."

"Right," Votrian said. "You used exactly the right words. 'Unfinished' business," he said, rising. "Speaking of business, I'll admit I'm a hardheaded businessman. I like a dollar as much as the next man, maybe more." Votrian faced Hash, grimacing, looking embarrassed. "I'll say it plainly, I'm stealing your money. It's not fair. I can't steal money from a man."

It figured, Hash thought. Nick knew, so this guy knew. This guy probably knew ahead of Nick. "A deal's a deal."

Votrian grimaced. "Sure, a deal's a deal," he said. "But both parties should be satisfied."

"I'll take my chances," Hash said.

"No, positively not," Votrian said, raising his hands and wigwagging. "It's not right. I can't let you do this. Look, that night in Riverside you saw a man who saw he had a flop on his hands, a drowning man. I was a drowning man." Votrian nodded, his head bobbing. "Looking for a lifeline." He stopped in front of Hash. "I'm not drowning." Votrian put his hands on his chest, fingers spread. "I'm healthy, I've got my health. I've still got my head on my shoulders. Tomorrow is another day. Today is another day. What's done is done." He raised his hand, shoving aside the past. "So we'll forget Riverside."

"Yeah," Hash said, taking an unmarked white envelope out of his inside jacket pocket. "Here's the hundred."

"I told you . . ." Votrian said, shaking his head. "No, no, I can't."

Nick removed two checks from the envelope. "Fifty grand each," he said. "They're out of two banks: Minden, Nevada, and the other one is from San Diego." Hash set the checks on Votrian's desk.

"You're not listening," Votrian snatched the envelope from Hash's hand. "Absolutely not. I couldn't live with myself," Votrian said, stuffing the checks into the envelope. "I couldn't take a man's money like this." He pushed the envelope into Hash's hand.

"Yeah." Hash slipped the 'flap into the envelope. The guy tired him out. He raised the envelope, wiggling it. "You sold me a picture, *Maiden Voyage*."

"Mr. Pertsick, I'm trying to tell you I don't hold you to this," Votrian said.

"Yeah." Hash dropped the envelope on the desk. Votrian swooped down on it. "Don't," Hash said. "And don't do any more talking either. We made a deal. You got the money. I got *Maiden Voyage*, me and my partner. Cash those checks. If you don't cash them checks, I'll still own *Maiden Voyage*, and if anyone asks, you'll say, 'That's right. He owns *Maiden Voyage*.' That's what you'll say." Hash reached for his hat.

Hearing Hash return, Nick went through the connecting door. "Did he make trouble?"

"How could he? A deal's a deal," Hash said.

Two weeks after *Maiden Voyage* came to Broadway, the motion picture opened in Chicago, Washington, Miami, Philadelphia, St. Louis, Los Angeles, and San Francisco. By the end of the week *Maiden Voyage* was the largest-grossing movie in each of those cities.

Polly seized upon the grosses, volunteering to work with the distributor every morning for the previous day's box office receipts. She woke before Loretta and often saw the newsboy delivering the *Los Angeles Times* as she drove down Roxbury Drive. She had coffee ready for Nick every morning, and she kept the door between the two offices open: hearing him move around, listening to his voice, brought him closer.

Hash missed her. He liked having her there when he came down to the patio, liked watching her in the pool or following the gardener. She knew a whole lot about the flowers out there. Now if he wanted to see her, he had to chase Polly down at Pleiades.

One afternoon Hash came into Nick's office. "Polly says Darryl Zanuck called. Why?"

"I suppose he has a deal."

"You suppose?" Hash took out a pack of cigarettes. "You didn't talk with him?"

"I had Michael Serlin here."

"The guy who wrote *Maiden Voyage*?" Hash asked. Nick nodded. "You stuck with the Hungarian over Zanuck?" Hash picked up the telephone. "The Hungarian's gone. That leaves Darryl Zanuck. Call him."

"You're a partner," Nick said. "You call him."

Hash returned to his office, and soon Nick's phone rang. "He'll get back to me," Hash said.

Hash sat at his desk until almost six o'clock. A few minutes afterward he returned to Nick's office. Behind him, Polly slid along the wall, stopping behind the doorjamb. "It's a deal, all right," Hash said. "The studio lawyer called. We stay independent, same as we are now. But we're on salary: three grand a week. Three grand *each*. Remember, we're only starting to talk. This is Zanuck's offer. We come back with an offer. They want us, kid. Zanuck's lawyer is talking for Spyros Skouras, the money man. They're giving us a studio, not this pisspot. And independent. You answer to nobody."

"Except Zanuck," Nick said.

Hash walked to the windows, facing the dusty studio street. "Will you talk to them?"

"You talked."

Hash looked back at the wetback. "You never were going to do it, were you? Listen to them?"

"One man makes a picture," Nick said. "Darryl Zanuck makes his pictures. I make my pictures."

"You're sweet, you are," Hash said. He lit a cigarette, holding the match. "What happened to 'we,' pal?"

"We are two sweet guys," Nick said.

Darryl Zanuck and Twentieth Century-Fox were only the first suitors to reach Pleiades. Adolph Zukor sent an emissary from Paramount who approximated Zanuck's offer of an independent unit, a share in the profits, and an enormous salary against profits. Jack Warner extended an invitation to lunch in his dining room on the Burbank lot. Nick agreed only to please Hash, who brought Polly.

In that same week the three lunched at R.K.O., and five days later they returned to the San Fernando Valley for a meeting with executives at Universal in Universal City. "All I'm doing is gaining weight," Hash said.

Their last offer was the accolade. Louis B. Mayer at Metro-Goldwyn-Mayer summoned them to Culver City. "No more," Nick said, patting Hash's middle. "You are too fat."

"We *can't* pass on this," Hash said. "This is Louis Mayer."

"The only true independent studio producer in the history of Hollywood was Irving Thalberg," Nick said. "When he died, Mayer celebrated."

"Let's settle this," Hash said. "If we're in the picture business, why aren't we making a picture?"

"We've started already," Nick said. "You heard of *Domino?*"

Hash could see Polly against the windows, smiling. Everyone knew about it except him. "The woman spy story?" Hash took a cigarette from his pack.

"Michael Serlin is writing a treatment."

"Hash, it's a wonderful story," Polly said. "Every actress in Hollywood would love to play *Domino.*"

Hash lit his cigarette. "You got a short memory, pal," he said to Nick. "You were fired out of Majestic because you wouldn't make that story. Milgrim owns that story."

"Nobody owns Domino," Nick said. "Nobody owns Napoleon or Abraham Lincoln or Caesar and Cleopatra."

"And nobody wants two pictures about the same dame," Hash said.

"I'm not making two," Nick said.

Hash dragged on his cigarette. "Are you trying to get even with Milgrim?"

Nick reached for the rubber ball in his pocket. "Me?"

The following afternoon, on a day of brutal heat, Polly came into Nick's office. "Would you like to drive out for a swim in our pool?"

"I never swim in my pool," Nick said.

The heat did not break. Later in the week, Polly said, "Let's have a picnic. Loretta can fix us a basket." Polly had never been forward with a man. "I know a place beyond Paradise Cove where we'll have the beach to ourselves."

"I'm working with Michael Serlin," Nick said.

Polly swore never to come near him again, but the following Monday, after a weekend which became an eternity, she arrived at the studio long before anyone else. She wrote, "Everyone says this is wonderful," across a *Variety* advertisement for the new Bogart movie. "Warner's is screening it at eight tonight."

Nick soon carried the trade paper into Hash's office. "Serlin invited me to dinner," he said, and afterward he telephoned to invite himself.

On Friday, beyond caring, Polly came to him with tickets for the Hollywood Bowl. "It's an all-Gershwin concert."

"Polly, I cannot," Nick said, hoping she would quit.

She almost tore up the tickets in front of him. She almost gave the tickets to a passerby in the studio street, an extra in a British commando uniform, his face and hands blackened. She drove toward Beverly Hills but turned at La Brea. She could not face Hash and Loretta and act cheerful all through dinner.

Polly ate a hamburger at a drive-in and drove to the Bowl, one of the first to park and climb the steps. She read every word in the program, including every word in the advertisements, and when the lights came up in the bandshell and the vast hollow darkened, she welcomed the night, sitting with her arm across the empty chair meant for Nick.

After the concert, in the convertible in the traffic jam on Highland Boulevard, Polly hummed a song, sharing Ira Gershwin's lovesick lyrics with Nick. Singing, her voice cracked and she began to cry, lowering her head to hide from the cars flanking her.

In that same week, Polly went to the Ringstrasse early one evening. During the shooting of Maiden Voyage, Nick had often brought her and Hash to the café from the studio. "You are Nick's friend," said Leopold Unger, who remembered every patron.

"There'll be two," Polly said. "My brother." She had never lied.

Leopold said, "Come," but she stopped him. "Could I—we—have something on the side?" she asked.

Leopold took her straight to a table near Nick's corner, seating her in a chair facing Nick's chair. "While you wait for your brother, I'll send you a vermouth cassis."

As she sipped the aperitif, the café filled. The sound of voices and laughter made Polly's longing unbearable. She vowed not to turn around and look for Nick, but three times in the next hour she tried to find him somewhere among the crowded tables. "Your brother is late?"

She looked up at Leopold. "He may not have received the message," she said.

"You must have dinner," he said.

"No, no." She could not stand to look at food. "I'll wait a little longer if you don't mind."

"I only mind if you leave," Leopold said.

Around eight o'clock he returned with a waiter carrying a tray. "Here is a tafelspitz," Leopold said, opening a napkin and dropping it in her lap. "If you find a good tafelspitz in Vienna, you are lucky. In Hollywood it is a miracle."

Polly could not escape. Leopold stood over the table, waiting for her endorsement. She could not disappoint him, and even when someone called him away, Polly continued to swallow the food dutifully, like medicine, until she could safely leave the table and the crowd and her glaring solitude, and slip unnoticed into the night.

When Hash came home later, he saw a light on in Polly's room. In the garage he looked at the clock in the La Salle dashboard. Almost two bells.

He couldn't go busting in on her. Christ, she was a college graduate. Hash got into bed and heard a noise, the bed creaking or Polly opening a window. He turned on his side, his back to her wall. He had a hell of a time falling asleep.

Hash woke early, early for him. He went downstairs in his robe, the first time ever. Loretta came out of the kitchen. "You all right?"

"Yeah, fine. Polly around?"

"Left a little while ago," Loretta said. "Nobody in this house eats anymore. Said she had to fix her suitcase."

Hash felt like someone had whacked him in the belly. He couldn't find a cigarette in the robe. "Suitcase?"

"She had this little suitcase," Loretta said. "Her favorite, she said. Said she spilled something in it way back and been meaning to do it over." Loretta didn't like the way he looked. He looked all out of gas. "How's about some coffee anyhow?"

"Yeah, coffee," he said. Hash walked through the house searching for cigarettes.

Around five o'clock that afternoon, Polly walked by Nick's office, waving good-bye. She drove from Pleiades into Cahuenga Boulevard, passing the entrance to the Hollywood Bowl and turning into a road which brought her to Mulholland Drive. She drove into the setting sun, twisting and turning for miles until she reached Benedict Canyon. Polly parked on a shoulder high above the orchards in the San Fernando Valley. She lowered the top on the convertible and locked the doors. Carrying her suitcase, Polly walked down into the canyon, darting onto the narrow dirt road leading to Nick's villa.

She stopped below the three levels of steps, head raised to the white Moorish castle with its minarets and battlements. Polly smiled, triumphant. She could hear Nick: "A lock cannot keep you safe. If someone is after you, he will find you." Polly climbed the steps and opened the heavy, arched door of the villa.

She saw signs of Nick everywhere: the stacks of manuscripts, a forgotten necktie, a forgotten drinking glass, newspapers on the floor. She walked through the villa slowly, like someone in a museum determined to see everything. She circled the lofty drawing room, touching the dart board, the darts in the basket, touching a chair, a table. Nick was all around her.

In his bedroom, Polly parted the drapes and raised the windows. She took the sheets and blankets from the bed, and found the linen closet facing the bathroom door.

She had been making her bed since her first summer at camp. When she finished, she carried the suitcase into the bathroom and undressed, folding her clothes neatly. Then she showered, drying herself with Nick's towel. She got into the nightgown Hash had sent her for Christmas. Polly had brought a book, George Eliot's *Silas Marner*, which she had always vowed to finish.

Polly left the bedroom door ajar. She pulled the drapes, shutting out the world. In bed she smoothed the covers, straightening the white collar of the top sheet over the blanket. She pushed herself up on the pillows and opened *Silas Marner*. She looked at the light from the bed lamp, which crossed the floor to the open door. Polly raised the book, determined to read.

As Nick turned off Benedict Canyon that night, he passed a black Buick Limited sedan. Hash squashed his cigarette in the ashtray. He had found the convertible on Mulholland Drive before telling Muley Rose where to park. "Give it awhile," Hash said. "Open your window some."

Hearing the door, Polly closed the book as though she had been caught. She could hardly breathe. "Hurry," she whispered.

Nick pulled off his jacket. He felt dry and went into the kitchen, where he filled a glass with ice cubes and water. He held the glass with both hands and then put it against his forehead. Nick drank deeply, almost emptying the glass.

He climbed the stairs, carrying his jacket. He saw the light from his bedroom, but the villa was dotted with lights he forgot to dim. He yawned as he pushed the door.

"Hello," Polly said.

Nick's immediate impulse was to yank her out of his bed and kick her behind. His annoyance gave way to anger, but she looked at him with such pathetic naïveté and hope that he only shook his head in bewilderment and defeat. "Where are your clothes?"

She did not reply. "You have clothes," Nick said. "Where did you leave them?" When she remained silent, he wheeled, plunging into the bathroom.

He found the open suitcase, then her folded clothes. He brought them into the bedroom. "Get dressed."

Nick started for the door, but Polly said, "No!" in such anguish that he could not leave her. He came to the bed knowing that anything he did would be cruel. "You thought—" he began, and broke off, rubbing his right hand with his left. "You believed if you . . . I—" he said, and stopped once more. "Put on your clothes."

"Don't leave!" Polly said. "Please don't leave me!"

"Polly, Polly, Polly. Nothing will happen here tonight," Nick said. "Nothing will happen if you are here tomorrow night."

She turned away. "Am I so undesirable?"

Nick sat down on the bed. "You are most desirable," he said. "You are beautiful. Young, alive, full of life, a beautiful child."

"Child!" Polly said, hating him and hating herself more. "I am not a child!"

"Listen to me," Nick said, taking her hand. His warm fingers on hers made her heart turn over. "We cannot," he said.

"Because I'm Hash's sister," she said.

"If you must have a reason, I will give you one," he said to end the fiasco. "You have never been with a man."

She hated him for his cruelty. "You're wrong!" Polly said in a fury. One of her nightgown straps slipped over her shoulder, and she pulled it back in place. "I have been with other men. I'm not a baby. I've been with many men," she said. "Here, and in New York, and . . . Boston," she said, remembering a night she had spent in a Boston hotel after a party to which a Harvard senior invited her.

"Still . . ."

"You think I'm lying," Polly said.

"I think you should go home," Nick said. "Now." He started to rise, but Polly grabbed him, sitting erect, wishing she could disappear, raging at herself and at him, unable to stop the tears which welled up in her eyes, and when Nick said, ever so gently, "We will forget tonight," something inside snapped. She raised her hands, making fists, and pummeled him.

Nick tried to grab her hands, but Polly was too quick, too furious. Weeping, she became frantic. Nick said, "Stop! Stop!" raising his arms in front of his face. She could not stop. Her little fists were like rocks pelting him, and when he struck out with both hands, she gasped and attacked again. Nick pushed her hard, and she fell into the pillows. Sobbing, she was lunging for him when she saw Hash come through the doorway.

She saw a man with Hash, saw Hash's face twist like something hurt. Her arms fell as Nick heard movement behind him. He sprang up from the bed, and Polly, facing Hash, wanted to die.

Muley said, "You sonofabitch," as Hash, facing the bed, raised his arm like a turnstile. Polly was alone between the sheets, and she was the only one without clothes. "Wait down below," Hash told Muley flatly. "Do it."

"You, too," Nick said. He stopped in front of Hash. "The lady must dress." He followed Hash, closing the bedroom door.

Muley stood at the foot of the stairs, watching Hash come down, watching the other fellow in case the bum tried something. "You made a big mistake," Nick said.

"Yeah."

"Take him and go," Nick said. "Quick, before she comes."

In the entrance hall Hash discovered his hat. He removed it, wiping the sweatband with his handkerchief. "Stuffy in here."

Nick opened the door wide. "Get out. You'll make it worse for her."

"Don't push," Hash said. He lit a cigarette, and as he waved the match to kill the flame, Polly appeared above them, carrying her suitcase. Nick stepped back, giving her room, but Hash didn't move.

Polly looked right through him as she walked across the entrance hall. "I'll see you in the morning," Nick said.

Hash nodded at Muley. "Close the door," and to Nick quietly, "You'll never see her." He dropped the cigarette onto the terrazzo floor and extended his hand. "Give me the piece."

"You . . . ?" Frowning, Muley said, and Hash sprang at him.

"Gimme!" Muley got the gun from his shoulder holster, and Hash took it. "I've never used one of these," Hash said. "I swore I'd never touch one, but you've made a liar out of me."

Hash raised the gun until the muzzle was inches from Nick's face. "I know you're tough," Hash said. "You seen it all over there in the old country. Here's something nobody ever saw, a rod in my hand. Stay away from her, pal. If she calls, hang up. If she shows up, run. Don't tell me you're innocent. I don't give a good fuck if you're Jesus. If I see her crying again, I'll kill you."

— 15 —

IN POLAND ALL THROUGH
the end of 1944, Fritz heard reports of Russian victories. At night, late
in December, Fritz heard German mechanized units, tanks and armored
vehicles, retreating on the Eastern Front. One morning as the prisoners
filed into the shoe factory, Fritz saw German troops in the distance. He
went to the guard commander's hut beside the gate for binoculars. The
gray soldiers looked like his Jews: gaunt, exhausted, shuffling across
the barren, frozen plain.

On Christmas Eve, alone in the commandant's house, Fritz heard
the hollow, muted booms of big guns. They kept him awake, and he
left the house at first light as the Russian artillery maintained the bombardment. Crossing the yard to the gate, Fritz saw a column of German
troops, and beside them a convoy of vehicles, all moving west. The
bombardment stopped later Christmas morning, but the retreat of men
and machines did not.

The retreat continued day after day. Fritz saw German troops constantly. One morning Lieutenant Jurgen Kuhl, the guard commander, joined him at the gate. "Another lost battalion," Fritz said.

"Four battalions, Commandant," Kuhl said, pointing with his cane. "You're looking at a regiment. Another *regiment.*"

"Don't give up, Jurgen," Fritz said.

"I took an oath to fight, Commandant, not to surrender."

"Good man," Fritz said. "If you run across Lemski, send him to me."

Around noon, Oscar Lemski came puffing into Fritz's office. The bedraggled Pole wore the same mismatched uniform and held the same overseas cap in his hands. "Here I am, Baron. Something wrong?"

"New Year's is upon us," Fritz said. He took money from his pocket. "Bring me some wine, Lemski. French, not a Polish farmer's pressing."

Lemski grimaced, turning the overseas cap in a circle and shifting his weight from one foot to the other. "Impossible, Baron. You can't find wine in these parts," Lemski said.

"Go into the city," Fritz said.

"Especially in the city," Lemski said. "Between their army and the Gestapo, they—"

Fritz clamped his hand over Lemski's mouth. "Three or four bottles," Fritz said, releasing him. "Not less than three."

Lemski didn't move. "I'm afraid, Baron," he said. "Hoarding means death and hoarding wine is torture, then death. You remember when they were here." Lemski waved his overseas cap. "Those two from the Gestapo sitting out there. They're bad. They were always bad, but now—"

Fritz interrupted, "I'm worse. Believe me, Lemski, I am worse. Three or four bottles."

On New Year's Day, Fritz left his office after the prisoners had been fed their noon gruel, crossing the yard to the factory. At one end, running the width of the building, stood the packing table. Here the finished shoes were inspected, tallied, and stacked by sizes for packing and shipping.

Fritz joined one of the packers, a tall, solid man with a friar's fringe of hair circling his bald head. "Mannheim?"

"Julius Mannheim, yes, sir," the man said. He appeared stronger and healthier than the others at the packing table or at the machines. "At your service, sir."

Fritz beckoned, walking away from the table. Mannheim followed. He had been a custom tailor in Frankfurt, a skilled craftsman much in vogue who had stayed afloat by volunteering to mend clothing for his captors regardless of rank. He remained eager and obliging, constantly soliciting work among the guards. Mannheim's nights were occupied with needle and thread. He worked in the guards' barracks, in the officers' quarters, in the mess hall, and there he managed to supplement the slop ladled out to the other prisoners. Mannheim had never gone hungry in his filthy prison stripes. "What can I do for you, Commandant?"

"Wear and tear, Mannheim," Fritz said. "Some minor repairs."

"I'll fetch my kit," Mannheim said.

"The Fatherland claims first priority on your talents," Fritz said. "Back to your duties. Come after the whistle."

Fritz went from the factory to his quarters. He took a suit from a hanger and removed the suit coat. He ripped a pocket, then the sleeve lining at the yoke. He took a razor and cut a trouser leg along the seam. He used the razor on his overcoat and on a heavy sports jacket. He made a mound of clothing for Mannheim. When the factory whistle sounded, ending the workday, Fritz carried the mutilated wardrobe into the small parlor, dumping it into the middle of the room. He could see Mannheim crossing the yard, carrying a small suede bag gathered at the top by a drawstring. As the tailor knocked, Fritz said, "Enter."

Mannheim dropped to his knees beside the clothing like a prospector before a mother lode. "Why have you waited, Commandant? You should have come to me long ago," Mannheim said.

"Agreed," Fritz said. "I've made a New Year's resolution to summon you at the first sign of a loose thread." He watched Mannheim choose the sports jacket from the pile and carry it to a chair. "Before you begin, Mannheim."

Fritz went into the kitchen, where he had opened a bottle of wine. He poured the wine into water glasses and carried them into the parlor. "To the new year." Fritz touched his glass to Mannheim's. "To the brotherhood of man."

"To the brotherhood of man," Mannheim said, and to himself, "To your extended agonizing death. May you become a leper with skin falling from your bones. May your eyes drop from their sockets." He sipped the wine. "May your insides rot with cancer. May your throat swell with vermin until you choke."

"Drink up, Mannheim," Fritz said.

The tailor obeyed, continuing his silent stream of venom until he drained his glass. "Thank you, Commandant."

As the tailor repaired the sports jacket, Fritz took Mannheim's glass. In the kitchen Fritz filled it, ignoring his, and carried both glasses back to join the tailor. Mannheim saw the commandant coming and began another mute litany of imprecation. He did not repeat himself. Long practice had made the tailor endlessly inventive. He heaped disease and despair, mishap and misfortune, suffering and agony, on his keeper. "To the new year, Commandant."

"To the new year," Fritz said. He wet his lips. "Not bad, if I say so myself."

"Excellent, sir," Mannheim said, raising his glass. He had hoped for food here in the commandant's quarters, and the wine without food made his head spin. But it kept out the chill.

Fritz moved a lamp. "Let me give you some light, old man." He stood behind the tailor. "Better?"

"Perfect, Commandant," Mannheim said.

Fritz went to the windows, parting the shabby curtains to look into the brightly lit factory yard. Then he swung around, crossing the narrow room. "What kind of host am I? Let me have your glass." He stood over Mannheim, hand extended. "Bottoms up."

Fritz carried the glasses into the kitchen, leaving his untouched. When he returned, Mannheim raised the sports jacket. "Finished, Commandant."

"Well done," Fritz said. "You've earned your reward." He offered Mannheim the tailor's glass and touched it with his own. "To the jacket."

Mannheim drank and looked down at the pile of clothing beside him. "Next?" he asked, moving his forefinger like a wand in a slow, wobbly circle. Fritz saw him swaying in the chair.

"These trousers," Fritz said, bending for the pants he had slit and dropping them in the tailor's lap. Fritz took a chair near the windows, setting his glass on the floor and watching Mannheim at work. The tailor bent over the trousers, sewing along the seam. When he raised the trousers in triumph, Fritz joined him. "You've earned your libation," Fritz said, waiting for the tailor to empty his glass.

After an hour or more, Fritz said, "I shouldn't have given you such a load."

"I am not complaining, Commandant," Mannheim said. He dug his hand into his pouch on the floor, and Fritz stepped forward, thinking Mannheim would fall. But the tailor toppled back into his chair, the wine sloshing in the glass.

"You're working too hard," Fritz said. "You are all working too hard." He began to pace, like a man beset with troubles. "The factory has been undermanned for more than a year. You know that. You have eyes in your head. You see the empty places in the barracks." Fritz stopped, looking into the empty kitchen and the two empty wine bottles. "I keep pleading for replacements, and Berlin keeps promising." Fritz crossed the parlor, stopping beside Mannheim. "You must be getting rusty."

Mannheim's skill with the needle made him the factory tattooist. Every worker in every factory in the Greater German Reich carried seven numbers on his left arm, tattooed when he arrived. "Me, rusty?" Mannheim bristled, fortified with wine. "I'm fast as anyone." He dug into the suede bag, raising his right hand. "Faster."

Fritz saw the steel skeleton Mannheim held, an instrument shaped like a handgun with a butt and a barrel. A needle protruded from the barrel, and suspended from it hung a slender rubber tube filled with indelible ink. An electric cord dropped from the butt. In Mannheim's hand the tattoo gun swayed from side to side like a snake's head. "I can put your name in your chest fast 's you can write it," Mannheim said.

"Maybe I should let you prove that," Fritz said.

In his chair Mannheim made a kind of bow. "At your service, C'mmandant." He put the gun in his lap. "Soon's I finish," he said, pulling the needle out of his striped blouse, where he had stuck it.

"Your devotion deserves a reward," Fritz said, taking Mannheim's glass.

Fritz brought the tailor more wine and watched him sewing the pocket of the suit coat. "Can I trust you, Mannheim?" As the tailor looked up, Fritz said, "I believe I can. I would not have asked if I didn't already have the answer." He squatted beside Mannheim, looking directly at the drunk. All drunks bared their souls. "In my heart I am one of you." Fritz pushed up the sleeve on his left arm over the elbow. "Make me one of you, my friend."

Mannheim dug into the leather bag, and Fritz lifted the tattoo gun from the tailor's lap. When Mannheim took the gun, Fritz reached for the electric cord and plugged it into a socket in the wall. He carried a chair across the parlor and sat down in front of Mannheim. "Are you ready?"

Fritz heard the whir of the motor in the butt of the tattoo gun. "Ready."

"Do, uh, three . . . uh, seven-two-nine-six-three-nine," Fritz said above the whir.

"Take a big drink, Commandant," Mannheim said.

"Nobody gave the others a drink, my friend," Fritz said, and raised his left arm, bending it across his chest. He felt Mannheim's fingers squeezing his wrist, saw Mannheim bend over him, lowering the gun, and felt the needle sting, ten times, a hundred times.

To himself Mannheim said, "In your heart, straight into your heart, into your balls, both balls, into your cock, all the way into your cock, through the pee hole into your cock, into your ass, Commandant, into your asshole, Commandant, up your nose, Commandant, up your nose and eyes and heart and cock and asshole, Commandant," and then, aloud, "Finished."

Fritz pulled down his sleeve hard. "Drink up, Mannheim. You've done enough for one night."

Mannheim raised a pair of trousers. "I have a few more items."

"Tomorrow, old friend," Fritz said. "Now I'll take you home."

Early the next morning, Fritz walked across the yard to the guard commander's hut. His left arm burned, and he kept his right hand over his coat sleeve. He could see steam rising from Jurgen Kuhl's coffeepot on the single electric burner. The lieutenant saw Fritz coming and poured a mug of coffee. "Morning, Commandant."

"Greetings," Fritz said, taking the mug. "Thank you, Jurgen." He looked through the gate. "No lost regiments today?"

"Only a lost Jew," Kuhl said. "Dead in his bunk. Mannheim the tailor."

"Damn. I'm shorthanded as it is," Fritz said. He drank his coffee. "Tell the doctor to bring me Mannheim's stripes. I'm still hoping for replacements."

In the following month, on February 14, 1945, Lemski trudged through Fritz's office. He said, hushed, "Baron," as though they might be overheard. "The Russians took Budapest yesterday, Baron. I heard it last night in town. Hungary is pfffttt. What's next?"

"We go to work," Fritz said. "Get out of here."

The temperature dropped all that day and continued to fall through the night. Early the next morning, Fritz summoned Lemski. "I need some fresh air. Take me to the country."

Lemski had long since accustomed himself to the baron's jokes. "It's freezing out, Baron. Look at the windows. The frost is so thick you can't see through the windows. You'll freeze out there, Baron."

"We'll freeze together," Fritz said. "Fill your gas tank and come back for me."

Sitting beside Lemski in the ancient truck, Fritz saw the guards at the gate, their gloved hands over their ears, hopping from one leg to the other, trying to stay warm. Lemski touched the horn, and the guards opened the gates wide, saluting when they saw the commandant.

A thin layer of clouds lay across the sky, shielding the lemony sun of the horizon. When Fritz could no longer see the factory, he said, "Turn at the next road."

"We never go that way, Baron," Lemski said. "It's like the moon that way. No farmers, nothing. Nothing can grow."

"You'll miss the turn," Fritz said.

Lemski swung onto the unfamiliar road, peering over the steering wheel. They rode away from the sun, heading west across the flat, empty prairie. "Where are we going, Baron?" Lemski had never seen him this way, this quiet. "Baron? Commandant?"

"Be still."

Lemski tried to obey, tried to stay warm in the rickety truck cab. The freezing cold enveloped him, coming through the open window, through the floorboard, through the windshield, which did not close completely. The baron sat beside Lemski like someone made of stone. "You must be getting hungry, Baron."

"You're drifting toward the shoulder," Fritz said.

"How's this?" Lemski asked, swinging out. The baron didn't answer. "I'm right in the middle, Baron." Missing a meal worried Lemski. "Maybe we ought to turn around," he said.

They rode on and on across the ghostly land. "Can't you say where we're going, Baron? I'd like to know," Lemski said. "Unless we turn soon, we'll still be out here when it gets dark."

"Stop," Fritz said.

"I can make it," Lemski said. "I'll just come over a little, see, and swing right around."

"Stop," Fritz said, putting his hand on the steering wheel. "Stop now." Lemski obeyed. "Check the tires," Fritz said. "You may have a flat tire."

"You want to leave me," Lemski said. "Why do—?" He broke off as Fritz shoved him into the door. "Out." Fritz reached over Lemski, opening the door and shoving. Lemski toppled, pawing for the door as his feet found the running board. Fritz put his hand in Lemski's face, pushing, and Lemski fell into the road. "I'll die out here! I'll freeze!" Lemski said, clambering to his feet. "Baron! Commandant!" The truck was moving. Lemski tried to run. "Commandant!"

The lumpy Pole, shouting and pleading, annoyed Fritz. He shifted through the gears quickly, picking up speed. Fritz drove until night fell.

He stopped on the road, curling up on the seat, trying to burrow into his coat, hugging himself in the bitter, penetrating cold.

When the first dull gray of daylight rose behind him, Fritz sat up, rubbing his arms and thighs against the cold. He stepped down from the truck, swinging his arms across his chest and running in place. His breath condensed in a shimmering cloud around him. Shivering, he climbed into the truck cab and turned the ignition key, listening to the slow groans of the engine. When the motor caught, he pumped the accelerator carefully before lowering the emergency brake. As he drove, he watched the gas gauge, and when the needle hovered over the empty mark, Fritz stopped the truck.

Standing beside the fender, Fritz first removed his coat, then his jacket and shirt, letting the garments fall to the frozen earth. Beneath his clothes he wore the filthy striped trousers and blouse which Doctor Kellerman had stripped from Julius Mannheim's body at Fritz's orders.

Fritz took the Beretta from his overcoat. He slipped the automatic into a sling he had made inside his striped pants. He picked up his shirt, carrying it to the gasoline tank at the rear of the truck. Fritz removed the gasoline cap and pushed a shirtsleeve down into the tank, soaking it with gasoline. He made a pile of his clothing and lit the shirtsleeve, dropping the matchbox into the flames, jumping aside as the fire grew. He wanted to warm his hands and feet, wanted to be engulfed by the blazing heat, but he left the truck behind, walking through the frozen fields, a tattooed Jew escaping from the Nazis and trying to stay alive, and when he came to a crossroad, Fritz turned south, following the advancing Russians.

Early on Christmas Eve, 1944, in the palace in Vienna, Zinn stopped in the doorway of the study. "Baroness."

Carly saw Zinn in his overcoat, holding his hat. "We're leaving, Baroness." Zinn wasn't certain she heard him. He said, "Baroness?" as Carly dropped Fritz's letter opener, springing to her feet like someone who had overslept.

"Your presents!" Carly said. "Do you have your presents?" she asked, and saw Matilda, bundled up for the street. Matilda raised a bulging mesh bag she used for the market.

"Everything is here, Baroness," Matilda said. Carly had given them their presents earlier in the day.

"Good," Carly said. Zinn stepped back to let her pass, and Carly took Matilda's arm. "Merry Christmas." Carly could not let them leave from the rear. She held on to Matilda, and with Zinn following, she took them through the palace, past the Great Hall, past the Petit Salon, down the marble steps into the circular entrance. "Merry Christmas." The pair were on their way to Matilda's sister, a nurse whose husband had been killed in Belgium. Carly kissed Matilda's cheek, and the cook, overcome, held her close.

"No one has been as kind," Matilda said.

Carly closed the massive doors behind them as though ridding herself of trespassers. Feeling cold, she hugged herself and then buttoned the cardigan she wore over a cashmere Fritz had given her on another Christmas. Carly felt safe, felt protected in the ancient palace.

In the study Carly wanted to stretch out on the window seat and cover herself with the afghan, but she could not remain. Taking the Christmas presents she had collected for her mother, she left the study to get her coat and snow boots.

In the blacked-out Himmelpfortgasse, Carly saw the glow of a cigarette across the street. The red dot fell into the snow, and Carly knew the Gestapo lookout was on his way to the telephone. She turned away, passing the Mercedes-Benz which would follow her. She had found the Gestapo car in Himmelpfortgasse the day after she lost Max. The Gestapo replaced Max.

Her mother heard Carly's key in the lock and scurried down the long corridor of the apartment. Helga's hair had turned completely gray in the months after her husband had leaped through the apartment window. She was thinner, and she had forsaken cosmetics after Klaus's death. Carly unwound the scarf around her neck. "Merry Christmas, Mama!" She got out of her coat.

"They've been asking for you all day!" Helga said. "They haven't stopped! Quickly!" She tugged at Carly's dress like a terrier.

Carly was weary of their demands. "It's Christmas."

"Later," Helga said, taking Carly through the kitchen and to the maids' rooms by the delivery entrance. Helga had nailed lengths of two-by-four studs across the entrance, top to bottom. They heard the English accent. "Quickly, Carly," Helga said, darting ahead to open a door.

Carly sat down in front of the wireless and took the small microphone. "This is Domino. Come in, Siegfried."

Helga listened, nodding her endorsement. In the week after Klaus's funeral, Helga had come to the palace. "I know everything now," she said. "You have no secrets from me," she said, adding in a whisper, "Domino." She stood over her daughter, who sat at Fritz's desk in the study. "Let me be with you, Carly." She bent forward. "Let me fight them, too!"

Because Carly was under constant surveillance, she had become a kind of messenger. She was ordered to assemble a wireless, gathering the components of the two-way radio from confederates all over Vienna. But she could not keep the wireless in the palace with Zinn and Matilda. When Carly went to her mother, Helga celebrated. "Bring it!" Helga said. "I'll kick my maids out tomorrow. I'll say I can't feed them. I'll say they should join the women's corps!"

Now, in a maid's room, Helga listened to Carly and the Englishman whose code name was Siegfried on the wireless. When Carly set down the microphone, Helga said excitedly, "Merry Christmas!"

Helga locked the room and hid the key in the kitchen. "Did you hear the Russians are in Hungary?" Helga said. "Mrs. Vollmer from the fifth floor told me this afternoon. Her nephew is back from the Eastern Front. He lost a leg. The Eastern Front will soon be the Western Front."

In the serving pantry, Helga took a candelabrum. "We have until eleven," she said. "Enough time for Christmas." Helga had cut long strips of colored paper and decorated a rubber tree. She arranged Carly's presents under the tree. Helga lit the candles. "Papa liked candlelight during Christmas," she said. "He liked the rubber tree. He watered it every Sunday and wound the clocks. On Sunday he became a householder."

They sat in front of the rubber tree opening presents. Helga made tea and brought out sweets she had baked, talking all the while, talking from the kitchen. Carly had long ago learned to retreat within herself before a mission and keep her mind blank. But the exchange on the wireless had transformed Helga. She was supercharged. Carly wanted to cover her ears. "I can do this alone, Mama."

"Impossible! It's too dangerous!" Helga said. They're watching you. I'm just an old housewife. It's Christmas Eve. It's normal for a mother and daughter to be together."

They left the apartment just after eleven o'clock, coming out of the building into the blackout. The long war, the continued bombings, the forced abdication of civic responsibility, had combined to make Vienna a ghost town. Carly and Helga walked through the Inner City, almost deserted at that hour, picking their way through refuse and rubble, through and around mounds of brick and mortar, girders and beams. Helga held on to Carly. "Here is Karntner Strasse."

They turned, entering the heart of Vienna. They encountered

other people walking in the street, and as they approached Stephans-platz, they became part of a crowd. "Can you see the cathedral?" Helga said.

Carly saw everything in the blackout: the outlines of St. Ste-phen's, like a mountain at the edge of the square, saw the open square in front of the mountain. In the blackout Carly could see Nick and hear him. "You brought me here to say good-bye," Nick said. "You're lying. You're still lying!"

She said in torment, "Hurry, Mama, hurry."

Carly could not escape. Nick followed her, and as she walked into the cathedral, Fritz joined them, leading her to the altar. She saw Fritz, saw Nick, and passing a chapel, saw Friedrich Varlingen and heard him. "Light a candle for me, Carly," Varlingen said, and louder, "Light a candle for me," and louder, "Light a candle—"

"Mama!" Carly startled her mother. "We'll sit here," Carly said, pushing her mother into a pew, trying to escape from the past.

"Look at them," Helga said. "Devils in a house of God."

Nazi uniforms filled the cathedral. The soldiers sat shoulder to shoulder, aisle after aisle, as though they were in formation. Carly was confounded. They had tortured and slaughtered millions, yet they came so God could forgive them. How could God forgive them? Carly saw the rows of stolid, scrubbed faces, men with wives and children who had murdered wives and children. Carly felt sick inside. She looked away, staring at the altar. So she did not see Der Chineser against the wall at her right.

He was shown the baroness sitting with her mother. "We have our people on both sides of her, and front and back," said the Gestapo agent who reported directly to Der Chineser morning and night. "She can't do anything here, Major. This is St. Stephen's. It's Christmas Eve. She's here for the midnight Mass like everyone else. We have a place for you, Major."

"Take it," said Der Chineser. The man talked too much. Der Chineser would have dumped him long ago, but he could not get re-placements. For the past two months Der Chineser had been losing men.

He moved back toward the rear of the cathedral, standing behind the pews where he had watched the baron marry her. Der Chineser watched her now. The baroness was like no one else. He didn't believe she had left the palace to mark the birth of the Christ child. Just then he saw the cardinal crossing the transept to begin the Mass.

Der Chineser didn't listen to the cardinal and Carly didn't listen.

She had to wait, and waiting, tried to banish memory. She could not be hindered by memory tonight. Sitting beside her mother, she abandoned the past, dropping into a kind of limbo, lulled by the sonorous cadence of the Mass. In the packed cathedral Carly was alone until her mother said, "Finally," rising as everyone rose.

Carly followed her mother, sidling out of the pew into the line inching toward the altar. Near the front the line of men and women turned left, and over her mother's shoulder Carly saw the priest distributing the wafers for communion. He was a tall young man who needed a haircut. As Helga stopped in front of the priest, she leaned forward and whispered, "Noon after Christmas. Zentralsriedhof," for the central cemetery, one of Vienna's largest. "At the hearse," Helga whispered. As the priest extended the wafer, Carly saw, gleaming, the oversized ring on his finger. She had seen such a ring on another American flyer. Carly followed her mother like someone on tiptoe, and facing the priest she whispered, "Ask the driver, 'Do you have room, Peter?' " On the ring, flanking the stone, were four numbers for the year he had been commissioned, and on the other side, U.S.M.A. for United States Military Academy. The young priest was telling the world he was a downed pilot.

As he offered her the wafer, Carly took his hand in both of hers, pulling the ring and dropping the wafer. "I'm sorry," she said, bending and dropping the ring into her snow boot. She straightened up slowly. The young American flyer gave her another wafer, and Carly moved aside, joining her mother.

Helga put her arm through Carly's, keeping her close. As they made their way toward the doors, Carly felt the big ring slip under her foot. She could not dislodge it, and she could not limp, drawing attention to herself. As they entered the nave, Helga whispered, "Look. Do you see him?"

Der Chineser stood with two Gestapo agents whom Carly recognized from Himmelpfortgasse. "I don't see him," Carly said, "and neither do you." They passed Der Chineser, leaving the cathedral.

"We'll stay with her, Major," said one of the agents.

"We'll all stay with her," said Der Chineser. "Where is your car?"

In Stephansplatz, Der Chineser sent his driver back to the motor pool. "Come for me at seven tomorrow."

"With permission, Major," said the driver. "Tomorrow is Christmas, sir."

"Seven," said Der Chineser, leaving him. The driver, a sergeant, watched him walk away. He hoped the Russians caught up with the nutty sadist.

Der Chineser rode in the front seat of the Gestapo Mercedes, keeping the driver a full block behind the baroness. She brought her mother back to Kruger Strasse. In the darkened lobby Carly took the American's ring from her snow boot and gave it to her mother.

"Here she comes," said the driver as Carly left the building and walked alone through the Inner City. "Lots of soldiers celebrating Christmas," he added. "Lonely soldiers. She's got nerve."

Der Chineser told the driver to stop near the palace. "Well, she's in for the night," said the other agent.

"Call me if she goes out again," said Der Chineser. "And call me if she leaves tomorrow. I'll be in the office."

In Vienna after Christmas in 1944, every day became more perilous than the previous one. The bombings were worse. The food shortages increased. The hospitals were reserved for the military, and the wounded came from every front. In the west the Allies advanced through France, and in the east the Russians advanced everywhere. In Vienna the thought of the approaching Russians terrified everyone.

One morning late in January, Der Chineser's secretary did not appear at the office. He sent his driver to her apartment. The driver returned in an hour. "She's gone, Major," he said. "The whole family's gone. The janitor said he saw them leave Sunday morning. He figured they were going to church, but they didn't come back. He let me into their apartment. They left everything, even the dishes on the table."

In that same week one of the Gestapo detail keeping the baroness under surveillance failed to report to Himmelpfortgasse. Der Chineser told the others to extend their tours. Five days later, another man in the detail disappeared. Der Chineser went to the Hotel Metropole. "I've lost two men."

He was given a requisition form. "You'll never get them," said the Gestapo chief.

One morning in February, Der Chineser's driver did not come for him. He called the motor pool, but there was no sign of his driver. "Send me another one."

"I don't have any, sir," said the sergeant commanding the detachment. "I don't have your car, either, Major. The Gestapo took your car this morning."

Der Chineser left his rooming house, walking to the trolley stop. He waited more than an hour and had to shove his way aboard. A mile from Ottakring he heard the sound of approaching aircraft. Someone yelled, "Bombers!" and someone else yelled, "Stop the trolley! Stop!" Der Chineser fought to keep his footing, and in the street he ran for shelter.

When the air raid ended, Der Chineser managed to find another trolley. Riding to his office, he saw a stream of men and women, some with children and all with luggage, leaving the city.

The exodus continued day after day, becoming an epidemic. The Viennese were running from the Russians. And as they left, they were replaced by Hungarians and Czechs, also fleeing the Russian troops and tanks.

Daily, Der Chineser saw the Greater German Reich collapsing around him. He could not muster a squad of military police. Desertions became commonplace, and those troops who remained were used to guard depots of arms and food against looters. The military police had orders to fire on anyone suspected of looting.

On the last Friday in March, Der Chineser had to walk most of the way to his office. Although he was late, the building was deserted. The only sounds were the sounds he made. Der Chineser left his office again and again, walking through the building, going from floor to floor, opening door after door on the chance he would find someone at his desk.

That night in the rooming house, Der Chineser carried his trunk up from the basement. He had been in uniform since the day German troops and tanks had rolled into Vienna for the Anschluss.

Very early the following morning, Der Chineser opened his trunk and put on civilian clothes for the first time in seven years. He took his overcoat and a cap from the trunk. Der Chineser opened the holster he had worn and removed the gun. Opening his wallet, he removed his identity card with his photograph in the upper quadrant. Der Chineser tore the card into pieces. He became a man without papers, free to construct a new past, but he knew, had always known, that his face condemned him.

Der Chineser remained in his room until he heard movement in the street. Although the end of March had brought warm weather and sunshine, Der Chineser kept his overcoat collar raised and wore his cap low with the bill shielding his face. Colonel Varlingen had taught him never to walk fast, drawing attention to himself: "Melt into the crowd, Emil." So Der Chineser became an idler that morning, strolling through the streets, taking twice the amount of time to reach his destination, a nondescript five-story building.

Der Chineser walked up three flights of stairs, down the end of the corridor, and knocked. He put his ear against the door but heard nothing. Then the door opened slightly, held by a chain. Der Chineser could not see beyond the door. "Let me in."

"Go away," she said.

"It's me," he said. "The major."

"I know it's you," she said. "The hell with you, all of you." She tried to close the door, but it hit his gun barrel.

"Let me in, or I'll shoot my way in," said Der Chineser. "Quick," he said, "or I'll shoot anyway."

She slipped the chain, freeing the door so Der Chineser could enter the apartment. He stepped back against the wall of the short hallway, hidden by the open door, and gestured with the gun. "Lock up," he said.

Zee Zee backed away from him, backed into the door, facing him. She felt for the door chain, watching Der Chineser. "Who are you supposed to be in that disguise?"

"Get away from the door," he said, waiting to follow her.

"You picked a hell of a time," Zee Zee said. Der Chineser had seen her only in a negligee, and when she removed it, in the bra she refused to forfeit for her customers. Now she wore old felt slippers, a dark wool dress, and a wool sweater. A towel lay across her shoulders. "I was ready to fix my hair," Zee Zee said. "Come on, then, but put the gun away."

Der Chineser followed her into the apartment. In the slippers, without her high heels, she seemed like a dwarf. "I'm not here for that," he said.

Zee Zee stopped beside the doorway to her bedroom. Der Chineser could see the big bed and the massive headboard. "Then why did you come?" she asked. "What're you doing here anyway? With your gun," she said. "Scaring the life out of me with your gun."

"I'm—" he said, and stopped. In seven years Der Chineser had never talked to her except in the bed. He had come and paid and gone. "I'm . . . here," he said. "I'm staying a couple of days, maybe longer." He raised the gun, pointing at the windows. "It's the Russians," he said. "They're on the way, they could be in Austria somewhere already." The rooming house had become a trap, like his face, and Der Chineser needed a temporary home.

Zee Zee began to cry, a little, pudgy woman without makeup, with streaks of gray in her dyed hair. She raised the towel around her neck, dabbing her face. "Why did you pick me? Why my place? I'm just an old whore," she said. Der Chineser had chosen Zee Zee for precisely that reason. "I'm all alone, alone in the whole world," she said.

"Stop crying," he said.

She rubbed her face, obeying him. "Now what?"

Der Chineser gestured with the gun. "Sit down," he said, and dropped into a chair.

"Sit down even if I don't want to sit," Zee Zee said, choosing a chair near the bedroom.

Der Chineser waved the gun. "Over on this side," he said.

"So you've made me your prisoner," Zee Zee said, trudging across the overstuffed room with its carpets covering carpets. She sat on a carved chair with a red cushion. "You and your gun," she said, and began to cry. "I can't stay in one place forever," she said. "I never could. I'm not like that."

"Stop crying and do something," he said.

She rose, watching him. "I was going to fix my hair."

"Fix it." Zee walked through the apartment and Der Chineser followed her. She went into the bathroom. "Don't close the door."

Der Chineser remained while Zee Zee began and completed her painstaking, protracted ritual. The fat, seedy little creature was transformed. Her hair sparkled. She became youthful. "I've worked up an appetite."

Zee Zee had made one corner of the apartment a kitchen, shielding the area with a screen. "Now I'll have to feed you," she said.

Der Chineser didn't want anything from the whore. "I'm not hungry."

"If you're not, you will be sooner or later," Zee Zee said. "Rabbit stew." She opened a window, taking a covered pot from the windowsill. While she heated the stew, she set plates and flatware on a small table against the screen. "You can't eat with a gun in your hand."

She emptied the pot onto the plates. They ate without speaking. Afterward, Zee Zee cleaned the kitchen, scrubbing the pot. "Most whores are spotless," she said. "Every once in a while you find a pig, but the rest are the cleanest people you'll find." She moved the screen. "Now I'm supposed to look at your gun the rest of the day."

Der Chineser let her talk. Her chatter was soporific. The familiar apartment became less dangerous than the rest of Vienna. Early that evening, Zee Zee boiled four eggs and shared some bread with Der Chineser. "What if someone comes to see me?" she asked.

"They're all afraid," said Der Chineser. "They're all hiding from the Russians."

"That's how much you know," she said. "Nothing stops a horny man. Someone could come to the door right now."

"Send him away," said Der Chineser.

"Send him away! I have to live," Zee Zee said. "I'm a poor woman, alone." She began to cry.

"Stop it," he said. He reached across the table, taking her arm and shaking it. "I've got money. I'll give you money."

When she had cleaned the kitchen again, she yawned. "Where do I sleep?"

"Where you always sleep," he said. "You can go to sleep."

She looked at him, then at the gun in his hand. "All right, I will," she said. She went into the bedroom, and as she began to undress, he joined her, carrying his overcoat. He closed the bedroom door and folded the overcoat, dropping it on the floor. She watched him lie down against the door, using the overcoat for a pillow. "You'll freeze down there," she said. She took a blanket from a chest and dropped it over him.

In the morning, Zee Zee held up a potato and a slab of bread. "Breakfast," she said. "And lunch and dinner. I have some tea. Enough for today."

As they were drinking tea, they heard a knock on the door. "Send him away," said Der Chineser.

"I've never had anyone this early," Zee Zee said. Der Chineser went to the door with her, standing against the wall. She slipped the chain, opening the door, hiding Der Chineser. "Well, Clara."

A woman said, "The Russians are in Koszeg! The radio says they're coming! With tanks!"

"They're not after you, Clara," Zee Zee said, closing the door. "My next door neighbor," she told Der Chineser. "She's old enough to be my mother, and no teeth."

Around noon, Zee Zee said, "There's no food. Are you going out for food?"

Der Chineser knew if he left the apartment, she would not let him return. He took money from his pocket. "Send the neighbor," he said. "But stay in the hall where I can see you."

"Where have you been? Not in Vienna," Zee Zee said. "What good is your money if it can't buy anything? She can't. I'm the only one in the neighborhood who gets a little food. The butcher is one of my customers."

"She can tell the butcher it's for you," said Der Chineser.

"The whole street can say it's for me," Zee Zee said. "You think everyone is dumb except you. If you want to eat, you'll have to trust me." She took the money from Der Chineser's hand. "Where would I go? To meet the Russians?"

He said, "Wait . . . ," and Zee Zee stopped, the money sticking up from her hand like a child's posy. Der Chineser was all alone. He had only this pariah, a derelict like himself. "All right," he said.

An hour after she left him, he went to the windows. He saw only an enclosure covered with refuse, and remembered she lived in the rear of the building. He went to the door, listening. Once he heard footsteps and stepped back, listening for her key in the lock. But the sound receded. He could not be still. He walked through the small apartment, returning to the door and slipping the chain. He saw half of another door across the corridor. Der Chineser went into the bedroom for his overcoat. He knew now Zee Zee would not return.

He did not know whom she might send in her place. He had forced his way into her apartment, her life. He had terrorized her, eaten her food, made her his prisoner. He was a deserter now, out of uniform, without papers. Der Chineser had sent hundreds of men and women without papers to camps, to their death. He had to run, but he could not leave the apartment yet, not in daylight when his face could convict him.

As night fell, Der Chineser got into his overcoat. He pulled his cap low over his forehead. He dropped the door chain. Holding the gun in his pocket, he stepped into the corridor, moving fast. He came down the three flights of stairs hugging the railing, his face averted, and in the street he hugged the building walls, heading for the outskirts of the city and the woods beyond Vienna.

One week later Carly returned to the palace after an afternoon with her mother. She was setting down two books she had taken from her father's library when she heard a man say, "May I take your coat?"

Carly swung around and saw Fritz. She said, "Where . . . ?" and flung herself at him.

Fritz felt Carly's arms around him, her face against his. He said, "Well . . ." taken aback by her fierce intensity. "Hello."

"Hello, hello, hello, hello," she said, and kissed him. She held on to Fritz, raising her head to look at him. He wore a black turtleneck sweater beneath a jacket of Harris tweed. He made Carly feel as though nothing had changed, as though she had left him after breakfast. Fritz grinned. "I'd know you anywhere."

"Where did you come from? You didn't write," Carly said. "I didn't know where you were, if you were . . . alive."

"Now you know," Fritz said, helping her with her coat.

"You were somewhere in Poland," Carly said.

"That's what I left behind," Fritz said, omitting the Russians. He put his arm around Carly's waist, taking her out of the entrance hall. He needed Domino now. The Russians were in Wiener Neustadt, twenty-five miles from the palace. They had started in Stalingrad, walking over their dead in the rubble of that city, soldiers and civilians, including children. The Russians had not often paused for prisoners, and they would not be a priority in Vienna. Nazis were the target, the Nazis who had slaughtered Russians from the Ukraine to the Neva. Fritz had commanded a factory making shoes for the Nazi army. The Russians could decide he was the enemy. But Domino had been a shining ally, his wife, the Baroness Von Gottisberg.

Fritz took Carly into the study. "This is where I lived," Carly said. "I was less alone here. This is your favorite place, so it became my favorite." He saw the color rise in her face and wondered if another woman in the world blushed like Carly.

"What have I missed? Tell me everything," Fritz said.

For a moment she did not reply. "I will, later," Carly said. "When all this is over, when it's really finished." Then her face brightened, and she smiled and clapped her hands. "Fritz, you're back! You're home!" Carly clasped her hands behind her, rocking from side to side, like a child with a happy secret. She was even more beautiful than he remembered.

"Show me the palace," Fritz said. "There hasn't been a day or night when I haven't longed to be here." He stopped beside her. "Do you mind? I must be certain nothing has changed."

Fritz took Carly through every room down into the wine cellar and high up under the eaves, to corners where he had played in childhood. "I always defended the palace against conquerors," he said. "I'm still defending it."

He had dropped his guard. He had never been as communicative. He had been alone so long, running and on the alert so long, that he forsook caution. He showed her the tattoo on his left arm. "I did not want to be mistaken for a Nazi," he said. Fritz talked all through dinner. Long afterward he stretched his arms. "Carly, your husband is leaving you for clean sheets. Clean sheets!" Fritz said. "I've dreamed of this."

They came up the stairs and Fritz stopped beside his door. "Now I'm home," he said quietly. "Good night, Carly."

"You said good night last time, and this is where I left you," she said, leading him into his bedroom.

When Fritz woke in the morning, he was alone. He got out of bed, stretching, luxuriating in whatever he touched: the floor beneath his feet, the bedpost, the bathroom tile beneath his feet, the lather he produced in the shaving mug, the water in the shower on his body.

He luxuriated in the sight of Carly, in her presence. "Is there anything special you would like to do?" she asked.

Fritz looked directly at her. "I am doing it," he said, grinning as the color rose in her cheeks.

Zinn appeared, rescuing Carly, and Fritz welcomed the interruption, welcomed the humdrum mechanics of the palace schedule. In the study later Fritz telephoned the schloss. "Tell me all runs smoothly, Fiegel," Fritz said.

"All runs smoothly, Baron," said the butler.

Fritz rose. "He's a man in a million," Fritz said, putting his arm around Carly's waist. "Lead on."

For two days the palace was an island of serenity, and then, late in the afternoon, they heard the heavy boom of artillery. "The Russians," Fritz said. "Good!"

Russian infantry reached Vienna in daylight on April 6, 1945. The Nazis fought fiercely. Vienna became a battlefield. In the palace they heard gunfire all through the days and nights. Adolf Hitler cherished the city of his youth, and the German army commanders had orders to stop the Russians.

The Red Army could not be stopped. Seven days after entering Vienna, they captured the city, and Russia's flag flew over the Hofburg.

Fritz opened doors and windows to hear the Russian sound trucks issuing orders to the population. He made Carly listen, summoned Zinn and Matilda. "Good-bye Anschluss!" Fritz said. "Good-bye thousand-year Reich!"

The elimination of the Nazis transformed Fritz. Zinn and Matilda commented among themselves on the baron's high spirits. The Russians had made him a different man. The baron had always lived in a hush. Now his voice could be heard all over the palace.

One morning in the first week of the Russian occupation, Fritz said, "I still haven't seen Vienna. Take me on a tour, Carly."

Fritz strode out of the palace like a drum major. "Look, Carly, no Nazis!" Carly had to move briskly to keep pace with him.

He was indefatigable, and as they continued, insatiable. He wanted to see all of Vienna, leading Carly to Schwartzenberg Platz, past the palace up to the Belvedere and through the gardens, then back down to the Staatsoper, the bombed ruins of the opera house. "We'll rebuild it," Fritz announced, as though he had an audience. "We'll rebuild Vienna."

He reminded Carly of Nick, the early Nick, before the hospital and the Anschluss. His extravagant pronouncements sounded like Nick, full of bombast and hyperbole. Carly wanted Fritz to stop, wanted to leave Nick behind, but he turned toward the Karntner Ring and Carly had to hurry after him. Fritz paused. "Forgive me. It's not every day Vienna is returned to us."

"You're dismissing the Russians," Carly said.

"They'll leave," Fritz said. "All the others left, and the Russians will leave. We'll watch them leave." He took Carly's hand. "Onward!"

Fritz could not check his euphoria, and Carly would not dampen his high spirits. They walked for hours, and when Carly saw the palace once more that afternoon, Fritz seemed ready to start over.

In the palace Zinn said, "Mail delivery began again, Baron."

They went into the study. A few envelopes lay on the desk. As Fritz examined them, Carly saw his enthusiasm evaporate. Fritz turned away and then turned back, as though he had forgotten something. He raised the letter and read again: "Help me, Emil."

"Is it bad news, Fritz?"

Carly forced him into familiar deception. "The pedestrian intrusion of life as usual," Fritz said. "One of our parishioners in the Tyrol pleads for aid. A needy tenant, Carly."

"Fiegel said there were no problems at the schloss," Carly said.

Fritz folded the letter, pushing it into the envelope. "No insoluble problems," he said. He slipped all the mail into his pocket.

On Monday of the following week, Fritz dressed carefully. "Wish me luck, Carly. I'm off to welcome General Tolbukhin," Fritz said. "Greeting foreign visitors is an old Von Gottisberg tradition. I'll probably have to wait my turn, so I'll be gone most of the day."

Fritz took the Daimler to Russian headquarters, leaving his card with General Tolbukhin's adjutant. "In Vienna the House of Von Gottisberg is his house, Colonel." Fritz smiled. "And yours."

An hour later, Fritz left the city. Emil Huebner, Der Chineser, had written from a monastery near the Czechoslovakian border. Fritz drove swiftly, watching the rearview mirror for military vehicles, scanning the countryside for any German soldiers who had eluded the Russians. He did not plan on any delays on his journey.

The monastery sat on the crest of a hill, a miniature sandstone attempt to copy the grandeur of Melk. A hamlet lay at the foot of the hill. A boy with a dog waved at Fritz, and he returned the greeting.

The road curved around the hill, ending at wooden gates built into the monastery, broad enough to admit a tank. An iron latch, thick as an ax handle, protruded from the doors. Fritz got out of the Daimler. He couldn't move the latch. He couldn't find a bell. He hit the door with his fist, but the thickness of the wood muffled the sound.

Fritz went back to the limousine, leaning into the car to put his hand on the horn. He stopped and pressed down again until he saw the latch rise. As he came forward, one door opened, and two monks appeared, both old, with unlined faces and smooth hands coupled against their chests. They stopped in front of the open door, and Fritz knew they would die to save the monastery from harm. One of them had steel gray hair cut short, and he said, "I am Father Bernard, sir, and I apologize for our abdication of hospitality. We are of an order which seeks out those who need us, and these doors are open to all. We close them with shame and dismay, not for our protection but for those who will perpetuate our order. The war has sealed us off from the world, sir."

So Fritz knew Father Bernard was the abbot. "You're too harsh on yourself, Father," Fritz said. "your world has been victimized by war. Faith and hope and charity are the first casualties."

"You are truly kind," said Father Bernard, and his companion murmured, "Alas, alas."

"Austria is a battlefield, Father," Fritz said, "and an army seeks the high ground always."

"Thank you," said the abbot. "How may we serve you?"

"I'm here as a toiler in your vineyard, Father. You have a guest, someone you've taken in and whom you protect, I'm certain. Emil Huebner." Fritz saw the two monks look at each other. "Father, my name is Fritz Von Gottisberg."

The old men squared their shoulders, and Father Bernard said, "Von Gottisberg?"

"We, too, seek out the unfortunate, Father," Fritz said. "Emil Huebner sent for me." Fritz extended Der Chineser's letter.

Father Bernard shook his head, waving his hands in front of him. He turned to his companion. "Go and fetch Emil."

"No!" Fritz stepped forward, ready to grab the monk. "Wait, Father—fathers. May I—?" Fritz broke off, gesturing at the monastery. "I've brought something. I'd like to . . . present it."

"As you wish, Baron," said the abbot.

Fritz went back to the Daimler. He took a dark, lidded wicker basket from the rear seat. "Lead on," Fritz said.

High above, beneath the western slope of the monastery roof, Der Chineser sat on the stool beside his cot. He had asked Father Bernard for chores, but the monks divided the maintenance of the monastery among themselves. Theirs was a scholarly order, with no need for physical labor. Der Chineser had fled into a life of idleness.

He felt the cat and, looking down, saw the monastery's pet rubbing against his leg. The ginger tom had adopted Der Chineser within days of his arrival, choosing his leg beneath the dining table, following him into the cloister when he walked, following him to the cell here beneath the roof.

Der Chineser watched the cat inching its way past his leg, rubbing against him. No animal had ever favored Der Chineser. So he was as uncomfortable with the ginger as with the people he avoided. But he did not chase away the tom, nor discourage it. Now and then, almost surreptitiously, Der Chineser lowered his hand to stroke the cat. As his fingers moved across its spine, he heard a single knock. "Emil?"

Father Bernard. "Yes, here," he said, as though he was answering a roll call. He crossed the shallow cell and opened the door. His heart stopped.

"You have a friend," said Father Bernard. Der Chineser didn't even see Father Bernard.

"Baron," said Der Chineser. He came to attention, hating his monk's cowl, his long hair, the scab on his face where he had cut himself shaving.

"Emil, greetings!" Fritz said. Father Bernard left them, and Fritz stepped into the cell carrying the wicker basket.

"Let me help you, Baron," said Der Chineser, bending, arms extended like an infielder after a ground ball.

Fritz let him take the basket. "You *can* help me, Emil." Der Chineser set the basket on the cot. The lid was fastened with a slender ivory hasp which extended from a cord and slipped through a wicker loop protruding from the basket. Fritz slipped the hasp, raising the lid. The basket was packed solid with delicacies which Fritz had scrounged, at exorbitant prices, since receiving Der Chineser's letter. "Yours, Emil," Fritz said. He raised a wrapped wedge. "Cheese," he said. He raised another package. "More cheese." He held up a jar. "Cornichons.

Beggars can't be choosers, Emil. There's still a war on." He picked up a wrapped cylinder. "Salami," he said, and took another cylinder. "Summer sausage." Fritz dropped both into the basket and pointed. "Liverwurst." He pointed. "Blutwurst. And bread. And sardines!" Fritz said, displaying the tin.

"Thank you, sir," Der Chineser said. "You didn't—"

"I did," Fritz interrupted. "And I have one request. Promise you'll share nothing I've brought you. I brought this for you. Give me your word, Emil." Fritz waited. "Emil, a monk becomes a monk to atone. Your hosts' only pleasures derive from deprivation."

"Yes," said Der Chineser. "You have my word, Baron." Der Chineser almost dropped to his knees. No one ever, anywhere, had been as kind to him.

"Good man," Fritz said. Something about Der Chineser's appearance had puzzled him. As he prepared to escape, Fritz solved the riddle. In his coarse monk's cowl and long hair, Der Chineser seemed at home, a Buddhist in his element. He had ceased being an oddity. "How can I help you?" Fritz asked. Fritz wanted to reach the palace in daylight.

"It's not very comfortable here, Baron. We can talk down below," Der Chineser said.

Der Chineser brought Fritz to the cloister. The court had an Oriental flavor, a rectangle of raked gravel crisscrossed by flagstones. Colonnades ran along all four sides of the court, and within, stone benches were spaced along the walls. Geraniums grew in twenty-four-inch clay pots placed in the four corners of the court. "Sit anywhere, Baron," said Der Chineser.

Fritz chose a bench facing the doors. Der Chineser sat beside him, asking questions about Vienna and Austria. Fritz answered patiently. Der Chineser could not be satisfied. "Emil, I am not a member of the Russian General Staff," Fritz said.

Der Chineser apologized but could not check himself. Fritz sat through a prolonged cross-examination. After more than an hour he said, "Emil, I have a question." Fritz took out his wallet. "How much do you need?"

"No money, Baron. I have more money than I can spend," said Der Chineser. "I . . . ," he said, and stopped as a lanky young monk entered the court carrying a watering pail. When he saw Emil with a visitor, he stopped. "Hello, Emil. I'm Father Casper," he said to the visitor. "Am I disturbing you? I can come back."

"Perish the thought," Fritz said. Father Casper went into a corner, raising the pot to water the geraniums. "Tell me, Emil," Fritz said.

"A gun, Baron," Der Chinese said. "Father Bernard took my gun when he put me in this . . ." Der Chineser tugged at the cowl. "He said a gun was a desecration in the monastery. He got rid of it somewhere, I don't know where."

Fritz watched Father Casper walking to another pot. "I don't travel with a gun," Fritz said.

"I need one," said Der Chineser. "I need protection when I leave, because I can't . . . hide like other people."

"Leave?" Fritz stared at Der Chineser. "Emil, you're safe here." Fritz rose. "Promise me you'll stay."

Der Chineser jumped up. "Sir, don't ask me to do that," he said. "I feel like a coward here. We're fighting in the west."

"Stay until I return with a gun," Fritz said. "Will you do that much?" Fritz slapped Der Chineser's shoulder. "I'll be back."

"Thank you, sir." Der Chineser walked beside the baron. "I know I shouldn't have bothered you, brought you all the way out from Vienna. Now you'll have to make another trip."

"Does the Daimler good," Fritz said. "Blows out the carbon." He raised his hand, waving at the monk. *"Wiedersehen,* Father."

Der Chineser stood at the open door watching the baron turn the limousine in a wide arc and start down the hill. The baron had changed everything. Der Chineser no longer felt like a prisoner, no longer felt trapped. He closed the big door and threw the bolt, and walking through the cloister he waved at Father Casper. "The flowers are beautiful, Father." Der Chineser had never spoken first.

He climbed the stone steps two and three at a time. Der Chineser decided to ask Father Bernard for a pair of scissors so he could cut his hair. He was still a soldier, at least he could look like a soldier. He opened his door and stopped on the threshold. He shook with fury. The contents of the wicker basket covered the floor. Many packages lay torn open. Der Chineser saw slices of salami half eaten, saw teeth marks in wedges of cheese. Der Chineser became homicidal. He plunged into the cell to kill the cat, and then he saw the animal on the cot, almost hidden by the open wicker basket. The big tom lay full length, its eyes wide open, and as Der Chineser came close, he saw the animal's mouth twisted in agony from the poison which had killed it.

16

ON MAY 8, 1945, IN HOL-lywood, Stage Three at Pleiades Pictures was wide open and so were the gates of the studio. So was the makeshift bar on the stage, happily thrown together by the studio grips. Everyone on the lot was on Stage Three, and all had called wives, husbands, brothers, sisters, friends, and acquaintances to the biggest wrap party in town.

The wrap party is a Hollywood tradition. "It's a wrap" signals the end of a day's shooting. And the final wrap, the end of the picture, is always followed by the producer's party for cast and crew.

When Hash Pertsick learned Adolf Hitler was officially finished, he sent Muley Rose off in the La Salle. Muley returned to Pleiades with a car full of whiskey. Muley's own car, the big Buick, had bartenders and enough food for an army.

Hash had always ducked crowds, but May 8 was different. Besides, it broke the monotony. He was half owner of a morgue, and the only stiffs in it were him and his partner. And all Nick had done since *Maiden Voyage* was work on the *Domino* script with his sidekick, Michael Serlin. And all Hash had to do at Pleiades was keep saying no to big-money offers around town.

Los Angeles was like the rest of the United States that day, noisy and happy and kissing and hugging, and Stage Three at Pleiades was among the happiest and noisiest.

Champ Gallagher came early. The director wore a red carnation, and his face almost matched the flower. He had a beautiful young woman on each arm when he confronted Nick. "Want you to meet my producer," Champ told the women. "Hey, Nick, buddy! Say hello to Flo and Jo." Champ looked from one woman to the other. "Eeny, meeny, miny, mo, who's Flo?"

The redhead on his right arm said, "I'm Flo, or some of my friends call me Flossie, for Florence."

"Hear that, Nick? Flo for Florence," Champ said. "And this is Jo." Champ winked. "Jo, the man-eater," he said, grinning at the blonde on his arm.

Jo giggled and slapped Champ's bald head. "Naughty."

"Christ, I hope so," Champ said. "Come on, Nick. The war's over. Get your feet wet."

"Sure," Nick said. "Have fun," he said, slipping away from the director and his harem.

"Sorehead," Champ said, and yelling, "I love ya, Nick, although I wish you'd make a picture!"

Nick felt cool hands over his eyes, felt someone behind him. "I, too, wish you would make a picture," said a woman. "Make *Domino.*"

Nick put his hands over hers and, turning, faced Sigrid Colstad. He had given her the script the previous week. She had called every day since reading the spy story. "I love it," she said. "Nick, I've never played a lead."

"And you are afraid," he said.

"You will protect me," Sigrid said, adding softly, "Why do you never come to protect me?"

She thought he would smile. "I am always with you," he said.

"Nick!" They heard the resonant command cutting through the stage.

Sigrid said, "Magda calls you."

"Surprise," he said, taking her with him, crossing the stage to Magda's section of the bar, a pair of two-by-twelve-inch planks set side by side on sawhorses. She held a tumbler of scotch.

Magda raised the glass. "So the little bastard from Linz is kaput," Magda said, and drank. "You're not celebrating."

"Soon," he said.

"The war is over, sonny," Magda said.

"I'm celebrating," Sigrid said. She turned to Nick, hesitant, suddenly shy and girlish. "Can I?" He nodded, and Sigrid, glowing, said, "Nick has given me the lead in *Domino*."

"Wonderful!" Magda said. She drained the whisky in the glass. "Come close, I'll kiss you," she said, and Sigrid bent forward for the accolade. "When do you shoot?"

Sigrid looked at Nick, who said, "After I scout locations. In Vienna."

"You fool!" Magda startled those around her. She banged the tumbler on the plank, summoning the bartender. "Now I know everything," she said. "You picked *Domino* only so you could go to Vienna. This time they will for sure kill you! Fool! They lost but they don't change!"

"Thanks for your advice," Nick said. The bartender set down Magda's glass. "For all your advice," Nick said.

Magda took the tumbler of scotch. "Dieter!"

Standing at the open stage door with Hash, Dieter said, "Magda is making friends. Help me."

At the bar Sigrid, frightened, touched Nick. "She said, *die*. What does she mean?"

"Tell her, sonny," Magda said, raising the glass to drink half the whisky.

Nick turned to leave them but was trapped by Dieter and Hash. "He is going to Vienna," Magda announced. "He picked *Domino* only so he can return to Vienna."

Dieter grimaced. "You're going back? You didn't have enough?"

"You're right," Nick said. "Magda is right. You're both right. Enjoy the party."

Hash took a cigarette out of his pack, forgetting everyone but his partner. "Who says we're going to Vienna?"

Nick moved Sigrid aside to face Hash. "I said. I am going to Vienna for locations. We are making this picture in Vienna."

Hash lit his cigarette. "I'm like the guy with the horns, the last one to find out. You talk to everyone in town except your partner. It's my turn, pal," Hash said, walking toward the rear of the stage. "You made *Maiden Voyage* without going across the street. Why Vienna?"

"This picture is about Vienna," Nick said.

Hash pointed to a gondola in the ways. "That's why we got art directors. They shot Venice here, water and all."

"*Domino* is not for a stage," Nick said.

"Yeah." Hash dragged on the cigarette. "So when're you leaving?"

"Hash!" Muley ran across the stage.

"I went for papers," Nick said. "They told me I am an enemy alien. I must wait."

Muley reached them. "You got company," he said, pointing. Hash looked over his shoulder and spun around. As he walked toward the open door, Nick saw Polly Pertsick standing beside a young man. Polly had not been on the lot since the fiasco in Nick's bed.

Coming closer, Hash saw she was with the same guy, George Goldberg. When he had begun to show up regularly, Hash had sent Muley down to Fairfax Boulevard, where George lived.

Muley took awhile, and when he came back, he said George had grown up down there and graduated from Fairfax High School. He went from there to UCLA. His folks had a little grocery store on Melrose near La Cienega. They lived in the neighborhood. The store was always open, and besides the parents, George and his younger brother worked there. George worked nights, studying with his books on the counter. He was graduating from UCLA in June, and had been accepted at Boalt, the law school up north in Berkeley. Hash didn't have to check out Boalt. "Hello, angel," he said, kissing Polly.

"Hello, Mr. Pertsick," George said.

"Hello, kid," Hash said, and then, because Polly was listening, "Hello, George. Glad you kids dropped by."

"You didn't tell me you were having a party," Polly said, looking past him.

"It just happened," Hash said. "On account of the war. The whole town's having a party. Anything I can get for you kids—folks?"

"We can help ourselves," Polly said. Hash watched them. She knew exactly where she was going, and so did Hash. What was she trying to prove?

She led George directly to Nick. "Hello."

"Polly, how are you? You are beautiful!" Nick said. "Welcome to the party."

"Thank you," she said. "I'd like you to meet my friend. This is George Goldberg."

"If he is your friend, I would like to meet him," Nick said. He extended his hand.

"Thank you, sir," George said as they shook hands.

"When I heard the surrender announcement I thought of you, of how happy you must feel," Polly said.

"Very happy," Nick said.

"Well—" Polly said, and broke off.

"You should have a drink," Nick said. He gestured at the bar. "You should both have a drink to celebrate."

Hash watched it all, watched Nick taking them to the bar, standing between her and the kid. Hash didn't see Champ return, having parked the two dames. "What's this I hear about shooting *Domino* in Vienna?"

"You know what I know," Hash said, watching Nick clink glasses with Polly.

"When do we leave?" Champ asked.

"Beats me."

Eight days after the victory party, Hash walked into Nick's office and dropped a large brown envelope on the desk. "This is from the Air Transport Command," Hash said. "You're flying out at seven o'clock tonight to Vienna. Adios, pal."

Late that night, Fritz returned to the study long after Carly and he had gone to bed. He had slipped the envelope into the dictionary, and he retrieved it, removing the letter from Father Bernard.

"My dear Baron," wrote Father Bernard. "I intrude out of deep concern for your welfare. I have today returned to the monastery after an absence brought on by the death of my beloved mother. So I have only just learned of Emil Huebner. He is gone! He disappeared the same day I was called away, the day after your visit, leaving only the cat which he strangled in a kind of mad frenzy. I fear Emil Huebner is mad. Our cat had befriended Emil as we had, as had you, Baron. Be on guard! I pray this warning, written in haste to catch the post . . ."

Fritz lowered the letter, walking into the Great Hall, moving sure-footedly in the darkness. He found matches beside the fireplace and lit the letter, dropping it into the andirons, lit the envelope and dropped it, watching the flames consume the paper as he had watched so much of his past burn. Der Chineser could be across the street waiting for him. In the morning, in daylight, Der Chineser could be anywhere in Vienna, on any rooftop, in any crowd. He had turned the city into a huge booby trap.

The following day, Fritz waited until Carly left the palace to keep a date with her mother before summoning Zinn to the study. "I've just talked with Fiegel," Fritz said. "There's an emergency at the schloss. Tell the baroness I'll call her when I arrive."

In the Daimler, Fritz locked all four doors. He set his Beretta automatic on the seat beside him and started the motor. The rooftops in the Alps were low and steeply pitched, and the schloss rested on a peak. In the Tyrol Fritz would see anyone coming.

As Fritz drove through Vienna, a C-54, the four-engine plane used by the Air Transport Command for moving men and materiel, flew east over the North Atlantic. Nick sat in a bucket seat behind the wing, one of only two civilians in the cabin. He had boarded the plane early the previous evening. In his seat in the dark, looking out at the blinking wing lights, his life in America began to blur. All that had happened in Hollywood receded. The past returned to claim him, returned vividly, as though there had been no break in his life.

The C-54 took on more passengers in Winnipeg, all bound for England. They flew north, crossing Hudson's Bay on the great circle route to Europe, flying through the night and into daylight, and late in the morning Nick dropped off to sleep.

The Air Corps sergeant acting as steward woke him. "Coming into Greenland," he said, walking through the cabin. "Buckle up." He checked the safety belt on each passenger and stopped beside Nick. "Buckle up, sir," he said. The sergeant leaned over Nick, "That's Bluie West Eight over there, sir. We'll be landing in about eighteen minutes."

Nick looked down. He saw only snow-covered mountains and felt his belly react as the pilot began to descend. The mountains seemed to rise. The plane lost altitude steadily until, without warning, it tilted sharply. All planes landing at Bluie West Eight had to make a dogleg around the mountain guarding the airstrip. For a little while the C-54 seemed to stand on its side, and then the pilot completed the turn, and Nick could hear the heavy, rasping grunt as the wheels were lowered.

Nick sat erect in the bucket seat, ready for the landing, ready for the refueling, ready for takeoff, for the flight to London, for the transfer to the Vienna plane in London. He tightened his seat belt. He could see Vienna.

When the C-54 stopped beside the cluster of Quonset huts which served as terminal and repair hangars, Nick saw soldiers pushing a boarding ramp out to the aircraft. The pilot cut the engines and the Air Corps sergeant, waiting beside the door, turned the big latch and pushed it open. The sergeant stepped out on the ramp while the cabin emptied. But he didn't see the foreign guy, the guy with the accent. The sergeant came back into the cabin, walking toward the tail. The guy had hardly been out of his seat since California. "You ought to get some fresh air, sir," said the sergeant. "Stretch your legs." Nick knew the sergeant would not go away. He came up from the seat.

"Sure," he said. "Stretch my legs."

When Nick came down the boarding ramp, a gasoline truck stood beside the C-54. Nick saw Air Corps enlisted men on the wing with the gasoline hoses. He began to circle the dull green aircraft as though he had been ordered to guard it. Nick kept moving, around and around, until the refueling had been completed and the hoses removed from the wing. He watched the gasoline truck move off. He stopped beside the boarding ramp, and as the copilot came out of the terminal hut, Nick climbed the steps and returned to his seat.

The C-54 filled with its passengers. Nick heard the engines starting, felt the aircraft vibrate from the enormous power of the four propellers. The roar of the engines filled the cabin until the sergeant latched the thick door. Nick felt the aircraft moving as the pilot turned and taxied along the airstrip.

In the cockpit the call-out had begun. The copilot was proceeding with the checklist as the pilot looked at the appropriate instrument on the enormous panel. At the head of the runway, the pilot turned the C-54 into the wind. "Flaps set for takeoff," said the copilot.

The pilot looked at the flap-angle indicator. The right wing showed a deflection of fifteen degrees. The left-wing indicator was dark. Without extended flaps to provide the lift, no aircraft can leave the ground.

Nick felt the aircraft moving once more, but it did not pick up speed. He looked out of the window and saw the Quonset huts. He leaned out into the aisle but didn't see the sergeant. Nick unbuckled his seat belt.

In his seat behind the cockpit, the sergeant saw the guy coming down the aisle while the plane was moving. "Sit down!" The guy kept coming. "Sit down!"

Nick cupped his mouth with his right hand, yelling, "Why are we going back?"

"Down!" said the sergeant. As he unbuckled his belt to go after the guy, Colonel Lawson, the ranking officer among the passengers, grabbed him.

Roland Lawson, an infantry officer, yelled, "Get back to your—" but broke off because he no longer had Nick, who squatted beside the sergeant.

"There must be a malfunction somewhere," the sergeant said as the C-54 stopped beside a repair hut.

The pilot left the plane first. On the ground he said, "There it is," pointing at the hydraulic fluid dripping from the wing. Beside him the crew chief said, "I'll lift the inspection plate and take a look, sir."

While the other passengers returned to the terminal, Nick watched the mechanics climb a ladder to the wing. They removed the screws holding a disc set flush into the wing. The crew chief came to the edge. "I see it, sir," he said to the pilot. "The leak is in the fitting there at the flap indicator. Take a couple hours, sir."

Nick went to the pilot. "I must be in London. I have a connection with an airplane for Vienna."

"There's another one tomorrow," the pilot said.

"Hey, the war's over," said the copilot.

"Thanks," Nick said. The pilots left him, following the passengers to the terminal hut. Nick stood below the engines, hearing the mechanics' footsteps on the wing above him. He turned slowly, walking to the boarding ramp and climbing the stairs to the empty cabin.

In Austria late in the afternoon that day, Der Chineser entered the railroad station in Bad Ischl, the spa which had been the favorite of Franz Josef. "Two adults and one child for Innsbruck," he told the ticket agent. "First class." Der Chineser kept his head averted, as though speaking to a companion beside him.

"How old is the child?"

"Six." Der Chineser pushed some money across the counter to the ticket agent.

Der Chineser had been in Bad Ischl since morning, deliberately avoiding the early train to Innsbruck, waiting to board in darkness.

When the train stopped that night, he found his car and came aboard. In his compartment he took a pad from his pocket and wrote, "Our son is very sick. His only chance for life is a specialist in Innsbruck. He must not be disturbed. The tickets are under the door." Der Chineser bent to push the tickets and the note under the door. He had avoided all unnecessary exposure since leaving the monastery, and he had come too close to his destination for any delay in his journey.

Twenty-four hours later, at the airport in Vienna, a sergeant came through the crowd, walking toward the eagles on an officer's shoulders. "Colonel Lawson, sir?"

"Lawson," said the colonel.

"Sergeant Ellis, sir. Headquarters motor pool." said the sergeant. "I've got a staff car, sir."

"Good man," said the colonel. "I'd given up."

"Sir, I almost had to give up myself," the sergeant said, "just getting near this place. Everybody's got a motor pool, sir, the French, the English. Them Russian drivers—excuse me for shooting off my mouth. This way, sir."

"Here we go, gang," Lawson said. In the terminal, waiting for his driver, the colonel had offered two Air Corps officers, a major and a captain, a lift into the city. Nick followed the colonel.

The sergeant led them to a gray sedan. He stowed the luggage in the trunk. "Where are you headed, sir?" He looked at Nick. "Sir? Where are you staying?"

"Staying," Nick said, and then, "Ah, the Imperial," he said, choosing Fritz's hotel, Hitler's hotel.

"Drop you first," said the sergeant. Colonel Lawson got in beside the driver, and Nick followed the major and captain into the rear.

The sergeant swung out away from the terminal. "I won't break any speed records, sir," he said to the colonel. "The roads are a mess. Whole place is a mess. It's worse at night."

"They took a beating, I guess," said the colonel. He looked back at Nick. "Are you from around here somewhere, Gallanz?"

"Somewhere," Nick said.

"They didn't worry much about precision bombing," the major said.

"Hit and run," said the captain. "That's my motto."

They rode in darkness. The only light came from the headlights of other military vehicles, going to and from Schwechat. As they came into the city, they passed a bombed-out trolley, burned-out cars, a toppled statue, another statue with half a horse and the marble figure of the rider in pieces at the base. Where some streetlights glowed, Nick saw block after block of bombed buildings with walls and roofs missing, collapsed store fronts. Nick remembered every street, every intersection, remembered the cheering crowds in the streets welcoming the Anschluss, the smiling women, the flower-throwing women, the swastikas everywhere, the Nazis everywhere. "Gallanz. What kind of name is that?" asked the major.

Nick looked past the captain. "A Jewish name," he said. "You are riding with a Jew. Stop the car and I will walk."

The colonel looked back. "Easy, man, he didn't say anything."

"I could swear I heard him," Nick said.

"Jesus," said the major under his breath.

"Another Jew," Nick said. He tapped the driver's shoulder. "Go left. Left is faster."

Near the Imperial the sergeant said, "Sir, this is about as close as I'll get. All the top brass is at the Imperial. There's four different armies in here, sir, all with cars."

"Sure," Nick said, opening the door.

"Hope you've got a reservation, sir," said the sergeant.

The colonel leaned out of the window. "Good luck."

The Imperial lobby was jammed. Nick saw every kind of uniform. He joined a crowd around the registration counter, and heard the room clerk. "Sorry. We have nothing. Sorry. Sorry." When Nick reached the counter, the clerk, an elderly man, said, "We are totally booked. Try the—"

"No," Nick interrupted. "I need a single. I am alone."

"We are completely booked," said the clerk. "We have no rooms."

"You'll find one," Nick said. "My name is Gallanz. I'll be back. Bring a bellhop for my bag."

"Bellhop!" said the old man. "We have no bellhops! We have no rooms!"

"Sure," Nick said. He looked at the nameplate on the counter. "Jan Lovenreid," he said. Nick set his suitcase on the counter. "Lovenreid. Code name, Weathervane," he said, low. "One of the Gestapo's—"

"Not true," said the room clerk, interrupting. "It's not—"

"Favorite of Herr Himmler," Nick said. "A key agent in the—"

"No!" said the clerk, his head swinging from side to side. "You are wrong! I was anti-Nazi!"

"Let the United States decide," Nick said, turning away. The room clerk fell across the counter, stopping him.

"I'm not! Wasn't! I swear to you!"

"I'll try to protect you," Nick said. He pushed the suitcase at the room clerk. "We'll talk later, in my room."

Nick made his way through the lobby like someone early for an appointment. He paused in front of the hotel. He felt strange, felt foreign to himself. He seemed lighter, seemed weightless. He could feel his heart pounding as he started for the Inner City.

In the kitchen in the palace, Zinn heard the bell, and as he rose, Matilda took his jacket from the hanger, holding it for him. "After nine o'clock," she said.

"Almost nine-thirty," Zinn said.

"Who would come now?" asked Matilda as Zinn left the kitchen.

The bell rang again as Zinn crossed the circular entrance. He opened the door and saw a man in rumpled clothes who looked like he was starving. The man needed a shave. Zinn decided he had lost his way. "Baron Von Gottisberg," Nick said.

"The baron is not at home," Zinn said. As he closed the door, Nick put his leg against it. "The baroness," he said.

"Who is calling?"

"I'm an old friend," Nick said, walking forward and shoving the butler back against the door.

"You can't—" Zinn said, and Nick interrupted:

"Sure, I can," Nick said, and flat, "Stand clear, Zinn, and I will not harm you."

As Nick left him, Zinn said, hushed, "Is it . . . ?" recognizing the derelict. Nick climbed the three marble steps, passing the study where Fritz had spoken of the Safe Conduct, where he had delivered the Safe Conduct, had offered the Daimler for the journey, had offered money for the journey. Nick passed the Petit Salon, where they had all dined, good friends, best friends. He saw the glow of lights from the Great Hall, and when he stopped, he saw the woman sitting with a book, saw Carly, the same Carly after seven years, hair falling over her shoulders, saw the same long, lithe body, and the same face, scrubbed and shining. He loathed her. He despised her. He loathed and despised her, and facing her, his body rigid, like a projectile primed for destruction, Nick discovered he loved her, had always loved her, would always love her. And loving Carly, hated her even more.

Carly heard footsteps, and when the footsteps ceased, looked up from her book. She saw the man at the head of the marble steps. "Who—? she began, and broke off. She set down her book and, standing, said, again, "Who—?"and broke off, looking hard and peering at the stranger. He came down the steps like someone on a tightrope, a smooth, graceful man moving with a dancer's poise and assurance. Carly shivered in the warm spring night. She came forward and then stopped, hardly breathing. She put her hands against her face, and her voice rose in a cry which pierced the far recesses of the palace. "Nick!" She cried, *"Nick!"* She cried, *"Nick!"* and ran.

Nick let her run, let her run, hair swinging across her back. "You're alive! You're alive!" Carly said. "Where did you come from? How did you get here? You're here! Nicki!" Carly took his arms, pulling him across the Great Hall to the lamp beside her chair. "Let me see you," she said. "Let me look at you. Let me *look* at you. Let me *look!*" she said. "Nick. Oh, Nick." She leaned forward to kiss him, but Nick moved and her lips barely brushed his.

She held on to him, afraid to let him go. "Seven years," Carly said. "Seventy years. Seven hundred. Every day was a year. I wrote to Rome, to California. You didn't write. Why didn't you write? Nick! Tell me everything. Tell me!"

"We'll wait for Fritz."

"Fritz is at the schloss," Carly said. "Finally, I thought you were dead. The letters came back, Addresse Unbekannt. Why? Why didn't you write?"

"I had a little accident," Nick said. He raised his right hand, and Carly took it. As she ran her fingers over the crater in his wrist, Nick exploded. Seven years of sorrow, of mourning, of anger and rage, of bewilderment and mystification, of helplessness and hopelessness, melded into a single convulsive eruption. He pulled his hand free, backing away from Carly, from the assassin.

"I couldn't write," Nick said. "A bullet made that hole in my hand. But I'm lucky, Baroness. Luckier than my mother, luckier than my father, luckier than Sam. The Nazis killed them. They're all dead. My family is dead, Baroness. That night, in a few minutes, two minutes, three minutes, they were gone. Murdered. My father died in Rome, but they killed him that night in the Alps."

Nick watched her. "You're surprised, Baroness," he said. "You look surprised, look shocked. You didn't know." He nodded. "Correct? You hear this for the first time." He nodded. "Correct? I'm bringing you this news after seven years. Correct? You would make a good actress." Nick took out his gun.

"Why did you do it, Baroness? Why did you kill them? You were rid of me," Nick said. "I was out of your life, out of Fritz's life. You would live happily ever after. Did my family need to die so you could live happily ever after? Why did you send the Nazis, Baroness? Tell me." Nick raised the Beretta. "You're going to tell me."

"You are wrong," Zinn said. "Every word is wrong." The butler stood beside the piano with Matilda huddled behind him as though she waited to be carried piggyback. "The baroness saved you, saved your life," Zinn said. "Without the baroness, you would have died, here in Vienna or in one of the camps. Do you believe the baron woke up one morning and said, 'I must help this man, Nicholas Gallanz, the Leopoldstadter?' Baron Fritz Von Gottisberg?" Zinn's head moved back and forth slowly. "Not the baron. The baroness saved you. She saved your *life*. The baroness kept you free of Hitler, of the Gestapo. She traded herself for you."

Matilda nudged Zinn. "You heard her."

"I heard her," Zinn said. "She stood there, beside the fireplace with the baron. She came with a bargain. I remember the word, 'bargain.' She would marry the baron if he arranged a passage out of Austria for you and your family."

"If he still wanted her," Matilda whispered.

"If he still wanted her," Zinn said. "And he accepted. And the next day you came. And the baron told you he would try for a Safe Conduct. The baron does not fail. He did not fail you."

Matila jabbed him. "Because the baroness did not fail you," she whispered.

"Because the baroness did not fail you," Zinn said. Matilda came out from behind Zinn, standing beside him. They were like two prisoners on the dock.

Carly said, "Thank you, Zinn. Matilda, thank you. I'm all right now. I'm in no danger." She faced Nick. "I'm in no danger."

The pair left the Great Hall. Carly said, "My head is whirling. You're here. *Here*. I can touch you," she said, putting her hand to his face, covering the scars left by the sutures.

Nick dropped the Beretta into his pocket and took her hand. "I came to kill you," he said. "Kill you both." He pressed her hand to his lips and released her. "I lost you and found you and have lost you again, lost you forever again."

"I couldn't let you die, couldn't have lived if you had died," Carly said.

"I must find the murderers," Nick said. "I've lived to come back and find these murderers. I'm going to the village."

"Then I'm going to the village," Carly said. "I'll call Fritz and tell him we're leaving in the morning."

"I am leaving now, Carly," he said.

"Now," she said, holding him as they left the Great Hall. In the study she kept Nick beside her as she telephoned.

In the schloss in the Tyrol, Fiegel came to the door of the breakfast room. "Excuse me, Baron. The baroness is calling."

Fritz set down the rifle. The breakfast room had become an armory. Fritz told Fiegel he intended to examine every weapon in the castle. "Now that the war is over, maybe the gunsmiths can resume some civilized work."

Fritz went to the telephone. "Carly . . . How nice!"

"Fritz, you'll never believe . . . you'd better sit down," Carly said. "Are you sitting?"

Fritz leaned against the wall. "I am," he said. "Fire away."

"Fritz, I'm in the study," Carly said. "I'm with *Nick! Nick* is here! Fritz, Nick is here beside me in the study!"

Fritz turned very slowly, as though he was looking for something he had lost. "*Our* Nick?"

"Yes, yes!" Carly said, and to Nick, "He said, 'Our Nick?' It's true, Fritz, it's true! He's lucky to be alive! He's the only one in his family—he'll tell you everything. We're coming to the schloss tonight." We're leaving tonight!"

"Carly . . ." Fritz said, and stopped.

"Yes, Fritz?" She listened. "Fritz?"

"Wonderful news," Fritz said. "Miraculous. Utterly miraculous. *Wiedersehen.*"

In the study, Nick said, "Come, Carly," turning away, ready to go, to hurry, hurry. He stopped at the door, looking back. "Carly?" She had not moved. He said, puzzled, "Carly?" watching her. He took a step toward her and stopped, and facing each other, they were reunited. They were together.

Carly left the desk. She had not spoken, nor did he speak again. She stopped beside him. She didn't touch him, nor did Nick move, yet they could not have been closer. In the still, hushed palace they were alone, isolated, in all the world only they remained.

Then Carly said, "I . . ." and, "You . . ." and stopped, and Nick said, "Yes," and Carly said, "Yes, yes, Nick, yes."

They left the study and Nick followed her through the darkened rooms. Their shadows were giants on the walls. Carly led him to the stairs, and as they came up the stone steps, the soft chimes of a clock tolling the hour pierced the silence.

Above, in the dim light of the corridor, Carly stopped, and as she opened a door, Nick said, "Not here," and stepped away.

"Stay," she said. "Stay. This is my room," she said, "Mine," bringing him with her.

Lights burned in Carly's room and the bed was turned down. Facing him beside the bed, Carly said, "I've prayed for this. I've thought of this night after night, every night." Looking into his eyes, she began to undress, and Nick took off his jacket.

She was naked first and helped him, raising his T-shirt, pulling it over his head and dropping it, pulling down his shorts. Carly took his hand, moving it across her lips, across her face, pressing his hand to her face, kissing the soft, warm flesh in the crook of his arm. Holding him, she took his other hand, cradling both hands in her arms, and pushing her arms with his hands into her breasts. She bent her head, kissing his hands as she pressed them to her breasts.

He said, his voice raw, "Oh, you . . ." trying to free himself, but she would not release him, had waited too long to release him.

She said, whispering, "Let me . . ." and touched his face, feeling his face as though she could not see. She moved her hands across his face, across his eyes, his lips, his neck, his chest, his belly, his hips, as though she needed proof that he was whole, had returned to her as he had gone, and when, slowly and carefully, she had moved over his entire body, she came forward. "Will you kiss me now?"

Nick put his arms around her, gathered her up carefully, brought her to him carefully, touched her lips with his, felt her lips open for his open lips, felt her breasts, felt the surge of elation of triumph and elation, of peace and safety and triumph and elation which set him afire. He said, "Carly! Carly! Carly!" as though he had, at that instant, discovered her in his arms, and bent to sweep her up, bringing her to the bed.

For a little while Nick stood beside the bed looking down at her. They were unlike lovers anywhere. Their union transcended physical coupling. Nick could feel Carly in every part of his body, feel her all through him. She galvanized him. He felt as though he was floating, felt as though he had stopped breathing, felt as though he must run, leap, vault over towering barriers, felt as though he would burst, would explode, would disintegrate, felt as though he must shout, must share his delight, and yet he remained mute, immobilized by Carly's presence, and only when she raised her arms did he lie down beside her.

Still he remained apart, propped on one elbow, facing her. Then Carly turned so her body touched his. She put her arm over him, bringing him down beside her. "Make me new, Nicki. Make me new."

He said, "Make us new," and kissing her, raised his leg, slipping his leg between hers. Kissing, he felt her legs closing around him with practiced ease, as though they had never been apart, felt her loins closing around his thigh, felt the first movement of her loins. He lowered his head as she cupped her breasts to nourish him, and as he feasted, his hands were never still. He heard her sighing, and then, softly, moaning, and he reached the soft, wet, hot core of her treasure.

He left her breasts, raising his leg and moving aside as he proceeded, but she was quicker, falling across his chest as her fingers floated across his belly and down, down until she said softly, "Pedro." She said, "You've brought Pedro back to me."

She did not release her trophy. "I've missed him," Carly said. "I've ached for him, Nicki." She said, "Hello, Pedro," and her head fell as Nick felt her take him. He felt her take him. He felt her lips, lips and tongue, felt her delicate embroidery, soft and smooth and hot, lips and tongue and mouth. She paused, raising her head, protecting her prize. "He remembers me," she said. "He's mine, Nicki. He belongs to me," Carly said, and returned, engulfing her prize.

Nick said, "Carly . . ." reaching for her, but she shook him off. She had waited too long, had been deprived for an eternity. She could not surrender. She had become mindless, and even when Nick turned and turned her, she continued.

With his arms around her hips, Nick brought her to him until he reached her font, and while she had him, he had her. He was no less famished than she. Carly felt him between her thighs, felt him burrowing, felt the first, tentative announcements of his appearance, felt him deeper, deeper, deeper, felt him gorging himself, and his hunger, his ravenous demands, only increased her needs. They could not be sated. Locked together, they became gluttonous.

Carly needed more of him, needed all of him. She freed him, freed herself to have more. She kneeled between his legs, looking down at him, eyes wide, wild, panting, her breasts rising and falling. "Go in me," she said, reaching out to guide him. "Go in me now," she said, and felt his buttocks rise against her as she welcomed him. She said, "Ah-h-h-h, yes. Yes. Yes, Nicki, like that."

"Let me see you," he said. He raised her head, holding her face in his hands so their faces touched, lips touched. "Now I have you," he said. "I have you now. I have you now. I have you."

She dropped down upon him, lost, and he thrust himself up at her, his body like a bow, raising them both and rolling with her until she lay beneath him.

Now she took him, took everything. She wanted more of him, wanted more, wanted more. She had to keep him, have him forever within her, raising her legs to dig the heels of her feet into his back, locking her hands in his back, imprisoning him as he imprisoned her.

So the endless night of his absence ended, the endless night of her absence ended. Both surrendered, surrendered together. A kind of indescribable, unimaginable delight, unimaginable joy took them away, took them far away, took them far, far away, took them far away and high, higher, higher, higher, took them where neither had ever been, where no one had ever been, where an incandescent, blinding splendor welcomed them, where both remained for a little while, numbed by the glory they shared.

They left the palace later that night, and with Nick beside her in the coupe, Carly drove to the Imperial for his luggage. When he returned, she stood beside the open trunk of the car. "I thought I had lost you," she said. "I thought I had imagined all this."

"I'm here," Nick said. "I am delivering you to Fritz."

She did not respond. They got into the coupe. Neither spoke, and they drove through the ruined city in silence. By the time they reached Schonbrunn, Carly said, "I feel as though we've escaped from everyone."

In the glow of the headlights Nick could see the Nazis burst out of the Alpenheutte near the Italian border, could hear the gunfire, hear his mother's cry, hear Sam's groans as his brother lay in the snow turning red with blood. "Nobody escapes," he said.

Early the next morning, Fritz summoned Fiegel. "The baroness is on her way," Fritz said. "She brings a guest, an old friend. It's a kind of reunion and deserves a celebration. We need to put on a festive face. Dig out something. Whatever you have."

"Any suggestions, Baron?"

Fritz set his beret on his head. "You're on your own, Fiegel. I promised that pest Gottschalk I'd look at a bull he's after. With my money." Jakob Gottschalk's family had farmed Von Gottisberg land for generations. "Today of all days."

"Can't you put him off?"

"I've put him off," Fritz said. "If Gottschalk loses that bull, I'll hear about it for the rest of my life. Or his. When the baroness arrives, extend yourself, Fiegel. I can count on you. I'll be back . . . when I get back."

Fritz left the Daimler, taking the small sedan Fiegel used for errands. The day was spectacular. Fritz smelled the tilled fields. He loved every acre, every tree, and every fence.

Fritz found Jakob Gottschalk in his barn. The farmer was a big man in middle age with clean clothes and scrubbed hands. "Baron!" Gottschalk whipped off his hat. "An honor, Baron! I didn't expect . . . I would have told Frau Gottschalk to prepare—"

"Calm down, Jakob. I'm making a neighborly visit," Fritz said.

"Welcome, Baron," Gottschalk said. "You saw the fields. Finally a crop we can keep. After seven years we'll feed Austrians, not Germans."

Fritz jabbed Gottschalk in the belly. "Good man," he said, and meant it. "Not Germans, not the French, not Americans, not Russians, not the bloody British. Austrians!" Fritz said, and, taken aback by his emotional lapse, "Put on your hat, man. You're not in church."

The heady smell of the barn raised Fritz's spirits. The barn took him far, far back to his childhood days, summer days when he had left the schloss early, running into the sun. "How is the herd, Jakob?"

"What's left of the herd," Gottschalk said, leading Fritz into another wing of the barn. "Six milkers," he said. Fritz saw the cows bunched together. There were twenty stalls on each side of the barn. "The Germans took eight in the last two weeks of the war."

"Forget the Germans," Fritz said. "They are gone. We're here. You need a bull, Jakob." The farmer's bull had died in 1943.

"Well, yes . . ." Gottschalk said. "Maybe in the fall. There's no money, Baron."

"There is now," Fritz said. "If you can find a bull, I can find the money."

The farmer's mouth opened and closed. He said, "Oh, my God."

"You can have your bull on one condition," Fritz said. "You came to me. I did not come to you. I can't start buying bulls for the entire Tyrol."

Miles from Jakob Gottschalk's farm, Carly rolled down the window of the coupe. "Seven years, Nick. I thought of you every day for seven years. I have a million questions, more than a million. What comes after a million?"

"A jillion?"

"I have a jillion questions," Carly said. "You were halfway around the world. How did you live? What did you do?"

"I waited for today," Nick said. "How much farther?"

"We're almost at the end," she said. The road narrowed, climbing constantly. Then they dropped into a meadow, and as Carly sped along the straightaway, Nick leaned forward, facing the hayfork where he had left Magda and his family that night. The entire planet had been altered, but the rusted steel skeleton remained untouched. "Soon," Carly said.

As the castle appeared above them, floating in the clouds, Carly said, "Fritz has been here all his life. He knows everyone. Everyone knows him. And trusts him. He'll find the people you're after. If they're still alive, he'll find them."

Minutes later, Fiegel heard the sound of a car, and at a window he saw the coupe. He walked through the castle, leaving the doors wide open. Fiegel saw the baroness with the stranger. Then the man turned and Fiegel remembered him. "Where is Fritz?" Carly asked.

"The baron had to keep an appointment with a tenant," Fiegel said. "You will want to freshen up before lunch."

"Sure," Nick said, forgetting the butler. "Can I take the car, Carly?"

"You're not alone," Carly said. "Not now."

In the coupe, Carly turned away from the castle. Nick said, "That night I started with Fritz's mechanic, in the garage where I delivered the Daimler."

"Kesselring," Carly said.

Nick sat on the edge of the seat as though he intended to jump. When they drove into the village, he said, "No more swastikas," and pointed. "There is the garage." Carly turned and stopped, facing the garage door. They could read the sign tacked to the door: "To INNS-BRUCK. BACK LATER."

Nick said, "He sent me to a club at the end of the street." Carly backed the coupe away from the garage. "It was on this same side," Nick said. "There. The hunt club." The paint was peeling on the walls of the chalet.

Inside, the bartender looked up at the pair coming through the door. Two men at a table watched the pair. "This is a private club," the bartender said.

"Sure," Nick said. "Were you here seven years ago?"

The bartender had pandered to the Nazis for seven years, bowing and scraping, taking their obscenity, their filth, and he had been angry since they fled. He reached under the bar for a club. "Turn around while you can."

"That club won't stop me," Nick said, ready to put his gun between the man's eyes. "Were you here seven years ago? Tell me fast while I still like you."

"Like me," said the bartender. He faced a madman. The Nazis had made a lot of people mad. "I was here seventeen years ago."

"Seven years ago I asked you for a guide," Nick said. "You sent me to the Rathaus, to the Nazis. Everybody laughed. No jokes today. Give me the name of the guide."

"Felix Nestroy was a guide," the bartender said. "But he's gone. They grabbed him for the army, sent him with Rommel in the desert. He was killed there."

"There were two," Nick said. "One wore a beret."

"Paul Grietze."

"Spell his name," Nick said. The bartender spelled Grietze. "Tell me where to find him," Nick said. "Slowly. I have been away from this language."

When they left the hunt club, Carly drove out of the village and into the mountains, into a rutted, narrow lane lined with boulders. The bartender had told them to continue for eight-tenths of a mile. When Carly stopped, they saw the roof of a house in a cluster of pine trees. Nick opened the door of the coupe. "At last."

Carly joined him. They walked through the trees to the house, climbing almost vertically. Wooden steps rose to an open porch. "Nick." Carly touched him. "Don't expect too much. This could be the beginning of the trail, not the end."

"I'm young," he said. "I have years left." On the porch he pulled a leather cord hanging from a bell. The door opened and they saw a woman wearing a white apron over her dress. "Paul Grietze," Nick said.

"Not home," she said. The man frightened Jenny Grietze. Everyone frightened her. She had never been out of the Tyrol.

"When will he be home?"

"He's gone hunting," she said, trying to hide behind the door. "For food. There is no food in the village."

"We'll wait," Nick said.

"Please," she said, "we were anti-Nazis."

Carly thought the woman would collapse. "We'll wait in the car," she said, recrossing the porch. She stopped on the stairs, looking up at Nick, and after a moment he followed.

"She could be lying," Nick said. "She could warn him, tell him to stay away."

"How? If she runs, she runs into us," Carly said. "And there is no telephone. There are no telephone lines."

"Have you become a detective?"

"I've become . . . something," Carly said.

He moved from side to side, unable to be still. "When I left Austria, the country was full of Nazis," Nick said. "Now it is full of anti-Nazis." He stopped, facing the house, and saw the woman in the window. She moved away, letting the curtains fall. Nick left Carly, looking up at the mountains and shading his eyes.

Hours passed. Carly got into the coupe. "Nick. You're too far away." He sat down beside her, one leg on the ground. "Try not to think," she said.

"I tried but I lost," he said, leaving the car. Carly joined him, leaning against the fender. The shadows lengthened and darkened. Late in the afternoon Jenny Grietze came out on the porch. "I can offer you tea."

Nick shook his head, and Carly thanked the woman, who went back into the house. As the door closed, Carly stepped away from the coupe and stopped, her head high like an animal smelling danger. She said, "Nick," raising her hand to silence him.

Nick didn't move. He listened fiercely until he heard the crackle of twigs. "There!"

Carly said sharply, "Quiet!"

A man emerged from the shadows. He carried a rifle over his shoulder, and rabbits hung from the other. More hung from his broad belt, from hip to hip. He wore heavy leather boots and a beret. "Paul Grietze?" Nick asked.

"Grietze," the man said, and Nick ran straight at him.

"Where's my wife?" Grietze asked, pushing the rabbits off his shoulder. He lowered the gun, keeping his finger inside the trigger guard. "Who the hell are you? What the hell do you want around here? I was an anti-Nazi."

"Sure," Nick said. "I didn't come for your wife or for you. She's safe and you're safe. We'll find out how safe you are, Paul Grietze, the guide."

Behind them, Carly turned on the headlights of the coupe, catching them in the beams. She walked toward the two men, stopping near them, with Nick on her left.

"This is about a night seven years ago," Nick said. "This is about a band of five pilgrims. They had a guide. He brought another guide. Did you take five pilgrims to Italy? Not to Italy, almost to Italy." Nick raised his right hand, pointing to the mountaintops. "Nazis came out of nowhere, came shooting." His voice rose. "Came killing!"

Grietze set down his rifle, resting it against his leg. "Felix Nestroy was with me."

Nick lunged at Grietze, grabbing him. "Who were they? Who sent them? Who made the ambush?" Nick began to shake Grietze, swinging him from side to side. "They killed my family! Killed . . . my . . . family!"

"Let go!" Grietze put his hands over Nick's, fighting him. "Let go!"

"Who betrayed us?" Nick shouted. "Tell me who betrayed us!"

"Nick!" Carly leaped between them, chopping with both hands, ramming Nick with her shoulder to drive him back, separating the two men.

"Paul!" Jenny Grietze screamed, running into the beams of the headlights, throwing herself at her husband.

Nick stood apart, his eyes wild. "Who did it?" The words echoed through the mountains. "Who betrayed us?"

"I can't." Grietze shook his head. "I don't know. You were there. Everything happened very fast. They were shooting, you were shooting, and they ran and we ran."

Below in the village, Otto Kesselring returned to the garage. He carried a canvas bag and used a cane. In the bag was a generator from a 1939 Peugeot and seven used spark plugs, the result of a full day's scrounging in the auto-repair shops in Innsbruck.

Kesselring dropped the bag beside the stove in the far corner of the garage. A kettle sat atop the stove. Kesselring liked a glass of hot water in the morning, but there was no firewood, and his arthritis kept him from getting into the mountains to cut fallen trees.

A table flanked the stove, and several odd chairs were grouped around the table and beside a cot against the wall. Since his wife's death two years earlier, Kesselring often slept in the garage, choosing the cot over the empty house in the village. The garage was usually empty as well. There were no parts for engines, and even when he managed to repair an engine, the owner usually left the car for weeks, until he could pay Kesselring. But the garage was familiar, and the aged man was comfortable with his cannibalized hulks.

The long day had tired him, and he needed to rest. Kesselring sat down on the cot and bent forward to take off his shoes. As he fumbled with the shoelaces, a shadow fell across the floor. He raised his head. "Hello?"

Someone stood out of the light. "Hello?" Kesselring pushed himself up from the cot, grunting. He teetered slightly before regaining his balance. "Baron?"

"Hello, Otto." Fritz stopped beside the stove. "Were you expecting anyone, Otto?"

"I? Expecting? Not I, Baron," Kesselring said. "For a long time now I've been alone. My daughters have decided I'm dead like their mother. Is it the Daimler, Baron? I hope it isn't the Daimler. There are no parts. I looked all over Innsbruck all day—" he said as Fritz shot him.

The aged man fell back. His legs hit the cot and he dropped against the wall. For a little while he sat against it as blood seeped through his clothes, spreading across his belly. Then, slowly as a tree, he toppled, lying on his side facing the stove, sprawled across the cot, one leg under him and the other dangling, his shoe scraping the floor. By that time Otto Kesselring was alone.

At the same time, Carly was inching the coupe down the mountain, driving in low gear, her foot on the brake, turning constantly to avoid the rocks. They were in darkness on the mountain. Night came quickly at those heights, almost immediately after the sun dropped below the jagged peaks. She glanced at Nick, who sat stiffly. "Nothing," he muttered, rubbing his right hand with his left.

"Fritz will help," Carly said. "You can depend on him."

"Sure," Nick said. Carly turned sharply, and Nick fell against her. He pushed himself back into his seat as though he rode with a stranger.

"We've just started," Carly said. "It's the first day."

"It's been two thousand days," Nick said.

"We'll talk with Fritz," Carly said. She had long since learned to expect miracles from him. He had never disappointed her. He was endlessly resourceful, and he was lucky. The war had taught Carly that luck was the decisive element in everyone's inventory, good luck or bad.

Carly saw the lights of the village and soon the village street at the foot of the narrow road. "Stop at the garage," Nick said. "Maybe the old man is back." Carly turned into the street. They passed the hunt club and the Rathaus, and Carly swung over to the side of the street, turning to face the garage. They could see the sign on the broad garage door. "Still in Innsbruck," Nick said.

"Maybe," Carly said, looking at the ancient Citroen beside the garage wall. "That car wasn't there before." As she turned off the ignition key, Nick scrambled out of the coupe.

He grabbed the handle with both hands, trying to raise the door. "Locked," he said. He kicked the door, shouting, "Kesselring! Otto Kesselring!"

Carly walked to the side of the building. "The big door is for cars. Maybe there's another door." She stopped beside the battered sedan and put her hand against the radiator. "Still warm," she said.

"Then he's here," Nick said, pulling Carly to the rear of the building. When they saw a rectangle of light on the ground, they began to run.

The light came from a door. Nick threw it wide open and stopped.

Carly froze as well. Kesselring lay on the floor on his belly, spread out like a turtle in the sand. He had rolled off the cot and crawled across the garage, leaving a wide swath of blood on the concrete floor. "He needs a doctor!" Carly said.

"Too late," Kesselring said. His head rose and fell like a toy's head. "I'm through," he said, groaning and bringing up blood.

"Not yet," Nick said, dropping to his knees beside the aged man.

"Finished," Kesselring said. "I—" he said, and could not continue.

Nick bent over him, talking into Kesselring's ear. "Listen, seven years ago I came here with the baron's car."

Kesselring's lips moved, trying to form words. Nick heard him making sounds. "I needed a guide," Nick said. "You remember," Nick said, then shouted, "You remember!"

"Daim . . . ler."

"The Daimler, correct!" Nick said, and saw Kesselring's eyes close. "Don't go! Listen! We walked into a trap! A Nazi trap! We were betrayed! Kesselring!" Nick took the aged man's shoulders, trying to lift him. "*Kesselring!*" He had come thousands of miles, had waited an unendurable lifetime.

Fifteen kilometers from the garage, Fritz made the last turn toward the schloss. He saw only the Daimler. Fritz got out of the sedan, and in the castle called for Fiegel. "Any word from the baroness? She should have been here hours ago."

"She is here," Fiegel said. "Not here, but she arrived, Baron. This morning. They came and went immediately."

"Gives me a chance to change clothes," Fritz said. He stood at the open doors.

"Did you forget something?" Fiegel asked.

"I hope not," Fritz said. "I wouldn't want to spoil the evening."

In his room, Fritz changed clothes quickly. As he pushed his gun into the pocket of the hunting jacket, he heard the coupe approaching.

Fiegel heard the car as well and came out of the castle to greet the baroness. "Is the baron here?" Carly asked, just before she saw Fritz.

"Carly! You had me worried," Fritz said. "Fiegel told me you came and went, zip, zip, before he could get your bags. Fiegel, get their bags." Fritz spread his arms wide. "Nick!" Fritz embraced him, and then stepped back, holding Nick's arms. "The same old Nick."

"Sure," Nick said. "The same old Fritz."

Fritz threw one arm over Nick's shoulder and the other over Carly's. "It's like old times," he said, bringing them into the castle. "It is old times. Come into the nave, as one of my ancestors called it. I never told you about him, Carly. Baron Hugo. An atheist who outraged his wife and everyone in the family. There he is," Fritz said, pointing at one of the portraits.

In front of the castle, Fiegel walked to the coupe and opened the trunk. He reached inside for the luggage and stepped back, a suitcase in each hand. As he came erect, Fiegel felt something cold under his arm. "Keep holding the bags," said Der Chineser, pushing a knife into Fiegel's neck and using his left hand to search him for a weapon. When Der Chineser finished, he said, "We're going inside. Not the front door, another door. Use the servants' door."

In the castle, at the safari bar Fiegel had set up near the fireplace, Fritz said, "For Carly, it's always vermouth." He took a bottle and a glass, and pouring, he said, "Isn't it unbelievable? We three together in the schloss? Where do we start?" Fritz asked. "Nick, tell us everything. Where were you? And why did you run off today?" Fritz set down the bottle, and when he looked up from the bar, he was facing the Beretta in Nick's hand.

"We've come from Kesselring," Nick said. "We were with the old man before he died." As Fritz lowered the glass of vermouth, Nick fired twice, shooting out the eyes of the sacrilegious Von Gottisberg on the wall. "Try it," Nick said.

Fritz raised his hands slowly, palms out. "You're smart," Nick said. "You were always smarter than everyone. You only made one mistake, and you made it today. You should have emptied the clip into Kesselring." Nick moved to his right, circling Fritz, and Carly stepped back, clear of both. "I'm going to empty this clip," Nick said. "I'm going to put these eleven rounds into your black heart."

Fritz watched him warily. He needed a diversion, two or three seconds to get his gun. He needed Fiegel!

"You called Kesselring that Saturday," Nick said, circling Fritz. "You put me into the Daimler, let me drive out, and went into the palace to warn Kesselring about the communist saboteurs!" Nick said, thinking of Sam and his father. "You told Kesselring the Daimler was packed with saboteurs on their way to join up with a gang near the border. You told him they would wipe out the Tyrol, dynamiting everything: electricity, telephones, water. You said the dynamite would make avalanches, burying everything." Nick stopped moving. "You killed my family. Why? You had Carly. You were rid of me."

Fritz wanted him to talk. The longer he talked, the less vigilant he became. Where was Fiegel?

Nick began to circle Fritz again. "What kind of creature are you? You're not a Nazi, you're worse," Nick said. "Hitler was what he was. Goering, Goebbels, Himmler, Von Ribbentrop, Julius Streicher, Heydrich, they were what they were. Who are you? You're like nobody who ever lived. You don't belong with people. You don't belong in this world, and I am going to save the world from you."

"Not you, Nick," Carly said. Fritz saw the automatic in her hand, and for the first time in his life he felt the sickening emptiness of fear. Carly waved at Nick, motioning him aside. "You're not a killer," she said. "You're clean. You'll stay clean. I'll keep you clean. We're the killers. Fritz and I. We're drenched in blood, all of us here, winners and losers. This is between Fritz and me, not between Fritz and you. Fritz is my . . . whatever he is. I came to Fritz. I started all this and I'll finish it."

"Stay out, Carly," Nick said. He had waited too long. He had come back to finish this. "Leave him for me," Nick said. "He is mine."

"You stay out," Carly said. "Get out and leave him with me."

Fritz saw both guns pointed at him. Where was that sonofabitch, Fiegel? Fritz had to keep them talking, had to make time. "Listen to her, Nick," he said. "Back off. You're an amateur. This is Domino, empress of the Underground. Domino, the flyers' fairy godmother, toast of the Allied air forces."

"So you knew that," Carly said.

"Your proudest admirer, Baroness," Fritz said, waiting to put a bullet between her eyes. He couldn't die, couldn't leave the schloss, leave the palace, to this tart.

"I should be surprised you are Domino, but I am not," Nick said, watching Fritz but speaking to Carly. "I should have known from the beginning, in Hollywood. Who else could be like Domino? Only you, Carly."

"Forget Domino," Carly said. "Fritz needs a conversation now, needs to keep us talking until he has a chance to run," she said, watching him. "You can't run," she said, taking a step toward the bar as Fritz saw Fiegel.

Then he saw someone with Fiegel, someone in a long coat and a big hat. He saw the knife in Fiegel's throat, and then he saw Der Chineser's face beneath the hat brim. A great, icy blast tore through him.

"Here's your master," said Der Chineser. "Yours and mine. My God. Baron Fritz Von Gottisberg. I would have died for you; I thought happily of ways I could die for you." Der Chineser shoved Fiegel aside, pulling a salami out of his coat pocket.

"This is from the hamper you brought me, Baron. Remember your orders? You said, 'Promise you'll share nothing I've brought you.' " Der Chineser tossed the salami at Fritz, and it fell beside the safari bar, at his feet.

Nick edged sideways, putting himself between Der Chineser and Carly. "I've come to break my word, Baron," said Der Chineser. "I'm going to share with you. I can't escape. My face won't let me escape. The baroness would kill me here and now. Correct, Baroness? And Gallanz would kill me for trying to kill him that night near the Zwischentheatre."

Nick was still watching Fritz. "You didn't know that, Gallanz," said Der Chineser. "Now you know. You didn't know your friend, the baron, sent me after you."

"He's lying," Fritz said. "Can't you see he's lying? He's crazy. Look at him." Fritz needed just a few more seconds.

"I've never lied," said Der Chineser. "A good soldier never lies." He pulled a summer sausage from his coat pocket. "Pick up the salami, Baron. Take a bite. You take a bite and then I'll take a bite." .

Fritz moved aside, clear of the bar. "Fiegel!"

"Pick up the salami, Baron," said Der Chineser.

"You're out of this," Nick told Der Chineser. "You and your knife. I'll blow the knife out of your hand. Your baron belongs to me. He belongs to me, Carly. My family bought him for me."

"Fiegel!" Fritz moved back. "Fiegel!"

"I can't stop them," Fiegel said. "I wouldn't if I could. You are a dark blot on this earth, Baron. You kill as easily as you breathe. You killed poor Otto Kesselring. You killed your innocent dog that day in the field. You killed your own dog. You're a monster, born a monster. I should have smothered you in your crib."

"Carly!"

"No," she said, and then, in a rage, "No! No!"

Fritz saw Der Chineser coming. He saw Nick raise his gun, saw Carly coming, raising her gun, saw Fiegel standing with his hands clasped behind him. Fritz stepped back. He had to escape from these vultures. "Wait," he said, moving back. "Wait . . . listen," he said. He couldn't let these hyenas . . . "Wait!" Fritz said, stepping back. "I didn't . . ." he said as they advanced on him.